THE CODEX

By Douglas Preston

Dinosaurs in the Attic*
Cities of Gold
Jennie
Talking to the Ground
The Royal Road
The Codex*
Tyrannosaur Canyon*

By Douglas Preston and Lincoln Child

Relic*
Mount Dragon*
Reliquary*
Riptide
Thunderhead
The Ice Limit
The Cabinet of Curiosities
Still Life with Crows
Brimstone
Dance of Death

*Available from Tom Doherty Associates

DOUGLAS PRESTON

THE CODEX

A TOM DOHERTY ASSOCIATES BOOK • NEW YORK

THE CODEX

Copyright © 2004 by Splendide Mendax, Inc.

A Forge Book
Published by Tom Doherty Associates, LLC
175 Fifth Avenue
New York, NY 10010

www.tor.com

Forge® is a registered trademark of Tom Doherty Associates, LLC.

Library of Congress Cataloging-in-Publication Data

Preston, Douglas J.
    The codex / Douglas Preston.
        p. cm.
    "A Tom Doherty Associates book."
    ISBN 0-765-31612-9
    EAN 978-0-765-31612-7
    1. Inheritance and succession—Fiction. 2. Pharmaceutical industry—Fiction.
3. Archaeological thefts—Fiction. 4. Manuscripts, Maya—Fiction. 5. Fathers and sons—
Fiction. 6. Mission persons—Fiction. 7. Treasure-trove—Fiction. 8. Tombs—Fiction. I. Title.

PS3566.R3982C63 2004
813'.54—dc22

                                                                                        2003049427

First Hardcover Edition: January 2004
First Trade Paperback Edition: September 2005

Printed in the United States of America

0 9 8 7 6 5 4 3 2 1

To

Aletheia Vaune Preston

and

Isaac Jerome Preston

Acknowledgments

There is one person above all others who must be thanked for the existence of this novel, and that is my good friend the inestimable Forrest Fenn—collector, scholar, and publisher. I will never forget that lunch of ours, many years ago in the Dragon Room of the Pink Adobe, when you told me a curious story—and thereby gave me the idea for this novel. I hope you feel I have done the idea justice.

Having mentioned Forrest, I feel it necessary to make one thing clear: My character Maxwell Broadbent is a complete and total fictional creation. In terms of personality, ethics, character, and family values, the two men could not be more different, a fact I wish to emphasize for anyone who fancies he sees a *roman à clef* in this novel.

Many years ago a young editor received a half-finished manuscript called *Relic* from a pair of unknown writers; he bought the manuscript and mailed the writers a modest editorial letter, outlining how he thought the novel should be rewritten and finished—a letter that propelled those two authors on the road to bestsellerdom and a number-one box-office hit movie. That editor was Bob Gleason. I owe a great debt to him for those early days and for guiding this novel to completion. In a similar vein I would like to thank Tom Doherty for welcoming back a prodigal son.

I wish to acknowledge here the incomparable Mr. Lincoln Child, truly the better half of our belletristic partnership, for his excellent and most insightful criticism of the manuscript.

I owe a great debt of gratitude to Bobby Rotenberg, not only for his insightful and detailed help with the characters and story, but also for his great and enduring friendship.

I would like to acknowledge my agents Eric Simonoff at Janklow & Nesbit in New York and Matthew Snyder in Hollywood. I want to thank Marc Rosen for helping me develop some of the ideas in this novel and Lynda Obst for her vision in seeing its possibilities in a seven-page treatment.

I owe a great debt to Jon Couch, who read the manuscript and made many helpful suggestions, particularly in regard to weaponry and firearms. Niccolò Capponi offered some of his usual brilliant ideas regarding several tricky scenes in the book. I am also indebted to Steve Elkins, who is searching for the real White City in Honduras.

Several books were useful to me while writing *The Codex*, in particular Redmond O'Hanlon's *In Trouble Again* and *Sastun: My Apprenticeship with a Maya Healer* by Rosita Arvigo—an excellent book that I would recommend to anyone interested in the subject of Mayan medicine.

My daughter Selene read the manuscript several times and offered top-notch criticism, for which I am immensely grateful. And I wish to thank my wife, Christine, and my other children, Aletheia and Isaac. I thank all of you for your constant love, kindness, and support, without which this book, and everything else wonderful in my life, wouldn't exist.

THE CODEX

1

Tom Broadbent turned the last corner of the winding drive and found his two brothers already waiting at the great iron gates of the Broadbent compound. Philip, irritated, was knocking the dottle out of his pipe on one of the gateposts while Vernon gave the buzzer a couple of vigorous presses. The house stood beyond them, silent and dark, rising from the top of the hill like some pasha's palace, its clerestories, chimneys, and towers gilded in the rich afternoon light of Santa Fe, New Mexico.

"It's not like Father to be late," said Philip. He slipped the pipe between his white teeth and closed down on the stem with a little click. He gave the buzzer a stab of his own, checked his watch, shot his cuff. Philip looked pretty much the same, Tom thought: briar pipe, sardonic eye, cheeks well shaved and after-shaved, hair brushed straight back from a tall brow, gold watch winking at the wrist, dressed in gray worsted slacks and navy jacket. His English accent seemed to have gotten a shade plummier. Vernon, on the other hand, in his gaucho pants, sandals, long hair, and beard, looked uncannily like Jesus Christ.

"He's playing another one of his games with us," said Vernon, giving the buzzer a few more jabs. The wind whispered through the piñon trees, bringing with it a smell of warm resin and dust. The great house was silent.

The smell of Philip's expensive tobacco drifted on the air. He turned to Tom. "And how are things, Tom, out there among the Indians?"

"Fine."

"Glad to hear it."

"And with you?"

"Terrific. Couldn't be better."

"Vernon?" Tom asked.

"Everything's fine. Just great."

The conversation faltered, and they looked around at each other, and then away, embarrassed. Tom never had much to say to his brothers. A crow passed overhead, croaking. An uneasy silence settled on the group gathered at the gate. After a long moment Philip gave the buzzer a fresh series of jabs and scowled through the wrought iron, grasping the bars. "His car's still in the garage. The buzzer must be broken." He drew in air. "Halloo! Father! Halloo! Your devoted sons are here!"

There was a creaking sound as the gate opened slightly under his weight.

"The gate's unlocked," Philip said in surprise. "He *never* leaves the gate unlocked."

"He's inside, waiting for us," said Vernon. "That's all."

They put their shoulders to the heavy gate and swung it open on protesting hinges. Vernon and Philip went back to get their cars and park them inside, while Tom walked in. He came face-to-face with the house—his childhood home. How many years since his last visit? Three? It filled him with odd and conflicting sensations, the adult coming back to the scene of his childhood. It was a Santa Fe compound in the grandest sense. The graveled driveway swept in a semicircle past a massive pair of seventeenth-century zaguan doors, spiked together from slabs of hand-hewn mesquite. The house itself was a low-slung adobe structure with curving walls, sculpted buttresses, vigas, latillas, nichos, portals, real chimney pots—a work of sculptural art in itself. It was surrounded by cottonwood trees and an emerald lawn. Situated at the top of a hill, it had sweeping views of the mountains and high desert, the lights of town, and the summer thunderheads rearing over the Jemez Mountains. The house hadn't changed, but it felt different. Tom reflected that maybe it was he who was different.

One of the garage doors was open, and Tom saw his father's green Mercedes Gelaendewagen parked in the bay. The other two bays were shut. He heard his brother's cars come crunching around the driveway, stopping by the portal. The doors slammed, and they joined Tom in front of the house.

That was when a troubled feeling began to gather in the pit of Tom's stomach.

"What are we waiting for?" asked Philip, mounting the portal and striding up to the zaguan doors, giving the doorbell a firm series of depresses. Vernon and Tom followed.

There was nothing but silence.

Philip, always impatient, gave the bell a final stab. Tom could hear the deep chimes going off inside the house. It sounded like the first few bars of "Mame," which, he thought, would be typical of Father's ironic sense of humor.

"Halloo!" Philip called through cupped hands.

Still nothing.

"Do you think he's all right?" Tom asked. The uneasy feeling was getting stronger.

"Of course he's all right," said Philip crossly. "This is just another one of his games." He pounded on the great Mexican door with a closed fist, booming and rattling it.

As Tom looked about, he saw that the yard had an unkempt look, the grass unmowed, new weeds sprouting in the tulip beds.

"I'm going to take a look in a window," Tom said.

He forced his way through a hedge of trimmed chamisa, tiptoed through a flower bed, and peered in the living room window. Something was very wrong, but it took him a moment to realize just what. The room seemed normal: same leather sofas and wing chairs, same stone fireplace, same coffee table. But above the fireplace there had been a big painting—he couldn't remember which one—and now it was gone. He racked his brains. Was it the Braque or the Monet? Then he noticed that the Roman bronze statue of a boy that held court to the left of the fireplace was also gone. The bookshelves revealed holes where books had been taken out. The room had a disorderly look. Beyond the doorway to the hall he could see trash lying on the floor, some crumpled paper, a strip of bubble wrap, and a discarded roll of packing tape.

"What's up, Doc?" Philip's voice came floating around the corner.

"You better have a look."

Philip picked his way through the bushes with his Ferragamo wingtips, a look of annoyance screwed into his face. Vernon followed.

Philip peeked through the window, and he gasped. "The Lippi," he said. "Over the sofa. The Lippi's gone! And the Braque over the fireplace! He's taken it all away! He's sold it!"

Vernon spoke. "Philip, don't get excited. He probably just packed the stuff up. Maybe he's moving. You've been telling him for years this house was too big and isolated."

Philip's face relaxed abruptly. "Yes. Of course."

"That must be what this mysterious meeting's all about," Vernon said.

Philip nodded and mopped his brow with a silk handkerchief. "I must be tired from the flight. Vernon, you're right. Of course they've been packing. But what a mess they've made of it. When Father sees this he's going to have a fit."

There was a silence as all three sons stood in the shrubbery looking at each other. Tom's own sense of unease had reached a high pitch. If their father was moving, it was a strange way to go about it.

Philip took the pipe out of his mouth. "What say, do you think this is another one of his little challenges to us? Some little puzzle?"

"I'm going to break in," Tom said.

"The alarm."

"The hell with the alarm."

Tom went around to the back of the house, his brothers following. He climbed over a wall into a small enclosed garden with a fountain. There was a bedroom window at eye level. Tom wrestled a rock out of the raised flower-bed wall. He brought it to the window, positioned himself, and hefted it to his shoulder.

"Are you really going to smash the window?" said Philip. "How sporting."

Tom heaved the rock, and it went crashing through the window. As the tinkling of glass subsided they all waited, listening.

Silence.

"No alarm," said Philip.

Tom shook his head. "I don't like this."

Philip stared through the broken window, and Tom could see a sudden thought blooming on his face. Philip cursed and in a flash had vaulted through the broken windowframe—wingtips, pipe, and all.

Vernon looked at Tom. "What's with him?"

Without answering, Tom climbed through the window. Vernon followed.

The bedroom was like the rest of the house—stripped of all art. It was a mess: dirty footprints on the carpet, trash, strips of packing tape, bubble wrap, and packing popcorn, along with nails and the sawed butt ends of lumber. Tom went to the hall. The view disclosed more bare walls where he remembered a Picasso, another Braque, and a pair of Mayan stelae. Gone, all gone.

With a rising feeling of panic he ventured down the hall, stopping at the archway to the living room. Philip was there, standing in the middle of the room, looking about, his face absolutely white. "I told him again and again this would happen. He was so bloody careless, keeping all this stuff here. So damn bloody careless."

"What?" Vernon cried, alarmed. "What is it, Philip? What's happened?"

Philip said, his agonized voice barely above a whisper, "We've been robbed!"

2

Detective Lieutenant Hutch Barnaby of the Santa Fe Police Department placed a hand on his bony chest and kicked back in his chair. He raised a fresh cup of Starbucks to his lips, the tenth one of the day. The aroma of the bitter roast filled his hooked nose as he looked out the window to the lone cottonwood tree. A beautiful spring day in Santa Fe, New Mexico, United States of America, he thought, as he folded his long limbs deeper into the chair. April 15. The Ides of April. Tax Return Day. Everyone was home counting their money, sobered up by thoughts of mortality and penury. Even the criminals took the day off.

He sipped the coffee with a huge feeling of contentment. Except for the faint ringing of a phone in the outer office, life was good.

He heard, at the edges of consciousness, the competent voice of Doreen answering the phone. Her crisp vowels floated in through the open door: "Hold on, excuse me, could you speak a little slower? I'll get you the sergeant—"

Barnaby drowned out the conversation with a noisy sip of coffee and extended his foot to his office door, giving it a little nudge shut. Blessed silence returned. He waited. And then it came: the knock.

Damn that phone call.

Barnaby placed his coffee on the desk and rose slightly from his slouched position. "Yes?"

Sergeant Harry Fenton opened the door, a keen look on his face.

Fenton was never one to like a slow day. The look was enough to tell Barnaby that something big had just come down.

"Hutch?"

"Hmmm?"

Fenton went on, breathlessly. "The Broadbent place was robbed. I got one of the sons on the phone now."

Hutch Barnaby didn't move a muscle. "Robbed of what?"

"*Everything.*" Fenton's black eyes glittered with relish.

Barnaby sipped his coffee, sipped again, and then lowered his chair to the floor with a small clunk. *Damn.*

As Barnaby and Fenton drove out the Old Santa Fe Trail, Fenton talked about the robbery. The collection, he'd heard, was worth half a billion. If the truth were anything close to that, Fenton said, it would be front-page-*New-York-Times*. He, Fenton, on the front page of the *Times*. Can you imagine that?

Barnaby could not imagine it. But he said nothing. He was used to Fenton's enthusiasms. He stopped at the end of the winding driveway that led up to the Broadbent aerie. Fenton climbed out the other side, his face shining with anticipation, his head forward, his huge hatchet nose leading the way. As they walked up the road, Hutch scanned the ground. He could see the blurred tracks of a semi, coming and going. They had come in bold as brass. So either Broadbent was away or they had killed him—more likely the latter. They'd probably find Broadbent's stiff in the house.

The road went around a corner and leveled out, and a pair of open gates came into view, guarding a sprawling adobe mansion set among a vast lawn dotted with cottonwoods. He paused to examine the gate. It was a mechanical gate with two motors. It didn't show any signs of having been forced, but the electrical box was open, and inside he could see a key. He knelt and examined it. The key was in a lock, which had been turned to deactivate the gate.

He turned to Fenton. "What do you make of that?"

"Drove a semi up here, had a key to the gate—these guys were professional. We're probably going to find Broadbent's cadaver in the house, you know."

"That's why I like you, Fenton. You're my second brain."

He heard a shout and glanced up to see three men crossing the lawn, coming toward him. The kids, walking right across the lawn.

Barnaby rose in a fury. "Jesus Christ! Don't you know this is a crime scene!"

The others halted, but the lead character, a tall man in a suit, kept coming. "And who might you be?" His voice was cool, supercilious.

"I'm Detective Lieutenant Hutchinson Barnaby," he said, "and Sergeant Harry Fenton. Santa Fe Police Department."

Fenton flashed them a quick smile that did little more than bare his teeth.

"You the sons?"

"We are," said the suit.

Fenton gave them another feral twitch of his lips.

Barnaby took a moment to look them over as potential suspects. The hippie in hemp had an honest, open face; maybe not the brightest bulb in the store but no robber. The one in cowboy boots had real horseshit on the boots, Barnaby noted with respect. And then there was the guy in the suit, who looked like he was from New York. As far as Hutch Barnaby was concerned anyone from New York was a potential murderer. Even the grandmothers. He scanned them again: Three more different brothers could not be imagined. Odd how that could happen in a single family.

"This is a crime scene, so I'm going to have to ask you gentlemen to leave the premises. Go out through the gate and go stand under a tree or something and wait for me. I'll be out in about twenty minutes to talk to you. Okay? Please don't wander around, don't touch anything, and don't talk to each other about the crime or what you've observed."

He turned, and then as an afterthought turned back. "The *whole* collection is missing?"

"That's what I said on the phone," said the suit.

"How much—ballpark—was it worth?"

"About five hundred million."

Barnaby touched the rim of his hat and glanced at Fenton. The look of naked pleasure on Fenton's face was enough to scare a pimp.

As Barnaby walked toward the house he considered that he had better be careful—there was going to be a lot of second-guessing on this one. The Feds, Interpol, God knows who else would be involved. He figured a quick look around before the crime-lab people arrived would be in order. He hooked his thumbs into his belt and gazed at the house. He wondered if the collection had been insured. That would bear some looking into. If so, maybe Maxwell Broadbent wasn't quite so dead after all. Maybe Maxwell Broadbent was sipping margaritas with some piece of ass on a beach in Phuket.

"I wonder if Broadbent was insured?" asked Fenton.

Hutch grinned at his partner, then looked back at the place. He looked at the broken window, the confusion of footsteps on the gravel, the trampled shrubbery. The fresh tracks were the sons', but there were a lot of older traces here as well. He could see where the moving van had parked, where it had laboriously backed around. It looked as if a week or two had passed since the robbery.

The important thing was to find the body—if there was one. He stepped inside the house. He looked around at the packing tape, bubble wrap, nails, discarded pieces of wood. There was sawdust on the rug and faint depressions. They had actually set up a table saw. It had been an exceptionally competent piece of work. Noisy, too. These people not only knew what they were doing, but they had taken the time to do it right. He sniffed the air. No sweet-and-sour-pork smell of a stiff.

Inside, the robbery felt just as old as it did outside. A week, maybe even two. He bent down and sniffed the end of a cut piece of lumber lying on the floor. It lacked that just-cut fresh-wood smell. He picked up a piece of grass that had been tracked into the house and crumbled it between his fingers—dry. Clots of mud tracked in by a lugged boot were also thoroughly dry. Barnaby thought back: Last rainfall was two weeks ago today. That's when it had happened; within twenty-four hours of the rain, when the ground was still muddy.

He wandered down the huge vaulted central hall. There were pedestals with bronze labels where statues had once stood. There were faint rectangles with hooks on the plastered walls where paintings had once been. There were straw rings and iron stands where antique pots had once sat, and empty shelves with dust holes where treasures had once stood. There were dark slots on the bookshelves where books had been removed.

He reached the bedroom door and looked at the parade of dirty footprints coming and going. More dried mud. Christ, there must've been half a dozen of them. This was a big moving job, and it must have taken a day at least, maybe two.

A machine sat inside the bedroom. Barnaby recognized it as a foam-in-place machine, of the kind you see at UPS. In another room, he found a shrink-wrapping machine for doing the really big stuff. He found stacks of lumber, rolls of felt, metal strapping tape, bolts and wing nuts, and a couple of skill saws. Couple of thousand dollars' worth of abandoned equipment. They hadn't bothered taking anything else; in the living room they'd left a ten-thousand-dollar television, along with a VCR, DVD, and two computers. He thought of his own crappy TV and VCR and the payments he was still making, while his wife and her new boyfriend were no doubt watching porno flicks on them every night.

He carefully stepped over a videotape cassette lying on the floor. Fenton said, "Lay you three to five the guy's dead, two to five it's an insurance scam."

"You take all the fun out of life, Fenton."

Someone must have seen the activity up here. The house, sitting on its mountaintop, was visible to all of Santa Fe. If he himself had bothered to look out the window of his double-wide in the valley two weeks ago he might have seen the robbery, the house ablaze all night long, the truck headlights winding down the hill. Again, he marveled at the moxie of the robbers. What made them so sure of pulling it off? It was too casual by half.

He glanced at his watch. He didn't have much time before the crime-scene van arrived.

He moved swiftly and methodically through the rooms, looking but taking no notes. Notes, he had learned, always came back to bite you. Every room had been hit. The job had gone to completion. In one room a bunch of boxes had been unpacked and paper lay scattered on the floor. He picked up a piece; some kind of bill of lading, dated a month ago, for twenty-four thousand dollars' worth of French pots and pans, German and Japanese knives. Was the guy starting a restaurant?

In the bedroom, in the back of a walk-in closet, he found a huge steel door, partway open.

"Fort Knox," said Fenton.

Barnaby nodded. With a house full of million-dollar paintings, it kind of made him wonder what was so valuable that it had to go into a vault.

Without touching the door he slipped inside. The vault was empty save some scattered trash on the floor and a bunch of wooden map cases. Slipping out his handkerchief, he used it to open a drawer. The velvet bore indentations where objects had once nested. He slid it shut and turned to the door itself, giving the lock a quick examination. There were no signs of a forced entry. None of the locked cases he'd seen in the rooms had been forced, either.

"The perps had all the codes and keys," said Fenton.

Barnaby nodded. This was no robbery.

He went outside and made a quick circle of the gardens. They looked neglected. Weeds were coming up. Nothing had been tended to. The grass hadn't been cut in a couple of weeks. The whole place had a seedy air about it. The neglect, it seemed to him, stretched back even more than the two weeks since the so-called robbery. It looked like the place had been going downhill for a month or two.

If insurance was involved, so were the sons. Maybe.

3

He found them standing in the shade of the piñon tree, arms crossed, silent and glum. As Barnaby approached, the guy in the suit asked, "Did you find anything?"

"Like what?"

The man scowled. "Do you have any idea what's been stolen here? We're talking hundreds of millions. Good God, how could anyone expect to get away with this? Some of these are *world-famous* works of art. There's a Filippo Lippi worth forty million dollars alone. They're probably on their way to the Middle East or Japan. You've got to call the FBI, contact Interpol, shut down the airports—"

He paused to draw in air.

"Lieutenant Barnaby has some questions," said Fenton, taking up the role he played so well, his voice curiously high and soft, with an undercurrent of menace. "State your names, please."

The one with the cowboy boots stepped forward. "I'm Tom Broadbent, and these are my brothers, Vernon and Philip."

"Look, officer," the one named Philip said, "these artworks are obviously headed for some sheik's bedroom. They could never hope to sell these paintings on the open market—they're too well known. No offense, but I *really* don't think the Santa Fe Police Department is equipped to handle this."

Barnaby flipped open his notebook and checked his watch. He still had almost thirty minutes before the crime-lab truck arrived from Albuquerque.

"May I ask a few questions, Philip? Okay if I use first names here?"

"Fine, fine, just get on with it."

"Ages?"

"I'm thirty-three," Tom said.

"Thirty-five," said Vernon.

"Thirty-seven," said Philip.

"Tell me, how is it that all three of you just happened to be here at once?" He directed his gaze toward the New Age type, Vernon, the one who looked like the least competent liar.

"Our father sent us a letter."

"What about?"

"Well . . ." Vernon glanced at his brothers nervously. "He didn't say."

"Any guesses?"

"Not really."

Barnaby switched his gaze. "Philip?"

"I haven't the slightest."

He swiveled his gaze to the other one, Tom. He found he liked Tom's face. It was a no-bullshit face. "So Tom, you want to help me out here?"

"I think it was to talk to us about our inheritance."

"Inheritance? How old was your father?"

"Sixty."

Fenton leaned forward to interrupt, his voice harsh. "Was he *sick?*"

"Yes."

"*How* sick?"

"He was dying of cancer," said Tom coldly.

"I'm sorry," said Barnaby, putting a restraining arm on Fenton as if to stop him from asking more tactless questions. "Any of you got your copy of the letter?"

All three produced the same letter, handwritten, on ivory laid paper. Interesting, Barnaby thought, that each one had his copy. Said something about the importance they attached to this meeting. Barnaby took one and read:

> Dear Tom,
>   I want you to come to my house in Santa Fe, on April 15, at exactly 1:00 P.M., regarding a very important matter affecting your future. I've asked Philip and Vernon as well. I have enclosed funds to pay for your travel. Please be on time: one o'clock sharp. Do your old man this one last courtesy.
>
> Father

"Any chance of a recovery from the cancer, or was he a goner?" Fenton asked.

Philip stared at Fenton and then turned to Barnaby. "Who is this man?"

Barnaby shot a warning glance at Fenton, who often got out of hand. "We're all on the same side here, trying to solve this crime."

"As I understand it," Philip said grudgingly, "there was no chance of recovery. Our father had gone through radiation treatments and chemotherapy, but the cancer had metastasized and there was no getting rid of it. He declined further treatment."

"I'm sorry," said Barnaby, trying unsuccessfully to summon up a modicum of sympathy. "Getting back to this letter, it says something here about funds. How much money came with it?"

"Twelve hundred dollars in cash," said Tom.

"*Cash?* In what form?"

"Twelve one-hundred-dollar bills. Sending cash like that was typical of Father."

Fenton interrupted again. "How *long* did he have to live?" He asked this question directly at Philip, thrusting his head forward. Fenton's was an ugly head, very narrow and sharp, with thick eyebrow ridges, deep-set eyes, a huge nose with each nostril projecting a thicket of black nosehairs, crooked brown teeth, and a receding chin. He had olive skin; despite the Anglo name, Fenton was a Hispano from the town of Truchas, way back up in the Sangre de Cristo Mountains. He was scary, if you didn't know he was the kindliest man alive.

"About six months."

"So he invited you here for what? To do a little eeny meeny meiny moe with his stuff?"

Fenton could be awful when he wanted. But the man got results.

Philip said icily, "That's a charming way of putting it. I suppose that's possible."

Barnaby broke in smoothly. "But with a collection like this, Philip, wouldn't he have made arrangements to leave it to a museum?"

"Maxwell Broadbent *loathed* museums."

"Why?"

"Museums had taken the lead in criticizing our father's somewhat unorthodox collecting practices."

"Which were?"

"Buying artwork of dubious provenance, dealing with tomb robbers and looters, smuggling antiquities across borders. He even robbed tombs himself. I can appreciate his antipathy. Museums are bastions of hypocrisy, greed, and cupidity. They criticize in everyone else the very methods they themselves employed to get their collections."

"What about leaving the collection to a university?"

"He hated academics. Tweedy-dums and tweedy-dees, he called them. The academics, especially the archaeologists, accused Maxwell Broadbent of looting temples in Central America. I'm not spilling any family secrets here: It's a well-known story. You can pick up just about any copy of *Archaeology* magazine and read about how our father was their version of the devil incarnate."

"Was he planning to sell the collection?" Barnaby pushed on.

Philip's lip curled with contempt. "Sell? My father had to deal with auction houses and art dealers all his life. He would die the death of a thousand cuts before he'd consign them one mediocre print to sell."

"So he planned to leave it all to you three?"

There was an awkward silence. "That," said Philip finally, "was the assumption."

Fenton broke in. "Church? Wife? Girlfriend?"

Philip removed the pipe between his teeth and, in a perfect imitation of Fenton's clipped style, answered him: "Atheist. Divorced. Misogynist."

The other two brothers broke out laughing. Hutch Barnaby even found himself enjoying Fenton's discomfort. It was so rare that any-one got the better of him during an interrogation. This Philip charac-ter, despite his pretensions, was tough. But there was something sad in the long, intelligent face, something lost.

Barnaby held out the bill of lading for the shipment of cookware. "Any idea what this is all about or where the stuff might have gone?"

They examined it, shook their heads, and handed it back. "He didn't even like to cook," said Tom.

Barnaby shoved the document into his pocket. "Tell me about your father. Looks, personality, character, business dealings, that sort of thing."

It was Tom who spoke again. "He's . . . one of a kind."

"How so?"

"He's a physical giant of a man, six foot five, fit, handsome, broad shoulders, not a trace of flab, white hair and white beard, solid as a lion with a roaring voice to match. People say he looks like Heming-way."

"Personality?"

"He's the kind of man who's never wrong, who rides roughshod over everyone and everything to get what he wants. He lives by his own rules in life. He never graduated high school, but he knows more about art and archaeology than most Ph.D.'s. Collecting is his reli-gion. He despises other people's religious beliefs, and that's one rea-son why he takes so much pleasure in buying and selling things stolen from tombs—and robbing tombs himself."

"Tell me more about this tomb robbing."

Philip spoke this time. "Maxwell Broadbent was born into a working-class family. He went to Central America when he was young and disappeared into the jungle for two years. He made a big dis-covery, robbed some Mayan temple, and smuggled the stuff back. That's how he got started. He was a dealer in questionable art and antiquities—everything from Greek and Roman statues that had been spirited out of Europe to Khmer reliefs chiseled out of Cambodian funerary temples to Renaissance paintings stolen in Italy during the war. He dealt not to make money but to finance his own collecting."

"Interesting."

"Maxwell's methods," Philip said, "were really the only way a person nowadays could acquire truly great art. There probably wasn't a single piece in his collection that was clean."

Vernon spoke: "He once robbed a tomb that had a curse on it. He quoted it at cocktail parties."

"A curse? What did it say?"

"Something like *He who disturbs these bones shall be skinned alive and fed to diseased hyenas. And then a herd of asses will copulate with his mother.* Or words to that effect."

Fenton let a laugh escape.

Barnaby shot him a cautionary glance. He directed his next question to Philip, now that he had the man talking. Funny how people liked to complain about their parents. "What made him tick?"

Philip frowned, his broad brow furrowing. "It was like this. Maxwell Broadbent loved his Lippi *Madonna* more than he loved any real woman. He loved his Bronzino portrait of little Bia de' Medici more than he loved any of his real children. He loved his two Braques, his Monet, and his Mayan jade skulls more than the real people in his life. He worshiped his collection of thirteenth-century French reliquaries containing the alleged bones of saints more than he worshiped any real saint. His collections were his lovers, his children, and his religion. That's what made him tick: beautiful things."

"None of that's true," said Vernon. "He loved us."

Philip gave a little snort of derision.

"You say he was divorced from your mother?"

"You mean our *mothers?* He was divorced from two of them, widowed by the other. There were also two other wives he didn't breed with and any number of girlfriends."

"Any fights over alimony?" Fenton asked.

"Naturally," said Philip. "Alimony, palimony, it never ended."

"But he raised you kids himself?"

Philip paused, then said, "In his own unique way, yes."

The words hung in the air. Barnaby wondered just what kind of father he might have been. Better stick to the main thread: He was running out of time. The SOC boys would be here any moment, and then he'd be lucky ever to set foot on the crime scene again.

"Any woman in his life now?"

"Only for purposes of mild physical activity in the evening," said Philip. "She will get nothing, I assure you."

Tom broke in. "Do you think our father is okay?"

"To be honest, I haven't seen any evidence of a murder here. We didn't find a body in the house."

"Could they have kidnapped him?"

Barnaby shook his head. "Not likely. Why deal with a hostage?" He glanced at his watch. Five, maybe seven minutes left. Time to ask the question. "Insured?" He made it sound as casual as possible.

A dark look passed over Philip's face. "No."

Even Barnaby couldn't hide his surprise. "*No?*"

"Last year I tried to arrange for insurance. No one would cover the collection as long as it was kept in this house with this security environment. You can see for yourself how vulnerable the place is."

"Why didn't your father upgrade his security?"

"Our father was a very difficult man. No one could tell him what to do. He had a lot of guns in the house. I guess he thought he could fight 'em off, Wild West style."

Barnaby shuffled through his notes and checked his watch again. He was disturbed. The pieces were not fitting together. He was sure it wasn't a simple robbery, but without insurance, why rob yourself? Then there was the coincidence of the letter to the sons, calling them in for this meeting at just this moment. He recalled the letter . . . *a very important matter affecting your future . . . very disappointed if you do not come . . .* There was something suggestive about the wording.

"What was in the vault?"

"Don't tell me they got into the vault, too!" Philip dabbed at his sweating face with a trembling hand. His suit had wilted, and the devastation on his face looked genuine.

"Yes."

"Oh, God. It held gemstones, jewelry, South and Central American gold, rare coins and stamps, all extremely valuable."

"The burglars seem to have had the combination to the vault as well as keys to everything. Any idea how?"

"No."

"Did your father have anyone he trusted—a lawyer, for example—who might have kept a second set of keys or had the combination to the vault?"

"He trusted nobody."

This was an important point. Barnaby looked at Vernon and Tom. "You agree?"

They both nodded.

"Did he have a maid?"

"He had a woman who came daily."

"Gardener?"

"A full-time man."

"Any others?"

"He employed a full-time cook and a nurse who looked in three days a week."

Fenton now interrupted, leaning forward and smiling in that feral way of his. "Mind if I ask you a question, Philip?"

"If you must."

"How come you're talking about your father in the past tense? You know something we don't?"

"Oh, for God's sake!" Philip exploded. "Who will rid me of this Sherlock Holmes *manqué?*"

"Fenton?" murmured Barnaby, casting him a warning glance.

Fenton looked over and saw Barnaby's look, and his face fell. "Sorry."

Barnaby asked, "Where are they now?"

"Where are who?"

"Maid, gardener, cook. This robbery took place two weeks ago. Somebody dismissed the help."

Tom said, "The robbery occurred *two weeks ago?*"

"That's right."

"But I only got my letter by Federal Express three days ago."

This was interesting. "Did any of you notice the sender's address?"

"It was some kind of drop-shipping place, like Mail Boxes Etc.," said Tom.

Barnaby thought for a moment. "I have to tell you," he said, "that this so-called robbery has insurance fraud written all over it."

"I already explained to you the collection wasn't insured," said Philip.

"You explained it, but I don't believe it."

"I *know* the art insurance market, Lieutenant—I'm an art historian. This collection was worth about half a billion dollars, and it was just sitting in a house in the country protected by an off-the-shelf security system. Father didn't even have a dog. I'm telling you, *the collection wasn't insurable.*"

Barnaby looked at Philip for a long time, and then he looked at the other two brothers.

Philip let out a hiss of air and looked at his watch. "Lieutenant, don't you think this case is a little big for the Santa Fe Police Department?"

If it wasn't insurance fraud, then what was it? This was no damn robbery. A crazy idea began to form, still vague. A truly nutty idea. But it was starting to take shape almost against his will, assembling itself into something like a theory. He glanced at Fenton. Fenton didn't see it. For all his gifts, Fenton lacked a sense of humor.

Barnaby then remembered the big-screen television, the VCR, and the videotape lying on the floor. No, not lying: *placed* on the floor, next to the remote. What was the hand-lettered title? WATCH ME.

That was it. Like water freezing, it all locked into place. He knew exactly what had happened. Barnaby cleared his throat. "Come with me."

The three sons followed him back into the house, into the living room.

"Have a seat."

"What's this all about?" Philip was getting agitated. Even Fenton was looking at Barnaby quizzically.

Barnaby picked up the tape and the remote. "We're going to watch a video." He flicked on the television set and slid the tape into the VCR.

"Is this some kind of joke?" Philip asked, refusing to sit, his face flushed. The other two stood nearby, confused.

"You're blocking the screen," said Barnaby, settling himself on the sofa. "Have a seat."

"This is outrageous——"

A sudden burst of sound from the video silenced Philip, and then the face of Maxwell Broadbent, larger than life, materialized on the screen. All three sat down.

His voice, deep and booming, reverberated in the empty room.

"Greetings from the dead."

4

Tom Broadbent stared at the life-size image of his father slowly coming into focus on the screen. The camera gradually panned back, revealing Maxwell Broadbent seated at the giant desk in his study, holding a few sheets of paper in his large hands. The room had not yet been stripped; the Lippi painting of the Madonna was still on the wall behind him, the bookshelves were still filled with books, and the other paintings and statues were all in their places. Tom shivered: Even his father's electronic image intimidated him.

After the greeting his father paused, cleared his throat, and focused his intense blue eyes on the camera. The sheets shook slightly in his hands. He seemed to be laboring under a strong emotion.

Maxwell Broadbent's eyes dropped back to the papers, and he began to read:

Dear Philip, Vernon, and Tom,
  The long and short of it is this: I've taken my wealth with me to the grave. I've sealed myself and my collection in a tomb. This tomb is hidden somewhere in the world, in a place that only I know of.

He paused, cleared his throat again, looked up briefly with a flash of blue, looked down, and continued reading. His voice took on that slightly pedantic tone that Tom remembered so well from the dinner table.

For more than a hundred thousand years, human beings have buried themselves with their most valuable possessions. Burying the dead with treasure has a venerable history, starting with the Neanderthals and running through the ancient Egyptians and on down almost to the present day. People buried themselves with their gold, silver, art, books, medicine, furniture, food, slaves, horses, and sometimes even their concubines and wives—anything they thought might be useful in the afterlife. It's only in the last century or two that human beings stopped interring their remains with grave goods, thus breaking a long tradition.

It is a tradition I am glad to revive.

The fact is, almost everything we know of the past comes to us through grave goods. Some have called me a tomb robber. Not so. I'm not a robber, I'm a recycler. I made my fortune on the wealth that foolish people thought they were taking with them to the afterworld. I've decided to do just what they did and bury myself with all my worldly goods. The only difference between me and them is that I'm no fool. I know there's no afterworld where I can enjoy my wealth. Unlike them, I die with no illusions. When you're dead you're dead. When you die you're just a duffel bag of rotting meat, grease, brains, and bones—nothing more.

I'm taking my wealth to the grave for another reason entirely. A very important reason. A reason that concerns the three of you.

He paused, looked up. His hands were still shaking slightly, and the muscles in his jaw were flexing.

"Jesus Christ," Philip whispered, half rising from his seat, his hands clenched. "I don't believe this."

Maxwell Broadbent raised the papers to read some more, stumbled over the words, hesitated, and then abruptly stood and tossed the papers onto the desk. *Screw this,* he said, shoving back the chair with a violent motion. *What I've got to say to you is too important for a damn speech.* He came around the desk with several great strides, his enormous presence filling the screen and, by extension, the room where they were sitting. He paced in front of the camera, agitated, stroking his close-cropped beard.

This isn't easy. I don't quite know how to explain this to you three.

He turned, strode back.

When I was your age, I had nothing. Nothing. I came to New York from Erie, Pennsylvania, with just thirty-five dollars and my father's old suit. No family, no friends, no college degree. Nothing. Dad was a good man, but he was a bricklayer. Mom was dead. I was pretty much alone in the world.

"Not *this* story again," moaned Philip.

It was the fall of 1963. I pounded the pavement until I found a job, a shitty job, washing dishes at Mama Gina's on East 88th and Lex. A dollar and twenty-five cents an hour.

Philip was shaking his head. Tom felt numb.

Broadbent stopped pacing, planted himself in front of the desk, and faced the camera, slightly hunched, glowering at them. *I can just see you three now. Philip, you're no doubt shaking your head sadly, Tom, you're probably up and swearing. And Vernon, you think I'm just plain nuts. God, I can just see the three of you. I feel sorry for you, I really do. This isn't easy.*

He resumed his pacing. *Gina's wasn't far from the Metropolitan Museum of Art. I went in there one day on a whim, and it changed my life. I spent my last dollar on a membership, and I began going to that museum every day. I fell in love with the place. What a revelation! I'd never seen such beauty, such*—He waved his large hand. *Christ, but you know all this.*

"We certainly do," said Philip dryly.

The point is, I started with nothing. Nada. *I worked hard. I had a vision for my life, a goal. I read everything I could get my hands on. Schliemann and the discovery of Troy, Howard Carter and King Tut's tomb, John Lloyd Stephens and the city of Copán, the excavation of the Villa of the Mysteries at Pompeii. I dreamed of finding treasures like these, digging them up, owning them. I cast around: Where in the world were there lost tombs and temples still to be found? The answer was Central America. There you could still find a lost city. There was still a chance for me.*

Now he paused to open a box on his desk. He withdrew a cigar, trimmed and lit it.

"Jesus Christ," said Philip. "The old man's *incorrigible.*"

Broadbent waved out the match, tossed it onto the desk, and grinned. He had beautiful teeth, and they glinted white. *I'm going to die anyway, why not enjoy my last few months. Right, Philip? Still smoking that pipe? I'd give it up if I were you.*

He turned and paced, trailing little puffs of blue. *Anyway, I saved my money until I had enough to go to Central America. I went there not because I wanted to make money—although that was part of it, I'll admit—but because I had a passion. And I found it. I found my lost city.*

He spun, turned, paced.

That was the beginning. That got me started. I dealt in art and antiquities only as a way to finance my collecting. And look:

He paused, gesturing open-palmed to the unseen collection in the house around him.

Look. Here's the result. One of the greatest private collections of art and antiquities in the world. These aren't just things. Every piece in here has a story, a memory for me. How I first saw it, how I fell in love with it, how I acquired it. Each piece is part of me.

He seized a jade object on his desk and held it toward the camera.

Like this Olmec head, which I found in a tomb in Piedra Lumbre. I remember the day . . . the heat, the snakes . . . and I remember seeing it for the first time, lying there in the dust of the tomb, where it had been for two thousand years.

Philip snorted. "The joys of theft."

He put the piece back down. *For two thousand years it had rested there— an object of such exquisite beauty it makes you want to cry. I wish I could tell you my feelings when I saw that flawless jade head just lying there in the dust. It wasn't created to vegetate in the darkness. I rescued it and brought it back to life.*

His voice cracked with emotion. He paused, cleared his throat, put the head down. Then he fumbled for the back of his chair and sat down, laying his cigar aside in the ashtray. He turned back to face the camera, leaning forward on the desk.

I'm your father. I've watched you three grow up. I know you better than you know yourselves.

"Not likely," said Philip.

As I've watched you grow up, I've been dismayed to see in you a feeling of entitlement. Privilege. A rich-kid's syndrome. A feeling that you don't have to work too hard, study too hard, exert yourselves—because you're the sons of Maxwell Broadbent. Because someday, without lifting a goddamn finger, you'll be rich.

He rose again, restless with energy. *Look, I know it's mostly my fault. I've catered to your whims, bought you everything you wanted, sent you to all the best private schools, dragged you around Europe. I felt guilty about the divorces and all that. I wasn't born to be a married man, I guess. But what have I done? I've raised three kids who, instead of living splendid lives, are waiting for their inheritance.* Great Expectations *redux.*

"Bullshit," said Vernon angrily.

Philip, you're an assistant professor of art history at a junior college on Long Island. Tom? A horse vet in Utah. And Vernon? Well, I don't even know what you're doing now, probably living in some ashram somewhere, giving your money to a fraudulent guru.

"Not true!" said Vernon. "Not true! Go to hell!"

Tom could say nothing. He felt a nauseous tightening somewhere in his gut.

And on top of that, the father went on, *you three don't get along. You never learned to cooperate, to be brothers. I started to think: What have I done? What have I done? What kind of father have I been? Have I taught my sons independence? Have I taught them the value of work? Have I taught them self-reliance? Have I taught them to take care of each other?*

He paused and fairly shouted out, *No!*

After all this, after everything, the schools, Europe, the fishing and camping trips, I've raised three quasi-failures. Christ, it's my fault that it ended up this way, but there it is. And then I found out I was dying, and that put me in a panic. How was I going to fix things?

He paused, turned. He was breathing hard now, and his face was flushed.

Nothing like having death poke his stinking mug into your face to make you think about things. I had to figure out what to do with my collection. I sure as hell wasn't going to give it to a museum or some university for a bunch of tweedy-dums to gloat over. And I wasn't going to let some scummy auction house or dealer get rich from all my hard work, break it up and disperse it to the four corners after I'd spent a lifetime assembling it. Absolutely not.

He mopped his brow, wadded up the handkerchief in a fist, and gestured at the camera with it.

I had always planned to leave it to you. But when it came down to it, I realized it would be the very worst thing I could do to you. No way was I going to hand over to you half a billion dollars that you hadn't earned.

He went back behind the desk, eased his enormous frame into the chair, and took another cigar from a leather box.

Look at me, still smoking. Too late now.

He clipped the end, lit it. The cloud of smoke confused the automatic focus on the camera, and it went blurry, shifting back and forth, trying to find its focus. When the smoke drifted leftward out of the frame, Maxwell Broadbent's square, handsome face leapt back into focus.

And then it came to me. It was brilliant. All my life I'd been excavating tombs and dealing in grave goods. I knew all the tricks for hiding tombs, every booby trap, everything. I suddenly realized that I, too, could take it with me. And then I could do something for you that would really be a legacy.

He paused, clasped his hands, and leaned forward.

You're going to earn this money. I've arranged to bury myself and my collection in a tomb somewhere in the world. I challenge you to find me. If you do, you can rob my tomb and have it all. That's my challenge to you, my three sons.

He inhaled, tried to smile.

I warn you: It's going to be difficult and dangerous. Nothing in life worth doing is easy. And here's the kicker: You'll never succeed unless you cooperate.

He brought his massive fist down on the desk.

That's it in a nutshell. I didn't do much for you in life, but by God I'm going to fix that with my death.

He got up again and walked over to the camera. His arm reached out to turn it off, and then, as an afterthought, he paused, his blurry face looming gigantically on the screen:

I've never been much on sentiment, so I'll just say to you, good-bye. Good-bye, Philip, Vernon, and Tom. Good-bye and good luck. I love you.

The screen went dead.

5

Tom remained on the sofa, momentarily unable to move. Hutch Barnaby was the first to react. He rose and coughed delicately by way of breaking the shocked silence.

"Fenton? Seems we're not needed here any longer."

Fenton nodded, rising awkwardly, actually blushing.

Barnaby turned to the brothers and politely touched the brim of his cap. "As you can see, this isn't a police matter. We'll leave you to, ah, sort things out on your own." They began edging toward the door archway that led to the hall. They couldn't wait to get away.

Philip rose. "Officer Barnaby?" His voice was half choked.

"Yes?"

"I trust you won't mention this to anybody. It wouldn't be helpful if . . . if the whole world started looking for the tomb."

"Good point. No reason to mention it to anyone. No reason at all. I'll call off the SOC boys." He backed out, and disappeared. A moment later they could hear the sound of the great front door of the house clanking shut.

The three brothers remained.

"The son of a bitch," Philip said quietly. "I can't believe it. The son of a bitch."

Tom glanced at his brother's white face. He knew that he'd been living rather well on his assistant professor's salary. He needed the money. And no doubt he had already been spending it.

Vernon said, "What now?"

The word hung in the silence.

"I can't believe the old bastard," Philip said. "Taking a dozen old master paintings to the grave like that, not to mention all that priceless Mayan jade and gold. I'm floored." He slipped a silk handkerchief out of his vest pocket and dabbed his brow. "He had no *right*."

"So what do we do?" Vernon repeated.

Philip stared at him. "We go find the tomb, of course."

"How?"

"A man can't bury himself with half a billion dollars of art without help. We find out who helped him."

"I don't believe it," Tom said. "He never trusted anybody in his life."

"He couldn't have done it on his own."

"It's so . . . *him*," said Philip suddenly.

"Maybe he left clues." Vernon strode over to the breakfront drawers, jerked one open, and rummaged through it, swearing. He pulled out a second, and a third, becoming so agitated that the drawer came out all the way, spilling its contents to the floor—playing cards, Parcheesi, chess, Chinese checkers. Tom remembered them all—the old games of their childhood, now yellowed and shabby with age. He felt a cold knot in his chest; this is what it had come to. Vernon cursed and gave the scattered mess a kick, sending pieces all over the room.

"Vernon, trashing the house is pointless."

Vernon, ignoring him, kept opening drawers, sweeping their contents onto the floor, moving on.

Philip slipped his pipe out of his trouser pocket and lit it with a shaking hand. "You're wasting your time. I say we go talk to Marcus Hauser. He's the key."

Vernon paused. "Hauser? Father hasn't been in contact with him in forty years."

"He's the only one who really knew Father. They spent two years together in Central America. If anyone knows where Father went, it's him."

"Father *hates* Hauser."

"I expect they had a reconciliation, with Father sick and all." Philip flicked open a gold lighter and sucked the flame into the bowl of his pipe with a gurgle.

Vernon moved into the den. Tom could hear cupboards being opened and shut, books being pulled from shelves, things crashing to the floor.

"I'm telling you, Hauser's involved. We've got to move fast. I've got debts—I've got obligations."

Vernon came back from the den carrying a boxful of papers, which he slammed down on the coffee table. "It figures you'd already be spending your inheritance."

Philip turned to him coolly. "Who was it took twenty grand from Father just last year?"

"That was a loan." Vernon started shuffling through the papers, rifling folders, scattering them on the floor. Tom saw their old elementary school report cards spilling from a file. It surprised him that their father had bothered to save those—particularly when he had been none too pleased with their grades to begin with.

"Have you paid it back yet?" Philip asked.

"I will."

"Of course you will," said Philip sarcastically.

Vernon colored. "What about the forty thousand that Father spent on sending you to graduate school? Have you paid that back yet?"

"That was a gift. He paid for Tom's veterinary school, too—right, Tom? And if *you* had gone to graduate school he would have paid for yours. Instead, you went and lived with that swami woo-woo in India."

There was a tense silence.

"Go to hell," said Vernon.

Tom stared from one brother to the other. It was happening, just as it had happened a thousand times before. Usually he stepped in and tried to be peacemaker. Just as often it did no good.

"The hell with you, too," Philip said. He put the pipe back between his teeth with a click and turned on his heel.

"Wait!" Vernon called, but it was too late. When Philip got mad, he left, and he was doing it again. The great door boomed shut with a dying rattle.

"For God's sake, Vernon, can't you pick a better time to fight?"

"Screw him. He started it, didn't he?"

Tom couldn't even remember who started it.

Back in the office, Hutch Barnaby sat in his chair, a fresh cup of coffee resting on his paunch, looking out the window. Fenton sat in the other chair, with his own cup, staring gloomily at the floor.

"Fenton, you gotta stop thinking about it. These things happen."

"I can't believe it."

"I know, it's some crazy shit, the guy burying himself with half a billion dollars. Don't worry. Someday someone in this town'll commit a *New York Times* front-page crime, and your name'll be there. This just didn't pan out."

Fenton nursed his coffee—and his disappointment.

"I knew it, Fenton, even before I saw that video. I figured it out. When I realized it wasn't an insurance scam, it was like a lightbulb went on in my head. Hey, it would make a great movie, don't you think? Rich guy takes his shit with him."

Fenton said nothing.

"How do you think the old guy did it? Think about it. He needed help. That was a lot of stuff. You can't move a few tons of artwork around the world without someone noticing."

Fenton sipped.

Barnaby glanced up at the clock and then down at the papers strewn about his desk. "Two hours to lunch. How come nothing interesting ever happens in this city? Look at this. Drugs and more drugs. Why don't these kids rob a bank for a change?"

Fenton drained the cup. "It's out there."

Silence.

"What are you trying to say? What do you mean by that comment? *It's out there.* So what? Lot of things are *out there.*"

Fenton crushed the cup.

"You aren't suggesting something, are you?"

Fenton dropped the cup in the trash can.

"You said, *It's out there.* I want to know what you meant by that."

"We go get it."

"And?"

"We keep it."

Barnaby laughed. "Fenton, I'm amazed at you. In case you didn't notice, we're *law enforcement officers*. Did that little fact slip your mind? We're supposed to be *honest*."

"Yeah," said Fenton.

"Right," said Barnaby after a moment. "Honesty. If you don't have that, Fenton, then what do you have?"

"Half a billion dollars," said Fenton.

6

The building wasn't an old brownstone as it would have been in a Bogart film but a glass and steel monstrosity that teetered into the sky above West Fifty-seventh Street, an ugly eighties skyscraper. At least, thought Philip, the rent would be high. And if the rent was high, it meant Marcus Aurelius Hauser was a successful private investigator.

Strolling into the lobby was like walking into a giant polished granite cube. The place reeked of cleaning fluids. A stand of sickly bamboo grew in one corner. An elevator whisked him up to the thirtieth floor, and he was soon at the cherry doors leading into the offices of Marcus Hauser, PI.

Philip paused inside the doorway. Whatever he had imagined as the office of a private investigator, this colorless postmodern interior of gray slate, industrial carpeting, and black polished granite was not it. How could anyone work in such a sterile space? The room appeared empty.

"Yeah?" came a voice from behind a half-moon wall of glass bricks.

Philip came around and found himself staring at the back of a man sitting at a vast kidney-shaped desk, which instead of facing the door to his office faced in the opposite direction toward a wall of windows that looked west over the dull zinc sheen of the Hudson River. Without turning, the man gestured toward an armchair. Philip crossed the floor, seated himself, and settled in to study Marcus Hauser: ex–Vietnam Green Beret; ex–tomb robber; ex-lieutenant, BATF, Manhattan field office.

In his father's photo albums he had seen pictures of Hauser as a young man, blurry and indistinct, dressed in jungle khakis, packing some kind of firearm on his hip. He was always grinning. Philip felt a little disconcerted finally seeing him in the flesh. He looked even smaller than Philip had imagined him, and he was overdressed in a brown suit with collar pin, vest, gold chain, and watch fob. A working-class man aping the gentry. There was the scent of cologne about him, and what little hair he had was excessively pomaded and curled, each strand individually arranged to provide maximal coverage to his bald spot. Gold rings winked on no fewer than four of his fingers. His hands had been manicured, his nails cleaned and polished, his nose carefully trimmed of hair. Even his bald pate, gleaming under the screen of hairs that covered it, gave every appearance of having been waxed and buffed. Philip found himself wondering if this was the same Marcus Hauser who had tramped through the jungles with his father in search of lost cities and ancient tombs. Perhaps there had been some mistake.

He cleared his throat. "Mr. Hauser?"

"Marcus," came the rapid reply, like a cracking good tennis volley. His voice was equally disconcerting: high, nasal, working-class accent. His eyes, however, were as green and cool as a crocodile's.

Philip felt flustered. He recrossed his legs and, without asking permission, took out his pipe and began to fill it. At this, Hauser smiled, slid open his desk drawer, turned out a humidor, and removed an enormous Churchill. "So glad you smoke," he said, rolling the cigar between his perfect fingers, sliding a gold monogrammed clipper out of his pocket, and giving the end a snip. "We mustn't let the barbarians take over." When he had lit up, he leaned back in his chair and, looking at him through a skein of smoke, said, "What can I do for the son of my old partner, Maxwell Broadbent?"

"May we speak in confidentiality?"

"Naturally."

"Six months ago my father was diagnosed with cancer." Philip paused, observing Hauser's face to see if he had already known. But Hauser's face was as opaque as his mahogany desk. "Lung cancer," Philip continued. "They operated, and he got the usual chemo and radiation. He gave up the stogies and went into remission. For a while it seemed like he had it licked, and then it came roaring back. He started on the chemotherapy again, but he hated it. One day he ripped out the IVs, decked a male nurse, and left. He picked up a box of Cuba Libres on the way home and never went back. They had given him six months to live, and that was three months ago."

Hauser listened, puffing on his cigar.

Philip paused. "Has he been in touch with you?"

Hauser shook his head, took another puff. "Not for forty years."

"Sometime last month," Philip said, "Maxwell Broadbent disappeared, along with his collection. He left us a video."

Hauser raised his eyebrows.

"It was a last will and testament of sorts. In it, he said he was taking it with him into the grave."

"He did *what*?" Hauser leaned forward, his face suddenly interested. The mask had fallen for a moment: He was genuinely astonished.

"He took it with him. Everything. Money, artwork, his collection. Just like an Egyptian pharaoh. He buried himself in a tomb somewhere in the world and then issued us a challenge: If we find the tomb, we can rob it. That, you see, is his idea of making us earn our inheritance."

Hauser leaned back and laughed long and loud. When he finally recovered, he took a couple of lazy puffs on his cigar, then reached out and tapped a two-inch ash off. "Only Max could come up with a scheme like that."

"So you don't know anything about this?" Philip asked.

"Nothing." Hauser seemed to be telling the truth.

"You're a private investigator," said Philip.

Hauser shifted the cigar from one side of his mouth to the other.

"You grew up with\Max. You spent two years with him in the jungle. You know him and how he worked better than anyone. I wondered if you'd be willing, as a PI, to help me find his tomb."

Hauser eased a stream of blue smoke out of his mouth.

Philip added, "It doesn't seem to me that this would be a difficult assignment. An art collection like that wouldn't travel inconspicuously."

"It would in the hold of Max's Gulfstream IV."

"I doubt he buried himself in his plane."

"The Vikings buried themselves in their ships. Maybe Max packed his treasure in an airtight, pressure-resistant container and ditched his plane in the ocean over the mid-Pacific abyssal plain, where it sank in two miles of water." He spread his hands and smiled.

Philip managed to say, "No." He dabbed his brow, trying to suppress the image of the Lippi, two miles deep, wedged in the abyssal muck. "You don't really believe that, do you?"

"I'm not saying that's what he did. I'm just showing you what ten seconds of thinking can turn up. Are you working with your brothers?"

"Half-brothers. No. I've decided to find this tomb on my own."

"What are their plans?"

"I don't know and frankly I don't care. I'll share what I find with them, of course."

"Tell me about them."

"Tom's probably the one to watch out for. He's the youngest. When we were children, he was the wild one. He's the kid who would be the first to jump off the cliff into the water, the first to throw the rock at the wasp's nest. Got kicked out of a couple of schools but cleaned up his act in college and has been on the straight and narrow ever since."

"And the other one, Vernon?"

"Right now he's in some pseudo-Buddhist cult run by an ex–philosophy professor from Berkeley. He was always the lost one. He's tried it all: drugs, cults, gurus, encounter groups. When he was a kid he'd bring home crippled cats, doggies that had been run over by cars, little birdies that had been pushed out of the nest by their bigger siblings—that sort of thing. Everything he brought home died. In school, he was the kid the others loved to pick on. He flunked out of college and hasn't been able to hold down a steady job. He's a sweet kid but . . . *incompetent* at adulthood."

"What are they doing now?"

"Tom went home to his ranch in Utah. The last I heard he had given up on searching for the tomb. Vernon says he's going to find the tomb on his own, doesn't want me to be part of it."

"Anyone else know about this besides your two brothers?"

"There were two cops in Santa Fe who saw the videotape and know the whole story."

"Names?"

"Barnaby and Fenton."

Hauser made a note. A light on the phone blinked once, and Hauser picked up the receiver. He listened for a long time, spoke softly and rapidly, made a call, another, and then another. Philip felt annoyed that Hauser was doing other business in front of him, wasting his time.

Hauser hung up. "Any wives or girlfriends in the picture?"

"Five ex-wives: four living, one deceased. No girlfriends to speak of."

A faint curl stretched Hauser's upper lip. "Max was always one with the ladies."

Again the silence stretched on. Hauser seemed to be thinking. Then, to Philip's annoyance, he made another call, speaking in low tones. Finally he set down the phone.

"Well now, Philip, what do you know about me?"

"Only that you were my father's partner in exploration, that you both knocked around Central America for a couple of years. And that you two had a falling-out."

"That's right. We spent almost two years in Central America together, looking for Mayan tombs to excavate. This was back in the early sixties when it was more or less legal. We found a few things, but it was only after I left that Max made his big strike and became rich. I went on to Vietnam."

"And the falling-out? Father never talked about it."

There was a faint pause. "Max never talked about it?"

"No."

"I can hardly remember it now. You know how it is when two people are thrown together for a long stretch of time, they get on each other's nerves." Hauser laid his cigar down in a cut crystal ashtray. The ashtray was as big as a dinner plate and probably weighed twenty pounds. Philip wondered if he had made a mistake coming here. Hauser seemed like a lightweight.

The phone blinked again, and Hauser picked it up. This was the last straw; Philip rose. "I'll come back when you're less busy," he said curtly.

Hauser wagged a gold-ringed finger at Philip to wait, listened for a minute, and then hung up. "So tell me, Philip: What's so special about Honduras?"

"Honduras? What's that got to do with anything?"

"Because that's where Max went."

Philip stared at him. "So you *were* in on it!"

Hauser smiled. "Not at all. That was the substance of the phone call I just received. Almost four weeks ago today his pilot flew him and a planeload of cargo to a city in Honduras called San Pedro Sula. From there he took a military helicopter to a place called Brus Lagoon. And then he vanished."

"You found all this out just now?"

Hauser generated a new and mighty cloud of smoke. "I'm a PI."

"And not a bad one, it seems."

Hauser emitted another meditative cloud. "As soon as I talk to the pilot, I'll know a lot more. Like what kind of cargo the plane was carrying and how much it weighed. Your father didn't make any effort to cover his tracks going down to Honduras. Did you know he and I were there together? I'm not surprised that's where he went. It's a big country with the most inaccessible interior in the world—thick jungle, uninhabited, mountainous, cut by deep gorges, and sealed off by the Mosquito Coast. That's where I expect he went—into the interior."

"It's plausible."

Hauser added after a moment: "I'm taking the case."

Philip felt irritated. He didn't recall having offered Hauser the job yet. But the guy had already demonstrated his competence, and since he now knew the story, he would probably do. "We haven't talked about a fee."

"I'll need a retainer. I expect the expenses in this case are going to run high. Anytime you do business in a shitcan Third World country you have to pay off every Tomás, Rico, and Orlando."

"I had in mind a fee based on contingency," Philip said quickly. "If we recover the collection, you get, say, a small percentage. I also should mention that I plan to divide it with my brothers: That's only fair."

"Contingency fees are for car-crash lawyers. I need a cash retainer up front. If I succeed, there will be an additional fixed fee."

"A retainer? Like how much?"

"Two hundred and fifty thousand dollars."

Philip almost laughed. "What makes you think I've got that kind of money?"

"I never *think* anything, Mr. Broadbent. I know. Sell the Klee."

Philip felt his heart stop for a moment. "What?"

"Sell the small Paul Klee watercolor you own, *Blau Kirk*. It's a beaut. I should be able to get you four hundred for it."

Philip exploded. "Sell it? Never. My father gave me that painting."

Hauser shrugged.

"And how did you know about that painting anyway?"

Hauser smiled and opened the soft white palms of his hand, like two calla lilies. "You do want to hire the best, don't you, Mr. Broadbent?"

"Yes, but this is blackmail."

"Let me explain how I work." Hauser leaned forward. "My first loyalty is to the case, not the client. When I take a case, I solve it, regardless of the consequences to the client. I keep the retainer. If I succeed, I get an additional fee."

"This discussion is irrelevant. I'm not selling the Klee."

"Sometimes the client loses his nerve and wants to back out. Sometimes bad things happen to good people. I kiss the babies and attend the funerals and keep going until the case is solved."

"You can't expect me to sell that painting, Mr. Hauser. It's the only thing I have of any value from my father. I love that painting."

Philip found Hauser gazing at him in a way that made him feel odd. The man's eyes were vacant, his face calm, emotionless. "Think of it this way: The painting is the sacrifice you need to make to recover your inheritance."

Philip hesitated. "You think we'll succeed?"

"I do."

Philip gazed at him. He could always buy the painting back. "All right, I'll sell the Klee."

Hauser's eyes narrowed further. He took another careful puff. Then he removed the cigar from his mouth and spoke.

"If successful, my fee will be one million dollars." Then he added, "We don't have much time, Mr. Broadbent. I've already booked us tickets to San Pedro Sula, leaving first thing next week."

7

When Vernon Broadbent finished chanting, he took a few moments to sit quietly in the cool, dark room with his eyes closed, allowing his mind to resurface after its long meditation. As consciousness returned, he began to hear the distant boom of the Pacific and smell the salt air just penetrating the myrrh-fragrant confines of the vihara. The glow of candles on his eyelids filled his internal vision with a reddish, flickering glow.

Then he opened his eyes, took a few deep breaths, and rose, still cradling the fragile feeling of peace and serenity that the hour of meditation had given him. He went to the door and paused, looking out over the hills of Big Sur, dotted with live oaks and manzanita, to the wide blue Pacific beyond. The wind off the ocean caught his robes and filled them with cool air.

He had been living at the Ashram for more than a year, and now, in his thirty-fifth year, he finally believed he had found the place he wanted to be. It had been a long journey, from those two years in India through Transcendental Meditation, Theosophy, EST, Lifespring, and even a brush with Christianity. He had rejected the materialism of his childhood and had tried to find some deeper truth to his life. What to others—especially his brothers—seemed a wasted life, had been to him a life of richness and striving. What else was the point of life, if not to find out *why?*

Now he had the chance, with this inheritance, to do some real good. Not just for himself this time but for others. It was his chance to do something for the world. But how? Should he try to find the tomb on his own? Should he call Tom? Philip was an asshole, but maybe Tom would want to join forces with him. He had to make a decision, and quickly.

He tucked up his linen robes and started down the path to the Teacher's hut—a sprawling redwood structure set in a gentle vale, nestled among a stand of tall oaks, with a view of the Pacific. On the way he passed Chao, the cheerful Asian boy who ran the Teacher's errands, bouncing up the trail carrying a bundle of mail. It was the life he sought: peaceful and uncomplicated. Too bad it was so expensive.

As he rounded the side of the hill, the Hut came into view. He paused—he was a little intimidated by the Teacher—but then resolutely carried on. He knocked on the door. After a moment, a low, resonant voice called out from the depths of the compound, "Come in, you are most welcome."

He removed his sandals on the veranda and stepped inside. The house was Japanese in style, simple and ascetic, with sliding screens of rice paper, floors covered with beige mats, and expanses of polished wood planking. The interior smelled of beeswax and incense. There was the gentle sound of water. Through a series of openings Vernon could see down the length of the house to a Japanese garden beyond, with mossy rocks standing among raked pebbles, and a pool with blooming lotus flowers. He could not see the Teacher.

He turned and peered down another hallway to his left, through successive doorways, which disclosed a teenage girl in bare feet and robes, with a long blond French braid down her back entwined with wilting flowers. She was chopping vegetables in the Teacher's kitchen.

"Are you there, Teacher?" he called.

The girl went on chopping.

"This way," came the low voice.

Vernon went toward the sound and found the Teacher sitting in his meditation room, cross-legged on a mat, his eyes closed. He opened them but did not rise. Vernon stood, waiting respectfully. The Teacher's fit, handsome figure was draped in a simple robe of undyed linen. A fringe of long gray hair, combed straight down, fell from a small bald spot, giving him a Leonardo da Vinci look. Astute blue eyes crinkled under strongly arched orbital ridges carved out of the broad dome of his forehead. A trimmed salt-and-pepper beard completed the face. When he spoke his voice was soft and resonant, underlain by a pleasing bed of gravel, with a faint Brooklyn accent that stamped him as a man of humble origins. He was about sixty—no one knew his exact age. Formerly a professor of philosophy at Berkeley named Art Brewer, he had renounced tenure to retreat into a life of the spirit. Here, at the Ashram, he had founded a community devoted to prayer, meditation, and spiritual growth. It was pleasantly nondenominational, loosely based on Buddhism, but without the excessive discipline, intellectualism, celibacy, and fatalism that tended to mar that particular religious tradition. Rather, the Ashram was a beautiful retreat in a lovely location, where under the gentle guidance of the Teacher each worshiped in his own way, at a cost of seven hundred dollars per week, room and board included.

"Sit down," the Teacher said.

Vernon sat.

"How can I help you?"

"It's about my father."

The Teacher listened.

Vernon collected his thoughts and took a breath. He told the Teacher about his father's cancer, the inheritance, the challenge to find his tomb. When he finished there was a long silence. Vernon wondered if the Teacher would tell him to forgo the inheritance. He remembered the Teacher's many negative comments about the evil effects of money.

"Let's have tea," said the Teacher, his voice exceptionally tender, placing his gentle hand on Vernon's elbow. They sat and he called for tea, which was brought in by the girl with the braid. They sipped silently, and then the Teacher asked, "How much, exactly, is this inheritance worth?"

"I figure that after taxes my share would probably be worth a hundred million."

The Teacher seemed to take a very long sip of tea, and another. If the sum surprised him he didn't show it. "Let us meditate."

Vernon, too, closed his eyes. He had trouble concentrating on his mantra, feeling agitated by the questions facing him, which only seemed to grow more complex as he thought about them. One hundred million dollars. One hundred million dollars. The phrase, not dissimilar in sound from the mantra, got tangled up with his meditating, preventing him from achieving either peace or internal silence. *One hundred million. Om mani padme hum. One hundred million.*

It was a relief when the Teacher raised his head. He took Vernon's hands and enclosed them within his own. His blue eyes were unusually bright.

"Few are given the opportunity that you have been given, Vernon. You must not let this opportunity pass you by."

"How so?"

The Teacher stood and spoke with power and resonance in his voice. "We need to recover that inheritance. We need to recover it now."

8

By the time Tom had finished doctoring the sick horse, the sun was setting over Toh Ateen mesa, casting long golden shadows across the sagebrush and chamisa. Beyond rose up a thousand-foot wall of sculpted sandstone, glowing red in the dying light. Tom gave the animal another quick lookover and patted him on the neck. He turned to the Navajo girl—the horse's owner. "He's going to make it. Just a touch of sand colic."

She broke into a relieved smile.

"Right now he's hungry. Lead him around the corral a few times and then give him a scoop of psyllium mixed in with his oats. Let him water afterwards. Wait half an hour, then give him some hay. He'll be fine."

The Navajo grandmother who had ridden on horseback five miles to the vet clinic to get him—the road was washed out, as usual—took his hand. "Thank you, doctor."

Tom gave a little bow. "At your service." He thought ahead to the ride back to Bluff with anticipation. He was glad the road had washed out, giving him the excuse for a long ride. It had wasted half his day, but the trail had taken him through some of the most beautiful red-rock country in the Southwest, through the Jurassic sandstone beds known as the Morrison Formation, rich with dinosaur fossils. There were a lot of remote canyons running up into Toh Ateen mesa, and Tom wondered if any paleontologists had ever explored up there.

Probably not. Someday, he thought, he'd take a little side trip up one of those canyons . . .

He shook his head and smiled to himself. The desert was a fine place to clear your mind, and he had had a lot of clearing to do. This crazy business with his father had been the biggest shock of his life.

"What do we owe you, doctor?" the grandmother asked, breaking his reverie.

Tom glanced aound at the shabby tar-paper hogan, the broken-down car half sunk in tumbleweeds, the skinny sheep milling in the pen.

"Five dollars."

The woman fished into her velveteen blouse and removed some soiled dollar bills, counting out five for him.

Tom had touched his hat and had just turned to get his horse when he noticed a tiny cloud of dust on the horizon. The two Navajos had also noticed it. A horse and rider were approaching fast from the north, from the direction he had come, the dark speck getting bigger in the great golden bowl of the desert. He wondered if it was Shane, his vet partner. It alarmed him. It would have to be one hell of an emergency for Shane to ride out there to get him.

As the figure materialized, he realized it wasn't Shane but a woman. And she was riding his horse Knock.

The woman trotted into the settlement, covered with dust from her journey, the horse lathered up and blowing. She stopped and swung down. She had been riding bareback without even a bridle across almost eight miles of empty desert. Absolutely, totally crazy. And what was she doing with his best horse and not one of Shane's glue-plugs? He was going to kill Shane.

She strode toward him. "I'm Sally Colorado," she said. "I tried to find you at your clinic, but your partner said you'd ridden out here. So here I am." With a rustle of honey-colored hair, she held out her hand. Tom, caught off guard, took it. Her hair had spilled down her shoulders over a white cotton shirt, now powdered with dust. The shirt was tucked in at a slender waist, which itself was snugged into a pair of jeans. There was a faint scent of peppermint about her. When she smiled it seemed her eyes had changed color from green to blue, so bright was the effect. She wore a pair of turquoise earrings, but the color in her eyes was even richer than the color of the stone.

After a moment Tom realized he was still holding her hand, and released it.

"I just had to find you," she said. "I couldn't wait."

"An emergency?"

"It's not a vet emergency, if that's what you mean."

"Then what kind of emergency is it?"

"I'll tell you on the ride back."

"Damn it," Tom exploded, "I can't believe Shane let you take my best horse and ride it like that, without a saddle or bridle. You could have been killed!"

"Shane didn't give him to me." The girl smiled.

"How did you get him, then?"

"I stole him."

It took a moment of consternation before Tom could bring himself to laugh.

The sun had set by the time they headed north, riding together, back to Bluff. For a while they rode in silence, and then Tom finally said, "All right. Let's hear what was so important that you had to steal a horse for it and risk your neck."

"Well . . ." she hesitated.

"I'm all ears, Miss . . . Colorado. If that's really your name."

"It's an odd name, I know. My great-grandfather was in vaudeville. He did the patent medicine circuit dressed as an Indian, and he took Colorado as his stage name. It was better than our old name— Smith—and so it kind of stuck. Call me Sally."

"All right, Sally. Let's hear your story." Tom found himself watching her ride with a feeling of pleasure. She looked like she'd been born on a horse. A lot of money must have gone into that straight, easy, and centered seat of hers.

"I'm an anthropologist," Sally began. "More specifically, I'm an ethnopharmacologist. I study indigenous medicine with Professor Julian Clyve at Yale. He was the man who cracked Mayan hieroglyphics a few years ago. A really brilliant piece of work. It was in all the papers."

"No doubt." She had a sharp, clean profile, a small nose, and a funny way of sticking out her lower lip. She had a little dimple when she smiled, but only on one side of her mouth. Her hair was dark gold, and it bent in a glistening curve over her slender shoulders before heading down her back. She was an amazingly beautiful woman.

"Professor Clyve has assembled the largest collection of Mayan writing in existence, a library of every inscription known in ancient Mayan. It consists of rubbings from stone inscriptions, pages from Mayan codices, and copies of inscriptions on pots and tablets. His library is consulted by scholars from all over the world."

Tom could just see the doddering old pedagogue shuffling among his heaps of dusty manuscripts.

"The greatest of the Mayan inscriptions were contained in what we call codices. They were the original books of the Maya, written in glyphs on bark paper. The Spanish burned most of them as books of the devil, but a couple of incomplete codices managed to survive here and there. A complete Mayan codex has never been found. Last year, Professor Clyve found *this* in the back of a filing cabinet that belonged to one of his deceased colleagues."

She drew a folded sheet of paper out of her breast pocket and handed it to him. Tom took it. It was an old, yellowing photocopy of a page of a manuscript written in hieroglyphics, with some drawings of leaves and flowers in the margins. It looked vaguely familiar. Tom wondered where he had seen it before.

"Writing was invented only three times independently in the history of the human race. Mayan hieroglyphics was one of them."

"My Mayan reading skills are a little rusty. What does it say?"

"It describes the medicinal qualities of a certain plant found in the Central American rainforest."

"What does it do? Cure cancer?"

Sally smiled. "If only. The plant is called the *K'ik'-te,* or blood tree. This page describes how you boil the bark, add ashes as an alkali, and apply the paste as a poultice to a wound."

"Interesting." Tom handed the sheet back to her.

"It's more than interesting: It's medically correct. There's a mild antibiotic in the bark."

They were now on the slickrock plateau. A pair of coyotes howled mournfully in a distant canyon. They had to go single file now. Sally rode behind while Tom listened.

"That page comes from a Mayan codex of medicine. It was probably written around 800 A.D., at the height of the Classic Maya civilization. It contains two *thousand* medical prescriptions and preparations, not just from plants but from everything in the rainforest—insects, animals, and even minerals. There may in fact be a cure for cancer in there, or at least some types of cancer. Professor Clyve asked me to locate the owner and see if I couldn't arrange for him to translate and publish the codex. It's the only complete Mayan codex known. It would be a stunning cap to his already distinguished career."

"And for yours, too, I imagine."

"Yes. Here's a book that contains all the medicinal secrets of the rainforest, accumulated over centuries. We're talking about the richest rainforest in the world, with hundreds of thousands of species of plants and animals—many still unknown to science. The Maya knew every plant, every animal, everything in that rainforest. *And everything they knew went into this book.*"

She trotted her horse alongside him. Her loose hair spilled and swung as she caught up. "Do you realize what this means?"

"Surely," said Tom, "medicine has advanced a long way from the ancient Maya."

Sally Colorado snorted. "Twenty-five percent of all our drugs originally came from plants. And yet, only one-half of one percent of the world's 265,000 plant species have been evaluated for their medicinal properties. Think of the potential! The most successful and effective drug in history—aspirin—was originally discovered in the bark of a tree used by natives to cure aches and pains. Taxol, an important anti-cancer drug, also comes from tree bark. Cortisone comes from yams, and the heart medication digitalis comes from foxglove. Penicillin was first extracted from mold. Tom, this codex could be the greatest medical discovery ever."

"I see your point."

"When Professor Clyve and I translate and publish this codex, it will *revolutionize* medicine. And if that doesn't convince you, here's something else. The Central American rainforest is disappearing under the loggers' saws. This book will save it. The rainforest will suddenly be worth a lot more standing up than cut down. Drug companies will pay those countries *billions* in royalties."

"No doubt keeping a tidy profit themselves. So what's this book got to do with me?"

A full moon was now rising over the Hobgoblin Rocks, painting them silver. It was a lovely evening.

"The Codex belongs to your father."

Tom stopped his horse and looked at her.

"Maxwell Broadbent stole it from a Mayan tomb almost forty years ago. He wrote to Yale asking for help in translating it. But Mayan script hadn't been cracked then. The man who got the letter assumed it was a fake and shoved it in an old file without even answering. Professor Clyve found it forty years later. He instantly knew it was real. No one could fake Mayan script forty years ago for the simple reason that no one could read it. But Professor Clyve could read it: He's the only man on earth, in fact, who can read Mayan script fluently. I've been trying to reach your father for weeks, but he seems to have dropped off the face of the earth. So finally in desperation I tracked you down."

Tom stared at her in the gathering twilight, and then he began to laugh.

"What's so funny?" she asked hotly.

Tom took a deep breath. "Sally, I've got some bad news for you."

When he had finished telling her everything, there was a long silence.

Sally said, "You've got to be joking."

"No."

"He had no right!"

"Right or not, that's what he did."

"So what are you going to do about it?"

Tom sighed. "Nothing."

"Nothing? What do you mean, *nothing?* You're not giving up your inheritance, are you?"

Tom didn't answer at once. They had reached the top of the plateau, and they paused to look at the view. The myriad canyons running down to the San Juan River were etched like dark fractals into the moonlit landscape; beyond, he could see the yellow cluster of lights of the town of Bluff and, at the edge of town, the cluster of buildings that made up his modest veterinary practice. To the left the immense stone vertebrae of Comb Ridge rose up, ghostly bones in the moonlight. It reminded him all over again of why he was here. In the days following the shock of learning what his father had done with their inheritance, he had picked up one of his favorite books: Plato's *Republic*. He read once again the passages on the myth of Er, in which Odysseus was asked what kind of existence he would choose in his next life. What had the great Odysseus, warrior, lover, sailor, explorer, and king, chosen to be? An anonymous man living in some out-of-the-way corner, "disregarded by the others." All he wanted was a life of peace and simplicity.

Plato had approved. And so did Tom.

That, Tom reminded himself, was why he had originally come to Bluff. Life with Maxwell Broadbent as a father was impossible: a never-ending drama of exhortation, challenge, competition, criticism, and instruction. He had come here to escape, to find peace, to leave all that behind. That, and of course, Sarah. Sarah: His father had even tried to select their girlfriends—disastrously.

He ventured a glance at Sally. A cool night breeze was stirring her hair, and her face was turned into the moonlight, her lips slightly parted in pleasure and awe at the stupendous view. One hand lay on her thigh, her slender body resting lightly on the horse's back. God, she was beautiful.

He angrily pushed that out of his mind. His life was now pretty much how he wanted it. He hadn't managed to become a paleontologist—his father had scotched that—but being a vet in Utah was the next best thing. Why screw it up? He'd been down that road before. "Yes," he finally responded. "I'm giving it up."

"Why?"

"I'm not sure I can explain it."

"Try."

"You have to understand my father. All my life, he tried to control everything my two brothers and I did. He *managed* us. He had big plans for us. But no matter what I did, what any of us did, it was never good enough. We were never good enough for him. And now this. I'm not going to play his game any longer. Enough is enough."

He paused, wondering why he was telling her so much.

"Go on," she said.

"He wanted me to become a doctor. I wanted to be a paleontologist, to hunt for dinosaur fossils. Father thought that was ridiculous— 'infantile,' he called it. We compromised on vet school. Naturally, he expected me to go to Kentucky and doctor million-dollar racehorses and maybe become an equine medical researcher, making great discoveries and putting the Broadbent name in the history books. Instead I came out here to the Navajo reservation. This is what I want to do; this is what I *love* doing. These horses need me and these people need me. And this landscape, southern Utah, is the most beautiful in the world, with some of the greatest Jurassic and Cretaceous fossil beds anywhere. But my father thought that me coming out here to the rez was a huge failure and disappointment. There was no money in it, no prestige, nothing *splendid* about it. Here I'd taken his money to go to vet school and cheated him by coming out here."

He stopped. Now he'd really said too much.

"And so that's it? You're just going to let the whole inheritance go, Codex and all?"

"That's right."

"Just like that?"

"Most people live their lives without a legacy. My vet practice isn't a bad living. I love this life, this country. Look around. What more could you want?"

He found Sally looking at him instead, her hair faintly luminous in the silvery light of the moon. "How *much* are you giving up, if I may ask?"

He felt a twinge, not for the first time, at the sheer size of it. "A hundred million, give or take."

Sally whistled. There was a long silence. A coyote howled somewhere in the canyons below them, answered by a further howl. She finally said, "Jesus, you've got guts."

He shrugged.

"And your brothers?"

"Philip's joined with my father's old partner to go find the hidden tomb. Vernon's going it alone, I hear. Why don't you team up with one of them?"

He found her looking at him rather intently in the dark. Finally she said, "I already tried. Vernon left the country a week ago, and Philip's also disappeared. They went to Honduras. You were my last choice."

Tom shook his head. "Honduras? That was fast. When they return with the loot, you can get the Codex from them. I'll give you my blessing."

Another long silence. "I can't risk it. They have no idea what it is, what it's worth. Anything could happen."

"I'm sorry, Sally, I can't help you."

"Professor Clyve and I need your help. The *world* needs your help."

Tom stared into the dark cottonwood groves in the floodplain of the San Juan River. An owl called from a distant juniper.

"My mind is made up," he said.

She remained looking at him, her hair in heavy disarray down her shoulders and back, her lower lip firmly set. The cottonwoods were casting a dappled moonlight over her body, the fuzzy silver spots of light rippling and shifting with the breeze. "Really?"

He sighed. "Really."

"At least give me a little help here. I'm not asking for much, Tom. Come to Santa Fe with me. You can introduce me to your father's lawyers, his friends. You can tell me about his travels, his habits. Give me two days. Help me do this. Just two days."

"No."

"Ever had a horse die on you?"

"All the time."

"A horse you loved?"

Tom immediately thought of his own horse Pedernal, who died from an antibiotic-resistant strain of strangles. He would never again own a horse as beautiful.

"Would better drugs have saved it?" Sally asked.

Tom looked toward the distant lights of Bluff. Two days wasn't much, and she did have a point. "All right. You win. Two days."

9

Lewis Skiba, CEO of Lampe-Denison Pharmaceuticals, sat motionless at his desk, looking down the file of gray skyscrapers along Avenue of the Americas in midtown Manhattan. A late-afternoon rain was darkening the city. The only sound in his paneled office was the mutter of a real wood fire in an eighteenth-century Siena marble fireplace, a sad reminder of fatter times. It was not a cold day, but Skiba had cranked up the A/C in order to have the fire. He found it soothing. It reminded him somehow of his childhood, of the old stone fireplace in the battenboard cabin by the lake, with the crossed snowshoes over the mantelpiece and the loons calling off the water. God, if only he could be there now . . .

Almost without knowing it, his hand unlocked the little front drawer of his desk and closed on a cool plastic bottle. He popped the top off with his thumbnail, fished out a dry little ovoid, put it in his mouth, and chewed. Bitter, but it cut the wait. That and a scotch chaser. Skiba reached to his left, slipped open a wall panel and took out a bottle of sixty-year-old Macallan and a whiskey glass, and poured himself a good slug. It was the color of rich mahogany. A dash of cool Evian released the flavor, and he brought it to his lips, sucked in a goodly amount, savoring the taste of peat, hops, the cold sea, the Highland moors, fine Spanish Amontillado.

As the feeling of peace stole over him he thought longingly of the big swim, of floating away on a sea of light. If it came to that, all it would take would be two dozen more of those tablets followed by the rest of the Macallan and he'd be sinking forever into the blue deep. No pleading the Fifth before Congress, no claiming to be just another poor misled incompetent CEO before the SEC, none of that Kenneth Lay shit. He'd be his own judge, jury, and executioner. His father, an army sergeant, had taught him the value of honor.

The one thing that could have saved the firm, but had sunk it instead, was that big breakthrough drug they thought they had. Phloxatane. With that in hand, the bean counters figured it was safe to start cutting long-term R&D to jack up current profits. They said the analysts would never notice, and at first they didn't. It worked like a dream, and their stock price shot through the roof. Then they started shifting current marketing costs to amortizable R&D, and still the analysts didn't notice and still the stock price rose. Then they assigned losses to paper-thin, off-the-books partnerships in the Cayman Islands and Netherland Antilles, booked loans as profits, and blew whatever cash was left over to buy back company stock to inflate the price even more—also inflating (naturally) the value of executive stock options. The stock soared; they cashed out, they made millions. God, it had been a heady game. They broke every law, rule, and regulation on the books and had a creative genius of a CFO who invented new ones to break. And all those high-flying stock pickers—they turned out to be about as perceptive as Br'er Bear. *Ize a-earnin' a dollah a minute.*

Now they'd come to the end of the line. There were no more rules to bend or break. Finally the market woke up, the stock crashed, and they had no more tricks up their sleeve. The carrion crows were circling above the Lampe Building at 725 Avenue of the Americas, cawing his name.

A shaking hand slipped the key into the lock; the drawer slid open. Skiba chewed up another bitter pill, took a second slug of scotch.

There came a buzz, announcing Graff.

Graff, the CFO genius who had gotten them to this point.

Skiba took a swig of Evian, swilled it around, swallowed, took another swig, and a third. He swept his hand over his hair, leaned back in the chair, and composed his face. He was already feeling that creeping lightness of being that started in his chest and moved outward to his fingertips, buoying him up, filling him with a golden glow.

He swiveled his chair, his eyes falling briefly on the photographs of his three bright little children smiling from their silver frames. Then his eye reluctantly traveled from the desk to rest on the face of Mike Graff, who had just entered the room. The man stood before Skiba, oddly delicate, encased from head to toe in impeccable worsted wool, silk, and cotton. Graff had been Lampe's rising young protégé, profiled in *Forbes*, courted by analysts and investment bankers, his wine cellar featured in *Bon Appetit* and his house in *Architectural Digest*. Now his protégé was no longer rising: He was holding hands with Skiba as they swan-dived off the edge of the Grand Canyon.

"What is it, Mike, that was so important it couldn't wait until our afternoon meeting?" Skiba spoke pleasantly.

"I've got a fellow outside you need to meet. He's got an interesting proposition for us."

Skiba closed his eyes. He suddenly felt tired almost unto death. All the good feeling was gone. "Don't you think we've had enough of your 'propositions,' Mike?"

"This one's different. Trust me."

Trust me. Skiba waved his hand in a gesture of futility. He heard the door open and looked up. There, standing in front of him, was a cheap hustler in a wide-lapel suit wearing too much gold. He was one of those types who combed five hairs across half a continent of bald skull and thought that solved the problem.

"Jesus Christ, Graff—"

"Lewis," said Graff, forging ahead, "this is Mr. Marcus Hauser, a private investigator formerly with the Bureau of Alcohol, Tobacco, and Firearms. He has something he wants to show us." Graff took a piece of paper from Hauser's hands and passed it to Skiba.

Skiba stared down at the page. It was covered with strange symbols, the margins drawn with curling vines and leaves. This was insane. Graff was cracking up.

Graff pushed on. "That's a page from a ninth-century Mayan manuscript. It's called a codex. It's a two-thousand-page catalog of rainforest drugs, how to extract them and use them."

Skiba felt a sensation of heat on his skin as the import sank in. It simply could not be true.

"That's right. Thousands of indigenous pharmaceutical prescriptions identifying medically active substances found in plants, animals, insects, spiders, molds, fungi—you name it. The medical wisdom of the ancient Maya in a single volume."

Skiba looked up, first at Graff, then at Hauser. "Where'd you get this?"

Hauser stood with his plump hands folded in front of him. Skiba was sure he smelled some kind of aftershave or cologne. Cheap.

"Let us just say I heard about it indirectly, through various twists and turns, from a professor up at Yale who likes to blow his own horn," said Hauser. His voice was high and irritating, with what sounded like a Brooklyn accent. A prepubescent Pacino.

Skiba said, "Mr. Hauser, it'll be ten years and half a billion in R&D before any of these drugs come on-line."

"True. But think what it'll do to your stock price *now*. As I understand it, you've got a bargeful of shit drifting down your little river here." He swept a plump hand in a circle, taking in the room.

Skiba stared at him. The insolent son of a bitch. He should throw him out now.

Hauser went on. "Lampe stock opened this morning at fourteen and three-eighths. Last December it was trading at fifty. You, personally, have two million stock options at a strike price of between thirty and thirty-five laddered out to expire over the next two years. All of which are now worthless unless you can get the stock price back up. On top of that, your major new cancer drug, Phloxatane, is a dog and is about to be disapproved by the FDA—"

Skiba rose from his chair, his face red. "How dare you speak these lies to me like this, in my office? Where are you getting this false information?"

"Mr. Skiba," said Hauser mildly, "let's cut the bullshit. I'm a private investigator, and this manuscript will be coming into my possession in about four to six weeks. I want to sell it to you. And I *know* you need it. I could just as easily take it to GeneDyne or Cambridge Pharmaceuticals."

Skiba swallowed hard. It was amazing how fast clearheadedness could return. "How do I know this isn't some kind of swindle?"

Graff said, "I've checked it out. It's as good as gold, Lewis."

Skiba stared at the huckster in the tasteless suit. He swallowed again, his mouth dry. This was how far they had sunk. "Tell me your proposal, Mr. Hauser."

Hauser said, "The Codex is in Honduras."

"So you're selling a pig in a poke."

"To get it, I need money, weapons, and equipment. I'm running a big personal risk. I've already had to undertake one urgent piece of business. This isn't going to come cheap."

"Don't hustle me, Mr. Hauser."

"Who's the hustler here? You're up to your neck in accounting irregularities as it is. If the SEC were to hear about how you and Mr. Graff here have been booking marketing costs as long-term amortizable R&D these past few quarters, you'd both be leaving the building in handcuffs."

Skiba stared at the man, and then at Graff. The CFO had turned white. In the long silence, a piece of wood popped in the fire. Skiba felt a muscle twitching somewhere behind his left knee.

Hauser went on: "When I deliver the Codex to you and you've authenticated it, as you will naturally insist on doing, you'll wire fifty million dollars to an offshore account of my selection. That's the deal I'm offering. No negotiations—just a yes or a no will suffice."

"Fifty million? That's totally insane. Forget it."

Hauser rose and headed for the door.

"Wait," Graff called, jumping up. "Mr. Hauser? None of this is engraved in stone." The sweat was trickling down from his well-groomed scalp as he chased after the man in the cheap suit.

Hauser kept walking.

"We're always open to—Mr. Hauser!"

The door closed in Graff's face. Hauser was gone.

Graff turned toward Skiba. His hands were shaking. "We've got to stop him."

Skiba said nothing for a moment. What Hauser had said was true: If they got their hands on the manuscript, the announcement alone would turn around their stock. Fifty million, however, was blackmail. Dealing with a man like this was odious. But some things couldn't be helped. Skiba said, "While there's only one way to pay a debt, there are a million ways not to pay it. As you well know, Mike."

Graff couldn't quite muster a smile through the sheen of sweat on his face.

Skiba spoke into his intercom. "That man who was just here, don't let him leave the building. Tell him we agree to his terms and escort him back up here."

He laid the phone back in its cradle and turned to Graff. "I hope for both of our sakes this guy is for real."

"He is," said Graff. "Believe me, I looked into this very thoroughly. The Codex exists, and the sample page is real."

In a moment Hauser was standing in the door.

"You'll get your fifty million," Skiba said brusquely. "Now take a seat and tell us your plan."

10

Charlie Hernandez felt drained. The funeral had been long, the interment longer. He could still feel the grit of the dirt on his right hand. It was always hell when one of their own had to be buried, let alone two. And he still had a court appearance and half a shift to get through. He glanced over at his partner, Willson, catching up on paperwork. Smart guy; too bad his handwriting looked like a kindergartner's.

The buzzer rang, and Doreen said, "Two people to see, ah, Barnaby and Fenton."

Christ, this was just what he needed. "What about?"

"They won't say. Won't talk to anyone but Barnaby and Fenton."

He sighed heavily. "Send them in."

Willson had stopped writing and was looking up. "You want me—?"

"You stay."

They appeared in the doorway, a stunning blond and a tall guy in cowboy boots. Hernandez grunted, sat up, smoothed a hand over his hair. "Sit down."

"We're here to see Lieutenant Barnaby, not—"

"I know who you're here to see. Please take a seat."

They sat down, reluctantly.

"I'm Officer Hernandez," he said, addressing the blond. "May I ask what your business with Officer Barnaby is?" He spoke with the practiced voice of officialdom, slow, stolid, and final.

"We'd prefer to deal directly with Officer Barnaby," said the man.

"You can't."

"Why not?" He flared up.

"Because he's dead."

They stared back at him. "How?"

God, Hernandez felt tired. Barnaby had been a good man. What a waste. "Automobile accident." He sighed. "Perhaps if you told me who you were and how I could help you?"

They looked at each other. The man spoke. "I'm Tom Broadbent, and about ten days ago Lieutenant Barnaby investigated a possible break-in at our house off the Old Santa Fe Trail. Barnaby handled the call, and I wondered if he filed a report."

Hernandez glanced over at Willson.

"He didn't file a report," Willson said.

"Did he say anything?"

"He said it had been some kind of misunderstanding, that Mr. Broadbent had moved some artworks and his sons mistakenly assumed they had been stolen. As I explained last week to your brother, a crime hadn't been committed, so there was no reason to open a file."

"My brother? Which one?"

"The name escapes me. Long hair, beard, hippie type—"

"Vernon."

"Right."

"Can we talk to his partner, Fenton?"

"He also passed away in the accident."

"What happened?"

"Car went off the Ski Basin Road at Nun's Corner."

"I'm sorry."

"So are we."

"So there's no paperwork, nothing on the investigation up at the Broadbent house?"

"Nothing."

There was a silence, and then Hernandez said, "Is there anything else I can do for you folks?"

11

Trash burned in a row of fifty-five-gallon drums along the filthy beach at Puerto Lempira, each sending a stream of acrid smoke into the town. A fat woman cooked on a comal over one of the drums; the smell of frying pork cracklings carried toward Vernon on a fetid breeze. He walked with the Teacher along the dirt street that paralleled the beach, trailed and jostled by a crowd of children, followed in turn by a groveling pack of dogs. The children had been trailing them for almost an hour, crying out "Gimme sweet!" and "Gimme dollar!" Vernon had dispensed several bags of candy and given out all his dollar bills in an effort to placate them, but the generosity had succeeded only in swelling the crowd to ever more hysterical proportions.

Vernon and the Teacher arrived at a rickety wooden pier that stuck out into the muddy lagoon, at the end of which was tied a gaggle of dugout canoes with outboard motors. Men lounged in hammocks, and dark-eyed women eyed them from doorways. A man pushed up to them, a boa wrapped around his neck.

"Snake," he said. "Fifty dollar."

"We don't want a snake," said the Teacher. "We want a boat. *Barca.* Boat. We're looking for Juan Freitag Charters. You *sabe* Juan Freitag?"

The man began unwrapping the snake and holding it out as if he were offering a string of sausages. "Snake. Thirty dollar."

The Teacher brushed past him.

"Snake!" the man cried, pursuing. "Twenty dollar!" His shirt was almost falling off his shoulders, it had so many holes. He clutched at Vernon with long brown fingers as he passed. Vernon, fishing in his pocket for change and dollar bills, could only find a fiver. He gave it to the man. The children surged forward, redoubling their hollering, streaming down to the quayside from the teeming barrios above.

"Damn you, stop handing out money," said the Teacher. "We're going to be robbed."

"Sorry."

The teacher seized an older child by the scruff of his neck. "Juan Freitag Charters!" he cried impatiently. "Where? *Donde?*" He turned to Vernon. "How do you say boat in Spanish again?"

"*Barca.*"

"*Barca! Donde barca?*"

The boy, frightened, pointed a dirty finger toward a cinderblock building across from the pier.

The Teacher released him and hurried along the dusty quayside, Vernon following, pursued by children and dogs. The door to the office was open, and they went in. A man behind a desk got up, went to the door with a flyswatter, swatted the pursuing children away from the door, and slammed it. By the time he had resumed his seat, he was all smiles. He had a small, neat head and body and blond, Aryan features. But when he spoke, it was with a Spanish accent.

"Please accommodate yourselves."

They took a couple of wicker chairs, next to an end table piled with copies of scuba magazines.

"What can I do for you, gentlemen?"

"We want to rent a couple of boats with guides," the Teacher said.

The man smiled. "Scuba diving or tarpon fishing?"

"Neither. We want to go upriver."

The smile seemed to gel on the man's face. "Up the Patuca?"

"Yes."

"I see. You are adventure travelers?"

The Teacher glanced at Vernon. "Yes."

"How far do you wish to go?"

"We don't know yet. A long way. Perhaps as far as the mountains."

"You must take motorized dugout canoes, because the river is too shallow for a regular boat. Manuel!"

After a moment a young man came in from the back. He blinked in the light. He had fish blood and scales on his hands.

"This is Manuel. He and his cousin Ramón will guide you. They know the river well."

"How long will it take to get upriver?"

"You can go as far as Pito Solo. One week. Beyond that is the Meambar Swamp."

"And beyond that?"

The man waved his hand. "You do not want to cross the Meambar Swamp."

"On the contrary," said the Teacher, "it's quite possible we do."

The man inclined his head, as if humoring crazy Americans was all in a day's work. "As you wish. Beyond the swamp are mountains and more mountains. You will need to take at least a month of supplies and food."

A wasp buzzed in the whitewashed room, tapping on the cracked window, swinging around, and colliding with it again. With a lightning motion the man smacked it with the flyswatter. It fell to the ground, writhing and stinging itself in agony. A polished shoe was extended from under the desk and ended its life with a little crunch.

"Manuel! Get Ramón." He turned to the Teacher. "We can outfit you here, señor, with everything you need. Tents, sleeping bags, mosquito netting, gas, food, GPS, hunting gear—everything. We can put it all on credit card." He laid his hand reverently on a brand-new credit-card machine connected to a shiny jack in the wall. "You do not worry about anything because we take care of it all. We are a modern operation." He smiled. "We give you adventure, but not too much adventure."

12

The car hummed northward through the San Juan Basin Desert toward the Utah border, along a vast and lonely highway between endless prairies of sagebrush and chamisa. Shiprock towered in the distance, a dark thrust of stone into blue sky. Tom, driving, felt a great relief that it was over. He had done what he promised, he had helped Sally find out where his father had gone. What she did next was up to her. She could either wait until his brothers came out of the jungle with the Codex—provided they found the tomb—or she could try to catch up to them herself. He, at least, was now out of it. He could get back to his life of peace and simplicity in the desert.

He cast a surreptitious glance at her sitting in the passenger seat. She had been silent for the past hour. She hadn't said what her plans were, and Tom wasn't sure he wanted to know. All he wanted to do was get back to his horses, to the routine of the clinic, to his cool adobe house shaded by cottonwoods. He had worked hard at creating the undemanding life he wanted, and he was more determined than ever not to let his father and his crazy schemes overturn it. Let his brothers have the adventure and, if they wanted, let them even keep the inheritance. He had nothing to prove. After Sarah, he wasn't about to jump into deep water again.

"So he went to Honduras," Sally said. "You still have no idea, no guess, as to where?"

"I've told you all I know, Sally. Forty years ago he spent some time in Honduras with his old partner, Marcus Hauser, looking for tombs and picking bananas to earn money. They got swindled, so I heard, buying a fake treasure map of some kind, and they spent a few months tramping through the jungle and nearly died. They had some kind of falling-out, and that was that."

"And you're sure he didn't find anything?"

"That's what he always said. The mountains of southern Honduras were uninhabited."

She nodded, her eyes looking ahead at the empty desert.

"So what are you going to do?" Tom finally asked.

"I'm going to Honduras."

"All by yourself?"

"Why not?"

Tom said nothing. What she did was her business.

"Did your father ever get in trouble for looting tombs?"

"The FBI investigated him on and off over the years. Nothing stuck. Father was too smart. I remember once when the agents raided our house and seized some jade figurines my father had just brought back from Mexico. I was ten at the time, and it scared the hell out of me, the agents pounding on the door before dawn. But they couldn't prove anything and had to return all the stuff."

Sally shook her head. "People like your father are a menace to archaeology."

"I'm not sure I see a big difference between what my father did and what archaeologists do."

"There's a big difference," said Sally. "Looters wreck a site. They remove things from their context. A dear friend of Professor Clyve was beaten in Mexico while trying to stop some local villagers from looting a temple."

"I'm sorry to hear that, but you can't blame starving people for trying to feed their children—and taking exception to some *norteamericano* coming down and telling them what to do."

Sally set her lip, and Tom could see she was angry. The car hummed along the shimmering asphalt. Tom cranked up the A/C. He would be glad when this was over. He didn't need a complication like Sally Colorado in his life.

Sally shook her heavy gold hair back from her head, unleashing a faint scent of perfume and shampoo. "There's something still bothering me. I just can't get it out of my head."

"What's that?"

"Barnaby and Fenton. Doesn't it seem strange to you that right after they investigate your father's so-called robbery they come up dead? There's something about the timing of their 'accident' that I don't like."

Tom shook his head. "Sally, it's just one of those coincidences."

"It doesn't feel right to me."

"I know the Ski Basin Road, Sally. Nun's Corner is a hellacious curve. They aren't the first ones to get killed there."

"What were they doing on the Ski Basin Road? Ski season's over."

Tom sighed. "If you're so worried, why don't you call that policeman, Hernandez, and find out?"

"I will." Sally slipped her cell phone out of her bag and dialed. Tom listened while she was transferred half a dozen times, from one slack receptionist to the next, until she finally reached Hernandez.

"This is Sally Colorado," she said. "You remember us?"

Pause.

"I wanted to ask you a question about Barnaby and Fenton's death."

Another pause.

"Why did they go up there to the ski basin?"

A very long wait. Tom found himself trying to listen, although he felt it was a waste of time.

"Yes, it was tragic," Sally said. "And where were they about to go on this fishing trip?"

A final silence.

"Thanks."

Sally slowly shut the phone and looked at Tom. Tom felt a knot in his stomach; her face had gone pale.

"They went up to the ski basin to check on a report of vandalism. Turned out to be phony. Their brakes failed on the way down. They tried to slow themselves down by banking off the guard rails, but the road was just too steep. When they reached Nun's Corner they were going close to ninety."

"Jesus."

"There wasn't much left of the car after the four-hundred-foot drop and explosion. No foul play is suspected. It was especially tragic, coming as it did the day before Barnaby and Fenton were about to go on the tarpon-fishing trip of a lifetime."

Tom swallowed and asked the question he didn't want to ask. "Where?"

"Honduras. A place called Laguna de Brus."

Tom slowed, checked his rearview mirror, and with a screech of tires, manipulating both the brakes and the gas, pulled a one-eighty.

"Are you crazy? What are you doing?"

"Going to the nearest airport."

"Why?"

"Because someone who would kill police officers could sure as hell kill my two brothers."

"You think someone found out about the hidden inheritance?"

"Absolutely." He accelerated toward the vanishing point on the horizon. "Looks like we're going to Honduras. Together."

13

Philip Broadbent shifted his position, trying to get comfortable in the bottom of the dugout, arranging some of the softer bundles of gear for the fourth or fifth time to form a chair of sorts. The boat slid upriver between two silent walls of green vegetation, the engine humming, the prow cutting the smooth black water. It was like traveling through a hot green cave, echoing with the unholy screeches, hoots, and whistles of jungle animals. The mosquitoes formed a permanent whining cloud around their boat, trailing behind. The air was dense, muggy, sticky. It was like breathing mosquito soup.

Philip removed the pipe from his pocket, reamed out the dottle, rapped it on the side of the boat, and refilled it from the Dunhill can he had stored in one of the pockets of his Barbour safari khakis. He took his time lighting it, then blew a stream of smoke into the mosquito cloud, watching it cut a clear area in the whining mass, which instantly closed up as the smoke drifted away. The Mosquito Coast had lived up to its name, and even the deet that Philip slathered on his skin and clothes provided less than adequate protection. On top of that it was oily and smelled frightful, and it was probably leaching into his bloodstream and poisoning him to boot.

He muttered a curse and took another hit off the pipe. *Father and his ridiculous tests.*

He adjusted himself, unable to get comfortable. Hauser, carrying a Discman, came back from the prow of the dugout and eased himself down next to him. He smelled of cologne instead of bug juice, and he looked as cool and fresh as Philip felt hot and sticky. He removed the earphones to speak.

"Gonz has been picking up traces of Max's passage all day. We'll learn more when we get to Pito Solo tomorrow."

"How can they follow a trace on a river?"

Hauser smiled. "It's an art, Philip. A cut vine here, a landing place there, the mark of a barge pole on a submerged sandbar. The river is so sluggish that marks on the bottom persist for weeks."

Philip sucked irritably on his pipe. He would endure this one last torture of his father's and then he would be free. Free, finally, to live the life he wanted to live without that old bugger interfering, criticizing, doling out niggardly parcels of money like Scrooge. He loved his father and at one level felt bad about his cancer and his death, but that didn't change his feelings about this scheme. His father had done many asinine things in his life, but this took the cake. It was vintage Maxwell Broadbent, this parting *beau geste*.

He smoked and watched the four soldiers in the front of the boat gambling with a greasy pack of cards. The other boat with its complement of eight soldiers was fifty yards ahead of them, laying a foul trail of blue exhaust over the water. Gonz, the lead "tracker," lay on his belly in the prow, staring down into the dark water, occasionally dipping a finger into the water to taste it.

Suddenly a shout went up from one of the soldiers in the front of their dugout. He had stood up and was pointing excitedly at something swimming in the water. Hauser winked at Philip and leapt to his feet, withdrawing the machete he kept strapped to his waist, and scrambled to the bow. The boat angled toward the swimming animal while Hauser positioned himself, legs apart, in the prow. As the boat drew alongside the now desperately swimming animal he leaned over and, with a sudden movement, slashed into the water with his machete, then reached down and pulled out an animal that looked like a two-foot-long rat. It had almost been decapitated by the blow, its head hanging by a flap of skin. It gave one convulsive jerk and then went still.

Philip watched with a vague sense of horror as Hauser tossed the dead animal toward him. It landed with a thud on the bottom, the head jouncing free, rolling to a stop at Philip's feet, mouth open, yellow rat's teeth gleaming, blood still draining out.

Hauser rinsed the machete in the river, stuck it back in his belt, and walked back to Philip, stepping over the dead animal. He grinned. "Ever eaten agouti?"

"No, and I'm not sure I care to begin."

"Skinned, gutted, split, and roasted over the coals—it was one of Maxwell's favorites. Tastes a bit like chicken."

Philip said nothing. That's what Hauser claimed about all the revolting bush meat they had been forced to eat—*tastes like chicken.*

"Oh!" said Hauser, looking at Philip's shirt. "I beg your pardon."

Philip glanced down. A single drop of fresh blood had struck his shirt and was now soaking into the material. Philip wiped at it, which only spread it. "I'd appreciate it if you were a little more careful when tossing around decapitated animals," he said, dipping his handkerchief into the water and giving the spot a scrubbing.

"It's so difficult to keep one's hygiene in the jungle," Hauser said.

Philip scrubbed a little more and then gave up. He wished Hauser would leave him in peace. The man was starting to give him the creeps.

Hauser slid a couple of CDs out of his pocket. "And now, to stave off the ever encroaching savagery surrounding us, would you care to hear some Bach, or some Beethoven?"

14

Tom Broadbent wallowed on an overstuffed sofa-chair in the "executive suite" in the Sheraton Royale de San Pedro Sula, examining a map of the country. Maxwell had flown with all his cargo to the town of Brus Laguna on the Mosquito Coast, at the mouth of the Río Patuca. And then he had disappeared. They said he had gone upriver, which was the only route into the vast, mountainous, and wild interior of southern Honduras.

He followed the wandering blue line of the river on the map with his finger, through swamps and hills and high plateaus until it vanished in a web of tributaries pouring out of a rugged line of parallel mountain ranges. The map showed no roads or towns; it was truly a lost world.

Tom had discovered they were at least a week behind Philip and almost two weeks behind Vernon. He was deeply worried about his brothers. It took balls to kill two police officers, and do it so quickly and successfully. The killer was clearly a professional. His two brothers were surely next on the killer's list.

Sally, wrapped in a towel, came out of the bath humming to herself and crossed their sitting room, her glossy wet hair spilling down her back. Tom followed her with his eyes as she disappeared into her bedroom. She was even taller than Sarah . . .

He stepped down hard on that thought.

In ten minutes she was back out, dressed in lightweight khakis, a long-sleeved shirt, a canvas hat with mosquito netting rolled down around her face, and a pair of heavy gloves, all bought during a shopping expedition that morning.

"How do I look?" she asked, turning around.

"Like you're in purdah."

She rolled up the mosquito netting and took off the hat.

"That's better."

She tossed the hat and gloves on the bed. "I have to admit I'm very curious about this father of yours. He must've been a real eccentric."

"He was."

"What was he like? If you don't mind me asking."

Tom sighed. "When he walked into a room, every head turned. He radiated something—authority, power, assurance. I'm not sure what. People were awed by him, even if they had no idea who he was."

"I know the type."

"Wherever he went, whatever he did, journalists chased him around. There were sometimes paparazzi waiting outside the gate to our house. I mean, here we were going to school and the damn paparazzi are chasing us down the Old Santa Fe Trail like we're Princess Diana or something. It was ridiculous."

"What a burden for you."

"It wasn't always a burden. At times it was even fun. Father's marriages were always big news, a time for head shaking and tongue clucking. He married extremely beautiful women no one had ever seen before—no models or actresses for him. My mother, before he met her, was a dental receptionist. He loved the attention. Once in a while, just for fun, he'd take a swing at some paparazzo and have to pay damages. He was proud of himself. He was like Onassis, larger than life."

"What happened to your mother?"

"She died when I was four. Some rare and sudden form of meningitis. She was the only one of his wives he didn't divorce—didn't have enough time, I guess."

"I'm sorry."

"I hardly remember her, except, well, as feelings. Warm and loving, that sort of thing."

She shook her head. "I still don't get it. How could your father do this to his sons?"

Tom stared down at the map. "Everything he did and everything he owned had to be extraordinary. That applied to us, too. But we didn't turn out like he wanted. Running off and burying himself with his money was his last gasp, trying to force us to do something that would ring down through history. Something that would make him proud." He laughed bitterly. "If the press ever got wind of this, it would be incredible. Gigantic. A half-billion-dollar treasure, buried in a hidden tomb somewhere in Honduras. The whole world would be down here looking for it."

"It must've been difficult having a father like that."

"It was. I don't know how many tennis matches I played when he left early because he didn't want to see me lose. He was a ruthless chess player—but if he realized he was going to beat one of us, he'd quit the game. He couldn't bear to see us lose, even to him. When the grades arrived he never said anything, but you could see the disappointment in his eyes. Anything less than straight A's was such a catastrophe that he couldn't bring himself to talk about it."

"Did you ever get straight A's?"

"Once. He laid his hand on my shoulder and gave me an affectionate squeeze. That was all. But it said volumes."

"I'm sorry, how terrible."

"Each of us found a refuge. I found mine first in fossil collecting— I wanted to be a paleontologist—and then in animals. They didn't judge you. They didn't ask you to be someone else. A horse accepts you for what you are."

Tom fell silent. It was amazing to him how much it hurt to think back on his childhood, even now at thirty-three.

"I'm sorry," said Sally, "I didn't mean to pry."

Tom waved his hand. "I don't mean to tear him down. He was a good father in his own way. Maybe he loved us too much."

"Well," said Sally after a moment, standing up. "At the moment, we need to find ourselves a guide to take us up the Patuca River, and I have no idea where to start." She picked up the phone book and began leafing through it. "I've never done this sort of thing before. I wonder if there's a listing in here for 'Adventure Travel' or something."

"I've a better idea. We need to find the local watering hole for foreign journalists. They're the savviest travelers in the world."

"Chalk one up to you."

She bent over and pulled out a pair of pants and tossed them at him, followed by a shirt, a pair of socks, and a pair of lightweight hiking shoes. They all landed in a pile in front of him. "Now you can take off those macho cowboy boots."

Tom scooped up his clothes and went into his room and put them on. They seemed to be mostly pockets. When he emerged, Sally eyed him sideways and said, "After a few days in the jungle, maybe you won't look quite so silly."

"Thanks." Tom went to the phone and called the front desk. The journalists, it seemed, hung out in a bar called Los Charcos.

Tom was surprised to find Los Charcos not the cheap dive he imagined but an elegant, wood-panelled affair off the lobby of a fine old hotel. It was air-conditioned to just above Arctic conditions, and the place was filled with the aroma of fine cigars.

"Let me do the talking," Sally said. "My Spanish is better than yours."

"You're better looking, too."

Sally frowned. "I don't find gender jokes very funny."

They took seats at the bar.

"*Hola*," said Sally cheerfully to the bartender, a man with a heavy-lidded face. "I'm looking for the man from the *New York Times*."

"Mr. Sewell? I haven't seen him since the hurricane, señorita."

"How about the reporter for the *Wall Street Journal?*"

"We have no *Wall Street Journal* reporter here. We are but a poor country."

"Well, what reporters do you have?"

"There is Roberto Rodriguez from *El Diario*."

"No, no, I'm looking for an American. Someone who knows the country."

"Would an Englishman suffice?"

"Fine."

"Over there," he murmured, pointing with his lips, "is Derek Dunn. He is writing a book."

"What about?"

"Travel and adventure."

"Has he written any other books? Give me a title."

"*Slow Water* was his last book."

Sally dropped a twenty-dollar bill on the bar and headed toward Dunn. Tom followed. *This is going to be good,* he thought. Dunn was sitting by himself in a snug, working on a drink, a man with a shock of blond hair over a beefy red face. Sally halted, pointed, and exclaimed, "Say, you're Derek Dunn, aren't you?"

"I have been known to answer by that name, yes," he said. His nose and cheeks were flushed a permanent pink.

"Oh, how exciting! *Slow Water* is one of my *favorite* books! I loved it!"

Dunn rose, exposing a robust frame, trim and fit, dressed in worn khaki pants and a simple short-sleeved cotton shirt. He was a handsome man of the British Empire type.

"Thank you very much indeed," he said. "And you are?"

"Sally Colorado." She pumped his hand.

She's already got him grinning like an idiot, thought Tom. He felt foolish in his new clothes that smelled of a menswear shop. Dunn, in contrast, looked like he had been to the ends of the earth and back.

"Won't you join me for a drink?"

"It would be an honor," cried Sally.

Dunn guided her into the banquette next to him.

"I'll have what you're having," she said.

"Gin and tonic." Dunn waved at the bartender and then glanced up at Tom. "You're welcome to sit, too, you know."

Tom took a seat, saying nothing. He was starting to lose his enthusiasm for this idea. He did not like the red-faced Mr. Dunn, who was looking very intently at Sally—and not just at her face.

The bartender came over. Dunn spoke in Spanish. "Gin and tonic for me and the lady. And—?" He glanced at Tom.

"Lemonade," said Tom sourly.

"*Y una limonada,*" added Dunn, his tone conveying exactly what he thought of Tom's choice of beverage.

"I'm so glad to have run into you!" Sally said. "What a coincidence!"

"So you read *Slow Water*," said Dunn, with a smile.

"One of the best travel books I've ever read."

"It certainly was," said Tom.

"You read it, too?" Dunn turned to him with an expectant look.

Tom noted that Dunn had already polished off half his drink.

"I certainly did read it," said Tom. "I especially liked the part where you fell in the elephant shit. That was hilarious."

Dunn paused. "Elephant shit?"

"Wasn't there elephant shit in your book?"

"There are no elephants in Central America."

"Oh. I must be mixing it up with another book. Beg your pardon."

Tom saw Sally's green eyes fixed on him. He couldn't tell if she was angry or suppressing a laugh.

Dunn turned in his chair, placing his square back to Tom, devoting his attention to Sally. "You might be interested to know I'm working on a new book."

"How exciting!"

"I'm calling it *Mosquitia Nights*. It's about the Mosquito Coast."

"Oh, that's just where we're going!" Sally clapped her hands in excitement, like a girl. Tom took a sip, regretting his choice of drink. He was going to need something a little stronger to get through this. He should never have agreed to let Sally do the talking.

"There are more than five thousand square miles of swamps and highland rainforest in eastern Honduras that remain completely unexplored. Parts of it are not even mapped by air."

"I had no idea!"

Tom shoved the lemonade aside and looked around for the waiter.

"My book chronicles a journey I took along the length of the Mosquito Coast, through the maze of lagoons that mark where the jungle meets the sea. I was the first white man to make the trip."

"Incredible. How on earth did you do it?"

"Motorized dugout. The only mode of transportation in those parts besides foot travel."

"When did you make this amazing journey?"

"About eight years ago."

"Eight years?"

"I've had a bit of publisher trouble. You can't rush a good book, you know." He polished off the drink and waved his hand for another round. "It's tough country down there."

"Really?"

Dunn seemed to take this as his cue. He leaned back. "For starters, there are the usual mosquitoes, chiggers, ticks, blackfly, and botfly. They don't kill you, but they can make life a trifle nasty. I had a botfly bite once, on my forehead. Felt like a mosquito at first. It began to swell and turn red. Hurt like the devil. A month later it erupted, and inch-long botfly maggots started squirming out and dropping to the ground. Once you're bitten, the best thing to do is let it run its course. If you try to dig 'em out you only make a muck of it."

"I sincerely hope the experience didn't affect your brain," said Tom.

Dunn ignored him. "Then there's Chagas disease."

"Chagas disease?"

"*Trypanosoma cruzi.* An insect carrying the disease bites you and shits at the same time. The parasite lives in the shit, and when you scratch the bite you infect yourself. You aren't aware anything is wrong—until ten or twenty years later. First you notice your belly swelling up. Then you become short of breath, can't swallow. Finally your heart swells up—and bursts. No known cure."

"Lovely," said Tom. He had finally got the waiter's attention. "Whiskey. Make it a double."

Dunn continued looking at Tom, a smile playing about his lips. "Are you familiar with the fer-de-lance?"

"Can't say that I am." Gruesome stories of the jungle, it seemed, were Derek Dunn's stock in trade.

"The most poisonous snake known to man. Brown and yellow bugger; the locals call it a *barba amarilla.* When young they live in trees and branches. Drop down on you when disturbed. The bite stops your heart in thirty seconds. Then there's the bushmaster, the largest poisonous snake in the world. Twelve feet long and as thick as your thigh.

Not nearly as deadly as the fer-de-lance—with a bushmaster bite, you might live, say, twenty minutes."

Dunn chuckled and took another gulp.

Sally murmured something about how dreadful it sounded.

"Naturally you've heard of toothpick fish? This isn't a story for the ladies." Dunn glanced over at Tom, winked.

"Do tell," said Tom. "Sally's no stranger to crudity."

Sally flashed him a look.

"Lives in the rivers around here. Let's say you go for a nice morning dip. The toothpick fish swims right up your johnson, then flares out a set of spines and anchors itself in your urethra."

Tom's drink paused halfway to his mouth.

"Blocks the urethra. If you don't find a surgeon damn quick, your bladder bursts."

"Surgeon?" Tom said weakly.

Dunn leaned back. "That's right."

Tom's throat had gone dry. "What kind of surgery?"

"Amputation."

The drink finally made it to Tom's mouth, where he took a slug, and then another.

Dunn laughed loudly. "I'm sure you've heard all about the piranhas, leishmaniasis, electric eels, anacondas, and that sort of thing." Dunn waved his hand disparagingly. "The dangers of those are greatly exaggerated. The piranhas only go after you if you're bleeding, and anacondas are rare this far north and don't eat people. There is one advantage to the Honduran swamps: no leeches. Watch out for the monkey spiders, though—"

"So sorry, but we'll have to leave the monkey spiders for another day," said Tom, looking at his watch. He realized that Mr. Derek Dunn had his hand under the table, resting on Sally's knee.

"Not having second thoughts are you, old chap? This is not a country for pantywaists."

"Not at all," said Tom. "It's just that I'd rather hear about your encounter with the toothpick fish."

Derek Dunn stared at Tom unsmiling. "That's a rather stale joke, my friend."

"Well!" said Sally brightly. "Did you make the trip alone? We've been looking for a guide and wondered if you could recommend someone."

"Where are you chaps headed?"

"Brus Laguna."

"You *are* getting off the tourist trail." Suddenly his eyes narrowed. "You're not a writer, are you?"

Sally laughed. "Oh no, I'm an archaeologist, and he's a horse vet. But we're just here as tourists. We like to have adventures."

"An archaeologist? There aren't many ruins around here. You can't build in a swamp. And no civilized people would ever live in those interior mountains. Up there in the Sierra Azul there's no denser rainforest on earth, and the hills are so steep you can hardly crawl up and down them. There isn't a flat place to pitch a tent for a hundred miles. You've got to cut your way through, and in a hard day of travel you're lucky to make a mile. A trail macheted through there will knit itself up so tight in a week you'd never know it existed. If it's ruins you're after, Sally, why don't you head over to Copán? Perhaps I could tell you more about it over dinner."

The hand was still on her knee, squeezing and rubbing.

"Right," said Sally. "Maybe. Getting back to the guide. Do you have any recommendations?"

"Guide? Oh yes. The man for you is Don Orlando Ocotal. A Tawahka Indian. Absolutely reliable. Won't cheat you like the others. Knows the country like the back of his hand. He was with me on my last trip."

"How do we find him?"

"He lives up the Patuca River, a place called Pito Solo, the last real settlement on the river before the big interior swamps begin. That's forty, maybe fifty miles upriver from Brus. Stay in the main channel of the river or you'll never get out alive. This time of year the forests are flooded, and there're a zillion side channels going every which way. That country is virtually unexplored, from the swamps all the way past the Sierra Azul down to the Guayambré River. Forty thousand square kilometers of terra incognita."

"We haven't really decided where we're going."

"Don Orlando. He's your man." Then Derek Dunn revolved in his seat and faced Tom with his big sweaty face. "Say, I'm a bit short of funds—royalty check in the mail and all that. Perhaps you could spot us another round, what say?"

15

On the computer screen nestled discreetly among the cherrywood paneling in his office, Lewis Skiba watched the progress of Lampe-Denison Pharmaceuticals on the New York Stock Exchange. Investors had been hammering the stock all day, and it was now trading at close to ten. Even as he watched, the stock ticked down another eighth of a point to trade at ten even.

Skiba did not want to see his company go into single digits. He flicked off the screen. His eyes flickered to the wood panel that hid the Macallan, but it was too soon for that. Too soon. He needed a clear head for the call.

Rumors were circulating that Phloxatane was in trouble at the FDA. The short sellers were all over the stock, like maggots on a corpse. Two hundred million dollars of R&D had gone into that drug. Lampe had worked with the best medical researchers and scientists at three Ivy League universities. The double-blind tests had been well conceived, the data massaged and patted into the best possible shape. Their friends at the FDA had been wined and dined. But nothing in the end would save Phloxatane. No matter which way you cut the data, Phloxatane was a failure. And here he was sitting on six million shares of Lampe stock he couldn't unload—no one had forgotten what happened to Martha Stewart—as well as two million paper options so far out of the money that they would be more useful as toilet tissue in his Carrara marble bathroom.

More than anything else in this world, Skiba loathed short sellers. They were the vultures, the maggots, the carrion flies of the market. He would give anything to see Lampe's stock turn against them and start rising; he would love to see their panic as they were forced to cover their positions. He would love to think of all the margin calls they would be receiving. It would be a beautiful thing. And when he got his hands on the Codex and made the announcement, this beautiful thing would happen. It would burn the short sellers so badly that it would be months, maybe years, before they came back.

A soft trill came from the phone on his desk. He glanced at his watch. The satellite call was right on time. He really hated talking to Hauser; he loathed the man and his principles. But he had to deal with him. Hauser had insisted on "keeping him in the loop"; even though Skiba was usually a hands-on CEO, he had hesitated. Some things were better left in the dark. But in the end he agreed, if only to keep Hauser from doing something stupid or illegal. When he got the Codex, he wanted it clean.

He picked up the receiver.

"Skiba here."

The voice of Hauser, made Donald-Duckish by the scrambler, came over the line. As usual, the PI wasted no time on pleasantries.

"Maxwell Broadbent went up the Patuca River with a bunch of highland Indians. We're on his track. We don't know yet where he was headed, but my guess is somewhere in the interior mountains."

"Any problems?"

"One of the sons, Vernon, jumped the gun and got ahead of us upriver. It seems the jungle might take care of that problem for us, though."

"I don't understand."

"He hired two drunken guides from Puerto Lempira, and they've gotten themselves lost in Meambar Swamp. It seems unlikely they will, ah, ever see sunshine again."

Skiba swallowed. This was a lot more information than he needed to know. "Look, Mr. Hauser, just stick to the facts and leave the opining to others."

"We had a minor setback with the other one, Tom. He's got a

woman with him, a graduate student in ethnopharmacology from Yale."

"Ethnopharmacology? She knows about the Codex?"

"You bet your ass she does."

Skiba winced. "That's rather inconvenient."

"Yeah, but it's nothing I can't handle."

"Look, Mr. Hauser," he said briskly, "I'll leave it all in your capable hands. I've got a meeting to go to."

"Those people will have to be taken care of."

Skiba didn't like the way the conversation kept doglegging back to that subject. "I don't have any idea what you're talking about, and I don't want to know. I'm content to let you handle the details."

There was a small chuckle at the far end. "Skiba, how many people are dying in Africa right now because you insist on charging twenty-three thousand dollars a year for that new TB drug that costs you a hundred and ten dollars to make? That's all I'm talking about. When I say 'take care of them,' all I mean is adding a few more numbers to your total."

"Damn you, Hauser, that's outrageous—" Skiba broke off and swallowed. He was just letting Hauser bait him. This was talk, nothing more.

"This is beautiful, Skiba. You want your Codex nice and clean and legal, you don't want anyone popping up to claim ownership, and you don't want anyone hurt. Don't worry, no white people will be killed without your permission."

"You listen to me. I will not countenance the killing of anyone, white or nonwhite. This reckless talk has got to stop." Skiba could feel the sweat trickling down his neck. How had he allowed Hauser to take control of the situation like this? His hand fumbled with the key. The drawer slid open.

"I understand," said Hauser. "Like I said—"

"I've got a meeting." Skiba ended the connection, his heart pounding. Hauser was down there, out of control, with no supervision, liable to do anything. The man was a psychopath. He bit down, chewed, washed the bitterness down with a slug of Macallan, and sat back, breathing deeply. The fire was burning merrily in the fireplace.

The talk of killing made him feel agitated, sick to his stomach. He gazed into the flames, seeking their soothing influence. Hauser had promised to ask his permission, and Skiba would never give it. Neither the company nor even his own personal fortune was worth taking that step. His gaze wandered over to the row of silver photographs on his desk: his three children, gazing back at him with towheaded grins. He regulated his breathing. Hauser was full of tough talk, but it was just that: talk. Nobody was going to get killed. Hauser would retrieve the Codex, Lampe would recover, and in two or three years he would be the toast of Wall Street for pulling his company back from the brink.

Skiba glanced at his watch: The markets had closed. With a feeling of anxiety and reluctance he flicked on the computer screen. Late bargain hunting had pushed the stock up in the last twenty minutes. It had closed at ten and a half.

Skiba felt a wisp of relief. It hadn't been such a bad day after all.

16

Sally looked skeptically at the junk heap of a plane being rolled out of the shabby hangar by two workers.

"Maybe we should have checked out the plane before we bought tickets," Tom said to her.

"I'm sure it's fine," said Sally, as if trying to convince herself.

The pilot, a lean expatriate American with a torn T-shirt, cutoffs, two long braids, and a beard, came sauntering over and introduced himself as John. Tom eyed him and then cast a sour look toward the plane.

"I know, I know. Looks like shit," John said with a grin, giving the plane's fuselage a rap with his knuckles, which made it rattle. "What matters is what's under the hood. I do all my own maintenance."

"You don't know how that reassures me," said Tom.

"So you're headed for Brus?"

"That's right."

John squinted at the luggage. "Going tarpon fishing?"

"No."

"Best tarpon fishing in the world. Not much else, though." John opened a compartment in the side of the plane and began shoving in their luggage with his skinny arms. "So what are you doing there?"

"We're not sure," Sally said quickly. The less said about what they were doing, the better. No sense in starting a treasure stampede upriver.

The pilot shoved the last bag in, gave it a few blows to make it fit, and slammed the hatch with a great noise of cheap tin. It took three tries before it latched. "Where you staying in Brus?"

"Haven't decided that either."

"Nothing like planning ahead," said John. "Anyway, there's only one place and that's La Perla."

"How many stars does Michelin give it?"

John gave a little laugh. He opened the passenger hatch and swung down the steps, and they climbed aboard. John followed, and as he entered Tom detected what he thought was a faint whiff of marijuana. *Great.*

"How long have you been flying?" Tom asked.

"Twenty years."

"Ever had an accident?"

"Once. Hit a pig in Paradiso. Jokers hadn't mowed the strip, and the damn thing was sleeping in the tall grass. And he was a *big* pig."

"Are you instrument rated?"

"Let's just say I know how to use my instruments. There isn't much call for official ratings down here, not for bush flights."

"Have you filed a flight plan?"

John shook his head. "All I have to do is follow the coast."

The plane took off. It was a splendid day. Sally felt a thrill as the plane banked and the sunlight shimmered off the Caribbean. They turned to follow the coastline, low and flat with many lagoons and offshore islands that looked like green pieces of jungle that had broken off the mainland and were drifting out to sea. Sally could see where roads ran up into the interior, bordered by irregular fields or ragged patches where the trees had recently been clear-cut. Deep in the interior, she could see a ragged line of blue mountains, their tops sprinkled in clouds.

Sally glanced at Tom. The sun had bleached his light brown hair, streaking it with gold, and he had a lean, tall, wiry, cowboy sort of way of moving that she liked. She wondered how someone could just kiss a hundred million dollars good-bye. That had impressed her more than anything else. She had lived long enough to realize that people who had money cared a lot more about it than people who had never had it.

Tom turned and glanced at her, and she quickly smiled and looked back out the window. As the coast ran farther eastward, the landscape below became wilder, the lagoons larger and more intricate. Finally the largest lagoon so far came into view, dotted with hundreds of tiny islands. A large river fed into the far end. As they banked to make their approach, Sally could see a town where the river joined the lagoon, a cluster of shining tin roofs surrounded by a hodgepodge of irregular fields lying on the landscape like torn bits of rags. The pilot circled once and aimed down toward a field, which as they approached resolved into a grass landing strip. He made his descent, but Sally thought it was awfully fast. Closer and closer they got to the ground, but the plane only seemed to accelerate. She gripped the armrests. The runway flashed underneath them, but still the plane did not drop. She watched the wall of jungle foliage at the far end approach at high speed.

"Jesus Christ," Sally yelled, "you're overshooting the runway!"

The plane made a quick easy rise, and the jungle came skimming past them, the treetops no more than fifteen feet below the plane. As they climbed, Sally heard John's dry laugh in her earphones. "Relax, Sal, just buzzing to clear the airstrip. I learned my lesson."

As the plane banked and came around again to land, Sally sat back, mopping her brow. "Nice of you to warn us."

"I *told* you about the pig, man."

They left their luggage at La Perla, a cinderblock barracks that called itself a hotel, and then went down to the river to see about renting a boat. They wandered down through the muddy lanes of Brus. It was afternoon, and the heat had rendered the air dead and listless. All was quiet, and steaming puddles of water lay on the ground. The sweat was dripping out of her sleeves, running down her back, and between her breasts. All sensible people were having a siesta, it seemed to Sally.

They found the river at the far end of town. It lay between steep earthen banks, about two hundred yards across and the color of mahogany. The river curved away between two thick walls of jungle, and it smelled of mud. The thick water moved sluggishly, the surface dimpled with whorls and eddies. Here and there a green leaf or a twig slowly made its way downstream. A trail made of logs descended the steep embankment, ending at a platform of bamboo sticks constructed over the water, forming a rickety dock. Four dugout canoes were tied up. They were each about thirty feet long and about four feet across, hewn from a single gigantic tree, tapering to a spearlike prow in front. The stern had been cut off flat and had a mounted board designed to accommodate a small outboard engine. Boards were laid athwartship fore and aft for seats.

They scrambled down the embankment to take a closer look. She noticed that three of the dugouts had six-horsepower Evinrude engines bolted to the sterns. The fourth, longer and heavier, sported an eighteen-horse.

"There's the local hotrod," said Sally, pointing. "That's the one for us."

Tom looked around. The place seemed deserted.

"There's somebody." Sally pointed to an open-sided bamboo shed fifty yards down the riverbank. A small fire smoked next to a pile of empty tin cans. A hammock had been strung between two trees in a spot of shade and inside the hammock a man slept.

Sally advanced. *"Hola,"* she said.

After a moment the man opened one eye. *"Sí?"*

"We want to talk to someone about renting a boat." She spoke in Spanish.

With a flurry of grunts and mutterings of displeasure he sat up in the hammock, scratched his head, and grinned. "I speak good American. We talk American. Someday I go to America."

"That's good. We're going to Pito Solo," said Tom.

He nodded, yawned, scratched. "Okay. I take you."

"We'd like to rent the big boat. The one with the eighteen-horsepower engine."

He shook his head. "That stupid boat."

"We don't care if the boat is stupid," said Tom. "That's the one we want."

"I take you in my boat. That stupid boat belong to army mans." He held out his hand. "Got candy?"

Sally removed a bag she had bought earlier, expressly for that purpose.

The man's face lit up in a smile. He put a withered hand into it, sorted through the candies, selected five or six, unwrapped them, and put them all in his mouth at once. They formed a great lump in his cheek. *"Bueno,"* he said in a muffled voice.

"We'd like to leave tomorrow morning," Tom said. "How long is the journey?"

"Three days."

"Three *days?* I thought it was forty or fifty miles."

"Water going down. Maybe get stuck. Have to pole. Much wading. Cannot use engine."

"Wading?" Tom asked. "What about that toothpick fish?"

The man looked at him blankly.

"Don't worry, Tom," Sally said, "you can wear tight underwear."

"Ah, *sí!* The candiru!" The man laughed. "That favorite gringo story. Candiru. I swim in river every day and I still got my *chuc-chuc*. It working fine!" He swayed his hips licentiously, winking at Sally.

"Spare me," said Sally.

"So this fish is a hoax?" Tom asked.

"No, it's real! But you got *piss* in river first. Candiru smell piss in river, swim up, and *chop!* If you no piss when you swim, you got no problem!"

"Anyone else come through here lately? Any gringos, I mean."

"*Sí.* We very busy. Last month, white man come with many boxes and Indians from the mountains."

"What Indians?" Tom asked excitedly.

"Naked mountain Indians." He spat.

"Where did he get his boats?"

"He bring many new dugouts from La Ceiba."

"And did the boats return?"

The man smiled, rubbed his fingers together in the universal gesture, and held out his hand. Sally put a five-dollar bill in it.

"Boats not return. Mans go upriver, never come back."

"Anyone else come through?"

"*Sí.* Then last week Jesus Christ came through with drunken guides from Puerto Lempira."

"Jesus Christ?" Sally asked.

"Yes, Jesus Christ with long hair, beard, robes, and sandals."

"That's got to be Vernon," said Tom, with a smile. "Was he with anyone else?"

"Yes. He with St. Peter."

Tom rolled his eyes. "Any others?"

"*Sí.* Then come two gringos with twelve soldiers in two dugouts also from La Ceiba."

"What did the gringos look like?"

"One very tall, smoke pipe, angry. Other one shorter with four gold rings."

"Philip," said Tom.

They quickly made a deal for a boat to Pito Solo, and Tom gave him a ten-dollar advance. "We leave at first light tomorrow."

"*Bueno!* I be ready!"

As they came back from the river to the cinderblock barracks that passed as the local hotel, they were surprised to see a jeep parked there with an army officer and two soldiers. Nearby a crowd of children, jostling and whispering, waited for something to happen. The landlady stood to one side, her hands clasped, her face pale with fright.

"I don't like the look of this," said Sally.

The officer stepped forward, a man with a very straight back, a spotless uniform, and little polished boots. He gave a crisp bow. "Do I have the honor of greeting Señor Tom Broadbent and Señorita Sally Colorado? I am Lieutenant Vespán." He took their hands, one at a time, then stepped back. The wind shifted, and Tom suddenly smelled a mixture of Old Spice, cigars, and rum.

"What's the problem?" said Sally.

The man smiled broadly, exposing a row of silver teeth. "I am devastated to inform you that you are under arrest."

17

Tom stared at the diminutive military officer. A little dog, which had taken a dislike to one of the soldiers, crouched in front of him, baring his teeth and yapping. The officer kicked it away with a dainty boot, and the soldiers laughed.

"On what charge?" Tom asked.

"We will discuss that back in San Pedro Sula. Now, if you will please come with me."

There was an awkward silence. Sally said, "No."

"Señorita, let us not make difficulty."

"I'm not creating any difficulties. I'm just not going. You can't force me."

"Sally," Tom said, "may I point out these men have guns?"

"Good. Let them shoot me and then explain it to the U.S. government." She spread her arms out to make a target.

"Señorita, I pray you."

The two soldiers with him shifted nervously.

"Go ahead, make my day!"

The officer nodded at his two men, and they set their guns down, briskly stepped forward, and seized Sally. She yelled and struggled.

Tom took a step forward. "Get your hands off her."

The two men hoisted her up and began carrying her, struggling, to the jeep. Tom took a swing at the first man and sent him flying. Sally wrenched free while Tom tackled the other man.

The next thing Tom knew he was lying on his back, looking up into the hot blue sky. The officer stood over him, red faced and angry. Tom could feel a throbbing sensation at the base of his skull where the man had struck him with the butt of his gun.

The soldiers pulled him roughly to his feet. Sally had stopped struggling and looked pale.

"Macho bastards," she said. "We're going to report your assault to the American Embassy."

The lieutenant shook his head sadly, as if at the folly of it all. "Now, may we please go peacefully?"

They allowed themselves to be taken to the jeep. The colonel shoved Tom into the backseat and pushed Sally in next to him. Their backpacks and bags had already been collected from the hotel and were piled in the back. The jeep started down the road to the airstrip. There, a shabby military helicopter was sitting on the grass. A metal panel on the side of the helicopter was off, and a man with a wrench was fiddling with the engine. The jeep came sliding to a stop.

"What are you doing?" the colonel asked sharply in Spanish.

"I am sorry, Teniente, but there is a small problem."

"What problem?"

"We need a part."

"Can you fly without it?"

"No, Teniente."

"Mary whore of Jesus! How many times does this helicopter have to break down?"

"Shall I radio for them to send a plane with the part?"

"By the balls of Joseph! Yes, you deficient, radio for the part!"

The pilot climbed into the chopper, radioed, and then came out. "It will be coming tomorrow morning, Teniente. That is the earliest."

The lieutenant locked them in a wooden shed at the airstrip and put the two soldiers outside to guard them. After the door clapped shut, Tom sat down on an empty fifty-five-gallon drum and held his aching head.

"How are you feeling?" Sally asked.

"Like my head is a brass gong that was just rung."

"That was a nasty blow he gave you."

Tom nodded.

There was a rattle, and the door was flung open again. The lieutenant stood aside while one of the soldiers tossed in their sleeping bags and a flashlight. "I truly regret the inconvenience."

"You'll truly regret the inconvenience when I report you," Sally said.

The lieutenant ignored this. "May I advise you not to do anything foolish. It would be disappointing if someone were shot."

Sally said, "You wouldn't dare shoot us, you tinhorn Nazi."

The lieutenant's teeth glinted silvery yellow in the feeble light. "Accidents have been known to occur, especially to Americans who come to La Mosquitia unprepared for the rigors of the jungle."

He backed out of the door, and the soldier slammed it. Tom could hear the muffled voice of the lieutenant telling the soldiers that if they fell asleep or drank on the job he would personally cut their testicles off, dry them, and hang them up as door knockers.

"Damn Nazis," said Sally. "Thanks for defending me back there."

"Didn't do much good."

"Did he hit you hard?" She looked at his head. "That's a nasty lump."

"I'm fine."

Sally sat down next to him. He felt the warmth of her presence. He looked at her and could see her faint profile, just outlined in the semidarkness of the shed. She looked at him. They were so close that he could feel the warmth of her face on his, see the curl of her lip, the faint dimple on her cheek, the scattering of freckles on her nose. She still smelled of peppermint. Without even thinking of what he was doing, he leaned forward, his lips just brushing hers. For a moment there was stillness, and then she sharply pulled away. "That's *not* a good idea."

What the hell was he thinking? Tom pulled away, angry and humiliated.

The awkward moment was interrupted by a sudden banging at the door. "Dinner," cried one of the soldiers. The door opened briefly, letting in light, then slammed shut. He heard the soldier relock the padlock.

Tom shined the flashlight over and picked up the tray. Dinner consisted of two warm Pepsis, some bean tortillas, and a heap of tepid rice. Neither of them felt like eating. For a moment they sat there in the darkness. The aching in Tom's head subsided, and as it did he began to get mad. The soldiers had no right. He and Sally had done nothing wrong. He felt that their phony arrest had probably been engineered by the nameless enemy who had killed Barnaby and Fenton. His brothers were in even more danger than he thought.

"Give me the flashlight."

He shined it around. The shed couldn't have been more shoddily built, just a post-and-beam frame with boards nailed over it and a tin roof. An idea began to take shape—a plan of escape.

18

At three o'clock that morning they took their places, Sally by the door and Tom braced at the back wall. He whispered a three-count and they both kicked simultaneously, Sally's assault on the door masking the sound of Tom's kick to the boards on the back wall. The combined blows sounded like one, ringing loudly in the confined space. The shabby board popped off, just as Tom hoped.

Dogs began to bark in the village, and one of the soldiers cursed. "What are you doing?"

"I have to go to the bathroom!" Sally cried.

"No, no, you must go in there."

Tom whispered the countdown again, *one, two, three, kick.* Sally gave the door another blow while he kicked out a second board.

"Stop!" said the soldier.

"But I have to go, *cabrón!*"

"Señorita, I am sorry, but you must take care of it in there. I am under orders not to open the door."

One, two, three, kick!

The third board popped off. The opening was now big enough to squeeze through. The dogs in town were barking hysterically.

"One more kick and I call the *teniente!*"

"But I have to go!"

"There is nothing I can do."

"You soldiers are barbarians."

"It is our orders, señorita."

"That's just what Hitler's soldiers said."

"Sally, let's go," hissed Tom, gesturing to her in the dark.

"Hitler was not such a bad man, señorita. He made the trains run on time."

"That was Mussolini, you idiot. You two will end up on the gallows, and good riddance."

"Sally!" Tom called.

Sally came back. "Did you hear what those Nazis just said?"

He pushed her through the hole and handed out their sleeping bags. They ran at a crouch down the jungle track toward the town. The town had no electricity, but the sky was clear and moonlight bathed the empty streets. The dogs were already barking, and they were able to pass through without creating a further alarm. Despite the noise nobody was stirring.

These people have learned to mind their own business, Tom thought.

In five minutes they were down by the boats. Tom flashed the light over the army dugout, the one with the eighteen-horse engine. It was in good order, with two large plastic tanks of gasoline, both full. He began untying the prow. Suddenly he heard a voice, speaking low, from the darkness.

"You no want that boat."

It was the man they had hired earlier that day.

"We sure as hell do," hissed Tom.

"Let stupid army mans take that boat. Water going down. At every bend in river they get stuck. You take my boat. You no get stuck. That way you escape." He leapt like a cat onto the dock and untied a slender dugout with a six-horsepower engine. "Get in."

"Are you coming with us?" Sally asked.

"No. I tell stupid army mans you rob me." He started unhooking the gas tanks from the army boat and loading them into the back of their dugout canoe. He also gave them the gas tank from the other boat. Tom and Sally climbed in. Tom fished in his pocket and offered the man some money.

"Not now. If they search me and find money, I get shot."

"How can we pay you?" Tom asked.

"You pay me million dollar later. My name Manuel Waono. I always here."

"Wait a minute. A million dollars?"

"You rich American, you easy pay me million dollar. I, Manuel Waono, save your life. You go now. Fast."

"How do we find Pito Solo?"

"Last village on river."

"But how do we know—"

The Indian wasn't interested in making any more explanations. He pushed them off with a big bare foot, and the boat slid into the blackness.

Tom lowered the engine into the water, primed it, choked it, gave it a pull. Instantly it roared into life. In the silence, the sound was high pitched and loud.

"Go!" said Manuel from shore.

Tom threw the boat into forward. He turned the throttle as far as it would go, and the tinny engine whined and shuddered. The long wooden canoe began to move through the water. Tom steered while Sally stood in the bow, probing the river ahead with the flashlight.

Not a minute later, back at the dock, Manuel began shouting in Spanish: "Help! I am robbed! My boat, they stole my boat!"

"Christ, he didn't wait long," Tom muttered.

Soon a cacophony of excited voices came drifting toward them over the dark river. Then the bright light of a gas lantern came bobbing down the embankment, along with flashlights, illuminating a knot of people gathering on the makeshift dock. There was some angry and confused shouting and then a sudden hush. A voice rang out in English: the voice of Lieutenant Vespán. "Turn around or I order my men to shoot, please!"

"He's bullshitting," said Sally.

Tom didn't feel quite so sure.

"Do not think I am joking!" the *teniente* shouted.

"He'll never shoot," said Sally.

"One . . . two . . ."

"It's a crock," said Sally.

"Three . . ."

There was a silence.

"What did I tell you?"

There was a sudden burst of automatic-weapons fire coming across the water, shockingly loud and close.

"Shit!" Tom yelled, throwing himself down. As the boat began to yaw, he quickly reached up with one hand and steadied the engine handle.

Sally was still standing in the prow, unconcerned. "Tom, they're shooting into the air. They're not going to risk hitting us. We're Americans."

There was a second burst of gunfire. This time Tom distinctly heard the slap of bullets hitting the water around them. Instantly Sally landed on the floor of the dugout next to him. "Jesus Christ, they *are* shooting at us!" she cried.

Tom reached up and shoved the tiller sideways, sending the dugout into a sharp evasive maneuver. There were two more short bursts of gunfire. This time he heard the whine of bullets overhead and to the left, like bees. They were evidently aiming for the sound of the engine, raking the water back and forth with their automatic weapons. And they were most definitely shooting to kill.

He steered the boat on a zigzag course, trying to throw the shooters off their aim. At each lull, Sally raised her head and shined the light ahead so they could see where they were going. They would be safe, at least for the moment, once they got around the bend in the river.

There was another burst, and this time several rounds nicked the gunwale, showering them with splinters.

"Shit!"

"We will come and get you!" rose up the voice of the lieutenant, fainter now. "We will find you, and then you will be very sorry for the very short remainder of your very miserable lives."

Tom counted to twenty and risked another look ahead. Slowly the boat came around the bend, out of the line of fire. Tom steered as close to the wall of vegetation as he dared. As they went around the bend, the lights at the little landing flickered through the leaves and then were gone.

They had made it.

There was another halfhearted burst of gunfire. Tom heard a snipping and cracking in the jungle to their left as the bullets were stopped
by the trees. The sounds echoed away and the river fell silent.

Tom helped Sally up. Her face looked white, almost ghostly, in the
dim light. He shined the flashlight around. Two walls of trees rose up
on either side of the dark river. A single star burned for a moment in
a patch of exposed sky, then blinked and flickered through the canopy
as they moved. The little engine whined away. For now they were alone
on the river. The dark, humid night enfolded them.

Tom took Sally's hand. He found it was shaking, and then he realized his own hand was shaking, too. The soldiers had shot at them,
trying to kill them. He had seen it a million times in the movies, but
to actually be shot at was something else entirely.

The moon was setting behind the wall of jungle, and darkness suffocated the river. Tom flicked on the flashlight to see what lay ahead,
guiding the boat around snags and riffles. A growing cloud of mosquitoes whined around them. They seemed to be sweeping up thousands
as they traveled.

"I don't suppose you have a can of bug repellent in one of those
pockets of yours?" Tom asked.

"As a matter of fact, I did manage to snag my fanny pack in the jeep.
I shoved it in my pants." She fished the small pack out of an enormous
pocket on her thigh and unzipped it. She began rummaging through,
pulling out a miscellany of things—a bottle of water-purification tablets,
some packs of waterproof matches, a roll of hundred-dollar bills, a
map, a chocolate bar, a passport, some useless credit cards.

"I'm not even sure what's in here."

She began sorting through the jumble of items while Tom held the
flashlight. There was no bottle of bug stuff. She swore and began putting everything back. As she did so, a photograph fell out. Tom shined
the light on it. It showed a strikingly handsome young man with dark
eyebrows and a chiseled chin. The grave expression that furrowed his
dark eyebrows, the firm full set of his lips, the tweed jacket, and the
way he tilted his head all showed him to be a man who took himself
very seriously indeed.

"Who's that?" Tom asked.

"Oh," said Sally. "That's Professor Clyve."

"That's Clyve? Why, he's so young! I imagined him to be some dotty old man in a cardigan puffing on a pipe."

"He wouldn't be happy to hear you say that. He's the youngest full professor in the history of the department. He entered Stanford at sixteen, graduated at nineteen, and had his Ph.D. by the time he was twenty-two. He's a true genius." She carefully tucked the photo back into her pocket.

"Why are you carrying around a photo of your professor?"

"Why," said Sally lightly, "we're engaged. Didn't I tell you?"

"No."

Sally looked at him curiously. "You don't have a problem with that, do you?"

"Of course not." Tom felt his face flushing and hoped the darkness would hide it. He was aware she was glaring at him in the dim light.

"You seemed surprised."

"Well, I was. After all, you're not wearing an engagement ring."

"Professor Clyve doesn't believe in those bourgeois conventions."

"And it was okay with him that you just come on this trip with me——?" Tom broke off, realizing he had said exactly the wrong thing.

"You think I have to get *permission* from 'my man' to go on a trip? Or are you somehow implying that I'm not to be trusted sexually?" She tilted her head, looking at him with narrowed eyes.

Tom looked away. "Sorry I asked."

"So am I. Somehow I thought you were more enlightened than that."

Tom busied himself driving the boat, hiding his embarrassment and confusion. The river was silent; the swampy night heat flowed past them. A bird cried in the darkness. In the silence that followed, Tom heard a noise.

Tom immediately switched off the engine, his heart pounding. The sound came again, the sputter of an outboard starter being pulled. A hush fell over the river. The boat coasted.

"They found some gas. They're coming after us."

The boat was starting to drift back down with the current. Tom unshipped a pole from the bottom of the boat and stuck it in the water. The boat swung a little to the current and steadied. Holding the boat still in the current, they listened. There was another sputter and then a roar. The roar subsided into a hum. There could be no doubt: It was the sound of an outboard.

Tom went to restart their engine.

"Don't," said Sally. "They'll hear it."

"We can't outpole them."

"We can't outrace them either. They'll be on us in five minutes with that eighteen-horse." Sally flashed the light along the wall of jungle on either side of the water. The water extended into the trees and spread out, drowning the jungle. "We can hide instead."

Tom poled the dugout toward the edge of the flooded forest. There was a small opening—a narrow lane of water that looked like it might have been a stream in drier times. He poled up it, and the boat promptly bumped into something: a sunken log.

"Out," Tom said.

The water was only a foot deep, but underneath it was another two feet of mud, which they sank into with a flurry of bubbles. A foul stench of marsh gas rose up. The back of the boat was still sticking out into the river, where it would be instantly spotted.

"Lift and push."

They struggled to get the nose of the boat up on the log and then, heaving together, pushed the boat across. Then they scrambled over it themselves and climbed back in. The sound of the Evinrude grew louder. The soldiers' boat was coming up the river fast.

Sally picked up the second pole, and they both poled forward, deeper into the flooded forest. Tom switched off the flashlight, and a moment later a powerful light came blinking through the trees.

"We're still too close," said Tom. "They'll see us." He tried to pole, but the pole sank into the muck and stuck. He jerked it out and laid it in the bottom of the boat, grabbing some hanging vines instead and using them to pull the boat deeper into the forest, halfway into a thicket of ferns and bushes. The Evinrude was almost on them. The spotlight flashed through the forest just as Tom grabbed Sally and pulled her down to the bottom of the dugout, and they lay side by side, his arm around her. Tom prayed that the soldiers wouldn't see their engine.

The sound of the motorboat grew very loud. The boat had slowed down, and the spotlight was probing the forest where they were hidden. Tom could hear the crackle of a walkie-talkie, the murmur of voices. The spotlight lit up the jungle around them like a movie set—and then slowly moved on. Blessed darkness returned. The sound of the engine passed and grew fainter.

Tom sat up in time to see the flash of the spotlight in the forest up ahead as the boat went around a bend. "They're gone," he said.

Sally sat up, brushing her tangled hair out of her face. The mosquitoes had gathered around them in a thick, whining cloud. Tom could feel them everywhere, in his hair, crawling into his ears, trying to get up his nose, crawling down his neck. Each blow killed a dozen, instantly replaced. When he tried to breathe, he breathed mosquitoes.

"We've got to get out of here," Sally said, slapping.

Tom began pulling dry twigs off the bushes around them.

"What are you doing?"

"Building a fire."

"Where?"

"You'll see." When he'd collected a pile of twigs, he leaned over the side and scooped up some mud from the swamp. He patted it into a pancake on the bottom of the dugout, covered it with leaves, and then built a small teepee of sticks and dry leaves on top.

"Match."

Sally handed him a match, and he lit the fire. As soon as it was going well, he added some green leaves and twigs. A curl of smoke drifted up and gathered in the still air. Tom plucked a large leaf from a nearby bush and used it as a fan to wave the smoke over Sally. The furious cloud of mosquitoes was driven back. The smoke had a pleasant smell, sweet and spicy.

"There's a nice trick," said Sally.

"My father showed it to me on a canoe trip in northern Maine." He reached up, yanked some more leaves off the bush, and added them to the fire.

Sally took out the map and began examining it by flashlight. "It looks like there are a lot of side channels to the river. I think we should stick to those until we reach Pito Solo."

"Good idea. And I think we'll have to pole from now on. We can't risk using the engine."

Sally nodded.

"You tend the fire," said Tom. "I'll pole, and then we'll switch off. We won't stop until we reach Pito Solo."

"Right."

Tom pushed the boat back into the river and poled close to the flooded forest, listening for the motorboat. Soon they came to a small side channel winding away from the main one, and took it.

Tom said, "Somehow I don't think Lieutenant Vespán had any intention of bringing us back to San Pedro Sula. I think he planned to have us fall out of his helicopter. If it weren't for that missing part, we'd be dead."

19

Vernon looked up into the vast canopy that arched above his head and noted that night was falling in the Meambar Swamp. With it came the whine of insects and a steamy miasma of rot that rose up from the shivery acres of muck that surrounded them, drifting like poison gas among the giant tree trunks. Somewhere in the depths of the swamp he could hear the distant shriek of an animal, followed by the roar of a jaguar.

It was the second night in a row that they could find no dry land to camp. Instead, they had tethered the dugout under a group of giant bromeliads in the hope that their leaves would help keep out a steady rain. They did no such thing, instead channeling the rain into streams that could not be avoided.

The Teacher lay in the bottom of the dugout, in the rain, huddled against the heap of supplies, wrapped in a wet blanket and shivering despite the suffocating heat. The cloud of mosquitoes that enveloped them in a mewling fog was especially thick about his face. Vernon could actually see them crawling about his mouth and eyes. Vernon reached out and spread some more deet on his face, but it was a hopeless task. If the rain didn't wash it off, the sweat did.

He glanced up. The two guides were in the front of the boat, playing cards by flashlight and drinking. They had hardly been sober since the beginning of the trip, and Vernon was horrified to discover that one of the ten-gallon plastic jugs that he thought contained water was actually full of homemade *aguardiente*.

Vernon hunched over, swaying and hugging himself. It wasn't quite dark; night seemed to be coming very slowly. There was no sunset in the swamp: The light went from green to blue to purple and then black. At dawn it was reversed. Even on sunny days there was no sun, just a deep green gloom. He felt desperate for a bit of light, a breath of fresh air.

After four days of wandering in the swamp, their guides had finally admitted that they were lost, that they had to turn around. And they had turned the boats around. But they only seemed to go deeper into the swamp. This certainly wasn't the way they had come. The guides were impossible to talk to; although Vernon spoke Spanish fairly well and the guides knew some English, they were often too drunk to speak any language. For the past few days, the more lost they seemed to become, the more loudly the guides denied it and the more they drank. And then the Teacher had gotten sick.

Vernon heard a curse from up front. One of the guides threw down his cards and staggered to his feet, rifle in hand. The boat rocked.

"*Cabrón!*" The other one had swayed to his feet, gripping a machete.

"Stop," Vernon yelled, but as usual they ignored him. They cursed and came together in a drunken scuffle; the rifle went off harmlessly, there was more grunting and scuffling, and then the two guides, none the worse for their altercation, settled back down in the boat, gathered up their spilled cards, and redealt as if nothing had happened.

"What was that shot?" the Teacher asked belatedly, opening his eyes.

"Nothing," said Vernon. "They're drinking again."

The Teacher shivered, drawing the blanket tighter. "You should take away that gun."

Vernon said nothing. It would be stupid to try to take away their gun, even when they were drunk. Especially when they were drunk.

"The mosquitoes," the Teacher whispered, his voice quavering.

Vernon squirted some more deet into his hands and gently smoothed it over the Teacher's face and around his neck. The Teacher sighed with relief, gave a quick shiver, and closed his eyes.

Vernon pulled his wet shirt about himself, feeling the heavy rain on his back, listening to the sounds of the forest, the alien cries of mating and violence. He thought about death. It seemed that the question he had been seeking an answer to all his life was about to be answered for him, in an unexpected and quite horrifying way.

20

For two days, a deep and protective cloak of mist lay on the river. Tom and Sally poled upstream, following winding side channels and keeping a strict policy of silence. They traveled day and night, taking turns sleeping. They had little to eat except Sally's two candy bars, which they rationed, bit by bit, and some fruit Sally collected on the way. They saw no sign of the soldiers pursuing them. Tom began to hope that they had given up and gone back to Brus, or had gotten hung up somewhere. The river was riddled with sandbars, mudbanks, and sunken logs to hang up a boat. Waono had been right.

The morning of the third day the mists began to lift, exposing two dripping walls of jungle lining the blackwater river. Shortly thereafter, they spied a house on stilts built over the water, with wattle walls and a thatched roof. Beyond that a riverbank appeared, with granite boulders and a steep embankment—the first dry land they had seen in days. A dock appeared at the water's edge like the one at Brus—a rickety platform of bamboo poles lashed to slender tree trunks sunk in the muck.

"What do you think?" Tom asked. "Should we stop?"

Sally stood up. A boy was fishing from a platform with a small bow and arrow.

"Pito Solo?"

But the boy had seen them and was already running away, abandoning his rod.

"Let's give it a try," said Tom. "If we don't get something to eat, we're finished." He poled into the dock.

Sally and Tom jumped out, and the platform creaked and swayed alarmingly. Beyond, a rickety gangplank led to a steep dirt bank, which rose out of the flooded jungle. There was nobody to be seen. They scrambled up the slippery embankment, slipping and sliding in the mud. Everything was soaking wet. At the top was a small open hut and a fire, with an old man sitting in a hammock. An animal was roasting on a spit of wood. Tom eyed it, smelling the delicious aroma of roasting meat. His appetite was tempered only slightly when he realized it was a monkey.

"*Hola,*" said Sally.

"*Hola,*" said the man.

Sally spoke in Spanish. "Is this Pito Solo?"

There was a long silence while the man looked at her blankly.

"He doesn't speak Spanish," said Tom.

"Which way is the town? *Donde?* Where?"

The man pointed into the mist. There was the sharp cry of an animal, and Tom jumped.

"There's a trail here," Sally said.

They started up the trail and soon came to the town. It sat on a rise above the flooded rainforest, a motley collection of wattle-and-daub huts with roofs of tin or thatch. Chickens strutted away from them, and skinny dogs slunk along the walls of the houses, eyeing them sideways. They wandered through the village, which seemed deserted. It ended as quickly as it began in a wall of solid jungle.

Sally looked at him. "What now?"

"We knock." Tom picked a door at random, knocked.

Silence.

Tom heard a rustle and looked around. At first he saw nothing, and then he realized that a hundred dark eyes were peering at him from the jungle foliage. They were all children.

"I wish I had my candy," Sally said.

"Take out a dollar."

Sally removed a dollar. "Hello? Who wants an American dollar?"

A shout went up, and a hundred children burst from the foliage, shouting and jostling, their hands extended.

"Who speaks Spanish?" asked Sally, holding up the dollar.

Everyone shouted at once in Spanish. Out of the hubbub an older girl stepped forward. "Can I help you?" she said, with great poise and dignity. She looked about thirteen and was pretty, wearing a tie-dyed T-shirt, a pair of shorts, and two gold earrings. Thick brown braids went down her back.

Sally gave her the dollar. A great *ahhh* of disappointment went up from the group, but they seemed to take it with good humor. The ice, at least, was broken.

"What is your name?"

"Marisol."

"That's a nice name."

The girl smiled.

"We are looking for Don Orlando Ocotal. Can you take us to him?"

"He went away with the *yanquis* more than a week ago."

"Which *yanquis*?"

"The tall angry gringo with the bites all over his face and the smiling one with the gold rings on his fingers."

Tom swore and looked at Sally. "Sounds like Philip got our guide first." He turned back to the girl. "Did they say where they were going?"

"No."

"Are there any grown-ups in town? We're going upriver and we need a guide."

The girl said, "I will take you to my grandfather, Don Alfonso Boswas, who is the head of the village. He knows everything."

They followed her. She had about her an air of self-possession and competence, reinforced by her straight posture. As they passed among the crooked huts, there was a smell of cooking that made Tom almost faint with hunger. The girl led them to what looked like the worst hut in the village, a leaning pile of sticks with almost no mud remaining in the cracks. It was built next to a muddy expanse that served as the town plaza. In the middle of the plaza stood a bedraggled cluster of lemon and banana trees.

The girl stood aside at the door, and they stepped inside. An old man sat in the center of the hut, on a stool too low for him, his bony knees sticking out of the great holes in his pants, a few wisps of white hair coming off his balding skull in random directions. He was smoking a corncob pipe, which had filled the hut with a tarry smell. A machete lay on the ground next to him. He was small and wore glasses that magnified his eyes, giving him a wide-eyed look of surprise. It was impossible to imagine he was the chief of the village; he looked, instead, like the village's poorest man.

"Don Alfonso Boswas?" Tom asked.

"Who?" The old man cried, picking up the machete and waving it about. "Boswas? That scoundrel? He's gone. They ran him out of town long ago. That good-for-nothing was living too long, and he just sat and smoked his pipe all day and looked at the girls passing his hut."

Tom stared at the man in surprise, then turned to look for the girl. She stood in the doorway, suppressing a giggle.

The old man laid down the machete and laughed. "Come in, come in. I am Don Alfonso Boswas. Sit down. I'm just an old man who likes to tell a joke. I have twenty grandchildren and sixty great-grandchildren, and they never come to visit me, so I must tell jokes to strangers." He spoke a curiously formal, old-fashioned Spanish, using the *usted* form.

Tom and Sally took two rickety stools. "I'm Tom Broadbent," he said, "and this is Sally Colorado."

The old man stood, bowed formally, and reseated himself.

"We're looking for a guide to go upriver."

"Humph," he said. "All of a sudden these *yanquis* are all crazy to go upriver and get lost in the Meambar Swamp to be eaten by anacondas. Why?"

Tom hesitated, nonplussed by the unexpected question.

"We're trying to find his father," said Sally. "Maxwell Broadbent. He came through here about a month ago with a group of Indians in dugout canoes. They probably had a lot of boxes with them."

The old man looked at Tom, squinting. "Come here, boy." He

reached out with a leathery hand and grasped Tom's arm in a viselike grip, drawing him closer. He peered at him, his eyes magnified grotesquely by the glasses.

Tom felt as if the old man were peering right into his soul.

After a moment's scrutiny, he released him. "I see that you and your wife are hungry. Marisol!" He spoke to her in an Indian language. The girl left. He turned back to Tom. "So that was your father who came through here, eh? You don't look crazy to me. A boy with a crazy father is usually crazy, too."

"My mother was normal," said Tom.

Don Alfonso laughed uproariously and slapped his knee. "That is good. You are a joker, too. Yes, they stopped here to buy food. The white man was like a bear, and his voice carried half a mile. I told him he was crazy to go on into the Meambar Swamp, but he did not listen. He must be a great chief from America. We had a good evening together with many laughs, and he gave me *this*."

He reached over to where some burlap sacks were folded up, fumbled about with his hands, and held something toward them in the palm of his hand. The sun struck it, and it glinted the color of pigeon's blood, with a perfect star shining in it. He placed it in Tom's hand.

"A star ruby," breathed Tom. It was one of the gems in his father's collection, worth a small, perhaps even a large, fortune. He felt a sudden rush of emotion: It was so like his father to make an extravagant gift to someone he liked. He had once given a panhandler five thousand dollars because the man amused him with a witty remark.

"Yes. A ruby. With it my grandchildren will go to America." He carefully squirreled it away among the dirty burlap sacks. "Why is your father doing this? He was as evasive as a coati when I tried to find out."

Tom glanced at Sally. How could he possibly explain it? "We're trying to find my father. He's . . . sick."

At this Don Alfonso's eyes opened wide. He removed his glasses, wiped them with a filthy rag, and put them back on, dirtier than before. "Sick? Is it infectious?"

"No. As you say, he's just a little *loco*, that's all. It's a game he wanted to play with his sons."

Don Alfonso thought for a while, then shook his head. "I have seen the *yanquis* do many strange things, but this is more than strange. There is something you're not telling me. If I am to help you, you must tell me all."

Tom sighed and glanced at Sally. She nodded. "He's dying. He went upriver with all his possessions to be buried, and he issued a challenge to us that if we wanted our inheritance, we would have to find his tomb."

Don Alfonso nodded, as if this were the most natural thing in the world. "Yes, yes, this is something we Tawahka Indians once did. We buried ourselves with our property, and it always made our sons angry. But then the missionaries came and explained to us that Jesus would give us new things in heaven so we didn't need to bury anything with the dead. So we stopped doing it. But I believe the old way was better. And I am not sure that Jesus has all these new things for people when they die. The pictures I have seen of him show a poor man without cooking pots, pigs, chickens, shoes, or even a wife." Don Alfonso sniffed loudly. "But then, perhaps it is better to bury yourself with your possessions than letting the sons fight over them. Even before you are dead they are fighting. That is why I already gave everything I owned to my sons and daughters and live like a wretch. This is the respectable thing to do. Now my sons have nothing to fight over, and, what is more important, they do not wish me dead."

He finished his speech and put his pipe back in his mouth.

"Did any other white people come by?" Sally asked.

"Ten days ago two dugouts with four men, two mountain Indians and two white men, stopped. I thought the younger one might be Jesus Christ, but at the missionary school they said he was only a type of person called a *hippie*. They stayed a day, and they went on. Then a week ago four dugouts with army soldiers and two gringos arrived. They hired Don Orlando to guide them and left. This is why I ask myself: Why are all these crazy *yanquis* suddenly going into the Meambar Swamp? Are they all looking for your father's tomb?"

"Yes. They're my two brothers."

"Why are you not cooperating?"

Tom didn't answer.

Sally spoke. "You mentioned mountain Indians with the first white man. Do you know where they come from?"

"They are naked savage Indians from the highlands who paint themselves red and black. They are not Christians. We are a little bit Christian here in Pito Solo. Not much, just enough to get by when the missionaries come with North American food and medicine. Then we sing and clap for Jesus. That is how I got my new glasses." He removed them and held them out to Tom for inspection.

Tom said, "Don Alfonso, we need a guide to take us upriver, and we need supplies and equipment. Can you help us?"

Don Alfonso puffed and puffed, then nodded. "I will take you."

"Oh no," Tom said, looking at the feeble old man with alarm. "That isn't what I was asking. We couldn't take you away from the village where you're needed."

"Me? Needed? The village would like nothing more than to get rid of old Don Alfonso!"

"But you're their chief."

"Chief? Puah!"

"It'll be a long, hard journey," said Tom, "not suitable for a man of your age."

"I am still as strong as a tapir! I'm young enough to marry again. In fact, I need a sixteen-year-old who will fit right in that empty place in my hammock and bounce me to sleep every night with little sighs and kisses—"

"Don Alfonso—"

"I need a sixteen-year-old to tease me and poke her tongue in my ear to wake me up in the morning so I get up with the birds. Do not concern yourselves any longer: I, Don Alfonso Boswas, will take you through the Meambar Swamp."

"No," said Tom as firmly as he could. "You will not. We need a younger guide."

"You cannot avoid it. I dreamed you would come and that I would go with you. So it is decided. I speak English and Spanish, but I prefer Spanish. English frightens me. It sounds like one is being choked."

Tom glanced at Sally, exasperated. This old man was impossible.

At that moment Marisol returned with her mother. They were each carrying wooden trenchers laid with palm leaves, on which were piled fresh hot tortillas, fried plantains, roasted meats and nuts, and fresh fruit.

Tom had never been so hungry in his life. He and Sally tucked into the feast, joined by Don Alfonso, while the girl and her mother watched in satisfied silence. All conversation ceased while they ate. When he and Sally had finished, the woman silently took their plates and refilled them, and then refilled them a third time.

When the meal was over, Don Alfoso leaned back and wiped his mouth.

"Now look," said Tom as firmly as he could. "Dream or no dream, you're not coming with us. We need a younger man."

"Or woman," said Sally.

"I will bring two young men with me, Chori and Pingo. I'm the only one besides Don Orlando who knows the way through the Meambar Swamp. Without a guide you will die."

"I must decline your offer, Don Alfonso."

"You don't have much time. The soldiers are after you."

"They were here?" Tom asked, alarmed.

"They came this morning. They will be back."

Tom glanced at Sally and then back to Don Alfonso. "We haven't done anything wrong. I'll explain—"

"You do not need to explain. The soldiers are evil men. We must start provisioning immediately. Marisol!"

"Yes, grandfather?"

"We will need tarpaulins, matches, petrol, two-cycle engine oil, tools, a frying pan, cooking pot, silverware, and water canteens." He continued to reel off the list of supplies and food.

"Do you have medicine?" Tom asked.

"We have much North American medicine, thanks to the missionaries. We did a lot of clapping for Jesus to get those medicines. Marisol, tell the people to come with the items for sale at fair prices."

Marisol ran off, her braids flying, and in less than ten minutes she returned, leading a file of old men, women, and children, each carrying something. Don Alfoso remained in the hut, aloof from the lowly business of buying and selling while Marisol handled the crowd.

"Buy what you want and tell the others to go away," Marisol said. "They will tell you the price. Do not bargain; it is not our way. Just say yes or no. The prices are fair."

She spoke sharply to the ragged line of people, and they shuffled together, standing up straighter.

"She's going to be chief of this village," Tom said to Sally in English, looking over the orderly row of people.

"She already is."

"We are ready," Marisol said. She gestured at the first man in line. He stepped forward and held out five old burlap sacks.

"Four hundred," said the girl.

"Dollars?"

"Lempiras."

"What's that in dollars?" said Tom.

"Two."

"We'll take them."

The next person stepped forward with a large sack of beans, a sack of loose dry corn, and an indescribably battered aluminum pot and lid. The original handle was missing, and in its place was a beautifully carved and oiled piece of hardwood. "One dollar."

"We'll take them."

The man laid them down and retreated, while the next one stepped forward, holding out two T-shirts, two pairs of dirty shorts, a trucker's hat, and a brand-new pair of Nikes.

"Here's my change of clothes," said Tom. He looked at the shoes. "Just my size, too. Imagine finding a brand-new pair of Air Jordans down here."

"They make them here," said Sally. "Remember the sweatshop scandals?"

"Oh yeah."

The procession of goods continued: plastic tarps, sacks of beans and rice, dried and smoked meats that Tom decided not to inquire too closely about, bananas, a fifty-five-gallon drum of petrol, a box of salt. Quite a few had arrived with cans of extra-strength Raid, the insect repellent of choice, which Tom declined.

Suddenly a hush fell over the crowd. Tom could hear the faint buzz of an outboard motor. The girl spoke rapidly.

"You must follow me into the forest. Quickly."

Instantly the crowd had dispersed, and the village fell silent, seemingly empty. The girl calmly led the way into the forest, following an almost invisible trail. A twilight mist drifted through the trees. There was swamp all around them, but the trail wound this way and that, keeping to high ground. The sounds of the village died away, and they were wrapped in the muffled cloak of the forest. After ten minutes of walking, the girl stopped.

"We wait here."

"How long?"

"Until the soldiers leave."

"What about our boat?" Sally asked. "Won't they recognize our boat?"

"We already hid your boat."

"That was a good idea. Thank you."

"You're welcome." The self-possessed girl turned her dark eyes back down the trail and waited, as still and quiet as a deer.

"Where do you go to school?" Sally asked, after a moment.

"The Baptist school down the river."

"A missionary school?"

"Yes."

"Are you a Christian?"

"Oh *yes*," said the girl, turning a serious face to Sally. "Aren't you?"

Sally blushed. "Well, ah, my parents were Christians."

"That is good," she said, smiling. "I wouldn't want you to go to hell."

"Well now," said Tom, speaking into the awkward silence. "I'm curious to know, Marisol, if there is anyone in the village besides Don Alfonso who knows the way across the Meambar Swamp."

She shook her head gravely. "He is the only one."

"Is it difficult to cross?"

"Very."

"Why is he so anxious to take us?"

She simply shook her head. "I do not know. He has dreams and visions, and this was one of them."

"He really did dream about us coming?"

"Oh yes. When the first white man came, he said the sons would soon follow. And here you are."

"A lucky guess," said Tom in English.

A distant shot echoed through the forest, then another. It rolled about like thunder, curiously distorted by the jungle, taking a long time to fade away. The effect on Marisol was terrible to see. She turned white, trembled, and swayed. But she said nothing and did not move. Tom was horrified. Had somebody been shot?

"They aren't shooting people?" he asked.

"I don't know."

Tom could see her eyes filling with tears. But she betrayed no other emotion.

Sally grabbed Tom's arm. "They might be shooting people on account of us. We've got to go give ourselves up."

"No," said the girl sharply. "Maybe they're shooting into the air. We can do nothing except wait." A single tear made a track down the girl's face.

"We never should have stopped here," said Sally, switching into English. "We had no right to put these people in danger. Tom, we've *got* to go back to the village and face those soldiers."

"You're right." Tom turned to go.

"They *will* shoot us if you go back," the girl said. "With soldiers, we are powerless."

"They'll never get away with this," Sally said, her voice shaking. "I'll report this to the American Embassy. Those soldiers will be punished."

The girl said nothing. She had fallen silent and was standing still again, like a deer, just barely trembling. Even her tears had stopped.

21

ewis Skiba remained alone in his office. It was still early in the afternoon, but he had sent everyone home to get them away from the
press. He had unplugged his office phone and shut the two outer doors
to his office. Now, while the company was crumbling around him, he
was locked in a cocoon of silence, wrapped in a golden glow of his own
making.

The Securities and Exchange Commission hadn't even waited until
the close of trading to announce the investigation into accounting
irregularities at Lampe-Denison Pharmaceuticals. The announcement
had fallen like a hammer blow on the stock, and now Lampe was at
seven and a quarter and ticking down. The company was like a dying
whale, paralyzed, wallowing, surrounded by a frenzied, mindless cluster of sharks—short sellers—tearing it apart, chunk by chunk. It was
a primitive, Darwinian feeding frenzy. And every dollar they chewed
out of the stock price ripped a hundred-million-dollar hole in
Lampe's market cap. He was helpless.

Lampe's lawyers had done their duty and issued the usual statement
that the allegations had "no merit" and that Lampe was eager to
cooperate and clear its name. Graff, the CFO, had played his part,
issuing a statement that Lampe had scrupulously followed generally
accepted accounting principals. Lampe's auditors expressed shock and
dismay, saying that they had relied on Lampe's financial declarations
and avowals and that if there were any irregularities they had been as

thoroughly deceived as everyone else. All the stock phrases Skiba had heard from every other crooked company and their legions of enablers got trotted out. It was all as stilted and programmed as a Japanese Kabuki drama. Everyone had followed the script but him. Now they all wanted to hear from him, the great and terrible Skiba. They wanted to jerk back the curtain. Everyone wanted to glimpse the charlatan working the controls.

It wasn't going to work that way. Not as long as he was still breathing. Let them jabber and haw; he would remain silent. And then, when the Codex arrived and their stock doubled, tripled, quadrupled . . .

He checked his watch. Two minutes.

Hauser's voice came in so clear over the satellite connection that the man could have been calling from next door, except that the scrambler made him quack like Donald Duck. Nevertheless the man's bully-boy bluster, his insolent familiarity, came through.

Hauser said, "Lewis! How're you doing?"

Skiba allowed a frosty moment to pass. "When am I going to have the Codex?"

"Skiba, here's the situation. The middle brother, Vernon, just as I thought, got his ass lost in the swamp, and he's probably done for. The other brother, Tom—"

"I didn't ask about the brothers. I don't care about the brothers. I asked about the Codex."

"You *should* care. You know the score. Anyway, as I was saying, Tom managed to slip past some soldiers I'd hired to stop him. They're pursuing him upriver and may yet catch him before he goes into the swamp, but he's proving a lot more resourceful than I anticipated. If he's going to be stopped, the last place to do it is at the far end of the swamp. I can't risk losing track of him and the girl in the mountains beyond. You follow?"

Skiba turned down the volume on the arrogant, quacking voice. He didn't believe he had ever hated a man as much as he hated Hauser right now.

"A second problem is the oldest son, Philip. At some point I'm going to have to deal with him. I'll need him for a while longer, but when he's outlived his usefulness, well, we can't have him 'popping up' (that was your phrase, or was it mine?) claiming ownership of the Codex. Nor can Vernon or Tom. And that goes for the woman Tom's traveling with, Sally Colorado."

There was a long silence.

"You do understand what I'm saying, don't you?"

Skiba waited, trying to control himself. These conversations were a colossal waste of time. Even more, they were dangerous.

"You there, Lewis?"

Skiba said angrily, "Why don't you just get on with it? Why these calls? Your job is to deliver the Codex to me. *How* you do it is your business, Hauser."

The chuckle swelled to a laugh. "Oh, that's beautiful. You're not going to get away so easily. You've known all along what has to happen. You've been hoping that I'd take care of it on my own. No such luck. There isn't going to be any deniability here, no selling out the little guy, no plea bargaining. When the time comes, you're going to *tell* me to kill them. It's the only way, and you know it."

"Stop this kind of talk immediately. There will be no killing."

"Oh, Lewis, Lewis ..."

Skiba felt sick. He felt the nausea contracting his stomach in waves. Out of the corner of his eye the stock was ticking down again. The SEC hadn't even halted trading, had hung Lampe out to twist in the wind. There were twenty thousand employees depending on him, millions of sick people who needed their drugs, there were his wife and children, his house, his own two million stock options and six million shares ...

He heard a loud honk on the line—evidently a laugh. He suddenly felt very weak. How had he allowed this to happen? How had this man escaped his control?

"Don't kill anyone," he said, swallowing before he could even finish the sentence. His stomach was going to heave at any moment. There was a legal way to do this; the sons would bring out the Codex, and then he'd negotiate with them, strike a deal ... But he knew it wouldn't happen, not with Lampe under a cloud of rumor and investigation, with a collapsing stock price ...

The voice suddenly became gentle. "Look, I know it's a tough decision. If you really feel strongly about this, I'll turn around and we'll forget all about the Codex. Really."

Skiba swallowed. That knot in his throat felt like it was going to choke him. His three towheaded sons smiled at him from the silver frames on his desk.

"Just say the word and we'll head back. Call it a day."

"There's to be no killing."

"Look, no decision has to be made just yet. Why don't you sleep on it?"

Skiba staggered to his feet. He tried to make it to his leather-covered gold-tooled Florentine wastebasket but only got as far as the fireplace. With the vomit crackling and sizzling in the fire, he came back to the phone, picked it up to say something, then changed his mind and slowly placed it back in its cradle with a shaky hand. The hand snaked out toward the top drawer of his desk, and searched out the cool bottle of plastic.

22

Thirty minutes later, Tom saw movement in the forest, and an old, shawled woman came tramping down the trail. Marisol rushed forward with a sob, and they spoke rapidly in their own language.

Marisol turned to Tom and Sally with a look of huge relief. "It is as I said. The soldiers just shot into the air to frighten us. Then they went away. We convinced them that you had not come to the village, that you had not passed by. They have gone back downriver."

As they approached the hut, Tom could see Don Alfonso standing outside, smoking his pipe, looking as unconcerned as if nothing had happened. His face broke into a big smile as they approached. "Chori! Pingo! Get out here! Come out and meet your new *yanqui* bosses! Chori and Pingo do not speak Spanish, they speak only Tawahka, but I yell at them in Spanish to show them my superiority, and you must yell at them, too."

Two magnificent specimens of manhood bowed out of the door of the hut, naked from the waist up, their muscled bodies gleaming with oil. The one named Pingo had Western-style tattoos on his arms and Indian tattoos on his face and held a three-foot machete in his fist, while Chori had an old Springfield rifle slung over his shoulder and carried a Pulaski—a firefighter's axe—in one hand.

"We will load the boat now. We must leave the village as soon as possible."

Sally glanced at Tom. "Looks like Don Alfonso's going to be our guide."

Shouting and gesticulating, Don Alfonso directed Chori and Pingo as they carried the supplies down to the river's edge. Their dugout was back, looking as if it had never been moved. In a half hour everything was all set, the supplies loaded in a great heap in the middle of the dugout and tied down with a plastic tarp. Meanwhile a crowd had been gathering on the bank, and cooking fires were lit.

Sally turned to Marisol. "You're a wonderful girl," she said. "You saved our lives. You could do anything in life you want, do you know that?"

The girl gazed at her steadily. "I only want one thing."

"What's that?"

"To go to America." The girl said no more but continued looking at Sally with her grave, intelligent face.

"I hope you do go to America," said Sally.

The girl smiled confidently and stood up straighter. "I will. Don Alfonso promised. He has a ruby."

The riverbank was now crowded with people. Their departure seemed to be turning into a festive occasion. A group of women was cooking a communal dinner over a fire. Children were running, playing, laughing, and chasing chickens. Finally, when it seemed that the whole village was assembled, Don Alfonso moved through the crowd, which parted for him. He was wearing a brand-new pair of shorts and a T-shirt that said "No Fear." His face was wreathed in smiles as he joined them on the bamboo dock.

"Everyone has come to say good-bye," he said to Tom. "You see how I am a beloved personage in Pito Solo. I am their special Don Alfonso Boswas. You see proof here that you chose the right person to guide you across the Meambar Swamp."

Some firecrackers went off nearby, and there was a squealing of laughter. The women began passing out food. Don Alfonso took Tom and Sally by the hand.

"We get into the boat now."

Chori and Pingo, still stripped to the waist, had already taken their places, one in the bow and the other the stern. Don Alfonso helped them while two boys stood at either end of the boat, holding the lines, ready to cast off. Then Don Alfonso got in himself. He steadied himself, turned, and faced the crowd. A hush fell: Don Alfonso was about to give a speech. When the silence was absolute, he started, speaking in a most formal Spanish.

"My friends and countrymen, many years ago it was prophesied that white men would come and I would take them on a long journey. And now they are here. We are setting off on a perilous journey across the Meambar Swamp. We will have adventures and see many strange and wonderful sights, never before seen by man.

"You may ask why we make this great journey! I will tell you. This American has come here to rescue his father, who lost his mind and abandoned his wife and family, taking with him all their possessions, leaving them destitute. His poor wife has been weeping tears for him every day and she cannot feed her family or protect them from the wild animals. Their house is falling down and the thatch has rotted, letting in the rain. No one will marry his sisters and they will soon be forced into whoredom. His nephews have taken to drink. This young man, this good son, has come to cure his father from his madness and bring him back to America, where he can live to a respectable old age and die in his hammock and not bring further dishonor and starvation to his family. Then his sisters will find husbands and his nephews and nieces will take care of his *milpas* and he will be able to play dominoes in the hot afternoon instead of working."

The village was spellbound at the speech. Don Alfonso, Tom thought, certainly knew how to tell a good story.

"Long ago, my friends, I dreamed a dream that I would leave you in this way, that I would go away on a great journey to the end of the earth. I am now one hundred and twenty-one years of age and finally this dream has come to pass. There are not many men who could do this thing at my age. I still have much blood in my veins, and if my Rosita were still alive she would be smiling every day."

"Good-bye, my friends, your beloved Don Alfonso Boswas is departing the village with tears of sadness in his eyes. Remember me always and tell my story to your children and tell them to tell their children, to the end of time."

A great cheer went up. Firecrackers went off, and all the dogs began barking. Some of the old men began beating sticks together in a complex rhythm. The boat was pushed out into the current, and Chori started the engine. The laden boat began nosing forward in the water. Don Alfonso continued standing, waving and blowing kisses to the wildly cheering crowd until long after the boat had rounded the first bend.

"I feel like we just took off in a balloon with the Wizard of Oz," said Sally.

Don Alfonso finally sat down, wiping tears from his eyes. "Ahee, you see how they love their Don Alfonso Boswas." He snugged himself into the heap of supplies, extracted his corncob pipe, packed it full of tobacco, and began to smoke, a pensive expression on his face.

"Are you really one hundred and twenty-one years old?" Tom asked.

Don Alfonso shrugged. "No one knows how old they really are."

"I know how old I am."

"You have counted every year you have lived since birth?"

"No, but others counted for me."

"So you *don't* really know."

"I do know. It's listed on my birth certificate, signed by the doctor who delivered me."

"Who is this doctor and where is he now?"

"I have no idea."

"And you actually *believe* some useless piece of paper, signed by a stranger?"

Tom looked at the old man, defeated by his crazy logic. "We have a profession for people like you in America," he said. "We call them *lawyers.*"

Don Alfonso laughed loudly, slapping his knee. "This is a good joke. You are like your father, Tomasito, who was a very funny man." He chuckled for a while, puffing his pipe. Tom took out their map of Honduras and examined it.

Don Alfonso eyed it critically and then snatched it out of his hand. He examined it first one way, then another. "What is this? North America?"

"No, it's southeastern Honduras. That's the Patuca River, and there's Brus. The village of Pito Solo should be here, but it's not marked. Neither, it seems, is the Meambar Swamp."

"So according to this map, we do not exist and the Meambar

Swamp does not exist. Take care to keep this very important map dry. We may need it to start a fire someday." Don Alfonso laughed at his humor, pointing to Chori and Pingo, who took the cue and belatedly began laughing along with him, even though they hadn't understood a word he'd said. Don Alfonso continued laughing uproariously, slapping his thigh, until the tears streamed.

"We have begun our journey well," he said when he had recovered. "There will be much humor and jokes on our trip. Otherwise the swamp will drive us mad, and we will die."

23

The camp had been set up with the usual military precision on an island of high ground surrounded by swamp. Philip sat by the fire, smoking his pipe and listening to the evening sounds of the rainforest. It surprised him how competent Hauser had proven to be at jungle-craft, organizing and laying out a camp and directing the soldiers about their various tasks. Hauser asked nothing of Philip and had rebuffed all his efforts to help. Not that Philip was anxious to go off wading in the muck hunting giant rats for dinner, as it seemed they were doing now. It was just that Philip disliked feeling useless. This was not the challenge his father had in mind, sitting by a fire smoking his pipe while others did all the work.

Philip kicked a stick back into the embers. The hell with the "challenge." It had to be the most asinine thing a father ever did to his children since King Lear divided his kingdom.

Ocotal, the guide they had picked up at that sorry town on the river, was sitting by himself, tending the fire and cooking rice. He was a strange fellow, this Ocotal—small, silent, utterly dignified. There was something about him that Philip found attractive; he seemed to be one of those men who had an unshakable, inner conviction of his own worth. He certainly knew his stuff, guiding them through an incredible maze of channels, day after day, without the slightest hesitation, paying no attention to Hauser's exhortations, comments, and questions. He was impervious to any attempts at conversation, whether on Philip's part or Hauser's.

Philip reamed out the dottle, glad he had thought to stock up on tins of Dunhill Early Morning, and repacked the pipe. He really should cut back, especially in light of his father's cancer. After the trip. For now, the smoke was the only way to keep off the mosquitoes.

There were shouts, and Philip turned to see Hauser coming back from the hunt, with a dead tapir slung on a pole, carried by four soldiers. They hoisted the animal up with a block and tackle from a tree branch. Hauser left the men and came to sit down next to Philip. There was a faint smell of aftershave, tobacco smoke, and blood. He took out a cigar, clipped it, and lit it. He took in a lungful of smoke and let it trickle back out of his nose, like a dragon.

"We're making excellent progress, Philip, don't you think?"

"Admirable." Philip slapped at a mosquito. He couldn't understand how Hauser managed to avoid getting bitten, despite the fact that he never seemed to use insect repellent. Maybe his bloodstream had a deadly concentration of nicotine. Philip noticed that he inhaled his fat Churchill cigars the way most people inhale cigarettes. Strange how one man dies of it, another lives.

"Are you familiar with Genghis Khan's dilemma?" Hauser asked.

"I can't say I am."

"When Genghis Khan was getting ready to die, he wanted to be buried as befitted the great ruler he was—with heaps of treasure, concubines, and horses to enjoy in the afterlife. But he knew that his tomb would almost certainly be robbed, depriving him of all the joys due him in the afterworld. He thought about this for a long time and could come up with no answer. He finally called in his Grand Vizier, the wisest man in his kingdom.

" 'What shall I do to keep my tomb from being robbed?' he asked the Vizier.

"The Vizier thought about it for a long time and finally came up with an answer. He explained it to Genghis Khan, and the ruler was satisfied. When Ghenghis finally died, the Vizier put the plan into action. He sent ten thousand laborers off to the remote Altai Mountains, where they built a great tomb hewn down into the living rock, filling it with gold, gemstones, wine, silks, ivory, sandalwood, and incense. More than a hundred beautiful virgins and a thousand horses were sacrificed for the great Khan's pleasure in the afterworld. There was a grand funeral with much feasting among the laborers, and then Genghis Khan's body was shut up in the tomb and the door carefully concealed. The area was covered with dirt, and then a thousand horsemen rode back and forth over the valley, obliterating all traces of their work.

"When the laborers and the horsemen returned, the Vizier met them with the Khan's army and killed them to a man."

"Nasty."

"Then the Vizier committed suicide."

"The fool. He could've been rich."

Hauser chuckled. "Yes. But he was loyal. He knew that even he himself, the most trustworthy of men, could not be trusted with such a secret. He might utter it at night in a dream, or it might be tortured out of him—or his own greed might eventually get the better of him. He was the weak link in the plan. Therefore, he had to die."

Philip heard a hacking noise and glanced over to see the hunters gutting the animal with machetes. The guts spilled to the ground with a wet sound. Philip winced and turned away. There was something to be said for the vegetarian lifestyle, he mused.

"Here's the rub, Philip, the weakness in the Vizier's plan. It required Genghis Khan to trust at least one other person with his secret." Hauser exhaled a cloud of pungent smoke. "My question to you, Philip, is *who was the one person your father trusted?*"

It was a good question, one that Philip had been considering for some time. "It wasn't a girlfriend or ex-wife. He constantly complained about his doctors and lawyers. His secretaries were always quitting on him. He had no real friends. The only man he trusted was his pilot."

"And I've already determined he wasn't in on the deal." Hauser held the cigar at a steep angle against his lips. "There's the rub, Philip. Did your father have some kind of secret life? A secret affair? A son born out of wedlock that he favored above you three?"

Philip felt himself go cold at this last suggestion. "I have no idea."

Hauser waved his cigar. "Something to think about, eh, Philip?"

He fell silent. The intimacy encouraged Philip to ask a question he had been wanting to ask for some time. "What happened between you and father?"

"Did you know we were childhood friends?"

"Yes."

"We grew up together in Erie. We played stickball together on the block where we lived, we went to school together, we went to our first whorehouse together. We thought we knew each other pretty well. But when you go out there into the jungle, when you're shoved up against the wall of survival, things come out. You discover things in yourself that you never knew were there. You find out who you really are. That's what happened to us. We got out there in the middle of the jungle, lost, bitten, starving, half dead with fever, and we found out who we really were. You know what I discovered? I discovered that I despised your father."

Philip looked at Hauser. The man returned the look, his face as calm and smooth and opaque as always. He felt his flesh creep. He asked, "So what did you discover in yourself, Hauser?"

He could see that the question took Hauser by surprise. The man laughed it off, threw the cigar butt into the fire, and rose. "You'll find out soon enough."

24

The dugout pushed through the thick black water, the engine whining with the effort. The river had divided and divided until it had become a labyrinth of channels and stagnant pools, with acres of exposed, black, stinking, shivery muck. Everywhere Tom could see whirling clouds of insects. Pingo stayed in the bow, shirtless, wielding a huge machete with which he took an occasional swipe at a vine hanging in the water. The channels were often too shallow to use the engine, and Chori would raise it and pole. Don Alfonso remained on his usual perch atop the canvas-covered heap of supplies and sat there cross-legged, like a wise man, puffing furiously on his pipe and peering ahead. On several occasions Pingo had to get out and chop a notch through a half-sunken log to allow the boat to pass.

"What are these hellish insects?" Sally cried, slapping furiously.

"Tapir-fly," said Don Alfonso. He reached into his pocket and extended a blackened corncob pipe toward her. "Señorita, you should take up smoking, which discourages the insects."

"No, thank you. Smoking causes cancer."

"On the contrary, smoking is very healthful and it leads to good digestion and a long life."

"Right."

As they proceeded deeper into the swamp, the vegetation seemed to press in from all sides, forming layered walls of glossy leaves, ferns, and vines. The air was dead and thick and smelled of methane. The boat pushed through it as if it were hot soup.

"How do you know this is the way my father went?" Tom asked.

"There are many pathways in the Meambar Swamp," Don Alfonso said, "but there is only one way through. I, Don Alfonso, know that way, and so did your father. I can read the signs."

"What do you read?"

"There have been three groups of voyagers before us. The first group came through a month ago. The second and third groups were only a few days apart, and they came through about a week ago."

"How can you tell all this?" Sally asked.

"I read the water. I see a notch chopped in a sunken log. I see a cut vine. I see a pole mark on a sunken sandbar or a groove made in the muddy shallows by a keel. Those marks, in this dead water, last for weeks."

Sally pointed to a tree. "Look, over there is a gumbo-limbo tree, *Bursera simaruba*. The Maya use the sap for bug bites." She turned to Don Alfonso. "Let's head over there and collect some."

Don Alfonso took his pipe out of his mouth. "My grandfather used to collect this plant. We call it *lucawa*." He gazed at Sally with a newfound respect. "I did not know you were a *curandera*."

"I'm not really," said Sally. "I spent some time in the north living with the Maya while I was in college. I was studying their medicine. I'm an ethnopharmacologist."

"Ethnopharmacologist? That sounds like a very big profession for a woman."

Sally frowned. "In our culture, women can do anything a man can. And vice versa."

Don Alfonso's eyebrows shot up. "I do not believe it."

"It's true," Sally said defiantly.

"In America, the women hunt while the men have babies?"

"That's *not* what I meant."

Don Alfonso, with a smile of triumph on his face, placed the stem of the pipe back in his mouth, argument won. He gave an exaggerated wink to Tom. Sally shot Tom a look.

And here I didn't say a thing, Tom thought, annoyed.

Chori brought the boat up alongside the tree. Sally gave the bark a chop with her machete and then peeled off a vertical strip of bark. The sap immediately began oozing out in reddish droplets. She scraped some off, rolled up her pants, and smeared it on her bug bites, then rubbed it into her neck, wrists, and the backs of her hands.

"You look a fright," said Tom.

She scraped some more of the gooey sap off the bark with the machete and held it out to him. "Tom?"

"You're not putting that stuff on me."

"Get over here."

Tom took a step over, and she rubbed it into the back of his badly bitten neck. The itching, burning sensation ebbed away.

"How does it feel?"

Tom moved his neck. "Sticky, but good." He liked the feeling of her cool hands on his neck.

Sally handed him the machete with its dollop of sap. "You can do your own legs and arms."

"Thanks." He smeared it on, surprised at how effective it was.

Don Alfonso also helped himself to the sap. "This is truly remarkable, a *yanqui* who knows the medicinal secrets of plants, a real *curandera*. I have lived one hundred and twenty-one years and still there are things I have not seen."

That afternoon they passed the first rock Tom had seen in days. Beyond, sunlight filtered down into an overgrown clearing made in an island of high ground.

"Here is where we will camp," announced Don Alfonso.

They brought the dugout alongside the rock and tied it up. Pingo and Chori leapt out with their machetes in hand, scrambled up and over the rocks, and began mowing down the new growth. Don Alfonso strolled around and examined the ground, scuffing it with a foot, picking up a vine or a leaf.

"This is amazing," Sally said, looking around. "There is some *zorillo*. Skunk root, one of the most important plants used by the Maya. They make an herbal bath from the leaves and use the root for pain and ulcers. They call it *payche*. And here is some *suprecayo*." She began plucking leaves from a bush, rolling them, and smelling. "And

over there is a *Sweetia panamensis* tree. This is amazing. It's a unique little ecosystem here. Anyone mind if I go collecting?"

"Be our guest," said Tom.

Sally went into the forest to collect more plants.

"It looks like someone camped here before us," Tom said to Don
Alfonso.

"Yes. This large area was first cleared about a month ago. I see a fire
ring and the remains of a hut. The last people were here perhaps a week
ago."

"All this grew up in a week?"

Don Alfonso nodded. "The forest does not like a hole." He poked
around the remains of the fire and then picked up something, handing
it to Tom. It was a cigar ring from a Cuba Libre, moldy and half dis-
solved.

"My father's brand," said Tom, looking at it. It gave him a strange
feeling. His father had come here, camped in this very spot, smoked a
cigar, and left this tiny clue. He put it in his pocket and began collecting wood for the fire.

"Before you pick up a branch," Don Alfonso advised him, "you
must beat on it with a stick to knock off the ants, snakes, and *veinte
cuatros*."

"*Veinte cuatros?*"

"It is an insect that looks like a termite. We call them *veinte cuatros*,
twenty-fours, because after their bite you are unable to move for
twenty-four hours."

"That's nice."

An hour later he saw Sally tramping out of the jungle with a long
pole slung over her shoulder on which were tied bundles of plants,
bark, and roots. Don Alfonso looked up from the parrot he was boiling in a pot to watch her arrive.

"Curandera, you remind me of my grandfather Don Cali, who used
to return just like that from the forest every day, except you are pret-
tier than he was. He was old and wrinkled while you are firm and
ripe."

Sally busied herself with her plants, stringing the herbs and roots
on a stick to dry near the fire. "There's an incredible variety of plants

here," she said excitedly to Tom. "Julian's going to be really pleased."

"Wonderful."

Tom turned his attention to Chori and Pingo, who were building a hut while Don Alfonso shouted directions and heaped criticism on them. They started by driving six stout poles into the earth, making a framework of flexible sticks, over which they tied the plastic tarps. The hammocks were strung between the poles, each with its own mosquito netting, and a final piece of plastic tarp was hung vertically, making a private room for Sally.

When they were done, Pingo and Chori stepped back while Don Alfonso examined the hut with a squinty eye, then nodded and turned. "There, I offer you a house as good as any in America."

"Next time," Tom said, "I'm going to help Chori and Pingo."

"As you wish. The *curandera* has her own private sleeping quarters, which can be enlarged for an additional guest, should she need company." The old man gave Tom another exaggerated wink. He found himself reddening.

"I am quite content to sleep alone," said Sally coldly.

Don Alfonso looked disappointed. He leaned over toward Tom as if to speak to him in private. His voice, however, was perfectly audible to everyone in the camp. "She is a very beautiful woman, Tomás, even if she is old."

"Excuse me, I'm twenty-nine."

"*Ehi*, señorita, you are even older than I thought. Tomás, you must hurry. She is almost too old to marry now."

"In our culture," Sally said, "twenty-nine is considered young."

Don Alfonso continued to shake his head sadly. Tom couldn't suppress a laugh any longer.

Sally rounded on him. "What's so funny?"

"The little culture clash here," he said, catching his breath.

Sally switched into English. "I don't appreciate this sexist little tête-à-tête between you and that dirty old man." She turned to Don Alfonso. "For a supposedly hundred-and-twenty-one-year-old man, you certainly spend a lot of your time thinking about sex."

"A man never stops thinking about love, señorita. Even when he grows old and his member shrivels like a yuco fruit left to dry in the sun. I may be one hundred and twenty-one, but I have as much blood as a teenager. Tomás, I would like to marry a woman like Sally, only she will be sixteen with firm, upturned breasts—"

"Don Alfonso," said Sally, interrupting, "don't you think you could make this girl of your dreams eighteen?"

"Then she might not be a virgin."

"In our country," said Sally, "most women don't marry until they're at least eighteen. It's offensive to speak of a sixteen-year-old girl getting married."

"I am sorry! I should have known that girls develop more slowly in the cold climate of North America. But here, a sixteen-year-old—"

"Stop it!" Sally cried, clapping her hands over her ears. "No more! Don Alfonso, I've had it with your comments about sex!"

The old man shrugged. "I am an old man, Curandera, which means I can talk and joke as I please. Do you not have this tradition in America?"

"In America old people do not talk constantly about sex."

"What do they talk about?"

"They talk about their grandchildren, the weather, Florida, that sort of thing."

Don Alfonso shook his head. "How boring it must be to get old in America."

Sally walked off and flipped back the door to the hut, flashing Tom an angry glance just before she disappeared. Tom watched her go, irritated. What had he done or said? He was being unjustly tarred with the brush of sexism.

Don Alfonso shrugged and relit his pipe and continued speaking in a loud voice. "I do not understand. Here she is twenty-nine and unmarried. Her father will have to pay an enormous dowry to get rid of her. And here you are, almost an old man, and you do not have a wife either. Why do you two not marry? Perhaps you are homosexual?"

"No, Don Alfonso."

"It is all right if you are, Tomás. Chori will accommodate you. He is not particular."

"No, thank you."

Don Alfonso shook his head in wonder. "Then I do not under-stand. Tomás, you must not let your opportunities slip by."

"Sally," said Tom, "is engaged to marry another man."

Don Alfonso's eyebrows shot up. "Ah. And where is this man now?"

"Back in America."

"He cannot love her!"

Tom winced, glancing toward the hut. Don Alfonso's voice had a peculiar carrying quality.

Sally's voice came from the hut. "He loves me and I love him, and I'll thank you both to shut up."

There was the sound of a rifle shot in the forest, and Don Alfonso rose. "That is our second course." He picked up his machete and went off toward the sound.

Tom rose and took his hammock into the hut to hang it up. He found Sally hanging some of the herbs from one of the poles inside.

"That Don Alfonso is a lecherous old man *and* a sexist pig," she said hotly. "And you're just as bad."

"He's getting us through the Meambar Swamp."

"I don't appreciate his little comments. Or you, smirking your agreement."

"You can't expect him to be up on the latest feminist PC."

"I didn't hear any talk about *you* being too old to marry—and you're older than I am by a good four years. It's only the *woman* who's too old to marry."

"Lighten up, Sally."

"I will *not* lighten up."

Don Alfonso's voice interrupted Tom's reply. "The first course is ready to eat! Boiled parrot and manioc stew. Tapir steaks to follow. It is all healthy and delicious. Stop arguing and come and eat!"

25

"B uenos *tardes*," murmured Ocotal, taking a seat next to Philip at the fire.

"*Buenos tardes*," Philip said, taking the pipe out of his mouth, surprised. It was the first time Ocotal had spoken to him the entire trip.

They had reached a large lake at the edge of the swamp and were camped on a sandy island that actually had a beach. The bugs were gone, the air was fresh, and for the first time in a week Philip could see more than twenty feet in one direction. The only thing that spoiled it was that the water lapping on the strand was the color of black coffee. As usual, Hauser was out hunting with a couple of soldiers while the others were at their own fire, playing cards. The air was drowsy with heat and the green-gold light of late afternoon. It was altogether a pleasant spot, thought Philip.

Ocotal abruptly leaned forward and said, "I overheard the soldiers talking last night."

Philip raised his eyebrows. "And?"

"Do not react to what I say. They are going to kill you." He said it so low and rapidly that Philip almost thought he hadn't heard properly. He sat there dumbfounded as the words sank in.

Ocotal went on. "They are going to kill me, too."

"Are you sure?"

Ocotal nodded.

In a panic, Philip considered this. Could Ocotal be trusted? Could it be a misunderstanding? Why would Hauser kill him? To steal the inheritance? It was quite possible. Hauser was no Mr. Rogers. Out of the corner of his eye he could see that the soldiers were still playing cards, their guns stacked against a tree. On the other hand, it seemed impossible. Like something out of a movie. Hauser was going to make a million dollars already. You didn't kill people just like that—did you? "What do you plan to do?"

"Steal a boat and run. Hide in the swamp."

"You mean *now?*"

"You want to wait?"

"But the soldiers are right over there. We'll never get away. What did you hear the soldiers say that made you think this? Perhaps it was just a misunderstanding."

"Listen to me, you deficient," Ocotal hissed. "*There is no time.* I go now. If you come, come now. If not, *adiós.*"

He rose easily, lazily, and began strolling down toward the beach where the dugouts were beached. In a panic Philip turned his eyes from him to the soldiers. They were still playing cards, oblivious. From where they were sitting, at the base of a tree, they could not see the boats.

What should he do? He felt paralyzed. A monumental decision had been thrust on him without warning or preparation. It was crazy. Could Hauser really be that cold-blooded? Was Ocotal himself trying to pull a fast one?

Ocotal was now sauntering along the beach, casually looking up into the trees. He stood by a boat and with his knee, slowly and without seeming to do so, began edging it into the water.

It was happening too fast. Really, it hinged on what kind of man Hauser was. Was he really capable of murder? He wasn't a nice man, that was true. There was something wrong with him. Philip suddenly remembered the pleasure he'd taken decapitating the agouti, the smile on his face when he saw the spot of blood on Philip's shirt, the way he'd said *you'll see.*

Ocotal now had the boat in the water and with a smooth motion stepped into it, picking up the pole at the same time and getting ready to shove off.

Philip stood and walked quickly down to the beach. Ocotal was already offshore, pole planted, ready to shove the boat into the channel. He paused long enough for Philip to wade out and climb in. Then, with a strong compression of his back muscles, Ocotal planted the pole into the sandy bottom and silently propelled them out into the swamp.

26

The following morning the fine weather had come to an end. Clouds gathered, thunder shook the treetops, and the rain came pouring down. By the time Tom and the rest had set off, the surface of the river was gray and frothing under the force of a violent downpour, the sound of rain deafening among the vegetation. The maze of channels they were following seemed to get ever narrower and more convoluted. Tom had never seen a swamp so thick, so labyrinthine, so impenetrable. He could scarcely believe that Don Alfonso knew which way to go.

By afternoon, the rain ended suddenly, as if a spigot had been turned off. For another few minutes the water continued running down the tree trunks, with a noise like a waterfall, leaving the jungle misty, dripping, and hushed.

"The bugs are back," Sally said, slapping.

"*Jejenes*. Blackflies," said Don Alfonso, lighting up his pipe and surrounding himself with a foul blue cloud. "They take a piece of your meat away with them. They are formed from the breath of the devil himself after a night of drinking bad *aguardiente*."

At times their way was blocked with hanging vines and aerial roots that grew down from above, forming thick curtains of vegetation that hung to the very surface of the water. Pingo remained in front, hacking them down with his machete while Chori poled from the back. Every blow of the machete dislodged tree frogs, insects, and other creatures that dropped into the water, providing a feast for the piranhas below, which thrashed and boiled around every hapless animal. Pingo, his great back muscles working, slashed left, right, then left, flicking most of the vines and hanging flowers into the water. In one particularly narrow channel, while Pingo was slashing away, he suddenly gave a cry, *"Heculu!"*

"Avispa! Wasps!" Don Alfonso cried, crouching down and putting his hat over his head. "Do not move!"

A compact, boiling cloud of black came racing out of the hanging vegetation, and Tom, crouching and protecting his head, immediately felt a tattoo of fiery stings on his back.

"Don't slap them," Don Alfonso cried. "It will make them madder!"

They could do nothing but wait until the wasps had finished stinging them. The wasps left as quickly as they had come, and Sally doctored the stings with more sap from the gumbo-limbo tree. They pushed on.

Around noon, a strange sound developed in the canopy above them. It sounded like a thousand smacking, gurgling noises, like a crowd of children sucking on candies, only much louder, accompanied by a rustling in the branches that grew in volume until it was like a sudden wind. There was the flashing of black shapes, just seen through the leaves.

Chori shipped his paddle, and instantly a small bow and arrow was in his hand and pointed skyward, tensed and ready to go.

"Mono chucuto," Don Alfonso whispered to Tom.

Before Tom could say anything, Chori had loosed his arrow. There was a sudden commotion above and a black monkey came falling out of the branches, still half alive, grasping and clutching and sliding through the foliage as it fell, finally landing in the water five feet from the dugout. Chori leapt up and snatched the bundle of black fur out of the water, just before a large swirl from underneath indicated something else had the same idea.

"Ehi! Ehi!" he said with a vast grin. "Uakaris! Mmmm."

"There are two!" said Don Alfonso, in a high state of excitement. "This was a very lucky strike, Tomasito. It is a mother and her baby."

The baby monkey was still clinging to the mother, squealing in terror.

"A monkey? You shot a monkey?" Sally said, her voice high.

"Yes, Curandera, are we not lucky?"

"Lucky? This is *awful!*"

Don Alfonso's face fell. "You do not like monkey? The brains of this monkey are truly a delicacy when roasted lightly in the skull."

"We can't eat a monkey!"

"Why not?"

"Why, it's . . . it's practically *cannibalism*." She rounded on Tom. "I can't believe you let him shoot a monkey!"

"I didn't let him shoot anything."

Chori, understanding nothing and still grinning proudly, dumped the monkey on the floor of the boat in front of them. It stared up at them, eyes filming over, tongue halfway out. The baby leapt off the dead body of its mother and crouched in terror, hands over its head, making a high-pitched scream.

"Ehi! Ehi!" Chori said, reaching to grab the baby monkey with one hand while raising the machete with the other, ready to deliver the coup de grace.

"No!" Tom snatched the little black monkey up into his arms. It nestled down and stopped screaming. Chori, his machete half raised, stared in surprise.

Don Alfonso leaned forward. "I do not understand. What is this about cannibalism?"

"Don Alfonso," Tom said, "we consider monkeys to be almost human."

Don Alfonso said something sharply to Chori, whose grin vanished in a look of disappointment. Don Alfonso turned back to them. "I did not know monkeys were sacred to North Americans. And it is true they are almost human, except that God put hands on their feet. I am sorry. If I had known, I would not have allowed it to be killed." He said something sharply to Chori and the boat moved on. Then he picked up the mother's body and tossed it into the water; there was a swirl and it was gone.

Tom felt the monkey nestling more vigorously into the crook of his arm, whimpering and trying to burrow into the warmth. He looked down. A little black face peeped back up at him, eyes wide, and a tiny hand reached out. The monkey was small—no more than eight inches long and weighing no more than three or four pounds. His hair was soft and short, and he had large brown eyes, a tiny pink nose, little human ears, and four miniature hands with delicate fingers as slender as toothpicks.

Tom found Sally looking at him with a smile on her face.

"What?"

"Looks like you've made a new friend."

"Oh no."

"Oh yes."

The little monkey had recovered from its terror. It crawled out on Tom's arm and began poking around his chest. Its little black hands went scurrying and plucking into the folds of his clothing while it made a smacking sound with its lips.

"He's grooming you," said Sally. "Looking for lice."

"I hope he's disappointed."

"Look, Tomás," said Don Alfonso, "he thinks you are his mother."

"How could you eat this beautiful creature?" Sally asked.

Don Alfonso shrugged. "All the creatures of the forest are beautiful, Curandera."

Tom could feel the monkey combing and picking through his shirt. The monkey crept about, using his buttons as handholds, and lifted up the flap of his giant, explorer-style vest pocket. He rummaged in there with a hand, made a smacking noise, and then climbed in it and wriggled himself into place. He sat there, his arms folded, peering around, his nose slightly elevated.

Sally clapped her hands together and laughed. "Oh, Tom, he *really* likes you now."

"What do they eat?" Tom asked Don Alfonso.

"Everything. Insects, leaves, grubs. You will not have any trouble feeding your new friend."

"Who says he's my responsibility?"

"Because he chose you, Tomasito. You belong to him now."

Tom looked down at the monkey, who was now peering around like a miniature lord surveying his domain.

"He's a hairy little bugger," said Sally in English.

"Hairy Bugger. That's what we'll call him."

That afternoon, at one particularly convoluted maze of channels, Don Alfonso stopped the boat and spent more than ten minutes examining the water, tasting it, dropping spitballs into it and watching them drift to the bottom. Finally he sat up.

"There is a problem."

"Are we lost?" Tom asked.

"No. *They* are lost."

"Who?"

"One of your brothers. They took that channel to the left, which leads to the Plaza Negra, the Black Place, the rotten heart of the swamp where the demons live."

The channel wound between enormous tree trunks and clumps of hanging vines, a layer of greenish mist hanging just above the black surface of the water. It looked like a watery pathway to hell.

It must be Vernon, Tom thought. Vernon was always getting lost, literally and figuratively. "How long ago?"

"At least a week."

"Is there a place to camp near here?"

"There is a small island a quarter mile further."

"We'll stop there and unload," said Tom. "We'll leave Pingo and Sally in camp, while you and I and Chori take the dugout on a search for my brother. We've no time to lose."

They landed on a sodden mud-island while a rain of such intensity that it was more like a waterfall poured down on them. Don Alfonso gestured and shouted, supervising the unloading and then reprovisioning of the boat, holding back the supplies they would need for their journey.

"We may be gone for two or three days," Don Alfonso said. "We must prepare to spend several nights in the dugout. There might be rain."

"No kidding," said Sally.

Tom handed Sally the monkey. "Take care of him while I'm gone, okay?"

"Of course."

The boat pulled away. Tom watched her in the pouring rain, a dim figure growing dimmer. "Tom, please take care of yourself," she called, just as her figure vanished.

Chori poled strongly down the channel, the unburdened boat moving swiftly. Five minutes later Tom heard a screeching noise in the branches above the boat, and a little black ball came bouncing from branch to branch and finally shot out of an overhead tree and landed on his head, shrieking like a lost soul. It was Hairy Bugger.

"You rascal, you didn't wait long to escape," said Tom, taking the tiny monkey back into his pocket, where he snuggled down and instantly fell silent.

The dugout pushed deeper into the rain-rotten swamp.

27

The storm reached a climax of fury as their dugout reached the channel to the Black Place. Flashes of lightning and bursts of thunder echoed through the forest, sometimes coming only seconds apart, like an artillery barrage. The tops of the trees, two hundred feet above their heads, shook and thrashed.

The channel soon divided into a maze of shallow waterways winding amid shivery expanses of stinking mud. Don Alfonso stopped from time to time to check for pole marks in the shallow bottom. The drenching rain never let up, and night came so imperceptibly that Tom was startled when Don Alfonso called a halt.

"We will sleep in the dugout like savages," Don Alfonso said. "Here is a good place to stop as there are no thick branches above us. I do not want to wake up to the rotten smell of jaguar breath. We must take care not to die here, Tomasito, for our souls would never find their way out."

"I'll do my best."

Tom bundled himself in his mosquito netting, found a place in their heap of gear, and tried to go to sleep. The rain finally ceased, but he was still soaked to the skin. The jungle was filled with the sound of dripping water, punctuated with the cries and moans and gasping shrieks of animals, some of which seemed almost human. Maybe they *were* human, the lost souls Don Alfonso had talked about. Tom thought of his brother Vernon, lost in this swamp, sick perhaps, maybe even dying. He remembered him as a boy who always had a hopeful, friendly, and perpetually lost look on his face. He subsided into a troubled night of dreams.

They found the dead body the next day. It was floating in the water, a hump with red and white stripes. Chori poled toward it. The hump turned out to be a wet shirt inflated with the gases of decomposition. As the dugout approached, a cloud of angry flies rose up.

Carefully, Chori brought the dugout alongside. A dozen dead piranhas floated around the corpse, their goggle eyes filmed over, their mouths open. The rain drizzled down.

The hair was short and black. It was not Vernon.

Don Afonso said something, and Chori prodded the body with a pole. The gas escaped from under the wet shirt with a blabbering sound, and there was a foul smell. Chori placed the pole under the corpse and, using the bottom as a fulcrum point, heaved it over. The flies roared up. The water boiled and flashed with silver as the fish that had been feasting underneath the body darted away in fright.

Tom stared with shock at the body, now face up in the water, if "face up" could even describe it. Piranhas had eaten the face off along with the entire ventral side of the body, leaving only the bones. The nose had been chewed down to a withered piece of cartilage; the lips and tongue were gone, the mouth a hole. A minnow, trapped in an eye socket, thrashed about, trying to escape. The smell of decomposition hit him like a wet rag. The water began to swirl as the fish began to work on the fresh side. Bits of cloth from the shirt floated to the surface.

"It is one of those boys from Puerto Lempira," said Don Alfonso. "He was bitten by a poisonous snake while clearing this brush. They left him here."

"How do you know he was killed by a snake?" Tom asked.

"You see the dead piranhas? Those are the ones who ate the flesh in the area of the snakebite. They were poisoned, and the animals that eat them will also be poisoned."

Chori pushed the body away with the pole, and they paddled on.

"This is not a good place to die. We must get out of here before nightfall. I do not want to meet that Lempira man's ghost in a dream tonight, asking me for directions."

Tom did not answer. The sight of the corpse had left him shaken. He tried to fight down a sense of foreboding. Vernon, who was panicky and disorganized to begin with, would be a basket case. God knows, he might even be dead, too.

"Why they do not turn around and leave this place, I cannot say. Perhaps a demon has gotten in the dugout with them and is whispering lies into their ears."

They continued on, making slow work of it. The swamp was endless, the boat grazing the muddy bottom and frequently getting stuck, forcing them to get out and push. Often they had to double back again and again, following tortuous channels. Toward midafternoon, Don Alfonso held up his hand, Chori stopped paddling, and they listened. Tom could hear a distant voice, distraught—someone crying hysterically for help.

Tom leapt to his feet and cupped his hands. "Vernon!"

There was a sudden silence.

"Vernon! It's me, Tom!"

There was a burst of desperate shouting that echoed through the trees, distorted and unintelligible.

"It's him," said Tom. "Hurry."

Chori paddled forward, and soon Tom could see the vague outlines of a dugout canoe in twilight of the swamp. A person was in the bow, screaming and gesturing. It was Vernon. He was hysterical, but at least he was standing.

"Faster!" Tom cried.

Chori pushed ahead. They reached the boat, and Tom pulled Vernon into their own.

Vernon collapsed into his brother's arms. "Tell me I'm not dead," he cried.

"You're okay, you're not dead. We're here now."

Vernon broke down sobbing. Tom, clasping his brother, had a sudden sense of déjà vu, the memory of a time when Vernon came home one day after school, having been chased by a gang of bullies. He threw himself into Tom's arms the same way, clutching and sobbing hysterically, his skinny body shaking. Tom had had to go out there and fight them himself—Tom, the younger brother, fighting his older brother's fights.

"It's okay," said Tom. "It's okay. We're here. You're safe."

"Thank God. Thank God. I was sure the end had come . . ." His voice trailed away into a choke.

Tom helped Vernon sit. He was shocked at his brother's appearance. His face and neck were swollen with bites and stings and smeared with blood from scratching. His clothes were indescribably filthy, his hair was tangled and foul, and he was even skinnier than usual.

"Are you okay?" Tom asked.

Vernon nodded. "Aside from being eaten alive I'm all right. Just scared." Vernon wiped his face with a filthy sleeve that left more dirt than it removed and choked another sob.

Tom took a moment to look at his brother. His mental state worried him even more than his physical state. As soon as they got back to camp, he would send Vernon back to civilization with Pingo.

"Don Alfonso," Tom said, "let's turn the boat around and get out of here."

"But the Teacher," Vernon said.

Tom stopped. "The Teacher?"

Vernon nodded toward the dugout. "Sick."

Tom leaned over and peered down. There, lying in a sodden sleeping bag in the bottom of the canoe, almost hidden among the mess of equipment and soggy supplies, was the swollen face of a man, with a wild head of white hair and a beard. He was fully conscious and stared back up at Tom with baleful blue eyes, saying nothing.

"Who's this?"

"My Teacher from the Ashram."

"What the hell is he doing here?"

"We're together."

The man stared up at Tom fixedly.

"What's wrong with him?"

"He's got a fever. He stopped speaking two days ago."

Tom pulled the medicine chest out of their supplies and stepped into the other dugout. The Teacher followed his every movement with his eyes. Tom bent over and felt the man's forehead. It was burning hot; a temperature of at least 104 degrees. The pulse was thready and fast. He listened with a stethoscope: The lungs sounded clear, the heart was beating normally, albeit very fast. Tom injected him with a broad-spectrum antibiotic and an antimalarial. Without access to any kind of diagnostic tests, it was the best he could do.

"What kind of fever does he have?" Vernon asked.

"Impossible to know without a blood test."

"Is he going to die?"

"I don't know." Tom switched into Spanish. "Don Alfonso, do you have any idea what disease this man has?"

Don Alfonso climbed into the boat and bent over the man. He tapped his chest, looked into his eyes, felt his pulse, examined his hands, then looked up. "Yes, I know well this disease."

"What is it?"

"It's called death."

"No," said Vernon, agitated. "Don't say that. He's not dying."

Tom was sorry he had asked for Don Alfonso's opinion. "We'll bring him back to camp in the dugout. Chori can pole that dugout, and I'll pole ours." Tom turned to Vernon. "We found one dead guide back there. Where's the other?"

"A jaguar dropped down on him at night and dragged him up into a tree." Vernon shuddered. "We could hear his screams and the crunching of his bones. It was . . ." The sentence finished in a choking sound. "Tom, get me out of here."

"I will," Tom said. "We'll send you and your Teacher back down to Brus with Pingo."

They arrived back at the camp just after nightfall. Vernon put up one of their tents, and they carried the Teacher up from the boat and put him inside. He refused all food and remained silent, staring at them in the most unsettling way. Tom wondered if the man was still sane.

Vernon insisted on spending the night with him in the tent. The next morning, as the sun was just catching the treetops, Vernon roused them all with a call for help. Tom was the first to arrive. The Teacher was sitting up in his sleeping bag, highly agitated. His face was pale and dry, and his eyes glittered like chips of blue porcelain, darting about wildly, focusing on nothing. His hands were grasping at the air.

All at once he spoke. "Vernon!" he cried, groping about with his hands. "Oh my God, where are you, Vernon? Where am I?"

With a shock Tom realized he must have gone blind.

Vernon grasped his hand and knelt. "I'm here, Teacher. We're in the tent. We're taking you back to America. You're going to be fine."

"What a goddamn fool I was!" the Teacher shouted, his mouth twisting with the effort to speak, causing spittle to fly.

"Teacher, please. Please don't excite yourself. We're going home, back to Big Sur, back to the Ashram . . ."

"I had everything!" the Teacher roared. "I had money. I had teenage girls to fuck. I had a house by the sea. I was surrounded by people who revered me. *I had everything.*" The veins were popping out on his forehead. Drool ran down and dangled from his chin. His whole frame trembled so violently that Tom fancied he could hear his bones rattling. The blind eyes roved madly in his head, like whirling pinballs.

"We're going to get you to a hospital, Teacher. Don't talk, everything's going to be all right, all right . . ."

"So what did I do? Ha! It wasn't enough! Like a fool I wanted more! I wanted a hundred million dollars more! *And look what happened to me!*" He roared out these last words and, having uttered them, fell back heavily, his body making the sound of a dead fish hitting the floor. He lay there, his eyes staring wide open, but the glitter was gone.

He was dead.

Vernon stared in horror, unable to speak. Tom put his hand on his brother's shoulder and found him shaking. It had been an ugly death.

Don Alfonso was badly shaken as well. "We must leave," he said. "A bad spirit came and took that man away, and he did not want to go."

"Prepare one of the boats to return," Tom said to Don Alfonso. "Pingo can take Vernon back to Brus while we go on—if you don't have any objections."

Don Alfonso nodded. "It is better this way. The swamp is no place for your brother." He began shouting orders to Chori and Pingo, who rushed about, equally terrified, only too happy to be leaving.

"I can't understand it," Vernon said. "He was such a good man. How could he die like that?"

Vernon was always being taken in by swindlers, Tom thought—financial, emotional, and spiritual. But now wasn't the time to point it out. He said, "Sometimes we think we know someone, and we don't."

"I spent three years with him. I *knew* him. It must have been the fever. He was delirious, out of his mind. He didn't know what he was saying."

"Let's bury him and move on."

Vernon went to work on digging a grave, and Tom and Sally joined in. They cleared out a small spot behind the camp, chopping through roots with Chori's axe and digging down into the soil underneath. In twenty minutes a shallow grave had been hollowed out of the hard-clay soil. They dragged the Teacher's body to the hole, laid him in, packed a layer of clay on top of him, then filled the grave with smooth boulders from the riverbank. Don Alfonso, Chori, and Pingo were already in the boats, fretting, waiting to go.

"Are you all right?" Tom asked, putting his arm around his brother.

"I've made a decision," Vernon said. "I'm not going back. I'm going on with you."

"Vernon, it's all arranged."

"What have I got to go back to? I'm dead broke, and I don't even have a car. I certainly can't go back to the Ashram."

"You'll figure out something."

"I've already figured out something. I'm coming with you."

"You're in no condition to come with us. You almost died back there."

"This is something I have to do," said Vernon. "I'm all right now."

Tom hesitated, wondering if Vernon really was all right.

"Please, Tom."

There was such a depth of pleading in Vernon's voice that Tom was surprised—and, despite himself, a little glad. He grasped Vernon's shoulder. "All right. We'll do this together, just as Father wanted."

Don Alfonso clapped his hands. "Enough talking? We go now?"

Tom nodded, and Don Alfonso gave the order to push off.

"Now that we have two boats," Sally said, "I'll do my share of the poling."

"Puah! Poling is a man's job."

"Don Alfonso, you are a sexist pig."

Don Alfonso crinkled his brow. "Sexist pig? What kind of animal is this? Have I been insulted?"

"You certainly have," said Sally.

Don Alfonso gave his boat a good pole, and it glided forward. He grinned. "Then I am happy. To be insulted by a beautiful woman is always an honor."

28

Marcus Aurelius Hauser examined his white shirtfront, and, finding a small beetle making its laborious way up it, he plucked it off, crushed it between spatulate thumb and forefinger with a satisfying chitinous crackle, and tossed it away. He turned his attention back to Philip Broadbent. All that archness, that fey effeteness, was gone. Philip squatted on the ground, shackled hand and foot, filthy, bug bitten, unshaven. It was disgraceful how some people just could not maintain their personal hygiene in the jungle.

He glanced over to where the guide, Orlando Ocotal, was being held by three of his soldiers. Ocotal had caused him considerable trouble. He had almost made good his escape, which Hauser had only prevented by the most dogged pursuit. A whole day had been wasted. Ocotal's fatal flaw had been in assuming a gringo, a *yanqui*, would not be able to track him in the swamp. He evidently hadn't heard of a place called Vietnam.

So much the better. Now it was out in the open. They were almost through the swamp anyway, and Ocotal had outlived his usefulness. The lesson he would teach Ocotal would be a good one for Philip, too.

Hauser inhaled the fecund jungle air. "Do you remember, Philip, when we were packing the boats? You wanted to know what we were going to do with these manacles and chains?"

Philip did not answer.

Hauser remembered how he had explained that the manacles were an important psychological tool to manage the soldiers, a sort of portable brig. Of course, he would never actually *use* them. "Now you know," Hauser said. "They were for you."

"Why don't you just kill me and get it over with?"

"All in good time. One doesn't kill the last in the family line lightly."

"What do you mean by that?"

"Delighted you asked. Shortly I'll be taking care of your two brothers, who are behind us in the swamp. When the last of the Broadbent line has been made extinct, I will take what is mine."

"You're a psychopath."

"I am a rational human addressing a great wrong that was once done to me, thank you."

"What wrong is this?"

"Your father and I were partners. He deprived me of my share of the loot from his first big discovery."

"That was forty years ago."

"Which only compounds the crime. While I struggled for forty years to make a living, your father bathed in luxury."

Philip struggled, rattling his chains.

"How wonderful is the turn of the wheel. Forty years ago your father cheated me out of a fortune. I went on to a lovely place called Vietnam while he went on to riches. Now I stand to gain it all back and more. The irony of it is delicious. And to think, Philip, you brought me this on a silver platter."

Philip said nothing.

Hauser inhaled again. He loved the heat and he loved the air. He never felt so healthy and alive as in the jungle. All that was missing was the faint perfume of napalm. He turned to one of the soldiers. "Now we will do Ocotal. Come, Philip, you won't want to miss this."

The two dugouts were already packed, and the soldiers shoved Ocotal and Philip into one. The soldiers fired up the engines, and they headed into the maze of pools and side channels at the far end of the lake. Hauser stood in the bow keeping an eye out.

"That way."

The boats motored on until they came to a stagnant pool, cut off from the main channel by the lowering water. The piranhas, Hauser knew, had been concentrated in the pool by the subsiding water. Long ago they had eaten all the available food and were now eating each other. Woe to any animal that blundered into one of those stagnant pools.

"Cut the engine. Drop anchor."

The engines sputtered off, and the ensuing silence was broken only by the two soft splashes of the rock anchors.

Hauser turned and looked at Ocotal. This was going to be interesting.

"Stand him up."

The soldiers pulled Ocotal to his feet. Hauser took a step forward and gazed on his face. The Indian, dressed in a Western shirt and shorts, was straight and cool. His eyes showed neither fear nor hatred. This Tawahka Indian, Hauser thought, had proven to be one of those unfortunate people motivated by superannuated notions of honor and loyalty. Hauser disliked such people. They were unreliable and inflexible. Max had also proven to be a person like that.

"Well, *Don* Orlando," Hauser said, giving the honorific an ironic emphasis. "Have you anything to say for yourself?"

The Indian gazed at him unblinkingly.

Hauser removed his pocketknife. "Hold him tight."

The soldiers grasped him. His hands were tied behind his back, and his feet were loosely tied together.

Hauser opened the little knife and sharpened the blade on a whetstone with a quick *zing, zing*. He tested it against his thumb and smiled. Then he reached out and scored a long cut across Ocotal's chest, cutting through the fabric of his shirt to his skin below. It wasn't a deep cut, but the blood began to run, turning the khaki black.

The Indian did not even flinch.

He made a second shallow cut on the shoulders, and two more cuts on the arms and back. Still the Indian showed nothing. Hauser was impressed. He hadn't seen such stamina since his days questioning captured Viet Cong.

"Give the blood a little time to flow," he said.

They waited. The shirt darkened with blood. A bird screamed somewhere in the depths of the trees.

"Throw him in."

The three solders gave him a shove, and he went over the side. After the splash there was a moment of calm, and then the water began to swirl, slowly at first, and then with more agitation, until the pool seethed. There were flashes of silver in the brown water like fluttering coins, until a red cloud billowed up, turning the water opaque. Tatters of khaki cloth and strings of flesh rose to the surface and bobbed on the chop.

The boiling went on for a good five minutes before it finally began to subside. Hauser was pleased. He turned to see Philip's reaction and was gratified by it.

Very gratified indeed.

29

For three days Tom and his group continued traveling through the heart of the swamp along an interconnecting web of channels, camping on mud-islands scarcely higher than the waterline, cooking beans and rice with wet wood over smoking fires because Chori could find no fresh game. Despite the endless rain the water had been going down, exposing waterlogged tree trunks that had to be chopped through before they could proceed. They carried along with them a permanent, malevolent humming cloud of blackflies.

"I'll think I'll take that pipe now," said Sally. "I'd rather die of cancer than endure this."

With a smile of triumph Don Alfonso removed it from his pocket. "You will see—smoking will lead to a long and happy life. I myself have smoked for over a hundred years."

There was a deep booming sound from the jungle, like a man with a cough, only louder and slower.

"What was that?"

"A jaguar. And a hungry one."

"It's amazing what you know about the forest," Sally said.

"Yes." Don Alfonso sighed. "But today no one wants to learn any more about the forest. My grandchildren and great-grandchildren, all they care about is soccer and those fat white shoes that rot your feet, the ones with the bird on the sides made in those factories in San Pedro Sula." He pointed at Tom's shoes with his lips.

"Nikes?"

"Yes. Up near San Pedro Sula there are entire villages of boys whose feet rotted and dropped off from wearing those. Now they have to walk around on wooden stumps."

"That's not true."

Don Alfonso shook his head, clucking disapprovingly. The boat moved on through curtains of vines, which Pingo slashed away at. Tom could see a patch of sunlight up ahead, a beam falling from above, and as they moved forward he saw that a giant tree had recently fallen, leaving a hole in the canopy. The trunk lay across the channel, blocking their path. It was the biggest tree they'd encountered yet.

Don Alfonso muttered a curse. Chori picked up his Pulaski and hopped out of the bow and onto the log. Gripping the slippery surface with his bare feet, he began to chop, the chips flying. In half an hour he had notched the log deep enough to slide the boats through.

They all climbed out and began to push. Beyond the log the water suddenly got deep. Tom waded through it, up to his waist, trying not to think of the toothpick fish, the piranhas, and all the diseases lurking in that soupy water.

Vernon was ahead of him, holding the gunwale and pushing the dugout forward, when Tom saw a slow undulation in the dark water to their right. Simultaneously he heard Don Alfonso's piercing cry. "Anaconda!" Tom scrambled in but Vernon was just a fraction too slow. There was a swirl of water, a sudden humplike rise, and with a scream—cut short—Vernon disappeared beneath the brown water. The snake's glossy back slid past, exposing briefly a body as thick as a small tree trunk, before it sank and disappeared.

"*Ehi!* He has Vernito!"

Tom pulled his machete out of his belt and dove into the water. He kicked, swimming down as deep as he could. He couldn't see more than a foot into the murky, brown glow. He scissors kicked toward the middle, feeling ahead with his free hand, trying to find the snake. He felt something cold, round, and slippery and slashed at it before he realized it was just a sunken log. Grasping it, he pulled himself forward, feeling around desperately for the snake or his brother. His lungs were about to burst. He shot to the surface and redove, groping ahead. Where was the snake?

How long had it been? A minute? Two? How long could Vernon survive? Desperation drove him forward, and he continued his mad search, feeling among the slimy sunken logs.

One of the logs suddenly flexed under his touch. It was a muscled tube, as hard as mahogany, but he could feel the skin moving, the waves of contracting muscles.

He shoved the machete into its soft underbelly, driving it in as deep as it would go. For a second, nothing: and then the snake exploded into a whiplike motion, which slammed him backward in the water, knocking out his air in a violent expulsion of bubbles. He clawed his way to the surface and sucked in more air. The surface was boiling as the snake thrashed. He realized he no longer had the machete. Now roiling coils of the snake flew out of the water in a glossy arc, and for a moment Vernon's hand appeared, clutched into a fist, followed by his head. A gasp, and he was gone.

"Another machete!"

Pingo tossed him one, handle first. He grabbed it and began slashing at the coils lashing about on the water's surface.

"The head!" Don Alfonso cried from the boat. "Go for the head!"

Where was the head in this mass of snake? Tom had a sudden idea and jabbed the snake with the tip of the machete, once, twice, prodding him into a fury—and then, rearing out of the water, came the brute's head, ugly and small, with a plated mouth and two slitty eyes, searching for the source of its torment. It lunged at him, mouth open, and Tom shoved the machete right into the pink cavity and straight down the monster's gullet. The snake jerked and twisted and bit down, but Tom, clutching the handle, held on even as his arm was being bitten, giving the machete one hard twist after another. He could feel the flesh yielding inside, the sudden gush of cold reptilian blood; the head began thrashing back and forth, almost jerking his arm out of its socket. With all his remaining strength he gave the machete a final massive twist, and the blade came out behind the snake's head. He rotated it and felt a spasmodic tremble in the jaws as the snake was decapitated from the inside. He pried open the mouth with his other hand and pulled his arm out, searching frantically for his brother amid the still-churning water.

Vernon suddenly rose to the surface of the pond, facedown. Tom grabbed him and turned him over. His face was red, his eyes closed. He looked dead. Tom dragged him through the water to the boat, and Pingo and Sally hauled him in. Tom fell in after him and passed out.

Sally was leaning over him when he came to, her blond hair like a waterfall swaying above him, cleaning the teeth marks in his arm, rubbing them with cotton soaked in alcohol. His shirt had been ripped off above the elbow, and there were deep scores on his arm. Blood was welling out.

"Vernon—?"

"He's okay," Sally said. "Don Alfonso's helping him. He just swallowed some water and got a nasty bite on his thigh."

He tried to sit up. His arm felt like it was on fire. The blackflies were swirling about him worse than ever, and he breathed them in with each breath. She pushed him back down with a gentle hand on his chest. "Don't move." She sucked in smoke from her pipe and blew it around him, chasing the flies away.

"Lucky for you anacondas have teensy weensy teeth." She scrubbed.

"Ouch." He lay back, looking up at the canopy slowly passing by. Nowhere could he see even a speck of blue sky. The leaves covered all.

30

Tom lay in his hammock that evening, nursing his bandaged arm. Vernon had recovered well and was cheerfully helping Don Alfonso boil some unknown bird that Chori had shot for dinner. It was stifling inside the hut, even with the sides rolled up.

Only thirty days had passed since Tom left Bluff, but it seemed like an eternity. His horses, the red sandstone buttes etched against the blue skies, the drenching sunlight and the eagles flying down the San Juan . . . It all seemed to have happened to someone else. It was strange . . . He had moved to Bluff with Sarah, his fiancée. She loved horses and the outdoors as much as he did, but Bluff turned out to be too quiet for her, and one day she'd packed up her car and left. He had just taken out a big bank loan and established his vet practice, and there was no way he could pull out. Not that he wanted to. When she left, he realized that given the choice between Bluff and her, he'd take Bluff. That was two years ago, and he hadn't had a relationship since. He told himself he didn't need one. He told himself the quiet life, the beauty of the land was enough for now. The vet practice had been intense, the work grueling, the compensation almost nil. He found it rewarding, but he could never quite shake the longing he had for paleontology, his childhood dream of hunting the bones of the great dinosaurs, entombed in the rock. Maybe his father was right, that it was an ambition he should have outgrown when he hit twelve.

He turned in his hammock, his arm throbbing, and glanced over at Sally. The partition was rolled up for ventilation, and she was lying in her hammock reading one of the books Vernon had brought, a thriller called *Utopia*. Utopia. That's what he'd thought he'd find in Bluff. But what he'd really been doing was running away from something—like his father.

Well, he wasn't running away from him anymore.

In the background he could hear Don Alfonso shouting orders to Chori and Pingo. Soon the smell of stewing meat came drifting through the hut. He glanced over at Sally and watched her read, turn the pages, brush back her hair, sigh, turn another page. She was beautiful, even if she was a bit of a pain in the neck.

Sally laid down the book. "What are you looking at?"

"Good book?"

"Excellent." She smiled. "How are you feeling?"

"Fine."

"That was a real Indiana Jones rescue back there."

Tom shrugged. "I wasn't going to stand around while a snake ate my brother." This wasn't really what he wanted to talk about. He asked, "Tell me about this fiancé of yours, this Professor Clyve."

"Well," Sally smiled at the memory. "I went to Yale to study with him. He's my doctoral thesis adviser. We just . . . Well, who wouldn't fall in love with Julian? He's brilliant. I'll never forget when we first met at the weekly Faculty Sherry. I thought he was just going to be another academic type, but—wow. He looked like Tom Cruise."

"Wow."

"Of course, looks mean nothing to him. What matters to Julian is the mind—not the body."

"I see." Tom couldn't help looking at her body: It put the lie to Julian's claims of intellectual purity. Julian was a man, like any other—just less honest than most.

"He had recently published his book, *Deciphering the Mayan Language*. He's a genius in the real sense of the word."

"Do you have a wedding date?"

"Julian doesn't believe in weddings. We'll go to a justice of the peace."

"What about your parents? Won't they be disappointed?"

"I don't have any parents."

Tom felt his face flush. "I'm sorry."

"Don't be," Sally said. "My father died when I was eleven, and my mother passed away ten years ago. I've gotten used to it—or at least as used to it as you can get."

"So you're really going to marry this guy?"

She looked at him, and there was a short silence. "What's that supposed to mean?"

"Nothing." *Change the subject, Tom.* "Tell me about your father."

"He was a cowboy."

Yeah, right, thought Tom. *A rich cowboy who raised racehorses, probably.* "I didn't know they still existed," he said politely.

"They do, only it's not what you see in the movies. A real cowboy is a laborer who just happens to work off the back of a horse, who makes less than minimum wage, who's a high school dropout, who's got a drinking problem, and who gets badly hurt or killed before he's forty. Dad was the foreman of a corporate-owned cattle ranch in southern Arizona. He fell off a windmill he was trying to fix and broke his neck. They shouldn't have asked him to go up there, but the judge decided it was his fault, because he'd been drinking."

"I'm sorry, I don't mean to pry."

"It's good to talk about it. At least that's what my analyst says."

Tom was unsure whether to treat this as a joke or not but decided to play it safe. Most people in New Haven probably went to analysts. "I figured your father would have owned the ranch."

"You thought I was a little rich girl?"

Tom colored. "Well, I did assume something like that. After all, here you are a Yalie, and with your riding ability . . ." He thought of Sarah. He'd had enough of rich girls to last him the rest of his life, and he'd just assumed she was another.

Sally laughed, but it was a bitter laugh. "I've had to fight for every little thing I have. And that includes Yale."

Tom felt his color deepening. He had been reckless in his assumptions. She wasn't like Sarah at all.

"Despite his shortcomings," Sally continued, "my father was a wonderful dad. He taught me how to ride and shoot, how to head, heel, and cut cattle. After he died my mother moved us to Boston, where she had a sister. She waited on tables at Red Lobster to support me. I went to Framingham State College because it was the only place I could get into after a pretty miserable public high school education. My mother died while I was in college. Aneurism. It was very sudden. For me, it was like the end of the world. And then finally something good happened. I had an anthropology teacher who helped me discover that learning was fun and that I was not just a dumb blond. She believed in me. She wanted me to become a doctor. I was pre-med, but then I got interested in pharmaceutical biology, and from there I went into ethnopharmacology. I busted my ass and got into Yale Graduate School. And at Yale I met Julian. I'll never forget when I first saw him. It was at the faculty sherry party and he was standing in the middle of the room, telling a story. Julian tells wonderful stories. I just joined the crowd and listened. He was talking about his first trip to Copán. He looked so . . . dashing. Just like one of those old-time explorers."

"Right," said Tom. "Sure."

"So what about your childhood?" Sally asked. "What was it like?"

"I'd prefer not to talk about it."

"No fair, Tom."

Tom sighed. "I had a very boring childhood."

"I doubt it."

"Where should I begin? We were to the manor born, so to speak. Giant house, pool, cook, gardener, live-in housekeeper, stables, a thousand acres of land. Father lavished us with everything. He had big plans for us. He had a shelf of books on child rearing, and he read every one. *Start with high expectations*, they all said. When we were babies he played Bach and Mozart and filled our rooms with reproductions of Old Master paintings. When we were learning to read he covered the house with labels for every little thing. The first thing I saw when I got up in the morning was TOOTH-BRUSH, FAUCET, MIRROR—labels staring at me from every corner of the room. At seven we each had to choose a musical instrument. I wanted to play the drums, but Father insisted on something classical, so I studied the piano. "Country Gardens" once a week with a shrill Miss Greer. Vernon studied the oboe, and Philip had to do the violin. On Sundays, instead of going to church—Father was a resolute atheist—we dressed up and played him a concert."

"Oh God."

"Oh God is right. It was the same thing with sports. We each had to choose a sport. Not for fun or exercise you understand, but to *excel* in. We were sent to the best private schools. Every minute of the day was scheduled: horseback-riding lessons, tutors, private sports coaches, soccer, tennis camp, computer camp, Christmas ski trips to Taos and Cortina d'Ampezzo."

"How awful. And your mother, what was she like?"

"Our three mothers. We're half-brothers. Father was unlucky in love, you might say."

"He got custody of all three of you?"

"What Max wanted, Max got. They weren't pretty divorces. Our mothers weren't a big part of our lives, and mine died when I was young anyway. Father wanted to raise us by himself. He didn't want any interference. He was going to create three geniuses who would change the world. He tried to choose our careers for us. Even our girlfriends."

"I'm sorry. What a horrifying childhood."

Tom shifted in his hammock, slightly annoyed at her comment. "I wouldn't call Cortina at Christmas 'horrifying.' We did get something out of it in the end. I learned to love horses. Philip fell in love with Renaissance painting. And Vernon—well, he just kind of fell in love with wandering."

"So he chose your girlfriends?"

Tom really wished he hadn't mentioned that particular detail. "He tried."

"And?"

Tom felt his face flushing. He couldn't stop it. The thought of Sarah—perfect, beautiful, brilliant, talented, wealthy Sarah—came flooding in.

"Who was she?" Sally asked.

Women always seemed to know. "Just some girl my father introduced me to. Daughter of a friend of his. It was, ironically, the one time I really wanted to do what my father wanted me to do. I went out with her. We got engaged."

"What happened?"

He looked at her closely. She seemed more than curious. He wondered just what that meant. "Didn't work out." He didn't add the part about him finding her riding some other guy in their own bed. What Sarah wanted, Sarah got, too. *Life is too short*, she said, *and I want to experience all of it. What's wrong with that?* She could deny herself nothing.

Sally was still looking at him curiously. Then she shook her head. "Your father was really a piece of work. He could have written a book on how not to raise children."

Tom felt the prickle of annoyance grow. He knew he shouldn't say it, he knew it would cause trouble, but he couldn't stop himself. He said, "Father would've *loved* Julian."

There was a sudden silence. He could feel Sally staring at him. "Excuse me?"

Tom went on against his better judgment. "All I meant is that Julian's just the kind of person Father wanted us to be. Stanford at sixteen, famous professor at Yale, 'a genius in the real sense of the word,' as you put it."

"I won't dignify that comment with an answer," she said stiffly, her face coloring with anger as she picked up her novel and began to read.

31

Philip was shackled to a tree, his hands manacled behind him. The blackflies were crawling over every square inch of exposed skin on his body, thousands of them, eating his face alive. There was nothing he could do as they crawled into his eyes, up his nose, into his ear canal. He shook his head, he tried to blink and twitch them off, but all efforts failed. His eyes were almost swollen shut already. Hauser was talking to someone in a low voice on his satellite phone. Philip couldn't hear the words, but he knew well that quiet, bullying tone of voice. He closed his eyes. He really was beyond caring. All he wanted now was for Hauser to end his misery soon—a quick bullet to the brain.

Lewis Skiba sat at his desk, his chair turned toward the window, staring southward over the peaks of the Manhattan skyline. He had not heard from Hauser in four days. Five days ago Hauser had said to sleep on it. Then silence. They had been the worst five days of his life. The stock was down to six; the SEC had delivered subpoenas and seized laptops and hard drives from their corporate headquarters. The bastards had even taken his own computer. The short-selling frenzy continued unabated. The *Journal* had now made it official that the FDA was set to disapprove Phloxatane. Standard & Poor's was about to downgrade Lampe's bonds to junk status, and for the first time there was public speculation of Chapter II.

That morning he'd had to tell his wife that, under the circum-
stances, they had to put the Aspen house on the market immediately. It
was, after all, their fourth house, and they only used it one week out of
the year. But she hadn't understood. She wept and carried on and ended
up sleeping in the guest room. Oh God, was this how it was going to
be? What would happen if they had to sell their real home? What
would she do if they had to pull their kids out of private school?

And all this time he hadn't heard from Hauser. What the hell was
he doing? Had something happened to him? Had he given up? Skiba
felt the sweat breaking out afresh on his brow. He hated the fact that
the fate of his company and his own fate were in the hands of a man
like that.

The scrambler phone rang, and Skiba literally jumped. It was ten
o'clock in the morning. Hauser never called in the morning. But
somehow he knew it was him.

"Yes?" He tried not to sound breathless.

"Skiba?"

"Yes, yes."

"How's it going?"

"Fine."

"Slept on it yet?"

Skiba swallowed. That lump was there again, that pig of lead in his
gut. He couldn't quite bring himself to speak, it was blocking his
throat. He'd already had his limit, but another sip wouldn't hurt.
Cradling the phone, he slid open the cabinet, poured a glass. He didn't
even bother with the water.

"Lewis, I know this is tough. But the time's come. Do you want the
Codex or not? I can call it quits right now, head back. What do you
think?"

Skiba swallowed the hot golden liquid and found his voice, but it
came out in a cracked whisper. "I've told you again and again, this has
nothing to do with me. You're five thousand miles away. I have no
control over you. You do what you want. Just bring me the Codex."

"I didn't catch that, with the scrambler and all . . ."

"Just do what you need to do!" Skiba roared. "Leave me out of it!"

"Oh no, no, no, no, noooo. No. I already explained it to you, Skiba. We're in this together, pard."

Skiba's hand gripped the phone with murderous force. His whole body was shaking. He almost imagined he could throttle Hauser if he squeezed hard enough.

"Do I get rid of them or not?" the jocose voice went on. "If I don't, even if I get the Codex, they'll be coming right back out and making a claim against you, and you know what, Lewis? *You can't win that one.* They'll take the Codex away from you. You told me you wanted it clean, no complications, no lawsuits."

"I'll pay them royalties. They'll make millions."

"They won't deal with you. They have other plans for the Codex. Didn't I tell you that? That woman, Sally Colorado, has got plans, *big* plans."

"What plans?" Skiba felt shaky all over.

"They don't involve Lampe, that's all you need to know. Look, Skiba, that's the problem with all you business guys. You don't know how to make the tough decisions."

"These are human lives you're talking about."

"I know. This isn't easy for me, either. Weigh the good against the bad. A few people disappear in an unknown jungle. That's on one side. The other side is lifesaving drugs for millions, twenty thousand people who still have work, shareholders who love you instead of crying for your blood, and you the darling of Wall Street for pulling Lampe back from the abyss."

Another swallow. "Give me another day to think about it."

"Can't. Things have reached a head. You remember what I said about stopping them before the mountains? Lewis, just to ease your mind, I'm not even going to do it myself. There are some Honduran soldiers down here, renegades, and I can hardly keep them in check as it is. These guys are crazy, liable to do anything. These things happen all the time down here. Hey, if I were to turn around now these soldiers would kill them anyway. So Lewis, what should I do? Get rid of them and bring you the Codex? Or turn around and forget about it? I've got to go. Your answer?"

"Just do it!"

There was a buzz of static.

"Say it, Lewis. Say what it is you want me to do."

"Do it! Kill them, goddamn you! Kill the Broadbents!"

32

Two and a half days after the snake attack, as they were poling along one more endless water channel, Tom noticed a brightening of the swamp, sunlight through the trees—and then with astonishing suddenness the two dugouts broke free of the Meambar Swamp. It was like entering a new world. They were on the edge of a huge lake, the water as black as ink. The late afternoon sun was breaking through the clouds, and Tom felt a surge of relief in finally being in the open, released from the green prison of the swamp. A fresh breeze swept away the blackflies. Tom could see blue hills on the far shore, and beyond them a faint line of mountains rising into the clouds.

Don Alfonso stood up in the bow of the boat and spread his arms, his corncob enclosed in one wrinkled fist, looking like a ragged scarecrow. "The Laguna Negra!" he cried. "We have crossed the Meambar Swamp! I, Don Alfonso Boswas, have guided well and true!"

Chori and Pingo lowered the boat engines and fired them up. The boats set off for the far end of the lake. Tom rested against the pile of supplies and enjoyed the delicious flow of air while his pet monkey, Hairy Bugger, climbed out of his pocket and rode on top of his head, eyes closed, smacking and chattering contentedly. Tom had almost forgotten what a breeze felt like on his skin.

They camped on a sandy beach at the far end of the lake. Chori and Pingo went hunting and returned an hour later with a gutted and quartered deer, the bloody chunks wrapped in palm fronds.

"Splendid!" cried Don Alfonso. "Tomás, we will eat deer chops tonight and smoke the rest for our overland journey."

Don Alfonso roasted the loin chops over the fire while Pingo and Chori built a smoking rack over a second fire nearby. Tom watched with interest as they expertly sliced off long pieces of meat with their machetes and flipped them over the rack, then piled wet wood on the fire, generating fragrant clouds of smoke.

The chops were soon done, and Don Alfonso served them out. As they ate, Tom raised the question he had been wanting to ask. "Don Alfonso, where do we go from here?"

Don Alfonso tossed a bone into the darkness behind him. "Five rivers flow into the Laguna Negra. We must find out which river your father went up."

"Where do they originate?"

"They have their sources in the interior mountain ranges. Some flow out of the Cordillera Entre Rios, some from the Sierra Patuca, and some flow out of the Sierra de las Neblinas. The Macaturi is the longest river, and it rises in the Sierra Azul, which is halfway to the Pacific Ocean."

"Are they navigable by boat?"

"The lower parts are said to be."

" 'Said to be'?" Tom asked. "You haven't been up them?"

"None of my people have been up them. The country back there is very dangerous."

"How so?" asked Sally.

"The animals are not afraid of people. There are earthquakes, volcanoes, and bad spirits. There is a city of demons from which no one ever returns."

"A city of demons?" Vernon asked, suddenly interested.

"Yes. La Ciudad Blanca. The White City."

"What kind of city is it?"

"Built by gods long ago, it lies in ruins."

Vernon gnawed on a bone, then tossed it into the fire. Matter-of-factly, he said: "There's the answer."

"The answer to what?"

"Where Father went."

Tom stared at him. "That's a rather big leap. How can you know?"

"I don't *know*. But that's just the kind of place Father would go. He'd love a story like that. He'd check it out for sure. And stories like that are often based in reality. I bet he did find a lost city there, some big old ruin."

"But there aren't supposed to be any ruins in those mountains."

"Says who?" Vernon pulled another roasted chop off the palm leaves and tucked in.

Tom remembered the very red-faced Derek Dunn and his breezy assertion that anacondas didn't eat people. He turned to Don Alfonso. "Is this White City common knowledge?"

Don Alfonso nodded slowly, his face contracted into a mask of wrinkles. "It is talked about."

"Where is it?"

Don Alfonso shook his head. "It has no fixed location but moves about the highest peaks of the Sierra Azul, always shifting and hiding in the mists of the mountain."

"So it's a myth." Tom glanced at Vernon.

"Oh no, Tomás, it's real. They say it can only be reached by crossing a bottomless gorge. Those who slip and fall die of fright, and then their bodies keep falling until they are bones, and the bones keep tumbling until they fall apart. In the end there is nothing left but a plume of bone dust, which will fall in the darkness for eternity."

Don Alfonso chucked a piece of wood into the fire. Tom watched as it smoked and then caught fire, the flames eating up its sides. The White City.

"There aren't any lost cities in this day and age," said Tom.

"That's where you're wrong," said Sally. "There are dozens, maybe even hundreds of them, in places like Cambodia, Burma, the Gobi Desert—and especially here, in Central America. Like Site Q."

"Site Q?"

"The loot has been pouring out of Site Q for thirty years now and it's driving the archaeologists crazy. They know it must be a great Mayan city, probably somewhere in the Guatemalan lowlands, but they can't find it. Meanwhile the looters are taking it apart stone by stone and selling it off on the black market."

"Father hung out in bars," Vernon said, "buying rounds for Indians, loggers, and gold prospectors, listening for gossip about ruins and lost cities. He even learned some Indian language. Remember, Tom, how he used to launch into it at dinner parties?"

"I always thought he was just making it up."

"Look," said Vernon, "think about it for a moment. Father wouldn't build a tomb from scratch to bury himself in. He'd simply reuse one of the tombs he robbed long ago."

Nobody said anything for a moment, and then Tom said, "Vernon, that's brilliant."

"And he got the local Indians to help him."

The fire crackled. There was a dead silence.

"But Father never mentioned anything about a White City," Tom said.

Vernon smiled. "Exactly. You know why he never mentioned it? Because *that's* where he made his big discovery, the one that got him started. He came down here dead broke, and he came back with a boatload of treasure and started his gallery business."

"It makes sense."

"You're damn right it makes sense. I bet you anything that's where he went back to be buried! It's a perfect plan. There must be any number of ready-built tombs in this so-called White City. Father knew where they were because he had robbed them himself. All he had to do was go back and install himself in one of them, with the help of the local Indians. This White City is real, Tom."

"I'm convinced," said Sally.

"I even know how Father bought the Indians' help," Vernon said, with a growing smile.

"How?"

"Remember those receipts that the Santa Fe policeman found in Father's house for all that fine French and German cookware that Father ordered just before he left? That's how he paid them: cooking pots for the natives."

Don Alfonso cleared his throat loudly and ostentatiously. When he had their attention, he said, "All this talk is silly."

"Why?"

"Because no one can go to the White City. Your Father never could have found it. Even if he did, it is inhabited by demons who would kill him and steal his soul. There are winds that would drive him back, there are mists that confuse the eyes and the mind, there is a spring of water that erases the memory." He shook his head vigorously. "No, this is impossible."

"Which river do you take to get there?"

Don Alfonso furrowed his brow. His big eyes behind the dirty lenses of his glasses looked very unhappy. "Why do you want to know this useless information? I am telling you it is impossible."

"It's not impossible, and that's where we're going."

Don Alfonso spent a long minute staring at Tom. Then he sighed and said, "The Macaturi will take you partway, but you cannot go father than the Falls. The Sierra Azul lies many days beyond the Falls, beyond the mountains and valleys and more mountains. It is an impossible journey. Your father could not have done it."

"Don Alfonso, you don't know our father."

Don Alfonso filled his pipe, his troubled eyes on the fire. He was sweating. His hand holding the pipe was shaking.

"Tomorrow," Tom said, "we're going up the Macaturi, and we're heading for the Sierra Azul."

Don Alfonso stared into the fire.

"Are you coming with us, Don Alfonso?"

"It is my fate to come with you, Tomás," he said softly. "Of course, we will all die before we reach the Sierra Azul. I am an old man, and I am ready to die and meet St. Peter. But it will be sad for me to see Chori and Pingo die, and Vernon die, and to see the Curandera die, who is so pretty with many fine years of lovemaking ahead of her. And it will be very sad for me to see you die, Tomás, because you are now my friend."

33

Tom could not sleep for thinking about the White City. Vernon was right. It all fit so perfectly. It was so obvious Tom wondered why he hadn't figured it out before.

While he tossed and turned, Bugger squeaked irritably, then finally climbed up the hammock pole and slept in the rafters over Tom's head. About four o'clock in the morning, Tom gave up. He rose from his hammock, built a fire in the ashes of the old, and put a pot on to boil. Bugger came down, still annoyed, climbed into his pocket, and tilted his head up to get scratched under the chin. Don Alfonso soon made an appearance, sitting down and accepting a cup of coffee. They sat in the jungle darkness for a long time without speaking.

"There's something I've been wondering," Tom said. "When we left Pito Solo, you talked as if you'd never be coming back. Why was that?"

Don Alfonso sipped his coffee, his glasses reflecting the flickering glow of the fire. "Tomasito, when the time comes, you will learn the answer to this question and many others."

"Why did you come on this trip?"

"It was prophesied."

"That's not a good reason."

Don Alfonso turned his face to Tom. "Destiny is not a reason. It's an *explanation*. We will speak no more of this."

. . .

The Macaturi was the broadest of the five rivers flowing into the Laguna Negra. It was a more navigable river than the Patuca, deep and clean, without sandbars or hidden snags. As they motored up the river the sun broke over the distant hills, tingeing them a greenish gold. Don Alfonso had taken his usual throne on top of the heap of supplies, but his mood was different. No longer did he offer philosophical reflections on life, talk about sex, complain about his ungrateful sons, or call out the names of the birds and animals. He just sat and smoked and gazed ahead with troubled eyes.

The two boats continued upriver in silence for several hours. As they rounded a bend, a large tree appeared, lying across the river, blocking their way. It had recently fallen, and the leaves were still green.

"This is strange," muttered Don Alfonso. He called out to Chori, and they slowed their boat to let Pingo's boat, which was behind them, catch up and pass. Vernon was amidships, leaning back against the gunwale, taking in the sun. He waved as they went by.

Pingo angled the dugout toward the far side of the river, where the fallen tree was thinnest and therefore easiest to chop through.

Suddenly Don Alfonso dove for the tiller and shoved it all the way to the right. Their dugout swerved and heeled almost to the point of capsizing. "Get down!" he screamed. "Down!"

At the same instant a burst of automatic-weapons fire rang out of the forest.

Tom threw himself on Sally and slammed her to the bottom of the boat as a line of bullets ripped through the side of the dugout, showering them with splinters. He could hear the bullets slapping the water around them and the shouts of the attackers. He twisted his head and saw Don Alfonso crouching in the stern, one hand still on the handle of the motor, steering them toward the shelter of an overhanging embankment.

An unearthly scream rose up from the boat behind them. Somebody had been hit.

Tom lay on top of Sally. He could see nothing but the mass of her blond hair and the scarred wooden hull beneath them. The screaming continued in the other boat—an inhuman wail of terror and pain. Tom thought, *It's Vernon. Vernon's been shot.* The firing continued, but now the bullets seemed to be passing above their heads. The boat scraped the bottom, scraped again, the propeller grinding on rocks in the shallows.

The firing and the screaming stopped at the same time. They had reached the cover of the embankment.

Don Alfonso scrambled back to his feet and looked behind. Tom could hear him shouting in Tawahka, but there was no answer.

Tom rose cautiously, lifting Sally. There were flecks of blood on her cheek where splinters of wood had cut her.

"Are you all right?"

She nodded mutely.

Their boat was now running alongside a high embankment of boulders and brush, almost underneath the overhanging bushes. He sat up and turned to the dugout behind, calling to his brother. "Vernon! Vernon! Are you hurt?" Tom could see there was a bloody hand clutching the tiller of the dugout behind. "Vernon!" Tom screamed.

Vernon rose up shakily from the center of the boat. He looked stunned.

"Vernon! My God, are you okay?"

"Pingo's hurt."

"How bad?"

"Really bad."

The cough and roar of a boat engine sounded upriver, and then a second one. Tom could hear distant shouts.

Don Alfonso steered the boat as close as possible to the embankment. Vernon had taken the tiller of his boat and was following.

"We can't outrun them," Tom said.

Sally turned to Chori. "Give me your gun."

Chori looked at her, uncomprehending.

Without waiting Sally grabbed the gun, checked to see it was loaded, slammed the bolt back, and crouched in the stern.

"You can't stop them with that," Tom cried. "They've got automatic weapons."

"I can sure as hell slow them down."

Tom could see their two boats coming around the bend in the river, the soldiers aiming their weapons.

"Down!"

Tom heard a single shot from Sally's gun just as a burst of gunfire raked the vegetation hanging down over them, showering them with leaves. The shot had the desired effect: The two boats veered off in a panic for the cover of the riverbank. Sally dropped down next to Tom.

Don Alfonso was steering their boat under the embankment, the propeller striking rocks and whining as it was forced out of the water. More bullets whizzed overhead, and there was a dull metallic clank as one of the rounds struck the engine. The engine spluttered, then there was a whoosh as it caught fire, the boat turning broadside to the sluggish current. The fire spread with incredible speed, the flames leaping up from the melting rubber gas lines. The prow of Pingo and Vernon's boat bumped into their hull from behind, jamming up against it as burning gas began to spread on the bottom of their boat, licking up around the gas tanks.

"Out!" said Tom. "They're going to blow. Grab what you can!"

They threw themselves over the sides and into the shallows along the riverbank. Vernon and Chori grabbed Pingo and carried him up the embankment. Another burst of gunfire slammed into the bank above them, sending dirt and pebbles cascading down, but Sally's shot had made the soldiers cautious, and they were keeping their distance. The fugitives scrambled up the dirt embankment and took cover beneath a mass of overhanging vegetation, stopping to catch their breath.

"We've got to keep going," Tom cried.

At the top of the embankment Tom looked back only once, to see their boats drifting downstream, flames leaping. There was a muffled explosion as the gas can in one of the boats exploded, sending a ball of flame skyward. Beyond, the boats with the soldiers were cautiously angling in toward shore. Sally, still carrying Chori's gun, dropped to a knee and fired a second shot through the screen of vegetation.

They retreated deeper into the jungle, taking turns carrying Pingo, forcing their way through the thick vegetation. From behind Tom could hear more shouting, followed by some random shooting through the forest and the muffled *crump* of another exploding gas tank. The men had evidently landed their boats and were half heartedly chasing them. But as they pushed deeper into the forest, the sporadic gunfire grew fainter until the sounds disappeared altogether.

They halted in a small grassy clearing. Tom and Vernon laid Pingo down, and Tom bent over him, desperately feeling for a pulse. There was none. He located the wound. It was horrifying. An expanding bullet had struck Pingo in the back, between the shoulder blades, and emerged with explosive force from his chest, leaving a gaping hole more than six inches across. It had passed directly through the heart. It was amazing he had lived for even a few seconds after a wound like that.

Tom glanced up at Chori. The man had an expression on his face that was absolutely cold.

"I'm sorry."

Don Alfonso said, "There is no time to be sorry. We must go."

"And leave the body here?"

"Chori will stay with it."

"But the soldiers are surely coming—"

Don Alfonso cut him off. "Yes. And Chori must do what he must do." He turned to Sally. "You keep his gun and ammunition. We will not see Chori again. Let us go."

"We can't leave him here!" Tom protested.

Don Alfonso grabbed Tom's shoulders. His hands were surprisingly strong, like steel clamps. He spoke quietly but with intensity. "Chori has unfinished business with his brother's killers."

"Without a gun?" Sally asked as Chori took out of his leather bag a tattered box of ammunition and handed it to her.

"Silent arrows are more effective in the jungle. He will kill enough of them to die with honor. This is our way. Do not interfere." Without a backward glance Don Alfonso turned, swiped his machete across a wall of vegetation, and plunged through the opening. They followed, struggling to keep up with the old man, who moved with the speed and silence of a bat. Tom had no idea where they were heading. They walked for hours up and down ravines, wading swift streams, at times hacking their way through dense stands of bamboo or ferns. Biting ants rained down on them and crawled down their shirts, and several times Don Alfonso impaled small snakes with his machete and flicked them aside. It rained briefly and they were soaked.

The sun came out and they steamed. Clouds of insects followed them, biting viciously. Nobody spoke. No one could speak. It was all they could do to keep up.

Hours later, when the light began to die in the treetops, Don Alfonso halted. Without a word he sat on a fallen tree trunk, fished out his pipe, and lit it. Tom watched the match flare up and wondered how many more they had. They had lost almost everything with the burning of the boats.

"What now?" Vernon asked.

"We camp," said Don Alfonso. He pointed with his machete. "Make a fire. There."

Vernon got to work and Tom helped.

Don Alfonso pointed his machete at Sally. "You: Go hunting. You may be a woman, but you shoot like a man and you have the courage of a man."

Tom looked at Sally. Her face was smudged, her long blond hair in tangles, the gun slung over her shoulder. He could see in her face everything he was feeling: the shock and surprise of the attack, horror at the death of Pingo, dread at the loss of all their supplies, determination to survive. She nodded and went off into the forest.

Don Alfonso looked at Tom. "You and I will build a hut."

An hour later, night had fallen. They were sitting around the fire, eating the last of a stew made from a large rodent Sally had shot. A small thatched hut sat nearby, and Don Alfonso sat in front of a pile of palm leaves, stripping them and weaving them into hammocks. He had been silent except for giving terse orders.

"Who were those soldiers?" Tom asked Don Alfonso.

Don Alfonso busied himself over the hammocks. "Those were the soldiers who came upriver with your other brother Philip."

"Philip would never permit an attack on us," said Vernon.

"No," said Tom. He felt his heart sink. There must have been a mutiny on Philip's expedition, or something else had happened. At any rate, Philip must be in grave danger—if not already dead. The unknown enemy, therefore, had to be Hauser. He was the one who had killed the two policemen in Santa Fe, who had arranged for their capture in Brus, who was behind this most recent attack on them.

"The question," Sally said, "is whether we go on or go back."

Tom nodded.

"It'd be suicide to go on," Vernon said. "We've got nothing—no food, no clothes, no tents, sleeping bags, or food."

"Philip's up ahead," said Tom. "And he's in trouble. It's pretty obvious that Hauser's the one behind the killing of the two policemen in Santa Fe."

There was a silence. "Maybe we should go back, resupply, and return. We won't be able to help him like this, Tom."

Tom glanced at Don Alfonso, plaiting deftly. He sensed from the studiously neutral expression on the old man's face that he had an opinion. He always looked that way when he was about to disagree. "Don Alfonso?"

"Yes?"

"Do you have an opinion?"

Don Alfonso laid the hammock down and rubbed his hands together. He looked Tom in the eye. "I do not have an opinion. I have instead a statement of fact."

"Which is?"

"Behind us is a deadly swamp in which the water is lowering every day. We have no dugout. It will take a week at least to make another. But we cannot stay in one place for a week, because the soldiers will find us, and the manufacture of a dugout creates clouds of smoke, which will be a signpost for all to see. So we must keep moving, on foot, through the jungle, toward the Sierra Azul. To go back is to die. That is my statement of fact."

34

Marcus Hauser sat on a log by the fire, Churchill in his mouth, field-stripping the Steyr AUG. The weapon didn't need it, but for Hauser it was a repetitive physical process that was almost a form of meditation. The rifle was mostly made of finely machined plastic, which Hauser liked. He retracted the cocking slide knob, grasped the barrel grip and, using his left thumb, pressed the barrel locking latch down. Then he rotated the barrel clockwise and pulled it forward. It came free with a satisfying smoothness.

From time to time he glanced into the forest where Philip was chained up, but there wasn't a sound. He had heard a jaguar roaring earlier in the day, a roar of frustration and hunger, and he didn't want his prisoner getting eaten, at least not before he had figured out where old Max had gone. He heaped some more wood on the fire to beat back the darkness and the prowling jaguar. To his right, the Macaturi River slid past the camp, making soft splashing and gurgling noises as it eddied and flowed. It was a beautiful night for a change, the velvety sky dusted with stars, which were reflected as faint dancing lights in the surface of the river. It was close to two o'clock in the morning, but Hauser was one of those fortunates who needed only four hours of sleep a night.

He chucked another log on the fire to increase the light and slid the bolt assembly out of the receiver. His hand lightly caressed the smooth pieces of plastic and metal—one warm, the other cold—and he savored the scent of gun oil and the clicks of the well-machined parts as they disengaged. A few more well-practiced moves and the rifle lay in front of him, stripped to its six basic parts. He hefted each piece, examining it, cleaning it, running his hands over it—and began putting them back together. He worked slowly, dreamily even: no boot-camp haste here.

He heard a faint sound: the whine of the returning boats. He paused, listening carefully. The operation had concluded, and the men were back right on time. Hauser was pleased. Not even a half-assed group of Honduran soldiers could have screwed up such a straightforward op.

Or could they? He saw, materializing out of the dark body of the river, the dugout, but with three instead of five soldiers in it. The boat docked at the large boulder that served as a landing stage. Two men hopped out, firelit forms moving against the darkness, and helped a third man out. He walked stiffly, and Hauser heard a groan of pain. Three men—and he had sent out five.

He refitted the butt plate, slid the bolt assembly back in, and reset the housing latch to the left, working by feel, his eyes fixed on the figures moving toward the fire. The men approached diffidently, nervously, one soldier supporting his wounded colleague. A three-foot-long arrow had passed through his thigh, the feathered end sticking out the back, the barbed metal point out the front. The pantleg had been torn and was stiff with dried blood.

The men paused, saying nothing, looking mostly at the ground, shuffling their feet in shame. Hauser waited. The enormity of his mistake—in trusting these men to perform the simplest of ops—was now obvious. He went back to reassembling his gun, rotating the barrel back into place and then reseating the magazine, sliding it into the stock with a click. Then he waited, weapon laid across his knees, an icy feeling in his heart.

The silence was excruciating. One of them would have to speak.

"*Jefe*—" the lieutenant began.

He waited for the excuses.

"We killed two of them, *jefe*, and burned their boats and supplies. Their bodies are in the canoe."

Hauser said, after a pause, "Which two?"

There was a nervous pause. "The two Tawahka Indians."

Hauser remained silent. This was a disaster.

"The old man with them saw the trap before we could open fire," the *teniente* went on. "They turned around. We chased them downstream, but they managed to land and escape into the jungle. We burned their boats and supplies. Then, as we pursued them into the jungle, we were ambushed by one of the Tawakha. He had a bow and arrow, so much the worse for us. We couldn't locate him until he got two of us and wounded the third, and then we killed him. You know how these jungle Indians are, *jefe*, silent as jaguars . . ."

His voice trailed off miserably. He shifted nervously, and the man with the arrow through his thigh let escape an involuntary groan.

"So you see, *jefe*, we killed two and drove the others into the jungle with no supplies, no food, nothing, where they will surely die—"

Hauser rose. "Excuse me, Teniente, this man needs immediate attention."

"Sí, señor."

With the rifle in one hand, Hauser rose and put his free arm around the wounded man, easing him off the soldier who had been supporting him. He leaned over and said gently, "Come with me. Let me take care of you."

The *teniente* waited by the fire, his face sagging.

Hauser supported the man and led him away from the fire. The man groaned, limping. His skin was hot and dry; he had a fever.

"Easy," said Hauser. "We'll just take you over here and fix you up." He led the man about fifty yards into the darkness beyond the campfire and eased him down on a log. The man staggered, groaned, but with Hauser's help was able to sit on the log. Hauser removed the man's machete.

"Señor, before you cut out the arrow, give me whiskey." The man whimpered, terrified of pain.

"This won't take but a second." He gave the man a gentle pat on the shoulder. "We'll have you fixed up in no time. I promise you, the operation will be painless."

"No, señor, please, whiskey first . . ."

Hauser bent over the arrow with the machete. The man stiffened, gritting his teeth, staring at the machete in terror and noticing nothing else. Meanwhile, Hauser raised the muzzle of the Steyr AUG to within an inch of the back of the man's head. He eased the trigger back to full auto fire and squeezed off a short burst. The fire struck the man obliquely, the force of it throwing him backward off the log where he landed, sprawled head down, unmoving. All was then silent.

Hauser returned to camp, washed his hands, and reseated himself by the fire. He picked up the half-smoked Churchill and relit it with a burning twig. The two soldiers were not looking at him, but some of the others, hearing the noise, had come out of their tents. They had their guns and were looking around, confused and alarmed.

"It is nothing," said Hauser, waving them away. "The man needed surgery. It was short, painless, and successful."

Hauser removed the cigar, knocked back a slug from his hip flask, and reinserted the wet tip of the cigar between his lips, drawing the smoke in. He felt only partly refreshed. It wasn't the first time he had made the mistake of entrusting a simple task to these Honduran soldiers only to see it fail. Unfortunately, there was only one of him and he couldn't do everything. It was always the same problem—always.

Hauser turned and smiled at the *teniente*. "I'm a very good surgeon, Teniente, should you ever have need of it."

35

They spent the following day in camp. Don Alfonso cut a gigantic stack of palm fronds and sat cross-legged next to them for most of the day, pulling them into fibrous strips and weaving palm-leaf backpacks and more hammocks. Sally hunted and brought back a small antelope, which Tom dressed and smoked over the fire. Vernon collected fruits and manioc root. By the end of the day they had a small supply of food for their journey.

They inventoried their supplies. Between them they had several boxes of waterproof matches, a box of ammunition with thirty rounds, Tom's daypack containing a tiny Svea backpacking stove set with an aluminum pots-and-pans set, two bottles of white gas, and a squeeze bottle of insect repellent. Vernon had escaped with a pair of binoculars around his neck. Don Alfonso had a pocketful of candy bars, three pipes, two packs of pipe tobacco, a small whetstone, and a roll of fishing line with hooks, all of which had been in his greasy leather bag, which he had snatched from the burning dugout. They all had their machetes, which they had been carrying tucked in their belts at the time of the attack.

The next morning they set off. Tom cleared the trail wielding a freshly sharpened machete, while Don Alfonso went behind, murmuring which way he was to go. After a few miles of bushwhacking they came out on what appeared to be an old animal trail running through a cool forest of smooth-barked trees. The light was dim, and there was almost no undergrowth. A hush lay over the forest. It was like walking through the columned interior of a vast green cathedral.

In the early afternoon the trail reached the base of a mountain range. The terrain pitched up from the forest floor, becoming a tangled slope of moss-covered boulders. The trail went almost straight up. Don Alfonso mounted it at astonishing speed, and Tom and the others struggled to follow, surprised at the old man's vigor. As they gained altitude the air became fresher. The stately trees of the jungle gave way to their dwarfish, twisted cousins of the mountains, their branches hung with moss. In the late afternoon they came out on a flat ridge, which ended in an outcropping of leaf-shaped rocks. For the first time they had a view back across the jungle they had just traversed.

Tom wiped his brow. The mountain fell away from them in one fantastic emerald declivity, plunging three thousand feet down to the green ocean of life below. Massive cumulus clouds moved above their heads.

"I had no idea we were so high," said Sally.

"Thanks to the Holy Mother we have journeyed far," said Don Alfonso, his voice subdued, setting down his palm-leaf backpack. "This is a good place to camp." He seated himself on a log, lit his pipe, and began to give orders.

"Sally, you and Tom go hunting. Vernon, first you will build the fire, and then you will build the hut. I will rest."

He leaned back, puffing lazily, his eyes half closed.

Sally slung the gun over her shoulder, and they set off, following what appeared to be an animal trail. "I haven't had a chance to thank you for shooting at those soldiers," he said. "You probably saved our lives. You've really got guts."

"You're like Don Alfonso—you seem surprised a woman might be handy with a rifle."

"I was talking about your presence of mind, not your shooting— but yes, I have to admit, I am surprised."

"Allow me to inform you that it's now the twenty-first century, and women are doing surprising things."

Tom shook his head. "Is everyone in New Haven so prickly?"

She turned a cool pair of green eyes on him. "Shall we get on with the hunting? Your chatter is scaring the game."

Tom suppressed a further comment and instead watched her slim body moving through the jungle. No, she was nothing like Sarah. Blunt, prickly, outspoken. Sarah was smooth; she never said what she really thought, never told the truth, was pleasant even to people she couldn't stand. For her, it was always so much more fun to deceive.

They went on, their footsteps silent in the wet, springy leaves. The forest was cool and deep. Through gaps in the trees, Tom could see the Macaturi River glinting in scimitarlike curves through the rainforest far below.

A cough sounded from the forested slopes above them. It sounded like a human cough, only deeper, throatier.

"That," said Sally, "sounds feline."

"Feline, as in jaguar?"

"Yes."

They moved side by side through the foliage, palming the leaves and ferns out of the way. The mountain slopes were curiously silent. Even the birds had stopped chittering. A lizard skittered up a trunk.

"It feels strange up here," said Tom. "Unreal."

"It's a cloudforest," said Sally. "A high-altitude rainforest." She moved ahead, the rifle at the ready. Tom fell behind her.

There was another cough: deep and booming. It was now the only sound in a forest that had become unnaturally silent.

"That sounded closer," said Tom.

"Jaguars are a lot more frightened of us than we are of them," said Sally.

They clambered across a slope covered with giant fallen boulders, squeezing through moss-covered faces of rock, and came out facing a thick stand of bamboo. Sally moved around it. Clouds were already pressing down on them, and tendrils of mist drifted through the trees. The air smelled like wet moss. The view below them had vanished into whiteness.

Sally paused, raised the gun, waited.

"What is it?" Tom whispered.

"Up ahead."

They crept forward. In front of them was a second cluster of giant mossy boulders, rolled and piled together, forming a honeycomb of dark holes and crawlspaces.

Tom stood behind Sally, waiting. The mists were rolling in fast, reducing the trees to silhouettes. The fog sucked the fantastical green from the landscape, turning it a dull bluish gray.

"There's something moving in those rocks." she whispered.

They waited, crouching. Tom could feel the mists collecting around him, soaking into his clothes.

After ten long minutes, a head appeared at a rock opening with two bright black eyes, and an animal that looked like a giant guinea pig came sniffing out.

The shot rang out instantly, and the animal squiffed loudly and rolled belly up.

Sally rose, unable to suppress a grin.

"Nice shooting," Tom said.

"Thanks."

Tom unsheathed his machete and went to examine the animal.

"I'll go on ahead."

Tom nodded and turned over the animal with his shoe. It was some kind of large rodent, with yellow incisors, round and fat and heavily furred. He slid out his machete, not at all looking forward to his job. He sliced it open, scraped and pulled out the guts and internal organs, cut off the paws and head, and skinned it. There was a strong smell of blood. As hungry as he was he began to lose his appetite. He wasn't squeamish—as a vet he'd seen plenty of blood—but he didn't like being part of the killing as opposed to the healing.

He heard another sound, this time a very low growl. He paused, listening. It was followed by a dainty series of coughs. It was hard to tell where they were coming from—somewhere upslope, in the rocks above them. He sought out Sally with his eyes and located her about twenty yards away, below the rockslide, a slender silhouette moving silently in the mist. She faded from view.

He quartered the animal and wrapped it up in palm leaves. It was depressing how little meat there actually was. It seemed hardly worth it. Maybe, he thought, Sally would bring down something bigger, like a deer.

As he finished wrapping the meat he heard another sound, a soft and gentle purr, so close that he flinched. He waited, listening, his whole body tense. Suddenly a bloodcurdling scream split the forest, trailing off into a hungry growl. He jumped up, machete in his hand, trying to identify where it came from, but the tree branches and rocks were all bare. The jaguar was well hidden.

Tom looked downslope to where Sally had vanished into the mists. He didn't like the fact that the jaguar hadn't gone away after the rifle shot. Picking up his machete, he left the chopped-up rodent and headed toward where Sally had disappeared.

"Sally?"

The jaguar screamed again, and this time it seemed to be right above him. He instinctively dropped to his knees, machete drawn, but all he could see were moss-draped rocks and disembodied tree trunks.

"Sally!" he called out more loudly. "Are you all right?"

Silence.

He began to run down the slope, his heart in a panic. "Sally!"

A faint voice answered, "I'm down here."

He continued downhill, slipping and sliding on the wet leaves, sending pebbles rolling down the steep slope. The mists were getting thicker by the minute. He heard another set of grunting coughs, behind him, very humanlike in sound. The animal was pursuing him.

"Sally!"

Sally emerged from the mists, carrying the gun, with a scowl on her face. "Your shouting caused me to miss a shot."

He pulled up short, then slid the machete back into his belt, embarrassed. "I was worried, that's all. I don't like the sound of that jaguar. It's hunting us."

"Jaguars don't hunt people."

"You heard what my brother said about what happened to his guide."

"Frankly, I don't believe it." She frowned. "We might as well go back. I'm not going to get anything more in this fog anyway."

They climbed back to the spot where the body of the rodent had been. The pieces were gone, leaving a few torn and bloody palm leaves behind.

Sally laughed. "That's all he was doing—chasing you away so he could eat our dinner."

Tom colored with embarrassment. "I wasn't chased away—I came looking for you."

"Don't worry about it," said Sally, "I probably would have run, too."

Tom noted with irritation the word *probably* but said nothing. But he suppressed a tart reply. He wasn't going to let her bait him anymore. They started back toward camp, following the trail they had come in on. As they approached the first rockpile, the jaguar screamed again, the sound oddly clear and crisp in the foggy forest. Sally stopped, her gun raised. They waited. Water drops were collecting and falling off the leaves, filling the forest with a soft pattering sound.

"He wasn't ahead of us before, Sally."

"You still think he's hunting us?"

"Yes."

"Nonsense. He wouldn't be making such a racket if he were. And besides, he just ate." She smirked at him.

They walked cautiously toward the rocks. Empty, but with a lot of dark holes and crevasses.

"Let's play it safe and skirt that rockfall," Tom said.

"All right."

They began climbing uphill, to go around it from above. The mists were getting thicker. Tom felt the wetness creeping through his only set of clothes. He stopped. There was a soft rustling sound.

Sally paused.

"Sally, get behind me," Tom said.

"I've got the gun. I should be in front."

"Get behind me."

"For heaven's sake." But she got behind him.

He drew his machete and moved forward. There were trees all around them, crooked trees with low branches hung with moss. The mists were so thick he could not see their upper reaches. Tom realized that they were now upwind of the jaguar. It had moved around them so that it could scent them, even if it could not see them.

"Sally, I can *feel* it hunting us."

"It's just curious."

Tom froze. There, about ten yards ahead, was the jaguar, suddenly exposing itself fully to their view. It was standing on a branch above their path, calmly looking at them, twitching its tail. Its magnificence took Tom's breath away.

Sally did not raise her gun to shoot, and Tom understood why. It was impossible to contemplate destroying such a beautiful animal.

After a moment's hesitation the jaguar leapt effortlessly to another tree branch and walked along it, eyeing them the whole time, its muscles rippling under its golden pelt, moving like flowing honey.

"Look at how beautiful it is," Sally breathed.

It *was* beautiful. With a movement of incredible lightness, the animal leapt to another branch, this one closer to them. There it stopped, slowly sinking down onto its haunches. It looked at them boldly, utterly unafraid, making no effort to hide, motionless except for the faintest twitching of the tip of its tail. There was blood on its muzzle. The look in its eye, Tom thought, was contemptuous.

"It's not afraid," said Sally.

"That's because it's never seen a human being before."

Tom backed up slowly, and Sally followed suit. The jaguar remained in its perch watching them, forever watching them, until it disappeared in the shifting mists.

When they got back to camp, Don Alfonso listened to their story about the jaguar, his brown face crinkling with concern. "We must be very careful," he said. "We must not talk about this animal anymore. Otherwise, he will follow us to hear what we say. He is proud and does not like to be spoken ill of."

"I thought that jaguars don't attack humans," Sally said.

Don Alfonso laughed and whacked Sally's knee. "That is a good joke. When he looks at us, what do you think he sees?"

"I don't know."

"He sees a weak, stupid, slow, perpendicular piece of meat without horns, teeth, or claws."

"Why didn't he attack?"

"Like all cats, he likes to play with his food."

Sally shuddered.

"Curandera, it is not pleasant to be eaten by a jaguar. They eat the tongue first, and not always before you are dead. Next time you have the opportunity to kill it, do it."

That night the forest was so quiet that Tom had trouble sleeping. Sometime after midnight, hoping a little air would help, he crept out of his hammock and ducked out the door of the hut. He was astonished at the sight that greeted him. The forest all around him was aglow with phosphorescence, as if glowing powder had been dusted over everything, outlining rotting logs and stumps, dead leaves and mushrooms, a luminescent landscape that stretched off into the forest, merging into one misty glow. It was as if the heavens had fallen to earth.

After five minutes he crept back into the makeshift hut and gave Sally a little shake. She rolled over, her hair a tangle of heavy gold. Like all of them, she was sleeping in her clothes. "What is it?" she said in a sleepy voice.

"There's something you have to see."

"I'm sleeping."

"You've got to see this."

"I don't *have* to do anything. Go away."

"Sally, just this once please trust me."

Grumbling, she got out of her hammock and stepped outside. She halted and stood there in silence, staring. Minutes passed. "My God," she breathed. "I've never seen anything so beautiful. It's like staring down at L.A. from thirty thousand feet."

The glow cast a faint illumination on Sally's face, barely outlining it against the darkness. Her long hair hung down her back like a cascade of light, silver instead of gold.

On an impulse, he took her hand. She didn't withdraw it. There was something amazingly erotic in just holding her hand.

"Tom?"

"Yes?"

"Why did you want me to see this?"

"Well," he said, "because I—" He hesitated. "I wanted to share it with you, that's all."

"That's all?" She looked at him for a long time. Her eyes seemed unusually luminescent—or maybe it was just a trick of the light. Finally she said, "Thank you, Tom."

All at once, the jaguar's scream split the night. A black shape slowly moved against the glowing background, like an absence of light itself. As it turned its great head toward them, they saw the faint gleam of its eyes reflecting the millions of points in two orbs, like two tiny galaxies.

Tom slowly pulled Sally back by her hand, toward the dull heap of coals that had been their fire. He reached down and heaped some brush on. As the yellow flames licked upward, the jaguar disappeared.

A moment later Don Alfonso joined them at the fire.

"He is still playing with his food," the old man muttered.

36

The next morning when they set off, the mists were so thick they couldn't see more than ten feet in any direction. They climbed farther up the mountain, still following the faint animal trail. They topped a secondary ridge and began to descend. Tom could hear the sound of roaring water at the bottom. In a few moments they came out on the steep banks of a river tearing down the mountainside, bursting over boulders on its way.

"We cut a tree," said Don Alfonso. He hunted around and found a slender tree that was positioned to fall in the right way. "Cut here," he ordered. They all joined in, and in fifteen minutes it had fallen, forming a bridge of sorts over the roaring cataract, where the river narrowed to a chute that ended in a boiling pool created by a logjam.

Don Alfonso gave a few whacks at a nearby sapling; in a moment he had fashioned it into a twelve-foot pole. He handed it to Vernon. "You first, Vernito."

"Why me?"

"To see if the bridge is strong enough," said Don Alfonso.

Vernon looked at him for a moment, and then Don Alfonso laughed, slapping his shoulder. "You must take off your shoes, Vernito. God gave us bare feet for a reason."

Vernon removed his shoes, tied the laces together, and draped them around his neck. Don Alfonso handed him the pole.

"Go slow, and stop if the log begins swaying."

Vernon crept out onto the log, balancing the pole like a tightrope walker, his feet white against the dark green. "It's as slick as ice."

"Slowly, slowly," Don Alfonso crooned.

As he crept out, the tree sagged and wobbled. In a few minutes he was over. Vernon threw the pole back across.

"Your turn," said Don Alfonso, handing the pole to Tom.

Tom removed his shoes and hefted the pole. He felt silly, like a circus performer. Cautiously he ventured onto the log, sliding his feet over the cold, slippery bark, one foot after the other. Every movement seemed to make the tree sway and tremble. He moved, waited, moved again. About halfway across, Bugger, who had been sleeping in his pocket, took the opportunity to poke his head out to take a look around; when he saw the torrent below, he let out a shriek and clambered out of the pocket and up Tom's face to nestle in his hair. Tom, startled, allowed one end of the pole to dip down. In a panic he heaved that end up; the inertia of it carried it up high; he took two quick steps trying to maintain his balance, which only caused the log to give a violent bounce.

He fell.

For a split second he was in the air, and then it was as if he had been swallowed by something black and freezing. He felt a violent tug as the current grabbed him, a terrifying weightless rush, and then a sudden pummeling roar. He flailed his arms, trying to struggle upward, but he didn't know which direction was up, and then he felt the current jam him into an underwater thicket of logs. He clawed about, feeling a terrible pressure on his chest, the air being forced out of his lungs. He tried to kick and pull himself free, but the logs surrounding him were slick and the pressure was fierce. It was like being buried alive. There were flashes of light in his vision, and he opened his mouth to scream, only to feel the pressure fill his mouth. He twisted his body, desperate for air, trying to propel himself out of the nest of branches, twisted again, but he had lost all sense of direction. He twisted and thrashed, but he could feel his energy fast ebbing; he was becoming lighter, weightless, going far, far away.

And then there was an arm around his neck and he was brutally pulled back to reality, manhandled through water, dragged over rocks, slung down. He found himself on the ground, staring up at a face he knew well, but it still took him a moment to realize it was Vernon.

"Tom!" Vernon shouted. "Look, his eyes are open! Tom, say something! Christ, he's not breathing!"

Sally was suddenly there, and he felt a sudden pressure in his chest. Everything looked strange and slow. Vernon bent over him. He felt him give his chest a big shove, and he felt his arms being raised. All at once the pressure seemed to break, and he coughed violently. Vernon rolled him to his side. He coughed, coughed again, felt a blinding icy headache take hold. Reality returned with a vengeance.

Tom struggled to sit up. Vernon put his arms under his shoulders and supported him.

"What happened?"

"This foolish brother of yours, this Vernito, jumped into that river and pulled you out from under those logs. I have never seen such craziness in my life."

"He did?"

Tom turned and looked at Vernon. He was soaked, and his forehead was cut. Blood and water ran together into his beard.

Vernon grasped him, and he stood up. His head cleared a little more, and the pounding headache began to subside. He look down into the roaring chute of water ripping into the frenzied pool jammed full of broken tree trunks and branches. He looked at Vernon again.

It finally sank in. "You," he said incredulously.

Vernon shrugged.

"You saved my life."

"Well, you saved mine," he said, almost defensively. "You decapitated a snake for me. All I did was jump."

Don Alfonso said, "By the Virgin Mary, I still cannot believe it."

Tom coughed again. "Well, Vernon, thanks."

"Isn't Death disappointed today," Don Alfonso cried, pointing to the small, wet, frightened monkey crouching on a rock by the water. "Why, even the *mono chucuto* cheated Death."

A miserable Bugger climbed back into Tom's pocket and took his accustomed place, making grumpy noises.

"Don't complain," Tom said. "It was your own damn fault."

The monkey answered with an insolent smack of his lips.

Past the river the trail went uphill again, and they continued to climb higher into the mountains. Darkness and a chill crept into the air. Tom was still soaked, and he began to shiver.

Don Alfonso said casually, "You know the animal I spoke to you about yesterday?"

It took Tom a moment to realize what he was referring to.

"It is a lady, and she is still with us."

"How do you know?"

Don Alfonso lowered his voice. "She has very bad breath."

"You *smelled* her?" Sally asked.

Don Alfonso nodded.

"How long is she going to follow us?"

"Until she eats. She is pregnant and hungry."

"Great. And we're the pickles and ice cream."

"Let us pray to the Virgin to send a slow anteater across her path." Don Alfonso nodded at Sally. "Carry loaded."

The trail continued to climb through a forest of gnarled trees that seemed to get denser as they gained altitude. At a certain point, Tom noticed the air becoming brighter. It seemed to smell different, carrying a faint odor of perfume. And then, quite suddenly, they walked out of the mist and into the sunlight. Tom paused, astonished. They were now looking out over a sea of white. On the puffy horizon the sun was sinking into an orange sea of fire. The forest was draped with brilliant flowers.

"We're above the clouds," cried Sally.

"We will camp at the top," said Don Alfonso, striking off with a newly invigorated step.

The trail crested the ridge in a broad meadow filled with wildflowers, rippled by a breeze, and all of a sudden they were at the summit, looking northwest over a rolling ocean of clouds. Fifty miles distant Tom could see a line of sharp blue peaks breaking through the clouds, like a chain of islands in the sky.

"The Sierra Azul," said Don Alfonso, in a small, queer voice.

37

Lewis Skiba stared into the flickering fire, losing himself in the shifting colors. He had done nothing all day, answered no phones, taken no meetings, written no memos. All he could think of was *Had Hauser done it? Had Hauser made him a murderer yet?* He held his head and thought back to the ivy-covered buildings of Wharton, the heady sense of possibility of those early days. The whole world was there, ahead of him, ripe for the plucking. And now . . . He reminded himself that he had brought jobs and opportunity to thousands, that he had grown his company and made drugs that cured people of terrible diseases and sicknesses. He had three fine sons. Yet for the past week the first thought that came into his mind when he woke up was *I am a murderer.* He wanted to take back his words. Except that he couldn't: Hauser hadn't called, and he had no way of contacting him.

Why had he told Hauser to do it? Why had he allowed himself to be bullied? Skiba tried to tell himself that Hauser would have done it anyway, that he himself had not caused anyone's death, that maybe it was just big talk. There were people like that who liked to talk violence, brag about their guns, that sort of thing. Sick people. Hauser might be one of those, all talk and no action.

The intercom buzzed, and with a shaking hand he pressed the button.

"Mr. Fenner from Dixon Asset Management for his two o'clock."

Skiba swallowed. This was the one meeting he couldn't miss. "Send him in."

Fenner looked like most of the other stock analysts of his acquaintance, small, dry, emanating overweening self-confidence. That was the key to his success: Fenner was a guy you just wanted to believe. Skiba had done a lot of little favors for Fenner, tipped some hot IPOs his way, helped get his kids into an exclusive Manhattan private school, given a couple of hundred thousand to his wife's favorite charity. In return, Fenner had been calling Lampe stock a "buy" all the way down, leading his hapless clients to the manure pile and shoving them in head first— all the while making millions himself. In short, he was a typical successful analyst.

"How are you, Lewis?" said Fenner, taking a seat by the fire. "This can't be much fun."

"It isn't, Stan."

"I don't want to bandy civilities at a time like this. We've known each other for too long. I want you to give me one reason why I should advise my clients to keep holding Lampe. I just need one good reason."

Skiba swallowed. "Can I offer you anything, Stan? Mineral water? Sherry?"

Fenner shook his head. "The investment committee is going to override me. It's fire-sale time. They're spooked and, frankly, so am I. I trusted you, Skiba."

What a crock. Fenner had known the company's real picture for months. He was just too tempted by all the tidbits Skiba was tossing his way and by the investment banking business Lampe gave Dixon. Greedy bastard. On the other hand, if Dixon went from "buy" to "hold" or "sell," that would finish Lampe. It would be Chapter 11.

He coughed, cleared his throat. He couldn't quite manage to get a word out, and he coughed again to cover his paralysis.

Fenner waited.

Finally Skiba spoke. "Stan, there is something I can give you."

Fenner tilted his head ever so slightly.

"It's privileged, it's confidential, and if you act on it it'd be a clear case of insider trading."

"It's only insider trading if you *trade*. I'm looking for a reason not to. I've got my clients up to their necks in Lampe stock, and I need to give them a reason to sit tight."

Skiba took a deep breath. "Lampe is going to announce, in the next few weeks, the acquisition of a two-thousand-page manuscript, a unique copy, compiled by the ancient Mayan Indians. This manuscript lists every plant and animal in the tropical rainforest with medically active properties, along with prescriptions on how to extract the active ingredients, dosages, side effects. The manuscript represents the sum total of ancient Mayan medical knowledge, refined over thousands of years from living in the richest pocket of biodiversity on the planet. Lampe will own it, lock, stock, and barrel. It will come to us free and clear, without royalty deals, partnerships, litigation, or encumbrances."

He stopped. Fenner's expression had not changed. If he was thinking, it didn't show on his face.

"When will you announce this? Can I have a date?"

"No."

"How certain is it?"

"Very."

The lie was easy. The Codex was their only hope, and if it fell through nothing else would matter anyway.

A long silence. Fenner allowed something that might have been a smile to form on the fine, astringent features of his face. He collected his briefcase and rose. "I thank you, Lewis. You take my breath away."

Skiba nodded and watched Fenner make his small, careful way out of the office.

If only he knew.

38

As they came down from the mountains, the rainforest changed. The terrain was extremely rough, a landscape cut by deep ravines and torrential rivers, with high ridges in between. They continued following the animal trail, but it was so overgrown that they had to take turns hacking their way forward. They slipped and fell going up the steep muddy trails and slid and fell going back down.

For days they struggled forward. There wasn't a level place to camp, and they were forced to sleep on slopes, hammocks strung between trees, sleeping all night in the rain. In the mornings the jungle was dark and foggy. In a hard day's travel they might make five miles, and by the end of each day they were all brutally exhausted. The hunting was almost nonexistent. They never had enough to eat. Tom had never been so hungry in his life. At night he dreamed of T-bone steaks and french fried potatoes, and by day he thought of ice cream and buttered lobsters, and all they talked about around the campfire at night was food.

The days began to run together. Not once did the rain stop or the mists lift. Their hammocks rotted and had to be rewoven, their clothes began to fall apart, chiggers infested their clothing and dug into their skin, and the stitches of their shoes unraveled. They had no change of clothes, and the jungle would soon reduce them to nakedness. Their bodies were covered with stings, bites, scrapes, cuts, scabs, and sores. On one climb out of a ravine Vernon slipped and grasped a bush to arrest his fall, causing a shower of fire ants to cascade over him; they bit him so viciously that he ran a fever for twenty-four hours and could barely walk.

The only redeeming quality of the rainforest was its plant life. Sally found a wealth of medicinal plants and was able to concoct an herbal ointment from them that worked wonders with bug bites, rashes, and fungal infections. They drank a tea she made that she claimed was an antidepressant, but it didn't keep them from feeling depressed.

And always, at night and even during the day, they could hear the coughing and prowling of the jaguar. No one spoke about it—Don Alfonso had forbidden it—but it was never far from Tom's mind. Surely there were other animals for it to eat in the forest. What did it want? Why did it follow and never strike?

On the fourth or fifth night—Tom had begun to lose count—they camped atop a ridge, wedged among massive rotting tree trunks. It had rained, and steam rose from the ground. They ate an early dinner—a boiled lizard with matta root. After dinner Sally stood up with the gun.

"Jaguar or no jaguar, I'm going hunting."

"I'm coming," Tom said.

They followed a small stream downhill from camp, through a ravine. The day was gray, and the forest around them was limp and bedraggled, the vegetation steaming. The sound of dripping water mingled with the hollow calls of birds.

For half an hour they picked their way down the ravine, over mossy boulders and tree trunks, until they reached a swift stream. They moved along it, Indian file, through the curling mists. Sally moved a bit like a cat herself, Tom thought, the way she silently insinuated herself through the understory.

Sally paused, held up her hand. Slowly she raised the gun, aimed, and fired.

An animal thrashed and squealed in the undergrowth, the sounds quickly subsiding.

"I don't know what it was, except that it was stout and furry." In the bushes they found the animal, lying on its side, its four legs sticking out horizontally.

"Some kind of peccary," said Tom, looking down at it in distaste. He would never get used to butchering animals.

"Your turn," said Sally, flashing him a smile.

He pulled out his machete and began cleaning the animal while Sally watched. Steam rose up from the internal organs as Tom scooped them out.

"If we parboil it back in camp, then we can scrape the hair off," Sally said.

"I can hardly wait," said Tom. He finished gutting it, cut a pole, and tied the legs together. They slid it on and hefted it over their shoulders. It didn't weigh more than thirty pounds, but it would make a fine meal with meat left over for smoking. They began heading along the ravine, backtracking the way they had come.

They hadn't gone more than twenty yards when they were stopped by the jaguar, standing in the middle of the trail directly in front of them. It stared at them with green eyes, the tip of its tail flicking back and forth.

"Back up," said Tom. "Nice and easy." But as they backed up, the jaguar took a step forward, and another, pacing them on padded paws.

"Remember what Don Alfonso said?"

"I can't do it," Sally whispered.

"Shoot over its head."

Sally raised the muzzle of the gun and squeezed off a round.

The sound was curiously muffled in the fog and heavy vegetation. The jaguar gave a small shiver but otherwise made no sign it had heard, just continued to stare at them, the tip of the tail twitching as rhythmically as a metronome.

"We'll go around it," Sally said.

They edged off the animal trail into the forest. The animal made no move to follow them except with its green eyes, and soon it was lost to sight. After a few hundred yards Tom began to cut back toward the ridgeline. They heard the cat cough twice off to their left, and they moved farther down from the ridge. They went a quarter mile and then stopped. They should have encountered the ravine with the stream, but it wasn't there.

"We should be cutting more to the left," said Tom.

They angled left. The forest became heavier, darker, the trees smaller and closer together.

"I don't recognize this area at all."

They stopped to listen. The jungle seemed to have fallen eerily silent. There was no sound of a stream, nothing but the patter of water dripping from branches.

A low, booming cough came from directly behind them.

Sally turned angrily. "Get out of here!" she yelled. "Scat!"

They went on, redoubling their pace, Tom in the lead, slashing a path through the undergrowth. From time to time he could hear the cat on his left keeping pace with them, making an occasional purring noise. It wasn't a friendly sound at all: It was low and thick and sounded more like a growl. He knew they were getting lost, that they weren't going in the right direction. They were almost running.

And then with a sudden flash of gold it seemed to congeal out of the mist ahead of them. It stood on a low branch, tensed.

They stopped, backed up slowly while the animal watched. Then, with a liquid movement, it leapt to one side of them, and in three bounds it had positioned itself on a branch behind them, blocking their retreat.

Sally kept her gun aimed at the jaguar, but she didn't shoot. They stared at the animal and the animal stared at them.

"I think maybe the time has come to kill it," Tom whispered.

"I can't."

Somehow, that was the answer Tom wanted to hear. Never had he seen an animal so vital, so supple, or so magnificent.

Then, all of a sudden, the jaguar turned and took itself away, jumping lightly from branch to branch, until it had disappeared into the forest.

They stood there silently, and then Sally smiled. "I told you she was just curious."

"That's some curiosity, following us for fifty miles." Tom looked around. Finally he tucked his machete back into his belt and picked up the pole holding the dead peccary. He felt unsettled, uneasy. It wasn't over.

They had gone five paces when the jaguar dropped down on them with a piercing shriek, like a shower of gold, landing on Sally's back with a muffled sound. The gun went off uselessly. Sally twisted while she fell; they hit the ground together, and the force of the blow knocked the jaguar off, but not before it had torn off half her shirt.

Tom threw himself on top of the animal's back, squeezing it between his legs like a bronco, clawing for its eyes with both thumbs to gouge them out; but before he could do it he felt the massive body flex and snap like a steel spring under him. The animal screamed again, leaping and twisting its body around in midair as Tom drew his machete. Then the animal was on top of him, a smothering of hot, rank fur bearing down on him and the pointed machete; Tom felt its flesh give; he could feel the blade slide up into the jaguar, and there was a powerful rush of hot blood in his face. The jaguar screamed, twisted, and with all his might Tom gave the machete a sideways jerk. The knife must have penetrated the animals' lungs, because the jaguar's scream turned into a suffocated gurgle. The animal went limp. Tom pushed it off him and pulled out the machete. The jaguar gave one more kick and then was still.

He rushed over to Sally, who was struggling to get up. She screamed when she saw him. "My God, Tom, are you all right?"

"Are *you* all right?"

"What did it do to you!" She tried to reach for his face, and he suddenly understood.

"It's not my blood, it's hers," he said weakly, bending over her. "Let me look at your back."

She rolled onto her stomach. The shirt was in tatters. There were four scores that ran across her shoulder. He pulled what remained of her shirt off.

"Hey, I'm fine," came her muffled voice.

"Quiet." Tom stripped off his own shirt and soaked one end in a puddle of water. "This is going to hurt."

She grunted slightly with pain as he cleaned out the wounds. They were not deep—the danger was mostly from infection. Tom took some moss and made a pad and tied it onto the wound with his shirt. He helped her put her shirt back on and sit up.

She looked at him again and winced. "My God, you're drenched in blood." She looked over at the jaguar, stretched out in all its golden glory on the ground, its eyes half open. "You killed her with your machete?"

"I had my machete out, and she jumped on it and did all the work herself." He put his arm around her. "Can you stand up?"

"Sure."

He helped her up, and she staggered a little, then recovered. "Give me my gun."

Tom fetched it. "I'll carry it."

"No, I'll just carry it over the other shoulder. You carry the peccary."

Tom didn't argue. He retied the peccary on the pole, slung it over his shoulder, and paused to take one last look at the jaguar stretched out on its side, its eyes glazed over, lying in a pool of blood.

"You're going to have one hell of a cocktail party story to tell when we get out of here," said Sally with a grin.

Back at the camp, Vernon and Don Alfonso listened to their story in silence. When Tom was finished Don Alfonso laid a hand on his shoulder, looked into his eyes, and said, "You are one crazy *yanqui*, Tomasito, you know that?"

Tom and Sally retreated into the privacy of the hut while he redoctored her wound with some of her own herbal antibiotics as she sat cross-legged on the ground with her shirt off, mending it with bark thread Don Alfonso had made. She kept looking at him out of the corner of her eye, trying to suppress a smile. Finally she said, "Have I thanked you for saving my life yet?"

"I don't need thanks." Tom tried to hide the flush in his face. It wasn't the first time he had seen her with her shirt off—they had long ago abandoned pretenses of privacy—but this time he felt an intense erotic charge. He noticed a blush creeping up her chest, spreading between her breasts, her nipples erect. Did she feel the same way?

"Yes, you do." She put down the shirt she was mending, turned around, put her arms around his neck, and kissed him softly on the lips.

39

Hauser halted his men at the river. Beyond he could see the blue flanks of the Sierra Azul rising into the clouds, like the lost world of Arthur Conan Doyle. He crossed the clearing himself and examined the muddy trail on the far side. The constant rain had washed away most marks, but it had the advantage of telling him that the bare footprints he saw must be very fresh—no more than a few hours old. It looked like a group of six men, a hunting party perhaps.

These, then, were the Indians that Broadbent had allied himself with. No one else lived in these godforsaken jungle mountains.

Hauser rose from his kneeling position and reflected for a moment. He would lose any cat-and-mouse chase in this jungle. He would get nothing from them by negotiation, either. That left only one sensible course of action.

He signaled the soldiers forward, taking the lead himself. They moved swiftly down the trail in the direction the men had gone. He had left Philip in the rear, well manacled, and guarded by a soldier. The Broadbent son was by now too weak to keep up and in no condition to escape, especially with manacles. It was a shame to lose the services of a soldier when he had so few competent ones, but when the time came Philip could be a useful bargaining chip. One should never underestimate the value of a hostage.

He ordered his men into double-time.

It unfolded exactly as he suspected. The Indians had heard them coming just in time and had melted into the forest—but not before Hauser had marked where they'd gone. He was an expert jungle tracker, and he pursued them at full press, a blitzkreig strategy that never failed to terrify even the most prepared enemy—let alone a group of unsuspecting hunters. His men split, and Hauser took himself and two others on a roundabout route, cutting off the Indians.

It was fast, furious, and earsplitting. The jungle shook. It brought back with such vividness his many firefights in Vietnam. In less than a minute it was over; trees were shattered and stripped, bushes smoking, the ground pulverized, an acrid haze drifting upward. One small tree had its branches hung with orchids and entrails.

It was amazing, really, what a couple of simple grenade launchers could do.

Hauser added up the body parts and determined that four men had been killed. Two others had escaped. For once his soldiers had acted competently. This is what they were good at: straight-ahead, uncomplicated killing. He would have to remember that.

There wasn't much time. He needed to reach the village shortly after the two survivors in order to strike at the moment of greatest confusion and terror, but before they could organize.

He turned and shouted to his men. *"Arriba! Vamonos!"*

The men cheered, heartened by his enthusiasm, finally in their element. "To the village!"

40

It rained for a week solid, without letup. Every day they pushed forward, up and down canyons, along precarious cliffs, across roaring streams, all of it buried in the thickest jungle Tom thought possible. If they made four miles it was a good day. After seven days of this Tom awoke one morning to find the rain had finally ceased. Don Alfonso was already up, tending a large fire. His face was grave. While they ate breakfast, he announced:

"I had a dream last night."

The serious tone in his voice gave Tom pause. "What kind of dream?"

"I dreamed that I died. My soul went up into the sky and began searching for St. Peter. I found him standing in front of the gates of heaven. He hailed me as I came up. 'Don Alfonso, is that you, you old rascal?' he asked. 'That's right,' I said. 'It is I, Don Alfonso Boswas, who died in the jungle far from home at the age of one hundred and twenty-one, and I want to come inside and see my Rosita.' 'What were you doing way out there in the jungle, Don Alfonso?' he asked. 'I was with some crazy *yanquis* going to the Sierra Azul,' I said. 'And did you get there?' he asked. 'No,' I said. 'Well then, Don Alfonso, you scoundrel, you'll have to go back.'"

He stopped, then added, "And so I came back."

Tom wasn't sure how to react. For a moment he thought the dream might be one of Don Alfonso's jokes, until he saw the serious look on the old man's face. He exchanged a glance with Sally.

"So what does this dream mean?" Sally asked.

Don Alfonso placed a piece of matta root inside his mouth and chewed thoughtfully, then leaned over to spit out the pulp. "It means I have only a few more days with you."

"A few more days? Don't be ridiculous."

Don Alfonso finished his stew and rose, saying, "Let us talk no more about this and go to the Sierra Azul."

That day was worse than before, for when the rains ceased the insects appeared. The travelers struggled up and down a succession of steep ridges on trails deep in muck, falling and sliding constantly, hounded by swarms. Toward afternoon they descended into another ravine echoing with the sound of roaring water. As they descended the roar became louder, and Tom realized a major river lay at the bottom. As the foliage broke at the banks of the river, Don Alfonso, who was in front, halted and retreated in confusion, motioning them to stay back in the trees.

"What's wrong?" Tom asked.

"There is a dead man across the river, under a tree."

"An Indian?"

"No, it is a person wearing North American clothing."

"Could it be an ambush?"

"No, Tomás, if it was an ambush we would already be dead."

Tom followed Don Alfonso to the riverbank. On the other side of the river, perhaps fifty yards up from the crossing point, there was a small natural clearing with a large tree in the middle. Tom could just see a bit of color behind the tree. He borrowed Vernon's binoculars to examine it more closely. A bare foot, horribly swollen, was visible, with part of a ragged pantleg in view. The rest of him was hidden behind the trunk. As Tom looked he saw a bluish puff of smoke drift from behind the tree, then another.

"Unless a dead man can smoke, that man's alive," said Tom.

"Mother of God, you are right."

They felled a tree across the river. The sound of the axe echoed through the forest, but whoever was behind the tree did not move.

After the tree had come crashing down, forming a wobbly bridge, Don Alfonso stared suspiciously across the river. "It may be a demon."

They crossed on the rickety tree using the pole. On the far side of the river they could no longer see the man.

"We must go on and pretend we have not seen him," whispered Don Alfonso. "I am sure now it is a demon."

"That's absurd," said Tom. "I'm going to check it out."

"Please do not go, Tomás. He will steal your soul and take it to the bottom of the river."

"I'll come with you," said Vernon.

"Curandera, you stay here. I do not want the demon to take all of you."

Tom and Vernon picked their way along the polished boulders on the riverbank, leaving Don Alfonso muttering unhappily to himself. They soon arrived at the clearing and stepped around the tree.

There, they beheld a wreck of a human being. He sat with his back against the tree, smoking a briar pipe, looking at them steadily. He did not seem to be an Indian, although his skin was almost black. His clothing was in tatters, and his face was scratched raw and bleeding from insect bites. His bare feet were cut and swollen. He was so thin, the bones of his body stuck out grotesquely, like a starving refugee's. His hair was stringy, and he had a short beard full of sticks and leaves.

He made no reaction to their arrival. He merely stared up at them out of hollow eyes. He looked more dead than alive. And then he gave a start, like a little shiver. The pipe came out of his mouth, and he spoke, his voice little more than a harsh whisper.

"How are you, brothers of mine?"

41

Tom jumped, he was so startled by hearing his brother Philip's voice coming from this living cadaver. He bent down to scrutinize the face, but he could find no point of resemblance. He recoiled in horror: Maggots were squirming in a sore on the man's neck.

"*Philip?*" Vernon whispered.

The voice croaked an affirmative.

"What are you doing here?"

"Dying." He spoke matter-of-factly.

Tom knelt and looked into his brother's face closer up. He was still too horrified to speak or react. He laid a hand on his brother's bony shoulder. "What happened?"

The figure closed its eyes for a moment, then opened them. "Later."

"Of course. What am I thinking?" Tom turned to his brother. "Vernon, go get Don Alfonso and Sally. Tell them we found Philip and that we're making camp here."

Tom continued looking at his brother, too shocked to speak. Philip was so utterly calm . . . it was as if he had already resigned himself to death. It was unnatural. There was the serenity of apathy in his eyes.

Don Alfonso arrived and, relieved to find that the river demon had turned out to be a human being, began clearing an area to set up camp.

When Philip saw Sally he removed the pipe and blinked.

"I'm Sally Colorado," she said, taking his hand in hers.

Philip managed a nod.

"We need to clean you up and doctor you."

"Thank you."

They carried Philip down to the river, laid him on a bed of banana leaves, and stripped him. Philip's body was covered with sores, many of which were infected and some of which were crawling with maggots. The maggots, Tom thought, examining the wounds, had actually been a boon, as they were consuming the septic tissue and reducing the chance of gangrene. He could see that in some of the wounds where the maggots had been at work there was already fresh granulation tissue. Others didn't look so good.

With an awful feeling he looked at his brother. They had no drugs, no antibiotics, no bandages, only Sally's herbs. They carefully washed him and then carried him back to the clearing and laid him down, stark naked, on a bed of palm leaves near the fire.

Sally began sorting the bundles of herbs and roots she had collected.

"Sally is an herbal healer," said Vernon.

Philip said, "I'd prefer an injection of amoxycillin."

"We don't have any."

Philip lay back on the leaves and closed his eyes. Tom doctored the sores, scraping out the necrotic flesh, irrigating and flushing out the maggots. Sally dusted the wounds with an herbal antibiotic and bandaged him up with strips of pounded bark that had been sterilized in boiling water and then smoke-dried in the fire. They washed and dried his tattered clothes and redressed him in them, having no others. They finished as the sun was beginning to set. They propped him up, and Sally brought in a mug of herbal tea.

Philip took the mug. He was looking better. He said, "Turn around, Sally, and let me check you for wings."

Sally blushed.

Philip took a sip and then another. Don Alfonso, meanwhile, had pulled a half dozen fish out of the stream and was now grilling them on skewers at the fire. The smell of roasting fish came wafting over.

"Strange how I have no appetite," said Philip.

"That's not uncommon when you're starving," said Tom.

Don Alfonso served out the fish on leaves. For a while they ate in silence, and then Philip spoke:

"Well well, here we are. A little family reunion in the Honduran jungle." Philip looked around, his eyes sparkling, and then he said: *"G."*

There was a silence and then Vernon said: *"H."*

Tom said *"O."*

Philip said *"S."*

There was a long silence and then Vernon said, "Goddamn it. *T."*

"Vernon has to wash the dishes!" crowed Philip.

Tom turned to Sally to explain. "It's a game we used to play," he said with a sheepish smile.

"I guess you three really are brothers."

"Sort of," said Vernon. "Even if Philip *is* an ass."

Philip let out a guffaw. "Poor Vernon. You always did end up in the kitchen, didn't you?"

"Glad to see you feeling better," said Tom.

Philip turned his hollow face to him. "I am."

"You feel like telling us what happened?"

Philip's face grew serious, losing all its archness. "It's a heart-of-darkness story, complete with a Mistah Kurtz. Are you sure you want to hear it?"

"Yes," said Tom. "We want to hear it."

42

Philip carefully filled his pipe from a tin of Dunhill Early Morning and lit it, his movements slow and deliberate. "The one thing they didn't take from me was my tobacco and pipe, thank God." He puffed slowly, his eyes half closed, gathering his thoughts.

Tom took the opportunity to examine Philip's face. Now that it had been cleaned up he could finally recognize his brother's long, aristocratic features. The beard gave him a raffish appearance that made him look curiously like their father. But the face was different: Something had happened to his brother, something so awful it had altered his basic features.

His pipe lit, Philip opened his eyes and began to speak.

"After I left you two, I flew back to New York and looked up Father's old partner, Marcus Aurelius Hauser. I figured that he would know better than anyone where Father might have gone. He was a private eye, of all things. I found him a rather plump, perfumed fellow. With two quick phone calls he was able to learn that Father had gone to Honduras, so I figured he was competent and hired him. We flew to Honduras; he organized an expedition and hired twelve soldiers and four boats. He financed it all by forcing me to sell the beautiful little Paul Klee watercolor that Father gave me—"

"Oh, Philip," Vernon said. "How could you?"

Philip closed his eyes wearily. Vernon fell silent. Then Philip continued: "So we all flew down to Brus and piled into dugout canoes for a jolly punt upriver. We picked up a guide in some backwater hamlet and proceeded across the Meambar Swamp. And then Hauser staged a coup. The pomaded prick had been planning it all along—he's one of those wicked micromanaging Nazi types. They chained me up like a dog. Hauser fed our guide to the piranhas and then set up that ambush to kill you."

At this his voice faltered, and he sucked on his pipe a few times, his bony hand trembling. The story was told with a certain humorous bravado that Tom knew well in his brother.

"After clapping me in chains, Hauser left five G.I. Josés behind on the Laguna Negra to ambush you all. He took me and the other soldiers up the Macaturi as far as the Falls. I'll never forget when the soldiers returned. There were only three of them, and one had a three-foot arrow sticking through his thigh. I couldn't hear all of what they said. Hauser was furious and took the man out, shot him point-blank in the head. I knew they had killed two people, and I was sure one or both of you were dead. I have to tell you, brothers of mine, that when you arrived, I thought I had died and gone to hell—and you were the reception committee." He gave a dry little laugh. "We left the boats at the Falls and followed Father's trail on foot. Hauser could track a mouse in the jungle if he had a mind to. He kept me around because he had the idea of using me as a bargaining chip with you. He ran into a group of mountain Indians, killed several, and chased the rest back to the village. He then attacked the village and managed to capture the chief. I didn't see any of this, I was kept behind under ball and chain, but I saw the results."

He shuddered. "Once he had the chief as a hostage, we made our way up into the mountains toward the White City."

"Hauser knows it's the White City?"

"He learned it from an Indian prisoner. But he doesn't know where the tomb is in the White City. Apparently only the chief and a few elders know the exact location of father's tomb."

"How did you escape?" Tom asked.

Philip closed his eyes. "Kidnapping the chief stirred up the Indians to war. They attacked Hauser while he was en route to the White City. Even with their heavy weapons Hauser and his men had their hands

full. He'd taken the chains off me to use them on the chief. At the
height of the attack I managed to get away. I spent the last ten days
walking—crawling, actually—back here, surviving on insects and
lizards. Three days ago I reached this river. There was no way to cross. I
was starving, and I couldn't walk anymore. So I sat down under a tree
to wait for the end."

"You were sitting under that tree for three days?"

"Three, four days—God only knows. They all ran together."

"My God, Philip, how awful."

"On the contrary. It was a refreshing feeling. Because I didn't care
anymore. About anything. I'd never felt so free in my life as while I
was sitting under that tree. I believe I might have actually been happy
for a moment or two."

The fire had died down. Tom added a few more sticks and stirred it
back to life.

"Did you see the White City?" Vernon asked.

"I escaped before they got there."

"How far is it from here to the Sierra Azul?"

"Ten miles, maybe, to the foothills, and another ten or twelve to the
city."

There was a silence. The fire crackled, hissed. A bird sang a mourn-
ful song in a distant tree. Philip closed his eyes and murmured, his
voice heavy with sarcasm, "Dear old Father, what a fine legacy you left
to your adoring children."

43

The temple lay buried in lianas, the front colonnade supported by square pillars of limestone streaked with green moss, holding up part of a stone roof. Hauser stood outside, looking at the curious hieroglyphics carved into the pillars, the strange faces, animals, dots, and lines. It reminded him of the Codex.

"Stay outside," he said to his men and slashed a hole in the screen of vegetation. It was gloomy. He shined a flashlight around. There were no snakes or jaguars, just a mess of spiders in one corner and some mice scurrying away. It was dry and sheltered—a good place to establish his headquarters.

He strolled deeper into the temple. At the back stood another row of square stone pillars framing a ruined doorway leading out to a gloomy courtyard. He stepped through. A few statues lay tumbled about, deeply eroded by time, wet in the rain. Great roots of trees snaked over the stones like fat anacondas, heaving apart walls and roofs, until the trees themselves became an integral part of what was holding the structure together. On the far side of the courtyard a second doorway led into a small chamber with a carved stone man lying on his back, holding a bowl.

Hauser came back out to his waiting soldiers. Two of them held between them the captured chief, a bowed old man, almost naked except for a loincloth and a piece of leather tied over his shoulder and belted around his waist. His body was one mass of wrinkles. He was just about the oldest-looking man Hauser had ever seen—and yet he knew he probably wasn't older than sixty. The jungle ages you fast.

Hauser gestured to the *teniente*. "We'll stay here. Have the soldiers clean this room out for my cot and table." He nodded to the old man. "Chain him in the small room across the courtyard and put a guard on him."

The soldiers hustled the old Indian chief into the temple. Hauser settled himself down on a block of stone and drew a fresh cigar tube from his shirt pocket, unscrewed the cap, and slid the cigar out. It was still covered in a cedarwood wrapper. He smelled the wrapper, crushed it in his hand, smelled it again, inhaling the exquisite fragrance, and then began the ritual that he loved so well of lighting the cigar.

As he smoked, he looked at the ruins of a pyramid directly in front of him. It was nothing like Chichén Itzá or Copán, but as Mayan pyramids went it was impressive enough. Important burials were often found in pyramids. Hauser was convinced old Max had reburied himself in a tomb he once robbed. If so, it had to be an important tomb, to hold all of Max's stuff.

The stairway going up the pyramid had been heaved apart by tree roots, which had levered out many blocks and sent them tumbling to the bottom. At the top was the small room held up by four square pillars, with four doors and a shallow stone altar where the Maya sacrificed their victims. Hauser inhaled. That would have been something to see, the priest splitting the victim at the breastbone, wrenching apart the rib cage, cutting out the beating heart and holding it up with a shriek of triumph while the body was tumbled down the stairs, to be hacked up by waiting nobles and made into corn stew.

What barbarians.

Hauser smoked with pleasure. The White City was fairly impressive even covered as it was by vegetation. Max had hardly scratched the surface. There was a great deal more worth taking here. Even a simple block with, say, a jaguar head carved on it could fetch a hundred grand. He'd have to be careful to keep the location secret.

In its heyday the White City would have been amazing—Hauser could almost see it in his mind's eye: the temples new and gleaming white, the ball games (where the losers lost their heads), the roaring crowds of spectators, the processions of the priests decked out in gold, feathers, and jade. And what had happened? Now their descendants lived in bark huts and their head priest was a man in rags. Funny how things change.

He drew in another lungful of smoke. It was true that not all had gone according to plan. No matter. Long experience had taught him that any op was an exercise in improvisation. Those who thought they could plan an op and execute it flawlessly always died following the book. That was his great strength: improvisation. Human beings were inherently unpredictable.

Take Philip. In that first meeting he had seemed all show in his expensive suit, with his affected mannerisms and phony upper-class accent. He could still scarcely believe the man had managed to escape. He would probably expire in the jungle—he was already on his last legs when he made off—but still, Hauser was concerned. And impressed. Perhaps a little of Max had rubbed off on the effete little bastard after all. Max. What a crazy old shit he'd turned out to be.

The main thing was to keep his priorities straight. The Codex, first, and then the rest of the stuff, later. And then third, the White City itself. Over the past few years Hauser had followed with interest the looting of Site Q. The White City was going to be his Site Q.

He examined the end of his cigar, holding it up so the curl of smoke tickled his nostrils. The cigars had weathered the journey through the rainforest well—you might even say they'd improved.

The *teniente* came out and saluted. "Ready, sir."

Hauser followed him into the ruined temple. The soldiers were fixing up the outer part, raking up the animal crap, burning out the cobwebs, sprinkling water to keep down the dust, and carpeting the ground with cut ferns. He ducked through the low stone doorway into the inner courtyard, passed by the tumbled statues, and went into the room in the back. The wizened old Indian was chained up to one of the stone pillars. Hauser shined the light on him. He was an old bugger, but he returned the gaze, and there wasn't even a trace of fear on his face. Hauser didn't like that. It reminded him of the face of Ocotal. These damn Indians were like the Viet Cong.

"Thank you, Teniente," he said to the soldier.

"Who will translate? He speaks no Spanish."

"I'll make myself understood."

The *teniente* withdrew. Hauser looked at the Indian, and once again the Indian returned the look. Not defiant, not angry, not fearful—just observing.

Hauser seated himself on the corner of the stone altar, carefully rubbed the ash off his cigar, which had gone out, and relit it.

"My name's Marcus," he said with a smile. He could already feel this was going to be a hard case. "Here's the situation, chief. I want you to tell me where you and your people buried Maxwell Broadbent. If you do, no problem, we'll just go in there, take what we want, and leave you in peace. If you don't, bad things will happen to you and your people. I'll discover the location of the tomb and rob it anyway. So which way do you want to go?"

He looked up at the man, puffing vigorously on the cigar, getting a good red tip going. The man hadn't understood a word. No matter. He was no fool: He knew what Hauser wanted.

"Maxwell Broadbent?" Hauser repeated slowly, enunciating every syllable. He made a universal gesture indicating a question, a shrug with hands turned up.

The Indian said nothing. Hauser rose and walked toward the old man, puffing vigorously on the cigar, getting a good long glow to the tip. Then he stopped, removed the cigar from his mouth, and held it up in front of the man's face. "Care for a cigar?"

44

Philip's story was over. The sun had set long ago, and the fire had fallen to a vermilion heap of coals. Tom could hardly believe what his brother had endured.

Sally spoke first. "Hauser's committing genocide up there."

There was an uneasy silence.

"We've got to do *something*."

"Like what?" Vernon asked. His voice sounded tired.

"We go to the mountain Indians, offer our services. In partnership with them, we can defeat Hauser."

Don Alfonso spread his hands. "Curandera, they will kill us before we can speak."

"I'll go into the village, unarmed. They won't kill an unarmed woman."

"Yes they will. And what can we do? We have one rifle against professional soldiers with automatic weapons. We are weak. We are hungry. We do not even have a change of clothes among us—and we have a man who cannot walk."

"So what are you suggesting?"

"It is over. We must go back."

"You said we'd never get across the swamp."

"Now we know they left their boats at the Macaturi Falls. We go and steal them."

"And then?" Sally asked.

"I go back to Pito Solo and you go home."

"And just leave Hauser up here, killing everyone?"

"Yes."

Sally was furious. "I don't accept that. He's got to be stopped. We'll contact the government, have them send in troops to arrest him."

Don Alfonso looked very tired. "Curandera, the government will do nothing."

"How do you know?"

"This man has already made arrangements with the government. We can do nothing except accept our powerlessness."

"I don't accept it!"

Don Alfonso gazed at her with old, sad eyes. He carefully scraped out his pipe, knocked the crumbs out, filled it, and relit it with a stick from the fire. "Many years ago," he said, "when I was a boy, I remember when the first white man came to our village. He was a small man with a big hat and a pointed beard. We thought he might be a ghost. He took out these turdlike yellow lumps of metal and asked if we had seen anything like it. His hands were shaking, and there was a crazy light in his eyes. We were frightened and said no. A month later in the annual flood his rotting boat floated back down the river, and there was nothing in it but his skull and his hair. We burned the boat and pretended it had never happened.

"The next year a man in a black dress and hat came up the river. He was a kind man, and he gave us food and crosses and dunked us all in the river and said he had saved us. He stayed with us for a few months and got a woman with child, and then he tried to cross the swamp. We never saw him again.

"After that came more of the men looking for the yellow shit, which they called *oro*. They were even crazier than the first, and they molested our daughters and stole our boats and food and went upriver. One came back, but he had no tongue, so we never knew what happened to him. Then came new men with crosses, and each one said the other men's crosses were not the good kind, that theirs was the only good one, the rest were junk. They dunked us in the river again, then the others redunked us saying the first ones had done it wrong, then others came and dunked us again, until we were thoroughly wet and confused.

Later, a white man came all by himself, lived with us, learned our language, and told us that all the men with crosses were deficients. He called himself an *anthropologist*. He spent a year prying into all our private business, asking us a lot of stupid questions about things like sex and who was related to who, what happened to us after we died, what we ate and drank, how we made war, how we cooked a pig. As we talked he wrote it all down. The wicked young men of the tribe, of which I was one, told him many outrageous falsehoods, and he wrote them all down with a serious face and said he was going to put them into a book that everyone in America would read and that would make us famous. We thought that was hilarious.

"Then men came upriver with soldiers, and they had guns and papers, and we all signed the papers, and then they said we had agreed to have a new chief, much bigger than the village chief, and that we had agreed to give him all the land and animals and trees and all the minerals and oil underground, if there was any, which we thought was very funny. They gave us a picture of our new chief. He was very ugly with a face as pockmarked as a pineapple. When our real chief protested, they took him into the forest and shot him.

"Then soldiers and men with briefcases came and said that there had been a *revolution* and that we had a new chief, that the old one had been shot. They told us to make marks on more papers, and then more missionaries came and made schools and brought medicines, and they tried to catch the boys and take them away to school, but they never could.

"In those days we had a very wise chief, my grandfather, Don Cali. One day he called everyone together. He said that we needed to understand these new people who acted like madmen but were as crafty as demons. We had to learn who these people really were. He asked for volunteers among the boys. I volunteered. The next time the missionaries came I let myself be captured and sent to boarding school in La Ceiba. They cut my hair and put me in itchy clothes and hot shoes and beat me for speaking Tawahka. I stayed there ten years, and I learned how to speak Spanish and English, and I saw with my own eyes who the white men were. That was my job: to understand them.

"I came back and told my people what I had learned. They said,

'This is terrible, what can we do?' And I said, 'Leave it to me. We will resist them by agreeing with them.'

"After that, I knew what to say to the men who came to our village with briefcases and soldiers. I knew how to read the papers. I knew when to sign the papers and when to lose them and act the fool. I knew what to say to the Jesus men to get medicine, food, and clothes. Every time they brought a picture of the new chief and told me to throw away the picture of the old chief, I thanked them and hung the new picture up in my hut with flowers.

"And that is how I came to be chief of Pito Solo. And so you see, Curandera, I understand how things are. There is nothing we can do to help the mountain Indians. We will be throwing away our lives for nothing."

Sally said, "I, personally, can't just walk away."

Don Alfonso laid a hand on hers. "Curandera, for a woman you are the bravest I have ever met."

"Don't start on that again, Don Alfonso."

"You are even braver than most men I have known. Do not underestimate the mountain Indians. I would not want to be one of these soldiers in the hands of the mountain Indians, with my last sight on earth that of seeing my manhood spit-roasting on an open fire."

No one spoke for a few minutes. Tom felt tired, very, very tired. "It's our fault, Don Alfonso, that this is happening. Or rather, our father's fault. We're responsible."

"Tomás, none of this means anything, this business of your fault, his fault, my fault. We can do nothing. We are powerless."

Philip nodded in agreement. "I've had it with this crazy journey. We can't save the world."

"I agree," said Vernon.

Tom found them all looking at him. A vote of sorts was being taken, and he had to decide. He found Sally looking at him with a certain curiosity. He just couldn't see himself giving up. He had come too far. "I'll never be able to live with myself if we just go back. I'm with Sally."

But it was still three against two.

. . .

Even before the sun rose, Don Alfonso was up and breaking camp. The usually inscrutable Indian was frightened out of his wits.

"There was a mountain Indian not half a mile from our camp last night. I saw his tracks. I am not afraid of death myself. But I have already caused Pingo's and Chori's deaths, and I do not want any more blood on my hands."

Tom watched Don Alfonso flinging together their meager belongings. He felt sick. It was over. Hauser had won.

Sally said, "Wherever Hauser goes with that codex, whatever he does, I'm going to be on his trail. He'll never escape me. We may be returning to civilization, but I'm coming back. This isn't over by any means."

Philip's feet were still infected, leaving him unable to walk. Don Alfonso wove a carrying hammock, something like a stretcher with two short poles that went across the shoulders. It didn't take long to pack. When the time came to leave, Tom and Vernon hoisted him up. They set off single file through the narrow corridor of vegetation, Sally in front wielding the machete, Don Alfonso taking up the rear.

"Sorry to be such a nuisance," said Philip, taking out his pipe.

"You are a damn nuisance," Vernon said.

"Allow me to beat my breast with remorse."

Tom listened to his two brothers. It had always been like this, a kind of half-joking banter. Sometimes it stayed friendly, sometimes not. Tom was glad, in a way, to see Philip well enough to start chaffing Vernon.

"Gee, I hope I don't slip and drop you in a mudhole," said Vernon.

Don Alfonso made one last pass among them, checking their packs. "We must be as silent as possible," he said. "And no smoking, Philip. They will smell it."

Philip swore and put the pipe away. It began to rain. Carrying Philip proved to be far more difficult than Tom anticipated. It was almost impossible to haul him up the slippery trails. Carrying him across wobbly logs laid across roaring rivers was an exercise in terror. Don Alfonso kept a vigilant eye out and enforced a strict regime of silence; even the use of the machete was forbidden. Utterly exhausted, they camped that afternoon on the only level piece of ground they could find, a wallow of mud. The rain poured buckets, the water streaming into the feeble hut Vernon built, and the mud covered everything. Tom and Sally went off to hunt and wandered through the forest for two hours, seeing nothing. Don Alfonso forbid the lighting of a fire, for fear of the smell. Their dinner than night was a raw root that tasted like cardboard and a couple of rotten fruits riddled with little white worms.

The rain continued to pour down, turning the streams into boiling torrents. Ten hours of grueling effort carried them only about three miles. The next day and the next were more of the same. The hunting was impossible, and Don Alfonso could not catch any fish. They subsisted on roots and berries and the odd rotten fruit that Don Alfonso was able to scrounge up. By the fourth day they had managed to travel less than ten miles. Philip, in his already half-starved condition, was weakening rapidly. The hollow look returned to his face. Unable to smoke, he spent most of his day staring up into the jungle canopy, hardly responding when spoken to. They weakened from the physical effort of carrying the hammock and had to rest ever more frequently. Don Alfonso seemed to shrink, his bones sticking out horribly, his skin loose and wrinkled. Tom forgot what it was like to have dry clothes.

On the fifth day, around noon, Don Alfonso called a halt. He reached down to pluck something off the trail. It was a feather with a tiny piece of plaited twine attached to it.

"Mountain Indians," he whispered, his voice quavering. "This is fresh."

There was a silence.

"We must get off the trail now."

Following the trail had been bad enough. Now walking became almost impossible. They pushed into a wall of ferns and lianas so thick that it seemed to push back at them. They crawled under and climbed over fallen trees, waded through boggy pools with the mud sometimes to their waists. The vegetation was riddled with ants and stinging insects, which when disturbed dropped down on them with a fury, crawling about their hair, falling inside their collars, stinging and biting. Philip suffered the most of all as his hammock was dragged and wrestled through the dense undergrowth. Don Alfonso insisted they travel off the trail.

It was pure hell. The rain never let up. They took turns hacking a path a few hundred yards long through the dense undergrowth; then two of them would carry Philip in his hammock along the path. There they would stop and take turns cutting another hundred yards through the forest. They proceeded this way at the speed of two hundred yards an hour for two more days, without a single letup in the downpour, wading through knee-deep mud, sliding and sometimes crawling uphill and falling and sliding back down again. Most of the buttons had come off Tom's shirt, and his shoes had fallen apart so badly that he had cut his feet on several occasions on sharp sticks. The rest were in a similar state of raggedness. The forest was empty of game. The days merged into one long struggle through twilight thickets and rain-loud swamps, where they were stung and bitten so continuously that their skin took on the raw texture of burlap. It now took all four of them to lift Philip, and sometimes they had to rest for an hour just to carry him a dozen yards.

Tom began to lose all track of time. The end was soon coming, he realized: the moment when they could go no farther. He felt strange, light-headed. The nights and days blended into one another. He fell in the mud and lay there until Sally pulled him up, and then, half an hour later, he would have to do the same for her.

They arrived at an open area where a giant tree had fallen, opening a hole in the forest canopy. The ground around it was, for once, relatively level. The giant tree had fallen in such a way that it was possible to shelter under its enormous trunk.

Tom could barely walk. By silent mutual consent, they all stopped to camp. He felt so weak that he wondered if, once having lain down, he'd be able to get up again. With the last of their strength the group cut poles and laid them against the trunk, thatching them with ferns. It seemed to be around noon. They crawled underneath and huddled together, lying directly on the wet ground in two inches of mud. Later, Sally and Tom made another attempt at hunting, but they returned well before dark empty-handed. They huddled under the log as the long darkness descended.

By the dying light Tom examined his brother Philip. He was in a desperate condition. He had been running a fever and had become semicoherent. There were great hollows where his cheeks used to be and heavy rings under his eyes; his arms were like sticks with swollen elbows. Some of the infections they had so carefully treated had reopened, and fresh maggots were there. Tom felt his heart breaking. Philip was dying.

Tom knew, in his gut, that none of them was going to be leaving that miserable little clearing.

The listless apathy of incipient starvation overtook them all. Tom lay awake most of that night, unable to sleep. The rain lifted during the night, and when dawn came the sunlight broke over the treetops. For the first time in weeks he could see blue sky—spotless blue sky. Sunlight streamed down through the opening in the treetops. Banners of light caught columns of insects, turning them into whirling tornadoes of light. Steam rose from the giant log.

It was so ironic: The break in the trees framed a picture-perfect view of the Sierra Azul. Here they had been struggling for a week in the opposite direction, and the mountains looked even closer than ever: the peaks rising through tatters of cloud, as blue as cut sapphires. Tom no longer felt hungry. *This is what starvation does to you,* he thought.

He felt a hand on his shoulder. It was Sally.

"Come over here." She spoke in a grave voice.

Tom was suddenly afraid. "It's not Philip?"

"No. It's Don Alfonso."

Tom got up and followed Sally down the length of trunk to where Don Alfonso had laid his hammock directly on the wet ground. He was lying on his side, staring at the Sierra Azul. Tom knelt and took his withered old hand. It was hot.

"I am sorry, Tomasito, but I am a useless old man. I am so useless that I am dying."

"Don't talk like that, Don Alfonso." He put his hand on Don Alfonso's forehead and was shocked by the heat.

"Death has come calling, and one cannot say to Death, 'Come back next week, I'm busy.'"

"Did you dream of St. Peter again last night or something?" Sally asked.

"One does not need to dream of St. Peter to know when the end has come."

Sally glanced at Tom. "Do you have any idea what he's got?"

"Without diagnostic tests, bloodwork, a microscope . . ." He swore and stood up, fighting a wave of faintness. *We've had it*, he thought. It made him angry in some vague way. It wasn't fair.

He brushed those useless thoughts out of his head and checked on Philip. He was sleeping. Like Don Alfonso he had a high fever, and Tom wasn't even sure he would ever awaken. Vernon got a fire going despite Don Alfonso's muttered entreaties not to light one, and Sally brewed a medicinal tea. His whole face had sagged, collapsing inward, the skin losing its color and taking on a waxy hue. His breathing was labored, but he was still conscious. "I will drink your tea, Curandera," he said, "but not even your medicine will save me."

She knelt. "Don Alfonso, you've talked yourself into dying. You can talk yourself out of it."

He took her hand. "No, Curandera, my time has come."

"You can't *know* that."

"My death was foretold."

"I don't want to hear any more absurdities. You can't see into the future."

"When I was a little boy, I had a bad fever, and my mother took me to a *bruja*, a witch. The *bruja* told me that my time of dying was not then, but that I would die far from home, among strangers, within sight of blue mountains." His eyes glanced up at the Sierra Azul, framed in the gap in the treetops.

"She could have been talking about any blue mountains."

"Curandera, she was talking about those mountains, which are as blue as the great ocean itself."

Sally blinked away a tear. "Don Alfonso, quit talking nonsense."

At this, Don Alfonso smiled. "It is a wonderful thing when an old man has a beautiful girl weeping at his deathbed."

"This isn't your deathbed, and I'm not crying."

"Do not worry, Curandera. This is no surprise to me. I came on this journey knowing it would be my last. I was a useless old man back in Pito Solo. I did not want to die in my hut a weak, foolish old person. I, Don Alfonso Boswas, I wanted to die as a *man*." He paused, drew a breath, shuddered. "Only I did not think I would die under a rotten log in the stinking mud, leaving you alone."

"Then don't die. We love you, Don Alfonso. The hell with that *bruja*."

Don Alfonso took her hand and smiled. "Curandera, there is one thing the *bruja* got wrong. She said I was going to die among strangers. This is not true. I die among friends."

He closed his eyes and murmured something, and then he died.

45

Sally wept. Tom stood up and looked away, feeling his unreasonable anger grow. He walked a little way into the forest. There, in a quiet glade, he sat on a log, clenching and unclenching his fists. The old man had no right to leave them. He had abandoned himself to his superstitions. He had talked himself into dying—just because he had glimpsed some blue mountains.

Tom thought back to the first time he saw Don Alfonso, sitting on the little stool in his hut, waving his machete and joking. It seemed a lifetime ago.

They dug a grave in the mucky ground. It was a slow, exhausting process, and they were so weak they could barely lift the shovel. Tom couldn't help thinking, *When will I be doing this for Philip? Tomorrow?* They finished the grave around noon, wrapped Don Alfonso's body in his hammock, rolled him into the waterlogged hole, and threw some damp flowers on top. Then they filled in the hole with mud. Tom fashioned a rough cross lashed with vines and planted it at the head of the grave. They stood around awkwardly afterward.

"I'd like to say a few words," said Vernon.

He stood, swaying a little. His clothes hung on his body, and his beard and hair were wild. He looked like a mendicant.

"Don Alfonso . . ." his voice trailed off. He coughed. "If you're still around somewhere, before heading up to the Pearly Gates, stick around a bit and help us out, will you, old man? We're in a bad way."

"Amen," Sally said.

Dark clouds began to roll in, ending their short, sunny respite. There was a roll of thunder and a scattered sound of drops in the canopy above.

Sally came to Tom. "I'm going hunting again."

Tom nodded. He took the fishing line and decided to try his luck in the river they had crossed about a mile back. Vernon stayed to take care of Philip.

They returned in the early afternoon. Sally had caught nothing, Tom returned with a single fish that weighed no more than six ounces. While they were gone Philip had developed a high fever and delirium. His eyes were open and glittered with heat, and he moved his head back and forth in a ceaseless pattern, mumbling disconnected phrases. Tom felt sure his brother was now dying. When they tried to get him to drink the tea Sally made, he began shouting incoherently and knocked the cup away. They boiled the fish in a pot with some manioc root and spoon-fed the stew to Philip, who finally accepted it after more shouting and thrashing. They divided the rest among themselves. After eating, they remained under the log as the rain poured down, waiting for darkness to come.

Tom was the first to wake, just before dawn. Philip's fever had worsened over the night. He tossed and mumbled, his fingers pluck-ing uselessly at his collar, his face looking collapsed and emaciated. Tom felt desperate. They had no medicine and no diagnostic tools, not even a medical kit. Sally's herbal medicines were ineffectual in the face of this raging fever.

Vernon built a fire, and they sat around it in a devastated silence. The dark ferns loomed about them like a menacing crowd, nodding their heads under the impact of the rain, casting a green dimness over their refuge.

Tom finally spoke. "We're going to have to stay here until Philip recovers."

Sally and Vernon nodded, although they all knew Philip was not going to recover.

"We'll make an all-out effort to hunt, fish, and gather edible plants. We'll use this time to build up our strength and get ready for the long trip home."

Again everyone agreed.

"All right," said Tom, rising. "Let's get to work. Sally will go hunting. I'm going to take the fishing line and hooks. Vernon, you stay here and take care of Philip." He looked around. "No giving up."

They all stood up shakily, and Tom was glad to see a rousing of energy among them. He collected the line and hooks and pushed off into the jungle. He went in a straight line away from the Sierra Azul, tearing notches in the sides of ferns as he passed to mark his trail and keeping an eye out for any edible plants. The rain was still falling steadily. Two hours later he arrived, exhausted, at a muddy cascade of water, having caught a small lizard to use as bait. He hooked the struggling reptile on the hook and tossed it into the boiling torrent.

Five hours later, with just enough light to get back to camp, he quit. He had lost three of six hooks and a good portion of fishing line and had caught nothing. He returned to camp before dark to find Vernon tending the fire. Sally was still out.

"How is Philip?"

"Not good."

Tom looked in on Philip and found him tossing in a restless sleep, drifting in and out of a dreamlike state, muttering snatches of conversation. The slackness in his face and lips scared Tom; it reminded him of Don Alfonso's last moments. Philip seemed to be having a one-sided conversation with their father, a broken series of grievances and accusations. His own name came into it, and Vernon's, and Philip's mother, whom he had not seen in twenty years. And then Philip seemed to be at a birthday party, a child's party. It was his fifth birthday, it seemed, and he was opening presents and exclaiming with joy.

Tom went away pained and saddened. He sat down next to Vernon at the fire. Vernon put his arm around him. "He's been like that all day." He handed him a mug of tea.

Tom took the mug and drank. His own hand looked like the hand of an old man, veiny and splotched. His stomach felt hollow, but he was not hungry.

"Sally hasn't come back?"

"No, but I heard a couple of shots."

As if on cue, they heard the rustle of vegetation and Sally appeared. She said nothing, just slung her rifle down and sat by the fire.

"No luck?" Tom asked.

"Bagged a couple of stumps."

Tom smiled and took her hand. "None of the stumps in the forest will be safe as long as the great hunter Sally stalks her prey."

Sally wiped the mud off her face. "I'm sorry."

"Tomorrow," said Tom, "if I leave early I might be able to hike back to the river where we found Philip. I'll be gone overnight, but that was a big river, and I'm sure I'll catch a mess of fish."

"Great idea, Tom," said Vernon, his voice strained.

"We're not going to give up."

"No," said Sally.

Vernon shook his head. "I wonder what Father would think if he saw us now."

Tom shook his head. He was past thinking of Maxwell Broadbent. If he knew what he'd done, sent his three sons to their deaths . . . It didn't bear thinking about. They'd failed him while he was alive, and now they'd failed him after his death.

Tom stared at the fire for a while and then asked, "Are you angry at Father?"

Vernon hesitated. "Yes."

Tom made a helpless gesture with his hand. "Do you think we'll be able to forgive him?"

"Does it matter?"

Tom woke up before dawn with a strange feeling of pressure at the base of his skull. It was still dark, and it was raining. The sound of the rain seemed to be crawling inside his head. He turned, turned again on the damp ground, and the pressure became a headache. He swung his feet around and sat up, only to find, with huge surprise, that he could barely keep himself upright. He sank back, his head reeling, staring up into the darkness, which seemed to fill with confused swirls of red and brown and the whispering of voices. He heard the soft, worried chatter of Bugger's voice near him. He looked around and finally, in the darkness, located the little monkey sitting on the ground near him, making anxious sucking noises. He knew something was wrong.

It was more than just the effects of hunger. Tom realized he was sick. *Oh God,* he thought, *not now.* He turned his head and tried to seek out Sally or Vernon in the swirling darkness, but he could see nothing. His nose seemed to be filled with the cloying smell of rotting vegetation, rain, and loam. The sound of the rain drumming on the forest leaves all around him was drilling into his skull. He felt himself drift off to sleep, and then he opened his eyes and there was Sally, peering at him with a flashlight in the dark.

"I'm going fishing today," Tom said.

"You're not going anywhere," she answered. She reached down and felt his forehead, and she was not able to hide from him the look of fright on her face. "I'll bring you some tea."

She came back with a steaming mug and helped Tom drink it down. "You sleep," she said.

Tom slept.

When he woke, it was brighter but still raining. Sally was crouching over him. When she saw his eyes open, she tried to smile.

Despite the suffocating heat under the log, he shivered. "Philip?" he managed to ask.

"The same."

"Vernon?"

"He's sick, too."

"Damn." He looked at Sally and felt alarmed. "And you? How are you?" Her face looked flushed. "You're not getting sick, too?"

Sally laid a hand on his cheek. "Yes, I'm getting sick, too."

"I'll get better," Tom said. "And then I'll take care of you. We'll get out of this mess."

She shook her head. "No, Tom, we won't."

The simple assertion of fact seemed to clear his throbbing head. He closed his eyes. That was it, then. They were going to die in the rain under that rotten log, and the wild animals would tear them apart. And no one would ever know what had happened to them. He tried to say this was the fever talking to him, that actually things weren't that bad, but deep down he knew it was true. His head swirled. They were going to die. He opened his eyes.

She was still there, her hand on his cheek. She looked at him for a long time. Her face was dirty, scratched, bitten; her hair tangled and dull, her eyes hollow. If there was any resemblance to the girl who had galloped after him bareback in Utah, it was gone—except the intense turquoise color of her eyes and the way her lower lip still stuck out a little.

Finally she spoke. "We don't have much time." She paused, looking at him steadily. "I need to tell you something, Tom."

"What?"

"It seems I've fallen in love with you."

Reality returned with sudden clarity. Tom couldn't quite speak.

She went on briskly. "Anyway, there—now it's said."

"But what about—?"

"Julian? He's the perfect dream guy, handsome, brilliant, with all the right opinions. He's the guy your parents want you to marry. He's my Sarah. Who wants that? The feeling I had for him isn't at all like what I feel for you, with all your . . ." She hesitated and smiled. "Imperfections?"

With those words all complications had been swept away, and now everything was clear and simple. He tried to speak, finally managed to croak out the words. "I love you, too."

She smiled, and a little glimmer of her former radiance came through. "I know that and I'm glad. I'm sorry I was cranky with you. I was in denial."

They were silent for a moment.

"I guess I loved you from the moment you stole my horse and came riding after me back there in Utah," said Tom. "But I really knew it when you wouldn't shoot that jaguar. I'll always love you for that."

"When you brought me outside to look at that glowing forest," Sally said, "that's when I realized that I was falling in love with you."

"You never said anything."

"It took me a while to work it out. As you may have noticed, I'm stubborn. I didn't want to admit I was wrong."

He swallowed. His head was beginning to spin. "But I'm just a normal guy. I didn't go to Stanford at sixteen—"

"Normal? A man who fights in hand-to-hand combat with jaguars and anacondas? Who leads an expedition into the heart of darkness with courage and good humor?"

"I only did those things because I was forced to."

"That's another one of your good points: You're modest. Being with you, I began to see what kind of a person Julian is. He didn't want to come with me because he figured it would be inconvenient. It would interrupt his work. And I think, underneath it all, he was afraid. Julian, I realized, is the kind of person who doesn't attempt anything unless he's absolutely sure he's going to succeed. You, on the other hand, would attempt the impossible."

His head began to swim again. He struggled to hold it still. He loved what he was hearing.

She smiled sadly and laid her head on his chest. "I'm sorry we've both run out of time."

He put his hand on her hair. "This is a hell of a place to fall in love."

"You're not kidding."

"Maybe in another life . . ." Tom struggled to maintain his hold on reality. "We'll have another chance, somehow . . . somewhere . . ." His mind began to whirl. What was he trying to say? He closed his eyes, trying to steady the vertigo, but that only made it worse. He tried opening his eyes, but there was nothing but a swirl of green and brown, and he wondered briefly if it all hadn't just been a dream, all of it, his father's cancer, the journey, the jungle, Sally, his dying brother. Yes, in fact it *had* been a dream, he realized, long and strange, and he was going to wake up in his own bed, a little boy again, his father shouting upstairs, "Good morning, good morning, another day is dorning!"

Thinking this, he drifted into oblivion, happy.

46

Marcus Hauser sat on a campstool in the doorway of the ruined temple, taking in the morning. A toucan screeched and hopped around in a nearby tree, waggling its enormous beak. It was a glorious day, the sky a limpid blue, the jungle a hushed green. It was cooler and drier up in these mountains, and the air seemed fresher. The perfume of an unknown flower drifted past. Hauser felt a semblance of peace returning. It had been a long night, and he felt drained, empty, and disappointed.

He heard footsteps rustling the fallen leaves. One of the soldiers brought him his breakfast—bacon, eggs, coffee, fried plantain—on an enamel plate with a sprig of some herb garnishing the side. He took the dish on his knees. The garnish irritated him, so he flicked it off, then picked up his fork and began to eat, his mind on the events of the previous night. It had been time to force the issue with the chief or fail. Not ten minutes into it he knew the old chief wouldn't crack, but he went through the motions anyway. It was like watching a pornographic film—unable to turn it off, yet in the end cursing the waste of time and energy. He had tried. He had done his best. Now he had to think of another solution to his problem.

Two soldiers appeared in the doorway, the body slung between them. "What should we do with it, *jefe?*"

Hauser pointed with his fork, his mouth full of eggs. "Into the gorge."

They went out, and he finished his breakfast. The White City was a big, overgrown place. Max could be buried almost anywhere. Problem was, the village was so stirred up that there wasn't much chance of taking another hostage and trying to squeeze the location of the tomb out of him. On the other hand, he didn't relish poking around these rat-infested ruins for the next two weeks himself.

He broke off, felt in his pockets, and slipped out a slender aluminum tube. In a minute the ritual was complete and the cigar was lit. He inhaled deeply, feeling the calming effects of the nicotine spreading from his lungs to his body. All problems could be broken down into options and suboptions. There were two: He could find the tomb on his own, or he could let someone else find it for him. If he let someone else find it, who might that person be?

"Teniente?"

The lieutenant, who had been waiting outside for his morning's orders, came in and saluted. "*Sí*, señor?"

"I want you to send a man back over the trail and check on the status of the Broadbent brothers."

"Yes, sir."

"Do not molest them or allow them to know of your presence. I want to know what state they're in, whether they're still coming or have turned around—as much as you can find out."

"Yes, sir."

"We're going to start on the pyramid this morning. We'll open this end with dynamite, working into it as we go. Organize the explosives and men and have them ready in an hour." He put his plate on the ground and rose, shouldering his Steyr AUG. He stepped out into the sunlight, looking up at the pyramid, already calculating where to set the charges. Whether he found Max in the pyramid or not, at least it would keep the soldiers busy—and entertained. Everyone liked a big explosion.

Sunlight. It was the first he had seen in two weeks. It would be pleasant to work in the sunlight for a change.

47

Death came for Tom Broadbent, but not cloaked in black carrying a scythe. It came in the form of a hideous savage face, striped in red and yellow, bristling with green feathers, with green eyes and black hair and pointed white teeth, peering down into his face and poking him with his fingers. But the death that Tom expected did not come. Instead, the terrifying figure forced some hot liquid down his throat, and forced it again. He struggled feebly and then accepted it and fell asleep.

He woke with a dry feeling in his throat and a throbbing headache. He was in a thatched hut in a dry hammock. He was dressed in a fresh T-shirt and shorts. The sun was shining outside the hut, and the jungle burbled with sounds. For a long moment he couldn't even remember who he was or what he was doing there, and then it came back, piece by piece: the father's disappearance, the strange will, their journey upriver, Don Alfonso's jokes and sayings, their little clearing with the view of the Sierra Azul, dying under the rotten log in the rain.

It all seemed to have happened so long ago. He felt renewed, reborn, as weak as a baby.

He gingerly lifted his head up, raising it only as much as his hammering headache would allow. The hammock next to his was empty. He felt his heart lurch. Who had been in that hammock? Sally? Vernon? Who had died?

"Hello?" he asked feebly, trying to sit up. "Anybody here?"

He heard a sound outside and then Sally came in, lifting up the flap. She was like a sudden eruption of gold. "Tom! I'm so glad you're feeling better."

"Oh, Sally, I saw that empty hammock and I thought . . ."

Sally came over and took his hand. "We're all still here."

"Philip?"

"Still sick, but much better. Vernon should be better tomorrow."

"What happened? Where are we?"

"We're still in the same place. You can thank Borabay when he comes back. He went out hunting."

"Borabay?"

"A mountain Indian. He found us and saved us. He nursed us all back to health."

"Why?"

"I don't know."

"How long was I sick?"

"We were all sick about a week. We've had a fever he calls *bisi*. He's a *curandero*. Not like me, but a real *curandero*. He gave us medicine, fed us, saved our lives. He even speaks a funny kind of English."

Tom tried to sit up.

"Not yet." She eased him back down. "Drink some of this."

She handed him a cup filled with a sweet beverage. He drank it down and felt his hunger intensify. "I smell something cooking that is positively delicious."

"Turtle stew à la Borabay. I'll bring you some." She laid her hand on his cheek.

He looked up at her, remembering everything now.

She leaned over and gave him a kiss. "We've still got a long way to go before this is over."

"Yes."

"Let's take it one step at a time."

He nodded. She brought him some turtle soup; Tom ate it and then fell soundly asleep. When he woke, his headache was gone and he was able to get out of his hammock and walk shakily out of the hut. His legs felt like rubber. They were in the same clearing with the same fallen tree, but it had been transformed from a dank thicket into a cheerful, open camp. The ferns had been cut and used to pave the muddy ground, forming a pleasant, springy carpet. There were two neat palm-thatch huts and a fire ring with logs for seats. The sun was streaming down through the hole in the treetops. The Sierra Azul loomed in the gap, deep purple against the blue sky. Sally was sitting next to the fire, and when he came out she leapt to her feet and took his arm, helping him sit down.

"What time is it?"

"Ten o'clock in the morning," said Sally.

"How's Philip?"

"He's resting in his hammock. He's still weak, but he'll be fine. Vernon's sleeping off the last stage of the fever. Eat some more stew. Borabay has been lecturing us that we have to eat as much food as we can."

"Where is this mysterious Borabay?"

"Hunting."

Tom ate some more turtle stew; there was a huge pot of it bubbling on the fire, filled not only with chunks of meat but also with a variety of strange roots and vegetables. When he was done he went to the other hut to see Philip. He pulled open the palm-thatch door, bent over, and stepped inside.

Philip lay in his hammock, smoking. He was still shockingly thin, but the sores had turned to scabs and his eyes no longer looked hollow.

"Glad to see you up and about, Tom," he said.

"How are you feeling?"

"A little weak in the knees but otherwise chipper. Feet are almost healed. I'll be walking in a day or two."

"Have you met this fellow, Borabay?"

"Oh yes. Queer chap, all painted up, disks in his ears, tattoos, the works. Sally would have put him up for canonization except I somehow doubt he's Catholic."

"You look like a new man, Philip."

"So do you, Tom."

There was an awkward silence, interrupted by a shout from outside. "Hallo! Brothers!"

"Ah, Borabay's back," said Philip.

Tom ducked out of the hut and saw the most amazing little Indian walking across the meadow. His upper body and face were painted red, with a circle of black around the eyes and ferocious yellow stripes painted diagonally across his chest. Feathers bristled from bands on his upper arms, and he was naked except for a breechclout. Two enormous plugs were inserted into stretched-out earlobes, which waggled with each step. An intricate pattern of scars ran across his belly, and his front teeth had been filed to points. He had black hair, cut off straight, and his eyes were a most unusual hazel color, almost green. The face was strikingly handsome and finely cut, the skin smooth and sculptural.

He stepped to the fire, small and dignified, holding a seven-foot blowgun in one hand and a dead animal—species unknown—in the other.

"Brother, I bring meat," Borabay said in English and grinned. Then he chucked the animal to the ground and strode over. He embraced Tom twice, with a kiss on each side of the neck, some kind of ritualized Indian greeting. Then he stepped back and placed a hand on his chest. "My name Borabay, brother."

"I'm Tom."

"Me, Jane," said Sally.

Borabay turned. "Jane? You not Sally?"

Sally laughed. "That was a little joke."

"You, me, him, we brothers." Borabay concluded by giving Tom another formal set of embraces, again kissing him on the sides of the neck.

"Thank you for saving our lives," Tom said. It sounded feeble as soon as he had said it, but Borabay seemed pleased.

"Thankee. Thankee. You eat soup?"

"Yes. Delicious."

"Borabay good cook. You eat more!"

"Where did you learn English?"

"My mother teach me."

"You speak well."

"I speak bad. But I learn from you and then I speak gooder."

"Better," said Sally.

"Thankee. I go to America someday with you, brother."

It amazed Tom that way out here, as far removed from civilization as any place on earth, people still wanted to go to America.

Borabay glanced at Bugger, who was in his usual place in Tom's pocket.

"This monkey cry and cry when you sick. What his name?"

"Hairy Bugger," said Tom.

"Why you not eat this monkey when you starve?"

"Well, I've gotten fond of him." said Tom. "He wouldn't have been more than a mouthful anyway."

"And why you call him Hairy Bugger? What is Hairy Bugger?"

"Er, that's just a nickname for an animal with hair."

"Good. I learn new word, *Hairy Bugger*. I want learn English."

Sally said, "I want *to* learn English."

"Thankee! You tell me when I mistake." The Indian held out his finger to the monkey. Bugger grasped it in a tiny paw and looked up at him, then squeaked and ducked down into Tom's pocket.

Borabay laughed. "Hairy Bugger think I want eat him. He know we Tara like monkey. Now I make food." He went back to where he had dropped his game and collected it along with a pot. He withdrew a ways from the camp, squatted down and began skinning and quartering the animal, chucking everything into the pot including the guts and bones. Tom joined Sally at the fire.

"I'm still a little discombobulated here," Tom said. "What happened? Where did Borabay come from?"

"I don't know any more than you. Borabay found us all sick and dying under that log. He cleared the area, built the huts, moved us in, fed us, doctored us. He collected a huge number of herbs and even some weird insects—you can see them all tied up in the rafters of his hut—and he used those to make medicines. I was the first person to get well. That was two days ago, and I helped him cook and care for the rest of you. The fever we all had, this *bisi*, seems to be short but intense. It's not malaria, thank God, and Borabay tells me it has no lasting effects and won't recur. If you don't die in the first two days it's over. It seems that *bisi* is what killed Don Alfonso—he says that old people are more susceptible."

At this reminder of their traveling companion, Tom felt a stab of pain.

"I know," Sally said. "I miss him, too."

"I'll never forget the old man and his offbeat wisdom. It's hard to believe he's gone."

They watched Borabay chopping and hacking up the animal and tossing the chunks into a pot. He was singing a chantlike tune that rose and fell with the breeze.

"Has he said anything about this Hauser fellow and what's going on in the Sierra Azul?"

"No. He won't talk about it." She looked at him and hesitated. "For a while back there I thought we were all finished."

"Yeah."

"Do you remember what I said?"

"I do."

She blushed deeply.

Tom asked, "You want to take it back?"

She shook her head, sending her blond hair aswirl, then gazed at him, her cheeks flushed. "Never."

Tom smiled. "Good." He took her hand. What they had gone through had deepened her beauty somehow, made her look spiritual, something he couldn't quite explain. That prickly, defensive edge seemed to have disappeared. Getting that close to death had changed them all.

Borabay came back with some raw tidbits of meat wrapped up in a leaf. "Hairy Bugger!" he called and made a sucking noise with his teeth that sounded uncannily like the monkey. Bugger popped his head out of Tom's pocket. Borabay extended his hand, and Bugger, after fretting and squeaking a bit, reached out, snatched off a little piece of meat, and crammed it into his mouth. Then he snatched another, and another, stuffing his face with both hands, his squeaks of pleasure muffled by the food.

"Hairy Bugger and I friend now," said Borabay, smiling.

Vernon's fever broke that night. He woke up the next morning, lucid but weak. Borabay fussed around him, forcing a variety of herbal tisanes and other concoctions down his throat. They spent the day resting in camp while Borabay went out collecting food. The Indian returned in the afternoon with a palm-leaf sack, from which he unloaded roots, fruits, nuts, and fresh fish. He spent the rest of the day roasting and smoking and salting the food, then bundling it in dry grass and leaves.

"Are we going somewhere?" Tom asked him.

"Yes."

"Where?"

Borabay said, "We talkee later."

Philip came limping out of the hut, his feet still bandaged, briar pipe in his mouth. "Glorious afternoon," he said. He came over to the fire and sat down. As he poured himself a cup of tea Borabay had made, he said, "This Indian chap should be put on the cover of *National Geographic*."

Vernon joined them, shakily settling down on the log.

"Vernon, eat!" Borabay immediately filled up a bowl with stew and passed it over. Vernon took it with trembling hands, mumbling thanks.

"Welcome back to the land of the living," said Philip.

Vernon wiped his brow and said nothing. He was pale and thin. He placed another spoonful of stew in his mouth.

"Well, here we are," said Philip. "My three sons."

There was a sudden edge to Philip's voice that Tom noted with unease. A piece of wood popped in the fire.

"And what a mess we have gotten ourselves into," Philip said. "Thanks to Dear Old Dad." He raised his cup in mock salute. "Here's a toast to you, Dear Old Dad." He tossed his tea down.

Tom looked more closely at Philip. He had recovered amazingly well. His eyes were finally alive—alive with anger.

Philip looked around. "What now, brothers of mine?"

Vernon shrugged. He was pale, his face sunken, gray circles under his eyes. He placed another spoonful of stew in his mouth.

"Do we scurry back out, tails between our legs? And let this Hauser fellow help himself to the Lippi, the Braques, the Monet, and all the rest?" He paused. "Or do we head on up into the Sierra Azul and maybe end up with our entrails hanging in the bushes?" He relit his pipe. "Those are our choices."

No one answered while Philip looked around, staring at each one in turn.

"Well?" Philip said. "I'm asking a serious question: Are we going to let that corpulent Cortez waltz in here and steal our inheritance?"

Vernon looked up. His face was still haggard from his illness, and his voice was weak. "Answer the question yourself. You're the one who brought Hauser up here."

Philip turned to Vernon with a cool look. "I should think the time for recriminations had passed."

"As far as I'm concerned, the time for recriminations has just begun."

"This isn't the time or place," said Tom.

Vernon turned to Tom. "Philip brought that psychopath up here, and he needs to answer for it."

"I was acting in good faith. I had no idea this man Hauser would turn out to be a monster. And I did answer for it, Vernon. Look at me."

Vernon shook his head.

Philip went on. "The real culprit here, since no one else seems inclined to admit it, is Father. Isn't anyone here just a *wee bit angry* at what Father's done to us? He nearly killed us."

Tom said, "He wanted to challenge us."

"You're not defending him, I hope."

"I'm trying to understand him."

"I understand him only too well. This Tomb Raider bullshit is just one more *challenge* in a long list of them. Remember the sports tutors, the ski instructors, the art history lessons and horseback lessons and music lessons and chess lessons, the exhortations and speeches and threats? Remember report card day? He thinks we're fuckups, Tom. He's always thought that. And maybe it's true. Look at me: thirty-seven years old and still an assistant professor at Gobshite Junior College—and you, doctoring Indian horses in Hayseed, Utah—and Vernon spending the prime of his life chanting with Swami Woo-Woo. We're *losers.*" He erupted in a harsh laugh.

Borabay rose to his feet. The action itself was simple, but it was done with such slow deliberation that it silenced them. "This not good talk."

"This doesn't involve you, Borabay," said Philip.

"No more bad talk."

Philip ignored him, speaking to Tom. "Father could've left us his money like any other normal person. Or he could have given it away. Fine. I could've lived with that. It was his money. But no, he had to come up with a plan to *torture* us with it."

Borabay glared at him. "Shut up, brother."

Philip turned on him. "I don't care if you did save our lives, *stay out of our family business.*" A vein pulsed in Philip's forehead; Tom had rarely seen him so furious.

"You listen me, little brother, or I wimp your ass." Borabay said defiantly, standing up to his full five feet of height, his fists balled.

There was a beat, then Philip began to laugh and shake his head. His body relaxed. "Christ, is this guy for real?"

"We're all a little stressed," said Tom. "But Borabay's right. This is no place to argue."

"Tonight," Borabay said, "we talk, very important."

"About what?" Philip demanded.

Borabay turned to the stewpot and began stirring, his painted face unreadable. "You see."

48

Lewis Skiba settled back in the leather armchair of his paneled den and shook out the *Journal* to the editorial page. He tried to read but the distant squeaks and blats of his son's trumpet practice kept him from concentrating. Almost two weeks had passed since Hauser's last call. The man was evidently playing with him, keeping him in suspense. Or had something happened? Had he . . . done it?

His eyes fastened on the lead editorial in an effort to drown out the rush of self-accusation, but the words just ran through his head without any of the meaning sticking. Central Honduras was a dangerous place. It was quite possible Hauser had slipped up somewhere, made a mistake, misjudged something, caught a fever . . . A lot of things could have happened to him. The point was, he had disappeared. Two weeks was a long time. Maybe he had tried to kill the Broadbents and they proved too good for him and killed him instead.

Skiba hoped against all hope that this was what had happened. Had he really told Hauser to kill them? What had he been thinking? An involuntary moan escaped him. If only Hauser was dead. Skiba now knew, too late, that he would rather lose everything than be guilty of murder. He was a murderer. He said it, *Kill them.* He wondered why Hauser had been so insistent on having him say it. Christ. How was it that he, Lewis Skiba, high school football star, graduate of Stanford and Wharton, Fulbright scholar, CEO of a Fortune 500 company—how was it that he had allowed himself to become trapped and bullied and dominated by a cheap polyester criminal? Skiba had always thought of himself as a man of moral and intellectual weight, a man of ethics, a *good* man. He was a good father. He didn't cheat on his wife. He went to church. He sat on boards and gave away a good portion of his earnings to charity. And yet a collar-sniffing gumshoe dick with a combover had somehow gotten the drop on him, pulled off his mask, shown him for what he really was. That's what Skiba could never forget and never forgive. Neither himself nor Hauser.

His mind drifted once again to his childhood summers at the lake, the battenboard cottage, the crooked dock running into the still water, the smell of woodsmoke and pine. If only he could roll back the clock, go back to one of those long summers and start his life anew. What he would give to do it all over again.

With a groan of agony he forced it all from his head, taking a sip from the glass of scotch at his elbow. It was gone, all gone. He had to stop thinking about it. What was done was done. He couldn't turn back the clock. They'd get the Codex, and maybe there would be a fresh beginning for Lampe and no one would ever know. Or Hauser was dead and they wouldn't get the Codex, but still no one would know. No one would know. He could live with that. He'd *have* to live with it. Except *he* would know. *He* would know that he was a man capable of murder.

He angrily shook out the paper and began the editorial again.

At that moment the phone rang. It was the corporate phone, the secure line. He folded the paper down, walked over, and picked it up.

He heard a voice speaking as if from far away, yet as clear as a bell. It was his own voice.

Do it! Kill them, goddamn you! Kill the Broadbents!

Skiba felt as if he'd been punched. He lost all his air in a rush; he couldn't breathe. There was a hiss, and then his voice repeated, like some ghost from the past:

Do it! Kill them, goddamn you! Kill the Broadbents!

Hauser's voice came on next, the scrambler back on, "Did you catch that, Skiba?"

Skiba swallowed, gasped, tried to get his lungs working.

"Hello?"

"Don't ever call me at home," Skiba croaked.

"You never told me that."

"How did you get the number?"

"I'm a private eye, remember?"

Skiba swallowed. No point in responding. Now he knew why Hauser had been so insistent on him saying it. He'd been trapped.

"We're there. We're at the White City."

Skiba waited.

"We know this is where Broadbent went. Had a bunch of Indians bury him in a tomb up here that he'd robbed forty years ago. Probably the same tomb he found the Codex in. How's that for irony? We're here now, in the lost city, and all we have to do is find the tomb."

Skiba heard a muffled *thump*, distorted by the scrambler into a long squawk. Hauser must have turned off the scrambler at just the right moment to record his words in his own voice. There'd be no stiffing Hauser now out of his fifty million. On the contrary, Skiba had a feeling he'd be paying more, a lot more—for the rest of his life. Hauser had him by the short hairs. What a goddamn fool he'd been, outmaneuvered at every turn. Unbelievable.

"Hear that? That's the beautiful sound of dynamite. My men are working over a pyramid. Unfortunately the White City is a big, overgrown place, and Max could be buried anywhere. Anyway, I called to tell you there's been a change. When we find the tomb and get the Codex, we're heading west, out over the mountains, through El Salvador to the Pacific. On foot and then downriver. It'll take a little more time. You'll have the Codex within a month."

"You said—"

"Yeah, yeah. Originally I was planning to helicopter the Codex out to San Pedro Sula. But all of a sudden we got a couple of dead Honduran army soldiers to explain. And you never know when some tinhorn general's going to expropriate your property as national patrimony. The only helicopters down here belong to the military, and just to fly out here you have to cross military airspace. So we're continuing west in an unexpected direction, nice and quiet. Trust me, it's the best way."

Skiba swallowed again. Dead soldiers? Talking to Hauser made him feel sick. He wanted to ask if Hauser had done it, but he couldn't bring himself to mouth the words.

"In case you're wondering, I haven't followed through on your order. The three Broadbent sons are still alive. Tenacious buggers. But I haven't forgotten. I promise you, I'll do it."

His order. That lump was forming in Skiba's throat again. He swallowed, just about choked on it. They were alive. "I've changed my mind," he croaked.

"What's that?"

"Don't do it."

"Don't do what?"

"Don't kill them."

There was a low chuckle. "It's *way* too late for that."

"For God's sake, Hauser, don't do it; I order you not to kill them, *we can work this out another way*—"

But the line had gone dead. He heard a noise and turned, his face crawling with sweat. There was his son standing in the doorway, in baggy pajamas, blond hair sticking out, trumpet dangling in one hand. "Don't kill who, Daddy?"

49

That night Borabay served them a three-course dinner, starting with a fish soup and vegetables, followed by roasted steaks and a mess of tiny boiled eggs with baby birds inside them, and then, for dessert, a gruel of cooked fruit. He urged second and third helpings on them, forcing them to eat almost to the point of becoming sick. When the last dish was consumed, the pipes came out against the insects of dusk. It was a clear evening, and a gibbous moon was rising behind the dark outline of the Sierra Azul. They sat in a semicircle around the fire, the three brothers and Sally, all smoking quietly, waiting for Borabay to speak. The Indian puffed for a while, then laid down his pipe and looked around. His eyes, glistening in the firelight, rested on each of their faces in turn. The evening frogs had begun to peep and croak, mingling with more mysterious night sounds—cries, hoots, drummings, shrillings.

"Here we are, brothers," said Borabay.

He paused. "I start story at very beginning, forty years ago, in year before I was born. In that year white man come up river and over mountains all alone. Arrive at Tara village almost dead. He first white man anyone see. They take him in hut, feed him, bring him back to life. This man live with Tara people, learn to speak our language. They ask why he come. He say to find White City, which we call Sukia Tara. It is city of our ancestors. Now we go there only to bury dead. They take him to Sukia Tara. They not know then that he want to steal from Sukia Tara.

"This man, he soon take Tara woman to be wife."

"Figures," said Philip with a sarcastic laugh. "Father was never one to pass up a little action on the side."

Borabay stared at him. "Who telling story, brother, you or me?"

"Fine, fine, go ahead." Philip waved his hand.

"This man, I saying, take Tara woman to be wife. That woman is my mother."

"He married your *mother?*" Tom said.

"Of course he marry my mother," Borabay said. "How else we be brother, brother?"

Tom was shocked speechless as the meaning of Borabay's words sank in. He stared at Borabay, really looking at him for the first time. His gaze took in the painted face, the tattoos, the pointed teeth, the disks in his ears—as well as the green eyes, the tall brow, the stubborn set of the lips, the finely cut cheekbones. "Oh my God," he breathed.

"What?" Vernon asked. "Tom, what is it?"

Tom glanced at Philip and found his older brother equally thunderstruck. Philip was slowly rising to his feet, staring at Borabay.

Borabay spoke, "Then after father marry mother, mother born me. I name Borabay, after Father."

"Borabay," murmured Philip, and then: "Broadbent."

There was a long silence.

"Don't you see? Borabay, Broadbent—they're the same name."

"You mean he's our *brother?*" Vernon asked wildly, finally getting it.

No one answered. Philip, now on his feet, took a step toward Borabay and leaned over to gaze into his face from close range, as if he were some kind of freak. Borabay shifted, took the pipe out of his mouth, and gave a nervous laugh. "What you see, brother? Ghost?"

"In a way, yes." He reached out and touched his face.

Borabay sat calmly, not moving.

"My God," Philip whispered. "You *are* our brother. You're the oldest brother. Good lord, I wasn't the first born. I'm the second son and I never knew it."

"It's what I say! We all brother. What you think I say when I say 'brother'? You think I joke?"

"We didn't think you meant it literally," said Tom.

"Why you think I save your lives?"

"We didn't know. You seemed to be a saint."

Borabay laughed. "I, saint? You funny, brother! We all brother. We all have same father, Masseral Borabay. You Borabay, I Borabay, we all Borabay." He thumped his chest.

"Broadbent. The name's Broadbent," corrected Philip.

"Borabeyn. I no speak well. You understand me. I been Borabay so long I stay Borabay."

Sally's laugh suddenly rose up into the sky. She was on her feet and walking in a circle around the campfire. "As if we didn't already have enough Broadbents around here! Now there's another one! Four of them! Is the world ready?"

Vernon, the last to understand, was the first to recover his presence of mind. He stood up and went over to Borabay. "I'm very glad to welcome you as my brother," he said, and gave Borabay a hug. Borabay looked a little surprised and then gave Vernon another pair of embraces, Indian style.

Then Vernon stood aside while Tom stepped forward and held out his hand. Borabay looked at it in puzzlement.

"Something wrong with hand, brother?"

He's my brother and he doesn't even know how to shake hands, Tom thought. With a grin he hugged Borabay, and the Indian responded with his ritual embraces. He stood back, looking into his brother's face—and now he could see himself in that face. Himself, his father, his brothers.

Philip followed. He held out his hand. "Borabay, I'm not one for hugging and kissing. What we gringos do is shake hands. I'll teach you. Hold out your hand."

Borabay held out his hand. Philip seized it and gave it a good shake. Borabay's arm flopped around, and when Philip released his hand Borabay withdrew it and examined it, as if to check for damage.

"Well, Borabay," said Philip, "join the club. The screwed-over-sons-of-Maxwell-Broadbent club. Membership roster growing daily."

"What this mean, this screwed-over club?"

Philip waved his hand. "Never mind."

Sally gave Borabay a hug herself. "I'm not a Broadbent," she said, with another smile, "thank heaven for that."

They settled back down around the fire, and there was an awkward silence.

"What a family reunion," said Philip, shaking his head with wonder. "Dear old Father, full of surprises, even after death."

"But that what I want to tell you," said Borabay. "Father *not* dead."

50

Night had fallen, but it made no matter in the depths of the tomb, where no light had reached for a thousand years. Marcus Hauser stepped over the shattered lintel in the deep space and inhaled the cool dust of centuries. Oddly enough it was a fresh, clean smell without a hint of decay or corruption. He shined the powerful halogen beam around, and the scattered glint of gold and jade came winking back at him, mingled with brown bones and dust. The skeleton lay on a stone burial platform carved with hieroglyphics, and it had once been richly adorned.

Hauser stepped over and picked up a gold ring, shaking out the fingerbone that it still encircled. It was magnificent, set with a piece of jade, carved into the shape of a jaguar head. He slipped it into his pocket and sorted through the other items left with the body—a gold collar, some jade pendants, another ring. He pocketed the smaller gold and jade items as he took a slow turn around the burial chamber.

The corpse's skull lay at the far end of the burial platform. Sometime in the span of centuries its jaw had come loose and fallen wide open, giving the skull a look of astonishment, as if it couldn't quite believe it was dead. The flesh was mostly gone, but a mess of braided hair lay loosely on the dome of the skull. He reached down and picked the skull up. The jaw swung down, hanging by dessicated threads of cartilage. The front teeth had been filed to points.

Alas, poor Yorick.

He swept the light over the walls. Dull frescoes, obscured by lime and mold, were painted on the walls. Pots lay in a corner, filled with dust, jostled together and broken by some ancient earthquake. Small roots had penetrated the ceiling and dangled in tangled masses into the dead air.

He turned toward the *teniente*. "Is this the only tomb in here?" he asked.

"On this side of the pyramid. We still have the other side to explore. If it is symmetrical perhaps there is another one like this."

Hauser shook his head. He wouldn't find Max anywhere in the pyramid. It was too obvious. He had buried himself like King Tut, in an unobvious place. That was how Max would do it.

"Teniente, gather the men. I want to talk to them. We're going to search this city from east to west."

"Yes, sir."

Hauser found he was still holding the skull. With one last look he tossed it aside. It struck the stone floor with a hollow pop, bursting as if it had been made of plaster. The lower jaw rolled, giving a few crazy turns before coming to rest in the dust.

A brute search of the city with dynamite, temple by temple. Hauser shook his head. He wished his man would get back from scouting the Broadbents. There was a better way to do this, a much better way.

51

Father's still *alive?*" Philip cried out.

"Yes."

"You mean he hasn't been buried yet?"

"I finish story, please. After Father stay with Tara for year, my mother born me. But Father, he talk about White City, go up there for days, maybe weeks at a time. Chief say it is forbidden, but Father not listen. He search and dig for gold. Then he find place of tombs, open tomb of ancient Tara king and rob it. With help of bad Tara mans he escape down river with treasure and disappear."

"Leaving your mother barefoot with a baby," Philip said sarcastically, "just like he did his other wives."

Borabay turned and looked at Philip. *"I telling story, brother. You and flapper take five!"*

Tom felt the shock of déjà vu. *You and your flapper take five* was a pure Maxwellism, one of his father's favorite expressions, and there it was coming out of the mouth of this outlandish, tattooed, earlobe-stretched, half-naked Indian. His mind reeled. He had gone to the very ends of the earth and what had he found? A brother.

"I never see Father again—until now. Mother die two years ago. Then little while ago, Father come back. Big surprise. I very glad to meet him. He say he dying. He say he sorry. He say he bring back treasure he stole from Tara people. In return, he want to be buried in tomb of Tara king along with treasure of white man. He talk to Cah, chief of Tara people. Cah say yes, okay, we bury you in tomb. You come back with treasure and we bury you in tomb like ancient king. So Father go away and later come back with many boxes. Cah send men to coast to bring up treasure."

"Did Father remember you?" Tom asked.

"Oh yes. He very happy. We go fishing."

"Really, now?" said Philip, irritated. "Fishing? And who caught the biggest fish?"

"I did," said Borabay proudly. "With spear."

"Bully for you."

"Philip—" Tom began.

"If Father had spent any time with Borabay," Philip said, "he would have come to hate him just as much as he hates us."

"Philip, you know Father didn't hate us," said Tom.

"I almost died back there. I was *tortured*. Do you know what it feels like to *know* you're going to die? This was Father's legacy to me. And now we suddenly have this painted Indian as an older brother, who goes *fishing* with Father while we're dying in the jungle."

Borabay said, "You finish being angry, brother?"

"I'll never finish being angry."

"Father angry man, too."

"You can say that again."

"You son most like Father."

Philip rolled his eyes. "Here's something new, a psychoanalyzing jungle Indian."

"Because you most like Father, you love him most and he hurt you most. And now you hurt again because you find you not oldest son after all. *I* oldest son."

There was a short pause and then Philip broke into a harsh laugh. "This is too much. How could I feel myself in competition with an illiterate, tattooed Indian with filed teeth?"

After a pause, Borabay said, "I continue story now."

"Be my guest!"

"Cah arrange everything for Father's death and funeral. When day come, there is big funeral feast for Father. Big, big feast. All Tara people come. Father there, too. Father enjoy his own funeral very much.

He give many presents. Everyone get cooking pots and pans and knives."

Tom and Sally looked at each other.

"He would love that," said Philip. "I can just see the old bastard lording it over his own funeral."

"You right, Philip. Father love it. He eat, drink too much, laugh, sing. Father open boxes so everyone can look at white man's sacred treasures. Everyone love sacred Mother Mary holding baby Jesus. White man have beautiful gods."

"The Lippi!" cried Philip. "Was it in good condition? Had it survived the journey?"

"It is most beautiful thing I ever see, brother. When I look at it, I see something in white man I not see before."

"Yes, yes, it's one of the finest things Lippi did. To think of it stuck in a damp tomb!"

Borabay went on: "But Cah trick Father. At end of funeral, he supposed to give Father special poison drink to make him die painless death. But Cah not do this. Cah give Father drink to make him *sleep*. No one know this except Cah."

"This sounds positively Shakespearean," said Philip.

"So sleeping Father is carried into tomb with treasure. They shut door, lock him in tomb. We all think he dead. Only Cah know he not dead, he only sleeping. So he later wake up in dark tomb."

"Wait a minute," said Vernon, "I'm not following this."

"I am," said Philip calmly. "They buried Father alive."

Silence.

"Not 'they,'" said Borabay. "*Cah*. Tara people know nothing about this trick."

Philip said, "With no food and water . . . *My God, how horrible.*"

"Brothers," said Borabay, "in Tara tradition, much food and water put in tomb for afterlife."

Tom felt a crawling sensation in his spine as the implications of this sank in. He finally spoke. "So you think Father's still alive, then, locked in the tomb?"

"Yes."

Nobody said a word. An owl hooted mournfully in the dark.

"How long has he been sealed in the tomb?" Tom asked.

"Thirty-two days."

Tom felt sick. It was unthinkable.

Borabay said, "This is terrible thing, brothers."

"Why in hell did Cah do this?" Vernon asked.

"Cah angry that Father rob tomb long ago. Cah was boy then, son of chief. Father humiliate father of Cah by robbing tomb. This is Cah's revenge."

"Couldn't you stop it?"

"I not know Cah's plan until later. Then I try to save Father. At tomb entrance is giant stone door. I cannot move. Cah find out I go to Sukia Tara to save Father. He very angry. Cah take me prisoner and he going to kill me. He say I dirty man, half Tara, half white. Then crazy white man and soldiers come and capture Cah, take him to White City. I escape. I hear soldiers talk about you, so I come back for you."

"How did you know we were here?"

"I hear soldiers talk."

The fire flickered as the night gathered about the five silent people sitting on the ground. Borabay's words seemed to hang in the air a long time after he had uttered them. Borabay's eyes traveled around the fire, looking at each one of them in turn. "Brothers, it is a terrible way to die. This death for rat, not for human being. He our *father*."

"What can we do?" Philip asked.

Borabay spoke after a long pause, his voice low and resonant: "We rescue him."

52

Hauser poured over the crude diagram of the city that he had drawn over the past two days. His men had surveyed the city twice, but it was so overgrown that making any kind of accurate map was almost impossible. There were several pyramids, dozens of temples and other structures, hundreds of places where a tomb could be hidden. Unless they got lucky, it could take weeks.

A soldier came to the doorway and saluted.

"Report."

"The sons are twenty miles back, sir, beyond the Ocata River crossing."

Hauser slowly laid down the map. "Alive and well?"

"They are recovering from sickness. There is a Tara Indian taking care of them."

"Weapons?"

"One useless old hunting rifle belonging to the woman. Bows and arrows and a blowgun, of course—"

"Yes, yes." Hauser, despite himself, felt a certain twinge of respect for the three sons, particularly Philip. By all rights they should be dead. Max had been like that, too, stubborn and lucky. It was a potent combination. A brief image of Max came into his mind, the man stripped to the waist, slashing his way through the jungle, his sweaty back peppered with chips, twigs, and leaves. For months they had hacked their way through the jungle, bitten, cut, infected, sick—finding nothing. And then Max had ditched him, gone upriver and found the prize for which they'd been searching for over a year. Hauser went home broke and had to enlist...He shook his head, as if to throw off the resentment. That was past. The future—and Broadbent's fortune—belonged to him.

The *teniente* spoke. "Shall I send back a detail of soldiers to kill them? This time we will be sure to finish them, *jefe*, I promise you."

"No," he said. "Let them come."

"I don't understand."

Hauser turned to the *teniente*. "Don't molest them. Leave them alone. *Let them come.*"

53

Philip recovered more slowly than the others, but after three more days of Borabay's ministrations he was able to walk. One sunny morning they broke camp and set off for the Tara village in the foothills of the Sierra Azul. Borabay's herbal concoctions, ointments, and teas had had a remarkable effect on them all. Borabay went first with his machete, setting a fast pace. By noon they had reached the broad river where they first discovered Philip, covering in five hours the distance that had taken them five days to travel on their desperate retreat. Beyond the river, as they got closer to the Sierra Azul, Borabay began to move more cautiously. They entered the foothills and began to gain altitude. The forest seemed to get sunnier, less somber. The limbs of the trees were decked with orchids, and cheerful patches of sun speckled the way ahead.

They spent the night in an old Tara encampment, a semicircle of palm-thatched shelters, sunken among rioting greenery. Borabay waded through the waist-high vegetation, his machete singing, clearing a path to the best-preserved cluster of huts. He ducked inside, and Tom heard the smack of the machete, the stomping of feet, and some muttered cursing, first in one small hut, and then in another. Borabay appeared with a small writhing snake impaled on the point of the machete, which he flicked into the forest. "Huts now clean. You go in, set up hammocks, get rest. I make dinner."

Tom looked at Sally. He felt his heart beating so strongly in his chest that it was almost audible. Without exchanging a word, they both knew what they were going to do.

They entered the smaller of the huts. It was warm inside and smelled of dry grass. Rays of sunlight pierced little holes in the palm thatch, dappling the interior with flecks of afternoon light. Tom hung up his own hammock and then watched her set up hers. The spots of light were like a handful of gold coins flung into her hair, which flashed on her as she moved. When she was done, Tom stepped toward her and took her hand. It was trembling slightly. He drew her to him, ran his fingers through her hair, and kissed her on the lips. She moved closer, her body touching his, and he kissed her again. This time her lips parted and he tasted her tongue, then kissed her mouth, her chin, the side of her neck, and she pulled him close and gripped his back as he kissed the top of her shirt, moving downward, kissing each button as he unfastened it. He freed her breasts and continued kissing them, first their soft sides and then around her nipples, hard and erect, and then slid his hands down her smooth belly. He could feel her hands massaging the muscles on his back. He unbuckled her pants and knelt, kissing her belly button and sliding the palms of his hands around to grip her from behind as he slid down her pants. She thrust her hips forward and parted her thighs with a short intake of breath as he continued kissing her, holding her buttocks, until he felt her fingers dig into his shoulders and heard her sharp intake of breath, a sudden gasp, her whole body shuddering.

Then she undressed him and they lay down together in the warm darkness and they made love while the sun set, the little coins of light turning red and then fading as the sun sank behind the trees, leaving the hut in a hushed darkness, the only sound the faint cries that filled the strange world around them.

54

They were awakened by Borabay's cheerful voice. Night had fallen, and the air was cooler, the smell of roasting meat drifting through the hut.

"Dinner!"

Tom and Sally dressed and emerged from the hut, feeling embarrassed. The sky was resplendent with stars, the great Milky Way arcing like a river of light over their heads. Tom had never seen the night so black or the Milky Way so bright.

Borabay was sitting by the fire, turning shish kebabs while he worked on a dry gourd, drilling holes in it and slicing a groove in one end. When he was finished he lifted it to his lips and blew. A sweet, low note came out, and then another and another. He stopped and grinned.

"Who want to hear music?"

He began to play, the wandering notes gathering into a haunting melody. The jungle fell silent as the pure, clean sounds spilled from the gourd, faster now, rising and falling, with runs of notes as clear and hurried as a mountain stream. There were moments of quiet while the melody remained suspended in the air around them, and then the song resumed. It ended with a series of low notes as ghostly as the moan of wind in a cave.

When he stopped, the silence lasted for minutes. Gradually the jungle noises began to enter the space vacated by the melody.

"Beautiful," said Sally.

"You must've inherited that ability from your mother," said Vernon. "Father had a tin ear."

"Yes. My mother sing very beautiful."

"You're lucky," said Vernon. "We hardly knew our mothers."

"You not have same mother?"

"No. They were all different. Father pretty much raised us himself."

Borabay's eyes widened. "I not understand."

"When there's a divorce . . . " Tom stopped. "Well, sometimes one parent gets the children and the other one disappears."

Borabay shook his head. "This very strange. I wish I had father." He turned the shish kebabs. "Tell me what growing up with Father like."

Philip laughed harshly. "My God, where to begin? When I was a kid I thought he was *terrifying*."

Vernon broke in. "He loved beauty. So much so that he sometimes wept in front of a beautiful painting or statue."

Philip gave another sarcastic snort. "Yeah, weeping because he couldn't have it. He wanted to *own* beauty. He wanted it for himself. Women, paintings, whatever. If it was beautiful he wanted it."

"That's putting it rather crudely," said Tom. "There's nothing wrong with loving beauty. The world can be such an ugly place. He loved art for itself, not because it was fashionable or made him money."

"He didn't live his life by other people's rules," Vernon said. "He was a skeptic. He marched to a different drummer."

Philip waved his hand. "Marched to a different drummer? No, Vernon, he whacked the different drummer upside the head, took his drum, and led the parade himself. That was his approach to life."

"What you do with him?"

Vernon said, "He loved taking us camping."

Philip leaned back and barked a laugh. "Appalling camping trips with rain and mosquitoes, during which he brutalized us with camp chores."

"I caught my first fish on one of those trips," Vernon said.

"So did I," said Tom.

"Camping? What is camping?"

But the discussion had outrun Borabay. "Father needed to get away from civilization, to simplify his existence. Because he was so complicated himself he needed to create simplicity around him, and he did that by going fishing. He loved fly-fishing."

Philip scoffed. "Fishing, next to Holy Communion, is perhaps the most asinine activity known to man."

"That remark is offensive," said Tom, "even for you."

"Come now, Tom! Don't tell me in your old age you've taken up that flapdoodle? That and Vernon's eightfold way. Where did all this religiosity come from? At least Father was an atheist. There's one good thing for you, Borabay: Father was born a Catholic, but he became a sensible, levelheaded, rock-ribbed atheist."

Vernon said, "There's a lot more to the world than your Armani suits, Philip."

"True," said Philip, "there's always Ralph Lauren."

"Wait!" cried Borabay, "you all talk at same time. I no understand."

"You really got us going with that question," said Philip, still laughing. "Got any more?"

"Yes. What you like as sons?" Borabay asked.

Philip's laugh died away. The jungle rustled beyond the light of the fire.

"I'm not sure what you mean," said Tom.

Borabay said, "You tell me what kind of father he is to you. Now I ask what kind of sons you are to him."

"We were good sons," said Vernon. "We tried to get with the program. We did everything he wanted. We followed his rules, we gave him damn musical concerts every Sunday, we went to all our lessons and tried to win the games we played, not very successfully, perhaps, but we *tried*."

"You do what he ask, but what you do that he not ask? You help him hunt? You help him put roof back on house after storm? You make dugout with him? *You help him when he sick?* "

Tom suddenly had the sensation of being set up by Borabay. This was what he had been getting at all along. He wondered what Maxwell

Broadbent had talked about with his eldest son in the last month of his life.

Philip said, "Father hired people to do all those things for him. Father had a gardener, a cook, a lady who cleaned the house, people to fix the roof. And he had a nurse. In America you buy what you need."

"That's not what he means," said Vernon. "He wants to know what we did for Father when he was sick."

Tom felt his face flushing.

"When he sick with the cancer, what you do? You go to his house? Stay with him?"

"Borabay," Philip said, his voice shrill, "it would have been utterly useless to impose ourselves on the old man. He wouldn't have wanted us."

"You let stranger take care of Father when he sick?"

"I'm not going to stand a lecture from you, or anyone, on my duties as a son," cried Philip.

"I not lecture. I ask simple question."

"The answer is yes. We let a stranger take care of Father. He made our lives miserable growing up, and we couldn't wait to escape from him. That's what happens when you're a bad father—your sons leave you. They run, they flee. They can't wait to get away from you!"

Borabay rose to his feet. "He *your* father, good or bad. He feed you, he protect you, he raise you. He *make* you."

Philip stood up in a fury himself. "Is that what you call that vile eruption of bodily fluid? Making us? We were accidents, each one of us. What kind of father is it who takes children away from their mothers? What kind of father is it who raises us like we're some kind of experiment in creating genius? Who drags us out into the jungle to die?"

Borabay took a swing at Philip, and it happened so fast that it seemed Philip just disappeared backward into the darkness. Borabay stood, five feet of painted fury, his fists clenching and unclenching. Philip sat up in the dust beyond the fire and coughed. "Ugh." He spat. His lip was bloody and swelling rapidly.

Borabay stared at him, breathing hard.

Philip wiped his face, and then a smile spread across it. "Well, well. The eldest brother finally asserts his place in the family."

"You no speak about Father like that."

"I'll speak about him any way I want, and no illiterate savage is going to make me change my mind."

Borabay clenched his fists but did not make a further move toward Philip.

Vernon helped Philip stand up. Philip dabbed at his lip, but the look on his face was triumphant. Borabay stood with uncertainty, seeming to realize that he had made a mistake, that by striking his brother he had somehow lost the argument.

"Okay," said Sally. "Enough talk about Maxwell Broadbent. We can't afford to fight at a time like this, and you all know it."

She looked at Borabay. "Looks like dinner's burned."

Borabay silently removed the blackened shish kebabs and began parceling them out on leaves.

Philip's harsh phrase rang in Tom's mind: *That's what happens when you're a bad father—your sons leave you.* And he wondered: Was that what they had done?

55

Mike Graff settled in the wing chair by the fire, folding his neat legs one across the other, an alert, pleasant expression on his face. It amazed Skiba how, in spite of everything, Graff managed to keep that crisp B-school aura of self-confidence. Graff could be paddling Charon's own boat down the River Styx toward the very gates of hell, and he'd still be sporting that fresh-faced look, persuading his fellow passengers that heaven was just around the corner.

"What can I do for you, Mike?" Skiba asked pleasantly.

"What's with the stock these past two days? It's gone up ten percent."

Skiba shook his head. The house was on fire while Graff was in the kitchen complaining about cold coffee. "Just be glad that we survived the piece in the *Journal* about Phloxatane."

"All the more reason to worry why our stock is going up."

"Look, Mike—"

"Lewis, you didn't tell Fenner last week about the Codex, did you?"

"I did."

"Christ. You know what a scumbag that guy is. We're in enough trouble as it is without adding insider trading to our bill of fare."

Skiba looked at the man. He really should have gotten rid of Graff before. Graff had so compromised them both that now dismissal was out of the question. What did it matter? It was over—for Graff, for the company, and especially for him. He wanted to scream at the irrelevancy of it. A bottomless gulf had opened below him—they were in free fall—and Graff still didn't know it.

"He was going to downgrade Lampe to a sell. I had to, Mike. Fenner's no fool. He won't breathe a word of it. Would he risk throwing his life away for a few hundred thousand on the side?"

"Are you kidding? He'd knock his own grandmother down to snatch a penny off the sidewalk."

"It's not Fenner, it's short sellers closing out their positions."

"That doesn't explain more than thirty percent of it."

"Contrarians. Odd-lotters. Widows and orphans. Mike, enough. *Enough.* Don't you realize what's happening? It's over. We're finished. Lampe is finished."

Graff looked at him, astonished. "What are you talking about? We'll weather this. Once we get the Codex, Lewis, it'll be clear sailing."

Skiba felt his blood run thick and cold at the mention of the Codex. "You really think the Codex will solve our problems?" He spoke quietly.

"Why not? Am I missing something here? Has something changed?"

Skiba shook his head. What did it matter? What did anything matter?

"Lewis, this defeatism is unlike you. Where's your famous fight?"

Skiba was tired, so very tired. This argument was useless. It was over and done with. There was no more point in talking. All they could do now was wait: wait for the end. They were powerless.

"When we unveil the Codex," Graff went on, "Lampe stock will go through the roof. Nothing succeeds like success. The shareholders will forgive us, and it'll take all the wind out of the sails of that Dudley Do-Right chairman of the SEC. That's why I'm concerned about insider trading. If someone said something about the Codex to someone who told his mother-in-law who phoned her nephew in Dubuque—that charge would stick. It's like tax evasion, it's what they nail everyone on. Look at what happened to Martha—"

"Mike?"

"What?"

"Get the fuck out."

. . .

Skiba turned out the lights, shut down the phones, and waited for darkness to come. On his desk were only three things: the little plastic pill bottle, the sixty-year-old Macallan, and a clean shot glass.

Time to take the big swim.

56

The following day they left the abandoned Tara settlement and entered the foothills of the Sierra Azul. The trail began to ascend by fits and starts through forests and meadows, passing some fallow fields overgrown with weeds. Here and there, hidden in the rainforest, Tom caught a glimpse of an abandoned thatched hut, sinking into ruin.

They entered a deep, cool forest. Borabay suddenly insisted on going ahead and, unlike his usual silent pace, proceeded noisily, singing, whacking unnecessarily at vegetation and stopping frequently to "rest," which looked to Tom more like reconnoitering. Something was making him nervous.

When they came to a small clearing, Borabay halted. "Lunch!" he cried and began to sing loudly while unpacking bundles of palm leaves.

"We had lunch two hours ago," said Vernon.

"We have lunch again!" The Indian unshouldered his bow and arrows, and Tom noticed that he laid them down at some distance from himself.

Sally sat down next to Tom. "Something's about to happen."

Borabay helped the others out of their backpacks and put them with the bow and arrows, on the far side of the clearing. Then he came over to Sally and put an arm around her, drawing her close. "Give me gun, Sally," he said in a low voice.

She unshouldered her gun. Borabay then took away all their machetes.

"What's going on?" Vernon asked.

"Nothing, nothing, we rest here." He began passing around some dried plantains. "You hungry, brothers? Very good banana!"

"I don't like this," said Philip.

Vernon, oblivious to the undercurrent of tension, tucked into the dried plaintains. "Delicious," he said, his mouth full. "We should eat two lunches every day."

"Very good! Two lunches! Good idea!" said Borabay, laughing uproariously.

And then it happened. Without any noise or apparent movement, Tom suddenly realized they were surrounded by men on all sides, with bows drawn to the limit, a hundred stone-tipped arrows pointing at them. It was as if the jungle had imperceptibly withdrawn, leaving the men exposed like rocks at low tide.

Vernon let out a scream and fell to the ground and was instantly surrounded by bristling, tense men, with fifty arrows drawn and poised inches from his throat and chest.

"No move!" Borabay cried. He turned and spoke rapidly to the men. Slowly, the bows began to relax and the men stepped back. He continued talking, less rapidly and at a lower pitch, but just as urgently. Finally the men took another step back and lowered their arrows completely.

"You move now," said Borabay. "Stand up. No smile. No shake hand. Look everyone in eye. *No smile.*"

They did as they were told, rising.

"Go get packs and weapons and knifes. Do not show you afraid. Make angry face but say nothing. Smile and you die."

They followed Borabay's orders. There was a brief flurry of raised bows as Tom picked up his machete, but when he sheathed it in his belt the bows went back down. Tom, following Borabay's instructions, raked the warriors near them with a baleful stare, and they stared back so ferociously that he felt weak in the knees.

Borabay was now talking in a lower voice, but he sounded angry. He was directing his comments to one man, taller than the others, with a brilliant set of feathers bristling from rings on his muscled upper arms. He wore a string around his neck, on which dangled as jewelry the detritus of Western technology, a CD-ROM offering six free months of AOL, a calculator with a hole drilled through it, a dial from an old telephone.

The man looked at Tom and stepped forward. Halted.

"Brother, take step toward man, tell him in angry voice he must apologize."

Tom, hoping that Borabay understood the psychology of the situation, scowled and stepped toward the warrior. "How dare you draw your bows at us?" he demanded.

Borabay translated. The man answered angrily, gesturing with a spear close to Tom's face.

Borabay spoke. "He say, 'Who are you? Why you come into Tara land without invitation?' You tell him in angry voice you come to save your father. Shout at him."

Tom obeyed, raising his voice, taking a step toward the warrior and shouting at him inches from his face. The man answered in an even angrier voice, shaking his spear in front of Tom's nose. At this, many of the warriors put up their bows again.

"He say Father cause big trouble for Tara and he very angry. Brother, you must be very angry now. You tell them to put down bows. Say you no talk unless they put arrows away. Make big insult."

Tom, sweating now, tried to push aside the terror he felt and feign anger. "How dare you threaten us?" he cried. "We have come into your land in peace, and you offer us war! Is this how the Tara treat their guests? Are you animals or people?"

Tom caught a flash of approval from Borabay as he translated—no doubt adding his own nuances.

The bows came down, and this time the men unnocked their arrows and put them back into their quivers.

"Now you smile. Short smile, not big smile."

Tom flashed a smile, then let his face settle back into sternness.

Borabay spoke at length, then turned to Tom. "You must hug and kiss that warrior in Tara way."

Tom gave the man an awkward hug and a pair of kisses on the neck, just as Borabay had done to him so many times. He ended up with red and yellow paint on his face and lips. The warrior returned the courtesy, smearing more paint on him.

"Good," said Borabay, almost giddy with relief. "Everything fine now! We go to Tara village."

The village consisted of an open plaza of packed dirt, surrounded by two irregular rings of thatched huts of the kind they had slept in a few nights before. The huts had no windows, just a hole in the peak. Cooking fires were burning in front of many of the huts, tended by women who, Tom noticed, were cooking with the French cooking pots, copper braising pans, and Meissen stainless steel cutlery that Maxwell Broadbent had brought them. As he followed the group of warriors into the center of the plaza, thatched doors popped open and various people came out to stand and gape at them. The small children were completely naked; the older ones wore dirty shorts or breechclouts. The women wore a piece of cloth tied around their waists and were naked above, with their breasts and chests smeared with red. Many had disks in their lips and ears. Only the men wore feathers.

There was no formal greeting ceremony. The warriors who had brought them in wandered off, going about their business with complete indifference, while the women and children of the village gaped.

"What do we do now?" Tom asked, standing in the middle of the dirt plaza and looking around.

"Wait," said Borabay.

A toothless old woman soon emerged from one of the huts, bent double from age, leaning on a stick; her short white hair made her look like a witch. She made her way toward them with excruciating slowness, her beady eyes never leaving their faces, sucking on her lips and muttering to herself. She finally arrived in front of Tom and peered up at him.

Borabay said quietly, "Do nothing."

She raised a withered hand and gave Tom a blow across the knees, then whacked him across the thighs, once, twice, three times— surprisingly painful blows for an old lady—all the while muttering to herself. She then raised her stick and struck him across the shins and again on the buttocks. She dropped the stick and reached up and groped him obscenely between his legs. Tom swallowed and tried not to flinch as she made a thorough check of his masculinity. Then she reached up toward Tom's head, making a motion with her fingers. Tom bent slightly, and she grabbed his hair and gave such a yank that tears sprang to his eyes.

She stepped back, the inspection apparently complete. She gave him a toothless smile and spoke at length.

Borabay translated. "She say contrary to apppearance you are definitely a man. She invite you and your brothers stay in village as guest of the Tara people. She accept your help for fight against bad men in White City. She say now you in charge."

"Who is she?" Tom glanced at her. She was peering up and down, examining him from head to toe.

"She is wife of Cah. Look out, Tom, she like you. Maybe she come to your hut tonight."

It broke the tension, and they all laughed, Philip most of all.

"What am I in charge of?" Tom asked.

Borabay looked at him. "You now war chief."

Tom was stunned. "How can that be? I've been here ten minutes."

"She say Tara warriors fail in attack against white man and many killed. You white man, too, maybe you understand enemy better. Tomorrow, you lead fight against bad men."

"Tomorrow?" Tom said. "Thanks, really, but I decline the responsibility."

"You not have choice," said Borabay. "She say if you do not, Tara warriors kill us all."

That night the villagers lit a bonfire, and a party of sorts got under way, starting with a multicourse feast, which arrived on leaves, culminating in a tapir roasted in a pit. The men danced and then gave a hauntingly strange orchestral performance on flutes, led by Borabay. Everyone went to bed late. Borabay roused them a few hours later. It was still dark.

"We go now. You speak to people."

Tom stared at him. "I have to give a *speech?*"

"I help you."

"This I've got to see," said Philip.

The bonfire had been heaped with fresh logs, and Tom could see that the whole village was standing, silently and respectfully, waiting for his speech.

Borabay whispered, "Tom, you tell me to get ten best warriors for fight."

"Fight? What fight?"

"We fight Hauser."

"We can't—"

"Be quiet and *do what I say*," Borabay hissed.

Tom gave the order, and Borabay then went through the crowd, clapping his hands, slapping the shoulders of various men, and in five minutes had ten warriors lined up with them, decked out in feathers, paint, and necklaces, each with a bow and quiver.

"Now you give speech."

"What should I say?"

"Talk big. How you going to rescue Father, kill bad mans. Don't worry, whatever you say, I fix up good."

"Don't forget to promise a chicken in every pot," said Philip.

Tom stepped forward and looked around at all the faces. The hubbub of talk died quickly. Now they were looking at him with hope. A shiver of fear ran through him. He had no idea what he was doing.

"Er, ladies and gentlemen?"

Borabay flashed him a disapproving look and then, in a martial voice, cried out something that sounded a lot more effective than the feeble opening he had managed. There was a rustling as everyone came to attention. Tom had a sudden feeling of déjà vu—he remembered Don Alfonso's speech to his people when they left Pito Solo. He had to give a speech like that, even if it was all lies and empty promises.

He took a deep breath. "My friends! We have come to the Tara lands from a distant place called America!"

At the word *America*, even before Borabay could translate, there was a rustle of excitement.

"We have come many thousands of miles, by plane, by dugout, and on foot. For forty days and nights we have traveled."

Borabay declaimed this. Tom could see he now had their undivided attention.

"A great evil has befallen the Tara people. A barbarian named Hauser has come from the other side of the world with mercenary soldiers to kill the Tara people and rob their tombs. They have kidnapped your head priest and killed your warriors. As I speak, they are in the White City, defiling it with their presence."

Borabay translated, and there was a loud murmur of agreement.

"We are here, the four sons of Maxwell Broadbent, to rid the Tara people of this man. We have come to save our own father, Maxwell Broadbent, from the darkness of his tomb."

He paused for Borabay's translation. Five hundred faces, lit by the firelight, gazed at him with rapt attention.

"My brother here, Borabay, will lead us up to the mountains, where we will observe the bad men and make plans for an attack. Tomorrow, we will fight."

At this there was an eruption of an odd sound like rapid grunting or laughing—the Tara equivalent, it seemed, of cheering and clapping. Tom could feel his monkey, Hairy Bugger, scrunching himself down into the bottom of his pocket, trying to hide.

Borabay then spoke to Tom, sotto voce. "Ask them to pray and make offering."

Tom cleared his throat. "The Tara people, all of you, have a very important role to play in the coming struggle. I ask you to pray for us. I ask you to make offerings for us. I ask you to do this every day until we return victorious."

Borabay's voice rang out with these declarations, and it had an electric effect. People surged forward, murmuring in excitement. Tom felt a kind of hopeless absurdity wash over him; these people believed in him far more than he believed in himself.

A cracked voice rang out, and the people instantly fell back, leaving the old woman, Cah's wife, standing alone, leaning on her stick. She looked up and fixed her eye on Tom. There was a long silence, and then she raised her stick, drew it back, and gave him a tremendous blow across the thighs. Tom tried not to flinch or grimace.

Then the old woman cried out something in a wizened voice.

"What'd she say?"

Borabay turned. "I do not know how to translate. She speak a strong Tara expression. It mean something like: *You kill or you die.*"

57

Professor Julian Clyve propped up his feet and creaked back in his old chair with his hands behind his head. It was a blustery May day, the wind twisting and torturing the leaves of the sycamore tree outside his window. Sally had been gone now for over a month. There had been no word. He hadn't expected to hear anything, but Clyve still found the long silence perturbing. When Sally left, they both expected the Codex would usher in one more academic triumph in Professor Clyve's life. But after thinking about it for a week or two, Clyve had changed his mind. Here he was a Rhodes scholar, a full professorship at Yale, with a string of prizes, academic honors, and publications that most professors didn't accumulate in a lifetime. The fact was, he hardly needed another academic honor. What he needed—let's face it—was *money*. The values of American society were all wrong. The real prize—financial wealth—did not come to those who deserved it most, to the intellectual movers and shakers: the brain trust that controlled, directed, and disciplined the great stupid lumbering beast that was the *vulgus mobile*. Who did make the money? Sports figures, rock stars, actors, and CEOs. Here he was, at the top of his profession, earning less than the average plumber. It was galling. It was unfair.

Wherever he went, people sought him out, crushed his hand, praised him, admired him. All the wealthy people of New Haven wanted to know him, to have him to dinner, to *collect* him and show him off as evidence of their good taste, as if he were an Old Master painting or piece of antique silver. Not only was it disgusting, but it was humiliating and expensive. Almost everyone he knew had more money than he did. No matter what honors he gained, no matter what prizes he won or monographs he published, he still wasn't able to pick up the tab at a reasonably good restaurant in New Haven. Instead *they* picked up the tab. *They* had him to their houses. *They* invited him to the black-tie charity dinners and paid for the table, brushing off his insincere offers of reimbursement. And when it was all over he had to slink back to his two-bedroom, revoltingly bourgeois split-level in the academic ghetto, while they went home to their mansions in the Heights.

Now, finally, he had the means to do something about it. He glanced at the calendar. It was the thirty-first of May. Tomorrow the first installment of the two million from the giant Swiss drug company, Hartz, was to arrive. The coded e-mail confirmation should be coming from the Cayman Islands soon. He would have to spend the money outside the United States, of course. A snug villa on the Costiera Amalfitana would be a nice place to park it; a million for the villa and the second million for expenses. Ravello was supposed to be nice. He and Sally could take their honeymoon there.

He thought back to his meeting with the CEO and the Hartz board, so very serious, so very Swiss. They were skeptical, of course, but when they saw the page Julian had already translated, their old gray mouths were almost watering. The Codex would bring them many billions. Most drug companies had research departments that evaluated indigenous medicines—but here was the ultimate medical cookbook, all nicely packaged, and Julian was about the only person in the world, apart from Sally, who could translate it accurately. Hartz would have to strike a deal with the Broadbents over it, but as the largest pharmaceutical company in the world it was in the best position to pay. And without his translation skills, what use would the Codex be to the Broadbents anyway? Everything would be done correctly: The company had of course insisted on it. The Swiss were like that.

He wondered how Sally would react when she learned that the Codex was going to disappear into the maw of some giant multinational corporation. Knowing her, she would not take it well. But once

they started enjoying the two million dollars Hartz had agreed to pay
him as a finder's fee—not to mention the generous remuneration he
expected to receive for doing the translation—she'd get over it. And he
would show her that this was the right thing to do, that Hartz was in
the best position to develop these new drugs and bring them to market. It *was* the right thing to do. It took money to develop new drugs.
Nobody was going to do it for free. Profit made the world go round.

As for himself, poverty had been fine for a few years while he was
young and idealistic, but it would become unendurable over thirty.
And Professor Julian Clyve was fast approaching thirty.

58

After ten hours of hiking into the mountains, Tom and his brothers topped a bare, windswept ridge. A stupendous view of mountains greeted their eyes, a violent sea of peaks and valleys, layered toward the horizon in deepening shades of purple.

Borabay pointed. "Sukia Tara, the White City," he said.

Tom squinted in the bright afternoon sun. About five miles away, across a chasm, rose two pinnacles of white rock. Nestled between them was a flat, isolated saddle of land, cut off on both sides by chasms and surrounded by jagged peaks. It was a lone patch of green, a lush piece of cloudforest that looked as if it had broken off from somewhere else to lodge between the two fangs of white rock, teetering on the brink of a precipice. Tom had imagined it would be a ruin with white towers and walls. Instead, he could see nothing but a thick, lumpy carpet of trees.

Vernon raised his binoculars, examined the White City, and passed them to Tom.

The green promontory leapt into magnification. Tom scanned it, slowly. The plateau was heavily covered in trees and what appeared to be impenetrable mats of vines and creepers. Whatever ruined city lay in that strange hanging valley was well covered by jungle. But as Tom scrutinized it, here and there, rising from the verdure, he could make out whitish outcrops that began to take on faint patterns: a corner, a broken stretch of wall, a dark square that looked like a window. And as he looked further at what he thought was a steep hill, he realized it was a ruined pyramid, heavily overgrown. One side of it had been gashed open, a white wound in the living green.

The mesa the city had been constructed on was, truly, an island in the sky. It hung between the two peaks, separated from the rest of the Sierra Azul by sheer cliffs. It looked cut off until he saw a thread of yellow curving across one of the chasms—a crude suspension bridge. As he examined it further he saw that the bridge was well guarded by soldiers who were using a ruined stone fortress evidently built by the original inhabitants to protect the White City. Hauser and his men had cut down a large swath of forest at the foot of the bridge to give themselves a clear field of fire.

On the opposite side of the White City, not far from the bridge, a small river ran down from the mountains and poured into the chasm, turning into a graceful filament of white and disappearing into the mists below. As Tom watched, mists billowed up from the chasm, obscuring the suspension bridge and then blocking their view of the White City itself. The mists cleared, then rose again, then cleared, in a never ending ballet of darkness and light.

Tom shivered. Their father, Maxwell Broadbent, had probably stood in the same place forty years ago. No doubt he had been able to pick out the faint outlines of the city amid the chaos of vegetation. Here was where he made his first discovery and began his life's work; and this was where he had ended up, shut up alive in a dark tomb. The White City was the alpha and the omega of Maxwell Broadbent's career.

He passed the binoculars to Sally. She examined the White City for a long time. Then she lowered the glasses and turned to Tom, her face flushed with excitement. "It's Maya," she said. "There's a central ball court, a pyramid, and some multistoried pavilions. It's High Classic. The people who built this city came from Copán, I'm sure of it— probably this is where the Maya retreated after the fall of Copán in A.D. 900. One great mystery solved."

Her eyes were sparkling, the sun shimmering off her golden hair. He had never seen her so vital. It was surprising, he thought, considering how little sleep they had been getting.

She turned and her eyes connected with his, and it seemed to him that she understood what he was thinking. Her face flushed slightly, and she looked away, smiling to herself.

Philip took the binoculars next and scanned the city. Tom heard an intake of breath. "There are men down there," he said. "Cutting trees at the base of the pyramid."

There was a faint *crump* of dynamite, and a puff of dust rose up from the city like a small white flower.

Tom said, "We're going to have to find Father's tomb before they do. Or . . ." He left the sentence unfinished.

59

They spent the rest of the afternoon in the cover of the trees, observing Hauser and his men. One group of soldiers was clearing trees from a stone temple at the base of the pyramid while another group dug and blasted into a smaller pyramid nearby. The shifting winds brought them the faint sounds of chainsaws and, every half hour or so, the distant rumble of explosives, followed by a rising cloud of dust.

"Where is Father's tomb?" he asked Borabay.

"In cliffs below city on far side. Place of dead."

"Will Hauser find it?"

"Yes. Trail down is hidden, but he find it in end. Maybe tomorrow, maybe two weeks."

As night fell, a pair of klieg lights went on in the White City, and another set illuminated the suspension bridge and the area around it. Hauser was taking no chances, and he had come well equipped with everything, including a generator.

They ate their dinner in silence. Tom could hardly taste the frogs or lizards or whatever dish it was Borabay had cooked for them. From what he could see from their vantage point on the ridge, the White City was well defended and well-nigh impregnable.

At the conclusion of the meal, it was Philip who spoke what was on everyone's mind. "I think we better get the hell out of here and come back with help. We can't do this on our own."

"Philip," said Tom, "when they find the tomb and open it, what do you think's going to happen?"

"They'll rob it."

"No, the first thing Hauser will do is murder Father."

Philip didn't answer.

"It's going to take us at least forty days just to get out of here. If we're going to save Father, we've got to act *now*."

"I don't want to be the one to say no to rescuing Father, but Tom, for God's sake, we have an old rifle, maybe ten rounds, and some painted warriors with bows and arrows. They have automatic weapons, grenade launchers, and dynamite. And they've got the advantage of defending an incredibly secure position."

Tom said, "Not if there's a secret way into the city."

"No secret way," said Borabay. "Only bridge."

"There has to be a second way," said Tom. "Otherwise, *how did they originally build the bridge?*"

Borabay stared at him, and Tom felt a flush of triumph.

"Gods build bridge," said Borabay.

"Gods don't build bridges."

"Gods build *this* bridge."

"Damn it, Borabay! The gods did not build that bridge, *people* built it, and to do that they had to be on both sides!"

"You're right," said Vernon.

"Gods build bridge," Borabay insisted. "But," he added after a moment, "Tara people also know how to build bridge from one side only."

"Impossible."

"Brother, you always so sure you right? I tell you how Tara build bridge from one side only. First, Tara shoot arrow with rope and hook. Get it stuck on tree on far side. Then send little boy across in basket on wheels."

"How does he get across?"

"He pull himself."

"How could a man possibly span a two-hundred-yard gap with an arrow trailing a rope and hook?"

"Tara use special big bow and special arrow with feather. Very important to wait for day with strong wind in right direction."

"Go on."

"When little boy across, man shoot second arrow with rope. Little boy tie two ropes together, put rope around little wheel—"

"A pulley."

"Yes. Then with pulley man can pull across many things. First he pull across heavy cable in basket, which uncoil as it go. Boy fix heavy cable to tree. Now man can come across on heavy cable. Now man and boy on far side. Man use second pulley to pull across three more cables, one at time. Now four cables across canyon. Now more men cross in basket—"

"That's enough," interrupted Tom. "I get the picture."

They fell into silence, the impossibility of their situation sinking in.

"Have the Tara warriors tried to ambush them and cut the bridge yet?"

"Yes. Many die."

"Have they tried burning arrows?"

"Cannot reach bridge."

"Let's keep in mind," said Philip, "that if the bridge is cut, Father's also trapped inside."

"I'm well aware of it. I'm just going over our options. Maybe we can offer Hauser a deal: Let Father out and Hauser can keep the tomb and its riches. We'll sign it all over to him and that's that."

Tom said: "Father would never agree."

"Even if it meant his life?"

"He's dying of cancer."

"Or our lives?"

Philip looked at them. "Don't even *think* of trusting Hauser or making a deal with him."

"All right," said Vernon, "we've eliminated getting into the White City by some other route, and we've eliminated it by a frontal attack. Anybody here know how to build a hang glider?"

"No."

"That leaves only one course of action."

"And what's that?"

Vernon smoothed out a place in the sand near the fire and began to draw a map while he explained his plan. When he was finished, Philip spoke first.

Philip shook his head. "This is a crazy plan. I say we go back, get help, and return. It may take them months to find Father's tomb."

Borabay interrupted. "Philip, maybe you no understand. If we run away now, Tara people kill us."

"Bosh."

"We make promise. Cannot break promise."

"I didn't make any bloody promises, that was Tom. Anyway, we can slip past the Tara village and be long gone before they even know we're missing."

Borabay shook his head. "That coward way, brother. That leave Father die in tomb. If Tara catch you, death for coward slow and ugly. They cut off—"

"We've already heard what they do," Philip said.

"There not enough food and water in tomb to last much longer."

The fire crackled. Tom glanced through the trees. Below and almost five miles distant, he could see a trio of diamond lights clustered in the White City. There was another faint explosion of dynamite. Hauser and his men were working around the clock. They really were up against the wall. There were no good options and only one mediocre plan. But it was the best they were going to get.

"Enough talk," said Tom. "We have a plan. Who's in?"

"I'm in," said Vernon.

Borabay nodded. "I'm in."

"I'm in," said Sally.

Now all eyes were on Philip. He made an angry gesture as if to sweep them all away. "For heaven's sake, you already know what my answer's going to be!"

"Which is?" Vernon asked.

"For the record, it's no, no, *no!* This is a James Bond plan. It'll never succeed in real life. Don't do it. For God's sake, I don't want to lose my brothers, too. Don't do it."

"We have to, Philip," said Tom.

"No one *has* to do anything! Maybe this is blasphemy, but isn't it just a little bit true that Father brought this down on himself?"

"So we just let him die?"

"I'm just asking you, please, not to throw your lives away." He threw up his hands and stomped off in the darkness.

Vernon was about to shout a reply, but Tom touched his arm and shook his head. Perhaps Philip was right and it was a suicide mission. But Tom personally had no choice. If he didn't do something now, he wouldn't be able to live with himself later. It was as simple as that.

Their faces flickered around the firelight, and there was a long, uncertain silence.

"There's no reason to wait," said Tom. "We leave tonight at two A.M. It should take us a couple of hours to get down there. Everyone knows what they have to do. Borabay, you can explain to your warriors their role." Tom glanced over at Vernon. The plan had been his, Vernon's, the brother who never took the lead. He reached out and grasped his brother's shoulder. "Good going," he said.

Vernon smiled back. "I feel like we're in *The Wizard of Oz* here.

"What do you mean?"

"I've found my brain. Tom, you've found your heart. Borabay's found his family. The only thing is, Philip hasn't quite found his courage."

Tom said, "Somehow I don't think a bucket of water is going to take care of Hauser, either."

"No," murmured Sally, "that it won't."

60

Tom rose from his hammock at 1:00 A.M. The night was black. Clouds had blotted out the stars and a restless wind rustled and mumbled through the trees. The only light came from the ruddy heap of embers in the fire ring, casting a reddish glow on the faces of the ten Tara warriors. They were still sitting in a circle around the fire, not having moved or spoken all night.

Before waking the others Tom collected the binoculars and stepped out of the trees to take one more look at the White City. The lights were still on at the suspension bridge, the soldiers in their ruined fort. Tom thought of what lay ahead. Perhaps Philip was right and it was suicide. Perhaps Maxwell Broadbent was dead in his tomb and they were risking their lives for nothing. All that was beside the point: He had to do it.

Tom went to wake the others only to find most of them up. Borabay unbanked the fire, piled in fresh sticks, and put a pot on to boil. Sally joined them soon afterward and began checking her Springfield by the light of the fire. Her faced looked drawn, tired. "You remember what General Patton said was always the first casualty of a battle?" she asked Tom.

"No."

"The battle plan."

"So you don't think our plan is going to work?" Tom asked.

She shook her head. "Probably not." She looked away, then back down at the rifle, giving it an unneeded polish with the cleaning rag.

"What do you think's going to happen?"

She shook her head wordlessly, sending waves through her heavy gold hair. Tom realized she was very upset. He placed his hand on her shoulder. "We have to do this, Sally."

She nodded. "I know."

Vernon joined them at the fire, and the four of them drank their tea in silence. When the tea was gone, Tom glanced at his watch. Two o'clock. He looked around for Philip, but his brother had not even come out of the hut. He nodded to Borabay, and they all rose. Sally threw the gun over her shoulder, and they shouldered small palm-leaf backpacks containing a supply of food, water, matches, camp stove, and other essentials. They set off single file, Borabay in the lead, the warriors bringing up the rear, moving down through the grove of trees and out into the open.

Ten minutes down from the camp, Tom heard the sound of running from behind, and they all stopped and listened, the warriors with their arrows nocked and drawn. In a moment Philip appeared, breathing hard.

"Here to wish us luck?" Vernon asked, an edge of sarcasm in his voice.

Philip took a moment to catch his breath. "I don't know why I would even think of joining this harebrained scheme. But damn it, I'm not going to let you go off to your deaths alone."

61

Marcus Aurelius Hauser felt in his musette bag for another Churchill and selected one, rolling it between thumb and forefinger before taking it out. He went through the sacrament of trimming, moistening, and lighting it, and then he held it out in the dark so that he could admire the big fat glowing tip while allowing the aroma of fine Cuban longleaf to surround him like a cocoon of elegance and satisfaction. Cigars, he mused, always seem to become better, richer, deeper tasting in the jungle.

Hauser was well hidden at a strategic point above the suspension bridge in a thicket of ferns, where he had a good view of the bridge and the soldiers in their little stone fort on the far side. He pushed aside some plants and raised a pair of binoculars to his eyes. He had a strong feeling that the three Broadbent brothers were going to make their break to cross the bridge tonight. They wouldn't wait; they couldn't wait. They had to get to the tomb before he did, if they wanted any chance at all of saving some of the masterpieces for themselves.

He puffed contentedly, thinking back to Maxwell Broadbent. He had lugged half a billion dollars' worth of fine art and antiquities up here, all on a whim. As outrageous as it was, it was perfectly in character. Max was the man of the big gesture, the spectacle, the show. He lived large and he died large.

Hauser remembered back to that defining fifty-day trek in the jungle, those harrowing days that he would never forget as long as he lived. They had heard there was a Mayan temple somewhere up in the Cerros Escondidos in the Guatemalan lowlands. Fifty days and fifty nights, hacking their way along overgrown trails, stung and bitten and scratched, starving and sick. When they stumbled into that Lacandon village, the villagers wouldn't talk. The temple was there somewhere, all right. No doubt about it. But the villagers were silent. Hauser had just about gotten a girl to the point of talking when Max had thwarted him. Pointed a gun right at his head, the bastard, disarmed him. That was the break, the final straw. Max had ordered Hauser away like he was some dog. Hauser had no choice but to give up their search for lost cities and go home—while Max went on to find the White City. He looted a rich tomb up here, and that tomb, forty years later, had become his own.

It had come full circle, though, hadn't it?

Hauser enjoyed another long suck on the cigar. In his years in combat, he had learned something important about people: When things got tough, you could never tell who was going to make it and who was going to fold. The big Army Ranger guys in their crew cuts and pumped-up Arnold Schwarzenegger pecs and big-dick talk sometimes fell apart like so much overcooked meat, while the geek in the company, the intel guy or the electronics nerd, turned out to be the real survivor. So you never knew. This was how it was with the three Broadbent kids. He had to hand it to them. They had done well. They would perform this final service and then their road would come to an end.

He paused, listened. There was a faint sound of ululating, whooping, and yelling. He raised the binoculars. Far to the left of the stone fort, he could see a shower of arrows come sailing out of the jungle. One of them struck a klieg light with a distant *ping!*

The Indians were attacking. Hauser smiled. It was a diversion, of course, designed to draw the attention of his soldiers away from the bridge. He could see his own men huddling behind the stone walls, guns at the ready, loading their grenade launchers. He hoped to hell they could pull it off. At least they had an assignment to fake what they were already good at: failure.

More arrows came sailing out of the forest, followed by another eruption of bloodcurdling yells. The soldiers answered with a panicky burst of gunfire, and another. A grenade went sailing uselessly into the forest, and there was a flash and a bang.

For once the soldiers were getting it right.

Now that the Broadbents had made their move, Hauser knew exactly how it was going to unfold. It was as predetermined as a series of forced moves in chess.

And there they were, right on schedule. He raised his binoculars again. The three brothers and their Indian guide were running low across the open ground behind the soldiers, heading for the bridge. How clever they thought they were, racing with all their hearts and souls into a trap!

Hauser just had to laugh.

62

Sally had crawled within two hundred yards of the soldiers guarding the bridge. She lay behind a fallen tree trunk, her Springfield resting on the smooth wood. All was quiet. She hadn't said good-bye to Tom; they had simply kissed and gone. She tried not to think about what was going to happen. It was a crazy plan, and she doubted they'd ever get across the bridge. Even if they did, and were able to rescue their father, they'd never get back.

This was exactly what she didn't want to be thinking about. She turned her attention to the rifle. The Springfield '03 dated back to before World War I, but it felt right, and the optics were excellent. Chori had taken good care of it. She had already calculated the distance from her hiding place to where the soldiers were hunkered down inside the ruined stone fort—210 yards—and she had adjusted the scope accordingly. The ammunition Chori had given her was standard military issue .30-06 with a 150-grain bullet, so no additional calculations were necessary, even if she had the adjustment tables handy, which she did not. She had also adjusted the knurled windage knob to her best estimate of the wind conditions. The fact was, 210 yards was not much of a challenge for her, especially with a stationary target as large as a man.

Since she had arrived at the log she had been thinking about what it would mean to kill another person and whether she could do it. Now, as the action was minutes from beginning, she knew she could. To save

Tom's life she would do it. Hairy Bugger was sitting in a little cage made of woven vines. She was glad he was there to keep her company, although he'd been fretting and grumping at Tom's absence and his own imprisonment. She took out a handful of nuts, gave a few to Bugger, and ate the rest herself.

It was about to begin.

Right on schedule she heard a distant yell from the forest on the far side of the soldiers, followed by a chorus of whoops, shrieks, and ululations that sounded more like a hundred warriors than ten. A shower of arrows flashed out of the dark woods, aimed high so they would come down on the soldiers at a steep angle.

She quickly fitted her eye to the scope to see the action better. The soldiers were scrambling in a panic, loading their grenade launchers and getting in position behind the stone wall. They began firing back, disorganized panicky bursts aimed willy-nilly at the wall of forest two hundred yards away. A grenade went sailing uselessly toward the forest, falling short and going off with a flash and bang. More grenades followed, bursting in the treetops and ripping the branches off the trees. It was an unusually incompetent display of military prowess.

To her left Sally saw a flash of movement. The four Broadbents were running at a crouch across the open area toward the bridgehead. They had two hundred yards of brush and fallen tree trunks to negotiate, but they were making good time. The soldiers seemed fully occupied with the feint attack on their flank. Sally continued watching through the scope, ready to provide covering fire.

One of the soldiers rose and turned to get more grenades. Sally aimed for his chest, finger on the trigger. He scurried back, dodging the rain of arrows, took two more grenades from the can, and came back—never having looked up.

Sally's finger relaxed. The Broadbents were now reaching the bridge. It spanned a gap of six hundred feet, and it had been well engineered, with four cables of twisted fiber, two above and two below, carrying the load. Vertical cords between the upper and lower sets of cables formed a kind of support for the surface of the bridge itself, formed from pieces of bamboo lashed midway between the two sets of cables. One by one the Broadbents swung underneath it, climbing out over the chasm on one of the lower cables, sidestepping their way and using the upright cords as handholds. The timing was right: The mists were rising heavily, and within fifty yards the four brothers had disappeared. The attack continued for another ten minutes, with more yells and showers of arrows, before dying away. It was a miracle. They had gotten across. The crazy plan had worked.

Now all they had to do was get back.

63

The rickety bamboo bridge stretched ahead of Tom, swaying and rattling in the updrafts, trailing vines and pieces into the great chasm that yawned below it. The mists were rising thickly, and Tom could see only twenty feet ahead of him. The sound of the waterfall echoed up from below like the deep distant roar of a furious beast, and the bridge shook with every step.

Borabay had gone first, Vernon was next, then Philip. Tom had followed last.

They sidestepped along the bottom cable, keeping out of sight below the surface of the bridge. Tom followed his brothers, moving as fast as safety would allow. The main cable was wet and slippery from the rising mist, the twisted fibers spongy and rotten, and many of the vertical cables had broken, leaving gaps. Every time a gust came up from below, the bridge swayed and shuddered, and Tom had to stop and cling until it had passed. He tried to focus on just the few feet of bridge in front of him and nothing else. *One step at a time,* he said to himself. *One step at a time.*

A rope, more rotten than most, gave way in his hand, and he experienced a brief sway of terror over the abyss before he could grasp another. He stopped, letting his hammering heart subside. As he cautiously moved forward, he began testing each rope with a tug before trusting it as a handhold. He looked ahead. His brothers were shadowy forms moving ahead of him, partially obscured in mists, bathed in a kind of shifting half-light from the powerful spotlight shining behind them in the fog.

The farther they edged out on the bridge, the more it shook and swayed, the bamboo squeaking and the cables groaning and sighing as if alive. In the middle of the bridge the wind currents grew stronger, buffeting them as they blew upward. Once in a while a turbulent gust caused the bridge to shake and twitch in the most terrifying way. Tom couldn't help but think of Don Alfonso's story of the bottomless chasm, the falling bodies turning around and around forever, disintegrating into dust. He shivered and tried to keep from looking down, but in order to place his feet he was forced to look into a dizzying space that plunged downward into columns of mist that disappeared into a bottomless dark. They were almost at the midpoint: He could see where the bridge reached the lowest point of its curve and began to rise back up to meet the far side of the chasm.

An exceptionally strong gust of wind billowed up, giving the bridge a sudden shake. Tom tightened his grip, almost slipping off. He heard a muffled cry and saw, ahead, two pieces of rotten cord drop into the chasm, spinning wildly in the updraft; and then Philip was suddenly dangling, holding on to the cable by the crook of one elbow, his feet twisting and milling over the void.

Oh my God, thought Tom. He hastened forward, almost slipping himself. There was no way his brother was going to be able to hold on like that for more than a few moments. He arrived at a point just above his brother. Philip was dangling silently, trying to throw his leg up and over, his face twisted, unable to speak with terror. The others had disappeared into the mists.

Tom crouched, one arm wrapped around the cable, the other trying to hook under Philip's arm. His own feet suddenly shot out from underneath him, and he momentarily dangled over the abyss before righting himself. He felt his heart pounding in his chest; his vision clouded with terror, and he could hardly breathe.

"Tom," his brother choked out, his voice as high as a child's.

Tom flattened himself on the cable above Philip. "Swing," he said to Philip, keeping his own voice calm. "Help me. Swing your body up. I'll grab you." He reached down with one arm, ready to snag Philip's belt.

Philip tried to swing himself back up and snag his feet on the cable but couldn't get a purchase, and the effort caused his arm to slip. He let out a short cry. Tom could see Philip's white knuckles clutching the cable, his hands locked together. A keening sound of terror escaped his lips.

"Try it again," Tom shouted. "Swing your body up. Up!"

Philip, grimacing, swung, and Tom tried to grab his belt, but his foot slipped again, and for one terrifying moment his leg dangled in space and he was holding himself on by one rotten cord. He hauled himself back up, trying to calm his pounding heart. A piece of bamboo, jarred loose by the activity, fell down, down, slowly turning around and around until it vanished from sight.

He's got about five seconds, thought Tom. This would be Philip's last chance. "Swing up. Give it all you've got, even if you have to let go. Get ready. One, two, three!"

Philip swung, and this time Tom let go with one arm, holding on to the rotten cord with the other, which allowed him to lean out far enough to snag Philip's belt with his hand. For a minute they were suspended, the two of them, most of their combined weight on the cord, and then with a tremendous heave Tom pulled Philip up on the cable, and he fell upon it, hugging it like a life ring.

They remained there, clutching the cables, both too terrified even to speak. Tom could hear Philip's harsh gasps.

"Philip?" he finally managed to say. "Are you okay?"

The rasping breaths began to subside.

"You're okay." Tom tried to make it a statement. "It's all right. It's over. You're safe."

There was another gust of wind, and the bridge shook. A sound, a gurgle, came from Philip, and his whole body tightened on the cable.

A minute passed. A very long minute.

"We've got to keep moving," Tom said. "You've got to stand up."

There was another gust, and the bridge danced and shimmied.

"I can't."

Tom understood what he meant. He himself had a powerful urge to wrap himself around the main cable and stay there forever.

The mists were thinning. More gusts came from below, very strong ones this time, and the bridge swayed. It wasn't a regular motion but a sway with a twist at the end, a snap, as it were, that each time threatened to twitch them off into the gloom below.

The shaking subsided.

"Stand up, Philip."

"No."

"You've got to. Now." Time was the one thing they didn't have. The mists had cleared. The klieg light was shining brightly. All the soldiers had to do was turn and look. He extended his hand. "Grab my hand and I'll lift you up."

Philip raised a shaking hand, and Tom grasped it and slowly pulled his brother up. The bridge swayed, and Philip clutched at the vertical cords. There was another series of gusts, and the bridge began to shudder and sway in that awful way again. Philip moaned in terror. Tom himself held on for dear life, his body thrown from side to side. Five minutes went by while the bridge shuddered, the longest five minutes of his life. He could feel his arms aching from the effort. Finally the shaking subsided.

"Let's go."

Philip moved one foot, gingerly placed it ahead on the cable, then another, then moved his hands, sidestepping along. In five minutes they had reached the far side. Borabay and Vernon had been waiting for them in the darkness, and together they plunged into the cloudforest, running as fast as they could.

64

orabay led the way through the forest, and his three brothers followed, moving in single file. Their way was lit by that strange phosphorescence Tom had seen earlier; every rotting stump and log was
etched in faint green light, shimmering like ghosts in the forest. It no
longer looked beautiful—only menacing.

After twenty minutes a broken stone wall loomed ahead. Borabay
stopped and crouched down, and suddenly there was a flare of light
and he stood up holding a burning bundle of reeds. The wall leapt
into view: It was made with giant limestone blocks, almost obscured
by a heavy mat of vines. Tom glimpsed a bas-relief—faces in profile, a
row of hollow-eyed skulls, fantastical jaguars, birds with huge talons
and gaping eyes.

"The city walls."

They walked along the wall for a moment and came to a small
doorway with vines hanging down across it like a beaded curtain.
Pushing the vines aside, they ducked through.

In the feeble light Borabay reached out, grasped Philip's arm, and
drew him toward him. "Little brother Philip, you brave."

"No, Borabay, I'm a dreadful coward and a hindrance."

Borabay gave him an affectionate slap on the arm. "Not true. I
scared out of shit there."

"Scared shitless."

"Thankee." Borabay cupped the brand and blew on it, brightening the flame. His face glowed in the light, making his green eyes golden, highlighting his Broadbent chin and finely formed lips. "We go to tombs now. We go find Father."

They passed through the doorway into a ruined courtyard. A staircase mounted up the side. Borabay flitted across the courtyard and climbed the stairs, and the others followed. He turned right, walked along the top of the wall, cupping the brand to obscure the light, and descended a staircase on the other side. There was a sudden shriek in the trees above and a commotion, the treetops thrashing and snapping. Tom jumped.

"Monkeys," whispered Borabay, but he paused, his face troubled. Then he shook his head and they went on, passing through a jumble of toppled columns into an inner courtyard. The courtyard was full of fallen blocks of stone, some measuring ten feet on a side, that had once formed a gigantic head. Tom could see a nose here, a staring eye there, an ear elsewhere, poking up helter-skelter from the riot of vegetation and snaking tree roots. They climbed over the blocks and passed through a doorway framed by stone jaguars into an underground passageway. The air moving through the corridor smelled cool and moldy. The brand flickered. The flame revealed they were in a tunnel of stone, the walls crusted with lime, the ceiling bristling with stalactites. Insects rustled and skittered across the damp walls seeking refuge from the light. A fat viper jerked itself into an S-coil with its head raised in striking position. It hissed, swaying slightly, its slitted eyes reflecting the orange flame. They gave the snake a wide berth and went on. Through cave-ins in the stone ceiling Tom could see a scattering of stars though the swaying treetops, lashed by wind. They went past an old stone altar littered with bones, out the far end of the tunnel, and across a platform dotted with broken statues, heads and arms and legs emerging from the tangle of vines like a crowd of monsters drowning in a sea of vines.

Suddenly they came to the edge of a vast precipice—the far side of the plateau. Beyond stretched a sea of jagged black mountain peaks, faintly backlit by starlight. Borabay paused to light a fresh brand. He tossed the spent torch over the cliff, where it flickered and disappeared into the blackness below. He led them along a trail skirting the edge, then through a cleverly hidden gap in the rock that seemed to lead over the sheer cliff. But as they came through the gap a trail appeared, chiseled into the cliff, becoming a steep staircase cut into the very rock of the mountain. It switchbacked down the cliff and ended at a terrace—a stone balcony of sorts—paved with smoothly fitted stones, made by an undercut into the cliff, which rendered it invisible from above. On one side the jagged cliffs of the White City mesa mounted up. On the other side was a sheer drop of thousands of feet into blackness. Hundreds of black doors riddled the cliffs above, with precipitous trails and staircases connecting them.

"Place of tombs," said Borabay.

The wind shivered and gusted around them, bringing with it the sickly-sweet smell of some nightblooming flower. Here they could not hear the sounds of the jungle above them—only the rising and falling of the wind. It was an eerie, haunting place.

My God, thought Tom, *to think that Father's up in those cliffs somewhere.*

Borabay led them through a dark doorway in the cliff, and they now ascended a spiral staircase cut into the rock. The cliff face was honey-combed with tombs, and the staircase passed open niches with bones inside them, a skull with a bit of hair, bony hands with rings winking on the fingers, mummified bodies rustling with insects, mice, and small snakes, disturbed by the light and retreating back into darkness. Several niches they passed contained fresh corpses, emanating a smell of decay; there the rustlings of animals and insects were even louder. They passed one corpse on which several large rats were crouched, eating.

"How many of these tombs did Father rob?" Philip asked.

"Only one," said Borabay. "But it was richest one."

Some of the tomb doors were smashed, as if broken into by grave robbers or shaken loose by ancient earthquakes. At one point Borabay stopped and picked something up off the ground. Silently he handed it to Tom. It was a shiny wing nut.

The staircase turned and ended on a ledge halfway up the cliff face, about ten feet wide. There was a massive stone door, the largest they had seen, which faced outward across the dark sea of mountains and the starry night sky above. Borabay held the burning brand up to the door, and they stood looking at it. All the other tomb doors had been unadorned; this one, however, had a small relief carved into its face, a Mayan glyph. Borabay paused, then took a step backward, saying something in his own language, like a prayer. Then he turned and whispered.

"Father's tomb."

65

The old gray men sat arrayed like mummies around the boardroom
table, high above the city of Geneva. Julian Clyve faced them across
the wilderness of polished wood, beyond which, through the wall of
glass, was spread the Lake of Geneva with its giant fountain, like a little white flower far below them.

"We trust," said the head man, "that you received the advance."

Clyve nodded. A million dollars. These days not a lot of money,
but more than what he was earning at Yale. These men were getting a
bargain and they knew it. No matter. The two million was for the
manuscript. They still had to pay him for the translation. Sure, there
were others who could now translate ancient Maya, but only he could
manage the difficult archaic dialect that the manuscript was written
in. He and Sally, that is. They hadn't yet discussed the particulars of
his translation fees. One step at a time.

"We called you here," the man continued, "because there is a
rumor."

They had been speaking in English, but Clyve decided to respond
in German, which he spoke fluently, as a way of throwing them off
balance. "Whatever I can do to help."

There was an uncomfortable shifting in the wall of gray, and the
man continued to speak in English. "There is a pharmaceutical company in the United States by the name of Lampe-Denison. Do you
know of it?"

Clyve continued in German. "I believe I do. One of the big ones."

The man nodded. "The rumor is that they are acquiring a ninth-century Mayan medicinal codex containing two thousand pages of indigenous medical prescriptions."

"There can't be two. It's impossible."

"That is right. There can't be two. And yet the rumor exists. The price of Lampe stock has risen more than twenty percent over the past week as a result."

The seven gray men continued looking at Clyve, waiting for his answer. Clyve shifted, crossed his legs, then recrossed them. He had a momentary frisson of fear. What if the Broadbents had somehow made other arrangements for the Codex? But they hadn't. Before she left, Sally had reported back to him in detail on how things stood, and since then the Broadbents had been incommunicado in the jungle, unable to strike deals. The Codex was free and clear. And he had great faith in Sally to do his bidding. She was bright, capable, and very much under his thumb. He shrugged. "The rumor's false. I control the Codex. From Honduras it'll be coming directly into my hands."

Another silence.

"We have deliberately refrained from inquiring into your affairs, Professor Clyve," continued the man. "But now you have one million of our dollars. Which means we are concerned. Perhaps the rumor isn't true. Very well. I would like an explanation for the very *existence* of this information."

"If you're implying that I've been careless, I can assure you I've spoken to no one."

"No one?"

"Except my colleague, Sally Colorado—naturally."

"And she?"

"She's deep in the Honduran jungle. She can't even contact me. How could she contact anyone else? And she is the soul of discretion."

The silence around the table stretched on for a minute. Was this what they had called him all the way to Geneva for? Clyve didn't like it. He didn't like it at all. He was not their whipping boy. He rose. "I am offended by the imputation," he said. "I'm going to keep my end of the bargain, and that's all you gentlemen need to know. You'll get the Codex, and you'll pay me the second million—and then we'll discuss my fees for translating it."

That was greeted with a further silence. "Fees for translating it?" the man repeated.

"Unless you intend to translate it yourselves." They looked like they'd just sucked lemons. What a gaggle of morons they were. Clyve despised businessmen like these: uneducated, ignorant, their slavering greed hidden behind a genteel facade of expensively tailored fabric.

"We hope for your sake, Professor, that you *will* do what you've promised."

"Don't threaten me."

"It is a promise, not a threat."

Clyve bowed. "Good day, gentlemen."

66

Seven weeks had passed since Tom and his two brothers had gathered at the gates to their father's estate—but it felt like a lifetime. They had finally made it. They had reached the tomb.

"Do you know how to open it?" asked Philip.

"No."

"Father must have figured it out, because he robbed the tomb once," said Vernon.

Borabay set some burning torches in niches in the rock walls, and together they made a minute inspection of the tomb door. It was solid stone, set into a doorway squared out of the white limestone of the cliffs. There was no keyhole, no buttons or panels or hidden levers. Surrounding the tomb, the rest of the rock had been left in its natural state, with the exception of a number of holes drilled into the rock on either side of the door. Tom held his hand over one and felt a cool flow of air—evidently airholes to the tomb.

The eastern sky brightened with a predawn light as they examined the area around the tomb. They rapped on the door, called, hammered and pressed and tried everything to open it. Nothing worked. An hour passed and the door remained immovable.

Finally Tom said, "This isn't working. We need a new approach."

They retired to a nearby ledge. The stars had disappeared, and the sky was brightening behind the mountains. It was a stupendous view across a fantastical wilderness of jagged white peaks, like teeth rising

from the soft green palate of the jungle. "If we take a look at one of
those broken tomb doors," said Tom, "maybe we can figure out how it
works."

They retraced their steps and, four or five tombs back, came to a
broken door. It had cracked down the middle, and one part had fallen
outward. Borabay lit another brand, then hesitated at the door.

He turned to Philip. "I coward," he said, handing him the brand.
"You braver than me, little brother. You go."

Philip gave Borabay a squeeze on the shoulder and took the brand.
He went into the tomb. Tom and Vernon followed.

It was not a large space, perhaps eight by ten feet. In the center was a
raised stone platform. On the platform sat a mummy bundle, still
upright, its legs drawn up to its chin, its arms folded in its lap. Its long
black hair was braided down its back, and the dried lips were drawn
back from its teeth. The mouth had fallen open, and an object had
dropped out. When Tom looked more closely he saw it was a piece of
jade carved in the shape of a chrysalis. One hand of the mummy held a
polished cylinder of wood about eighteen inches long, decorated with
glyphs. Ranged around were a small selection of grave goods: terra-
cotta figurines, broken pots, some carved stone tablets.

Tom knelt down and examined how the door worked. There was a
groove in the stone floor; set into the groove were polished stone
rollers on which the door rested. They were loose, and Tom picked
one out and handed it to Philip. He turned it over in his hand.

"It's a simple mechanism," he said. "You get the door rolling and it
opens by itself. The trick is, how do you start the door rolling?"

They examined it all around, but there was no obvious answer.
When they emerged from the tomb Borabay was waiting for them, an
anxious expression on his face.

"What find?"

"Nothing," said Philip.

Vernon emerged from the tomb holding the cylinder of wood that
the mummy had been clutching. "What's this, Borabay?"

"Key to underworld."

Vernon smiled. "Interesting." He carried it back along the passageway to their father's tomb. "Funny that the stick should fit so perfectly

into these airholes," said Vernon, shoving the stick in several holes, almost losing it in one. "You can feel the air coming out of these holes. See?" He went from hole to hole, testing with his hand the flow of air from each one. Finally he stopped. "Here's an airhole with no breeze coming out of it."

He inserted the stick. It went in about fourteen inches and stopped, leaving four inches exposed. Vernon picked up a heavy, smooth rock. He handed it to Philip.

"You do the honors. Whack the end of the stick."

Philip took the rock. "What makes you think this'll work?"

"A wild guess, that's all."

Philip hefted the rock, braced himself, drew back his arm, and brought the rock down hard against the protruding end of the stick. There was a *chunk* as he drove the stick into the hole, and then silence.

Nothing happened. Philip examined the hole. The wooden dowel had gone all the way in and stuck.

"Damn it!" Philip cried, losing his temper. He rushed at the tomb door and gave it a savage kick. "Open up, damn you!"

A sudden grinding noise filled the air, the ground vibrated, and the stone door began to slide open. A dark crack appeared and gradually widened as the door moved in the groove along its stone rollers. In a moment, with a clunk, it came to a halt.

The tomb was open.

They all waited, staring into the yawning black rectangle. The sun was just breaking over the distant mountains, pouring golden light across the rocks, at an angle too oblique to penetrate into the tomb itself, which remained in utter blackness. They stood without moving, paralyzed, too afraid to speak or call out. A pestilential cloud of corruption—the stench of death—came drifting out of the tomb.

67

Marcus Aurelius Hauser waited in the pleasing dawn light, his finger stroking the blunt trigger of his Steyr AUG. The weapon was perhaps the most familiar object he knew besides his own body, and he never felt quite normal without it. The metal barrel, warmed from constant contact, felt almost alive, and the plastic stock, polished by his own hands for years, was as smooth as a woman's thigh.

Hauser had tucked himself into a comfortable niche along the trail that led down the cliff. While he couldn't actually see the Broadbents from his vantage point on the trail above, he knew they were below and would have to come back the same way. They had done exactly what he hoped. They had led him to old Max's tomb. And not just one tomb, but a whole necropolis. Unbelievable. He would have found this trail eventually, but it might have taken a long time.

The Broadbents had now served their purpose. There was no rush; the light was not high enough, and he wanted to give them plenty of time to get comfortable, to relax, to assume they were safe. And he, Hauser, wanted to think this op through. One of the great lessons he had learned in Vietnam was patience. That was how the Viet Cong had won the war—they were more patient.

He gazed around with delight. The necropolis was stupendous, a thousand tombs filled with grave goods, a tree laden with fruit ripe for the plucking. Not to mention all the valuable antiquities, stelae, statuary, reliefs, and other treasures in the White City itself. On top of that, there was the half billion dollars' worth of art and antiquities in Broadbent's tomb. He would bring the Codex out with some of the lighter stuff and finance his return with the proceeds. Yes, he would definitely be back. There were billions to be made in the White City. Billions.

He felt into his musette bag, fondled a cigar, and with regret allowed it to remain undisturbed. It would not do for them to smell cigar smoke.

One had to make certain sacrifices.

68

The four brothers stood rooted to the ground, staring into the rectangle of darkness. They could not move, they could not speak. The seconds ticked on into minutes as the flow of foul air ebbed. No one made a move to go inside the tomb. No one wanted to see what horror lay within.

And then there was a sound: a cough. And another: the shuffle of a foot.

They were paralyzed, mute with anticipation.

Another shuffle. Tom knew it then: Their father was alive. He was coming out of the tomb. Still Tom could not move, and neither could the others. Just as the tension became unbearable, in the center of the black rectangle, a ghostly face began to materialize. Another shambling step, and now an apparition appeared in the gloom. Another step brought the figure into reality.

He was almost more horrifying than a corpse. The figure halted before them unsteadily, blinking his eyes. He was stark naked, shrunken, stooped, filthy, cadaverous, smelling like death itself. Snot ran from his nose; his mouth hung open like a madman's. He blinked, sniffed, blinked again in the dawn light, his colorless eyes vacant, uncomprehending.

Maxwell Broadbent.

The seconds ticked by, and still they remained rooted to the ground, speechless.

Broadbent stared at them, one eye twitching. He blinked again and straightened up. The hollow eyes, sunken in great dark pools of flesh, were darting from each of their faces to the next. He took a long, noisy breath.

No matter how much he wanted to, Tom could not move or speak. He stared as their father straightened up a bit more. The eyes roved once again across their faces, more penetrating. He coughed, the mouth worked a bit, but no sound came. Broadbent raised a trembling hand, and finally a cracked sound came from his lips. They leaned forward, straining to understand.

Broadbent cleared his throat, rumbled, and took a step closer. He inhaled again and finally spoke:

"What the hell took you so long?"

It roared out, ringing off the cliffs, echoing back out of the tomb. The spell was broken. It was their old father, there in the flesh after all. Tom and the others rushed forward and embraced the old man. He gripped them fiercely, all at once and then each one in turn, his arms surprisingly strong.

After a long moment Maxwell Broadbent stepped back. He seemed to have expanded to his usual size.

"Jesus Christ," he said, wiping his face. "Jesus, Jesus Christ."

They all looked at him, unsure how to respond.

The old man shook his great gray head. *"Christ almighty,* I'm glad you're here. God, I must stink. Look at me. I'm a mess. Naked, filthy, revolting!"

"Not at all," said Philip. "Here, let me give you this." He pulled off his shirt.

"Thank you, Philip." Maxwell put on Philip's shirt and buttoned it up, his fingers fumbling clumsily. "Who does your laundry? This shirt is a disgrace." He attempted a laugh and ended up coughing.

When Philip began taking off his pants, Broadbent held up a large hand. "I'm not going to strip my own sons."

"Father—"

"They buried me naked. I'm used to it."

Borabay reached into his palm-leaf pack and pulled out a long piece of decorated cloth. "You wear this."

"Going native, am I?" Broadbent awkwardly fitted it around his waist. "How do you tie it up?"

Borabay helped him tie it around his waist with a knotted hemp cord.

The old man knotted it and stood there, saying nothing. Nobody knew what to say next.

"Thank God you're alive," said Vernon.

"At first I wasn't so sure myself," Broadbent said. "For a while there I thought I'd died and gone to hell."

"What, you? The old atheist now believing in hell?" said Philip.

He looked up at Philip, smiled, and shook his head. "So much has changed."

"Don't tell me you found God."

Broadbent wagged his head and clapped a hand on Philip's shoulder. He gave it an affectionate shake. "Good to see you, son."

He turned to Vernon. "And you, too, Vernon." He looked around, turning his crinkly blue eyes on each of them. "Tom, Vernon, Philip, Borabay—I'm overwhelmed." He placed a hand on each of their heads in turn. "You made it. You found me. My food and water were almost gone. I could only have lasted a day or two more. You've given me a second chance. I don't deserve it but I'm going to take it. I did a lot of thinking in that dark tomb . . ."

He looked up and out over the purple sea of mountains and the golden sky, straightened up, and inhaled.

"Are you okay?" Vernon asked.

"If it's the cancer you're talking about, I'm sure it's still there—just hasn't kicked in yet. I've still got a couple of months. The son of a bitch got into my brain—I never told you that. But so far, so good: I feel great." He looked around. "Let's get the hell out of here."

Tom said, "Unfortunately, it's not going to be that simple."

"How so?"

Tom glanced at his brothers. "We've got a problem, and his name is Hauser."

"Hauser!" Broadbent was astonished.

Tom nodded and told their father all the details of their respective journeys.

"Hauser!" Broadbent repeated, looking at Philip. "You teamed up with that bastard?"

"I'm sorry," said Philip. "I figured . . ."

"You figured he'd know where I went. My fault: I should have seen that was a possibility. Hauser's a ruthless sadist, almost killed a girl once. The biggest mistake in my life was partnering with him." Broadbent eased himself down on a shelf of rock and shook his shaggy head. "I can't believe the risks you took getting here. God, what a mistake I made. The last one of many, in fact."

"You our father," said Borabay.

Broadbent snorted. "Some father. Putting you to a ridiculous test like this. It seemed like a good idea at the time. I can't understand what got into me. What a damn stupid, foolish old bastard I've been."

"We haven't exactly been My Three Sons," said Philip.

"Four sons," said Borabay.

"Or . . . perhaps there are more?" Vernon asked, raising one eyebrow.

Broadbent shook his head. "Not that I know of. Four fine sons if only I'd had the brains to realize it." He fixed his blue eyes on Vernon. "Except for that beard, Vernon. Good Christ, when are you going to trim that hairy appendage? You look like a mullah."

Vernon said, "You don't look too clean-cut yourself."

Broadbent waved his hand and laughed. "Forget I said that. Old habits die hard. Keep your damn beard."

There was an awkward silence. The sun was rising higher above the mountains, and the light was turning from gold to white. A flock of chattering birds flew past, dipping and rising and swerving in unison.

Tom turned to Borabay. "We need to think of our plan of escape."

"Yes, brother. I think of this already. We wait here until dark. Then we go back." He glanced up at the clear sky. "It rain tonight, give us cover."

"What about Hauser?" Broadbent asked.

"He search for tomb in White City. He not yet think of looking in cliffs. I think we get by him. He not know we here."

Broadbent looked around. "You didn't bring any food with you, by any chance? That stuff they left me in the tomb wasn't fit for an in-flight meal."

Borabay unpacked food from his palm-leaf backpack and began setting it out. Broadbent shuffled over a little unsteadily. "Fresh fruit. My God." He picked up a mango and bit into it, the juice running out of his mouth and dripping onto his shirt. "This is heaven." He crammed the mango into his mouth, ate a second one, and then polished off a couple of *curwa* fruits and some smoked lizard fillets.

"Borabay, you could open a restaurant."

Tom watched his father eat. He could hardly believe that the old man was still alive. There was something unreal about it. Everything, and nothing, had changed.

Broadbent finished his meal and leaned back against the stone wall, gazing out over the mountains.

"Father," Philip asked, "if you don't mind telling us, what happened to you in that tomb?"

"Philip, I'll tell you how it was. We had a big funeral—no doubt Borabay told you all about it. I drank Cah's infernal drink. The next thing I knew, I was waking up. It was pitch-black. As a good atheist I'd always believed death was the end of consciousness. That was it. But here I was, *still conscious*, even though I was sure I was dead. I've never been so frightened in my life. And then, as I fumbled around in the darkness in a total panic, I had a sudden thought: *Not only am I dead, but I've gone to hell!*"

"You didn't really believe that," said Philip.

He shook his head. "I did. You have no idea how terrified I was. I wailed and howled like a lost soul. I begged God, I prayed on my knees, I repented, I swore I'd be good if only he'd give me one more chance. I felt like one of those poor sods in Michelangelo's *Last Judgment* crying out for forgiveness while being dragged down by demons into a lake of fire.

"And then, when I was all tired out with wailing and self-pity, I began to recover a bit of my sanity. That's when I crawled around and realized I was in the tomb—and it dawned on me that I wasn't dead after all, that Cah had buried me alive. He'd never forgiven me for what I'd done to his father. I should have known it; Cah always struck me as a shifty old fox. When I found the food and water I knew I was in for a long ordeal. I had planned this whole thing to be a lighthearted challenge for the three of you. And then suddenly my life depended on your success."

"A lighthearted challenge?" Philip repeated skeptically.

"I wanted to shock you into doing something more important with your lives. What I didn't realize is that each of you *is* doing something important—that is, living the life that *you* want to live. Who am I to judge?" He paused, cleared his throat, shook his head. "Here I was locked up with what I thought was my treasure, my *life's work*—and it was crap. It was useless. Suddenly it meant nothing. In the dark I couldn't even look at it. Being entombed alive shook me to the core. I found myself looking back on my whole life with a kind of loathing. I had been a bad father to you, a bad husband, greedy, selfish—and then I found myself praying."

"No," said Philip.

Broadbent nodded. "What else was there to do? And then I heard voices, a bang, then a rumbling sound, and the light came in, and there you all were! My prayers had been answered."

"You mean," Philip asked, "you found religion? You're a believer?"

"You're goddamn right I found religion!" He lapsed into silence, looking out over the vast landscape stretching below, the endless mountains and jungles. He shifted, coughed. "Funny, I feel like I've died and been reborn."

69

From his hiding place, Hauser could hear the murmur of their voices carried up on the wind. He couldn't make out individual words, but he had no doubt what was going on: They were having a grand old time looting their father's tomb. No doubt they were planning to take out the smaller stuff—including the Codex. The woman, Colorado, knew what it was worth. That would be the first thing they would take.

In his mind, Hauser ran through the list of other treasures in the tomb. A great deal of Maxwell Broadbent's collection would be portable, including some of the most valuable items. There were some rare carved gemstones from the Indian subcontinent. There was a large collection of Inca and Aztec gold artifacts, most of which were small, as were the ancient Greek gold coins. There were two extremely valuable Etruscan bronze figurines, each about ten inches high, that weighed less than twenty pounds apiece. All these things could be carried on the back of a single man. Value: between ten and twenty million.

They would be able to carry out the Lippi and the Monet. These two paintings were relatively small—the Lippi was twenty-eight by eighteen inches, the Monet thirty-six by twenty-six. Both had been packed unframed. The Lippi, painted on gessoed wood, weighed ten pounds and the Monet eight pounds. The two boxes that held them weighed no more than thirty pounds apiece. Both boxes could be tied together, strapped on a pack frame, and carried out on one person's back. Value: upward of one hundred million.

There were, of course, many treasures they could not take. The Pontormo, worth perhaps thirty or forty million, was too large. So was the Bronzino portrait. The Mayan stelae and the Soderini bronzes were too heavy. But the two Braques were portable. The smaller of the two was one of Braque's earliest cubist masterpieces, which might fetch five or ten million. There was a late Imperial Roman bronze statue of a boy, half life-size, that weighed a hundred pounds—probably too much to carry out. There were Cambodian temple figurines in stone, a couple of early Chinese bronze urns, some Mayan inlaid turquoise plaques . . . Max had had a good eye, and he had gone for quality, not quantity. Over the years, a lot of art had passed through his hands, and he had shortstopped only the very best for himself.

Yes, Hauser thought, if it weren't for him the four of them below could remove on their backs artworks amounting to perhaps two hundred million dollars. Almost half the value of the entire collection.

He shifted, stretching his cramped legs. The sun was bright and hot. He glanced at his watch. Five to ten. He had decided to move out at ten o'clock. Time had little meaning out here, but the habits of discipline gave him pleasure. It was, he thought, more a philosophy of life than anything else. He stood up, stretched his arms, and took a few deep breaths. He did a rapid check of his Steyr AUG. It was, as usual, in perfect working order. He smoothed his hair again, then examined his cuticles and nails. There was a rim of dirt under one of them; he scraped it out with the end of his nail file and flicked it away. Then he examined the backs of his hands, which were smooth, hairless, and white and showed only the faintest trace of veins; they were the hands of a thirty-year-old, not a man of sixty. He had always taken good care of his hands. The sun glistened off the array of heavy gold and diamond rings on his fingers. He flexed his hands five times, balling and opening them, and then shook out the creases in his khaki pants, rotated his ankles, rolled his head around on his neck five times, opened his arms wide, and inhaled again. Exhaled. Inhaled. He examined his crisp white shirt. He would consider this op successful if, at the end, his shirt was free of spots. It was such a trial keeping one's clothes clean in the jungle.

Hauser eased the Steyr AUG back on his shoulder and headed down the trail.

70

The four brothers and their father rested in the shade along a shelf of rock to the side of the tomb door. They had eaten most of their food, and Tom passed around a canteen of water. There was so much Tom had wanted to say to his father, and he had no doubt his brothers felt the same way—and yet, after the initial outburst of talk, they had fallen silent. Somehow it was enough to be together. The canteen made the rounds, with a gurgle as each one drank, and ended up back with Tom. He screwed the top on and shoved it back in his small rucksack.

Finally Maxwell Broadbent spoke. "So Marcus Hauser is out there, looking to rob *my* tomb." He shook his head. "What a world."

"I'm sorry," said Philip again.

"It was my fault," said Broadbent. "No more apologies. Everything is my fault."

This was something new, Tom thought: Maxwell Broadbent admitting he was wrong. He seemed to be the same gruff old man, but he had changed. Definitely, he had changed.

"There's only one thing I want right now, and that's for my four sons to get out of here alive. I'm going to be a drag on you. You leave me here and I'll take care of myself. I'll greet that man Hauser in a way that he'll remember."

"What!" Philip exclaimed. "After all we did to rescue you?" He was genuinely outraged.

"Come now. I'm going to be dead in a month or two anyway. Leave me to deal with Hauser while you escape."

Philip rose up, furious. "Father, we didn't come all this way to abandon you to Hauser."

"I'm a sorry reason to risk your lives."

"Without you, we no go," Borabay said. "Wind come from east, bring storm tonight. We wait here till dark, then go. Get across bridge during storm."

Broadbent exhaled and wiped his face.

Philip cleared his throat. "Father?"

"Yes, son?"

"I don't mean to bring up an unwelcome subject, but what are we going to do about the stuff in your tomb?"

Tom immediately thought of the Codex. He had to bring it out, too—not only for himself, but for Sally and for the world.

Broadbent gazed at the ground for a moment before speaking. "I hadn't thought about that. It just doesn't seem important to me anymore. But I'm glad you brought it up, Philip. I suppose we should take the Lippi and anything else that's easy to carry. At least we can keep a few things out of that greedy bastard's hands. It kills me to think he's going to get most of the stuff, but I guess it can't be helped."

"When we get out, we'll report it to the FBI, Interpol—"

"Hauser's going to get away with it, Philip, and you know it. Which reminds me. There was something odd about the boxes in the tomb, something that I've been wondering about. As much as I hate to go back in there, there's something I've got to check out."

"I'll help you," Philip said, springing to his feet.

"No. I need to go in there alone. Borabay, give me a light."

Borabay lit a bundle of reeds and handed it to his father.

The old man disappeared through the doorway, and Tom could see the yellow halo moving about in the tomb among the crates and boxes. Maxwell Broadbent's voice boomed out. "God knows why all this bloody crap was so important to me once."

The light moved deeper into the darkness and vanished.

Philip stood up and walked a tight circle, stretching his legs.

He lit his pipe. "I hate to think of Hauser getting his hands on the Lippi."

A voice, cool and amused, came floating toward them:

"I say, did someone mention my name?"

71

Hauser spoke softly, soothingly, his weapon leveled and ready to go at the slightest movement. The three brothers and the Indian, sitting on the far side of the open tomb door, turned their heads toward him, blank terror in their eyes.

"Do not discommode yourselves by rising. Do not move at all, except to blink your eyes." He paused. "Philip, so good to see you recovered. You've come a long way from the effete little snit that walked into my office two months ago, with that ridiculous briar pipe."

Hauser took a light step forward, braced, ready to mow them down at the slightest movement. "How kind of you to guide me to the tomb. And you've even opened the door for me! Very considerate. Now listen carefully. If you follow my directions no one will be hurt."

Hauser paused to examine the four faces in front of him. No one was panicking, and no one was gearing up to play the hero. These were sensible people. He said, as softly and pleasantly as possible, "Someone tell the Indian he needs to put his bow and arrows down. Slowly and smoothly—no sudden movements, please."

Borabay took off his quiver and bow and let them fall in front of him.

"So the Indian understands English. Good. And now I will ask each of you fellows to unsheath and drop your machetes one at a time. You first, Philip. Remain seated."

Philip unsheathed his knife and dropped it.

"Vernon?"

Vernon did the same and then Tom.

"Now, Philip, I want you to go over to where you have piled your packs, get them, and bring them to me. Easy does it." He made a little gesture with the muzzle of his gun.

Philip collected the packs and placed them at Hauser's feet.

"Excellent! Now let's empty our pockets. Turn the pockets inside out and leave them that way. Drop everything on the ground in front of you."

They complied. Hauser was surprised to see that they had not, as he supposed, been loading up on treasure from the tomb.

"And now you'll stand up. All at once, in unison, in *slow* motion. Good! Now, just moving your legs from the knees down, taking small steps, keeping your arms *very* still, you will move back. Keep in a group there, that's right. One step at a time."

As they shuffled back in this ridiculous fashion, Hauser stepped forward. They had bunched up, instinctively, as people did when in danger—especially family members herded under gunpoint. He had seen it before, and it made everything so much easier.

"Everything's just fine," he said softly. "I don't want to hurt anybody—all I want is Max's grave goods. I'm a professional, and like most professionals I dislike killing." *Right.* His finger caressed the smooth plastic curve of the trigger, found its place, began to tighten it back to full auto position. They were in place. There was nothing they could do now. They were as good as dead.

"Nobody's going to get hurt." And then he couldn't help adding: "Nobody's going to feel a thing." He squeezed for real now, felt that imperceptible *give* in the trigger that he knew so well, that millisecond release after the feeling of resistance, and simultaneously Hauser saw a swift movement in his peripheral field of vision, and there was an explosion of sparks and flame and he fell, firing wildly as he went, the bullets ricocheting off the stone walls, and he had a terrifying glimpse of what had struck him before he hit the stone ground.

The thing had come straight out of the tomb, half naked, face white as a vampire, sunken-eyed, stinking of decomposition, its bony limbs as gray and hollow as death, holding aloft a burning brand that it had just struck him with, and it was still coming at him with a shrieking mouth full of brown teeth.

Damned if it wasn't the ghost of Maxwell Broadbent himself!

72

Hauser rolled when he hit the ground, still clutching his weapon. He twisted, trying to get back into firing position, but it was too late and the ragged specter of Maxwell Broadbent had fallen on top of him, roaring and stabbing and slashing him across the face with the burning brand; there were showers of sparks, and he smelled burning hair as he tried to ward off the blows with one hand, clutching his gun with the other. It was impossible to get off a shot while the attacker was trying to gouge out his eyes with the burning brand. He managed to wrench free, and then fired blindly, from on his back, wildly sweeping the muzzle back and forth, hoping to hit something, anything. But the specter seemed to have vanished.

He stopped firing and gingerly sat up. His face and right eye felt like they were on fire. He yanked the canteen out of his pack and doused his face.

Christ, how it hurt!

He dabbed the water off his face. Hot coals and sparks from the brand had lodged inside his nose, under one eyelid, in his hair and his cheek. The monstrous thing that had come out of the tomb—could it really have been a *ghost?* He opened, painfully, his right eye. As he gently probed around it with his fingertip, he realized the damage was all to the eyebrow and lid. The cornea was intact, and he hadn't lost his vision. He poured some water into his handkerchief, wrung it out, and blotted his face.

What the hell happened? Hauser, who always expected the unex-pected, had never been more shocked in his life. He *knew* that face, even after forty years; he knew every detail of it, every expression, every tic. There was no doubt: It was Broadbent himself who had come shrieking out of that tomb like a banshee—Broadbent, who was supposed to be dead and buried. White as a sheet, ragged hair and beard, hollow, skeletal, wild.

Hauser swore. What had he been thinking? Broadbent was alive and at this very moment escaping. Hauser shook his head in a sudden fury, trying to clear it. What the hell was wrong with him? He had allowed himself to be blindsided and now, sitting here, he'd given them at least a three-minute head start.

He quickly reshouldered his Steyr AUG, took a step forward, and stopped.

There was blood on the ground—an attractive, half-dollar-sized splotch. And farther along another generous splash. Hauser felt the semblance of calm return. As if he needed further confirmation, the so-called ghost of Broadbent was bleeding real blood. He had man-aged to hit him and perhaps some of the others after all, and even a grazing shot from the Steyr AUG was no joke. He took a moment to analyze the spray pattern, the amount, the trajectory.

The wound was not trivial. All in all, the advantage was still very much his.

He looked up the stone staircase and began running, taking it two steps at a time. He would get on their trail, he would track them down, and he would kill them.

73

They ran up the carved staircase, the sound of the shots still echoing from the distant mountains. They reached the trail at the top of the cliffs and sprinted for the green walls of lianas and creepers that covered the ruined ramparts of the White City. As they reached the covering shade, Tom saw his father stumble. Streaks of blood were running down one of his legs.

"Wait! Father's hit!"

"It's nothing." The old man stumbled again and grunted.

They stopped briefly at the base of the wall.

"Leave me alone!" the old man roared.

Ignoring him, Tom examined the wound, wiping away the blood, locating the entrance and exit wounds. The bullet had passed through the right lower abdomen at an angle, traversing the rectus abdominus and coming out the back, where it seemed to have avoided the kidney. It was impossible to tell yet whether the peritoneal cavity had been nicked. He pushed that possibility aside and palpated the area; his father groaned. It was a serious wound and he was losing blood, but at least no arteries or major veins had been cut.

"Hurry!" Borabay cried.

Tom took off his own shirt and with one savage pull tore a strip of cloth away, then another. He bound them as best he could around his father's midriff, trying to stem the loss of blood.

"Put your arm around my shoulder," Tom said.

"I'll take the other," Vernon said.

Tom felt the arm go around him—it was skinny and hard, like a cable of steel. He bent forward to take some of his father's weight. He felt his father's warm blood trickling down his leg.

"Let's go."

"Uff," Broadbent said, staggering a little as they set off.

They jogged along the base of the wall, looking for an opening. Borabay plunged through a liana-draped doorway, and they scrambled across a courtyard, through another doorway, and along a collapsed gallery. With the double support of Tom and Vernon, Maxwell Broadbent was able to move rapidly enough, wheezing and grunting with pain.

Borabay headed straight into the thickest, deepest part of the ruined city. They ran through dark galleries and half-collapsed underground chambers with massive roots bursting through their coffered stone ceilings. As they ran, Tom thought of the Codex and all the other things they were leaving behind.

They took turns supporting Broadbent as they moved on, passing through a series of dim tunnels, Borabay leading them in sharp turns and doubling back in an effort to throw off their pursuer. They came out into a grove of giant trees, surrounded on two sides by massive stone walls. Only the dimmest green light filtered down. Stone stelae, decorated with Mayan glyphs, dotted the grove like sentinels.

Tom heard his father's ragged breath and a muffled curse.

"I'm sorry that it hurts."

"Don't worry about me."

They traveled for another twenty minutes and arrived at a place where the jungle became riotously luxuriant and thick. Creepers and climbing vines smothered the trees, giving them the appearance of huge, muffled green ghosts. At the top of each suffocated tree, tendrils of vine seeking a new purchase grew straight out, like spiky hair. Heavy flowers hung everywhere. Water dripped incessantly.

Borabay paused, peering around. "This way," he said, pointing to the thickest part.

"How?" Philip said, looking at the impenetrable wall of growth.

Borabay dropped to his knees and crawled ahead, into a small opening. They did likewise, Max grunting with pain. Tom saw that hidden under the matted vines was a network of animal trails, tunnels going every which way through the vegetation. They crawled into the thickest of it, squeezing through the tunnels the animals had made. It was dark and rank. They crawled for what seemed like an eternity, but was probably no more than twenty minutes, through a fantastical maze of branching and rebranching trails, until they came to an open area, a cave in the vegetation underneath a vine-choked tree whose lower branches created a tentlike space, impenetrable on all sides.

"We stay here," Borabay said. "We wait until night."

Broadbent sagged back against the tree trunk with a groan. Tom knelt over his father, stripped off the blood-soaked bandages, and examined the wound. It was bad. Borabay knelt next to him and carefully examined it himself. Then he took some leaves he had plucked from somewhere during their flight, crushed and rubbed them between his palms, and made two poultices.

"What's that for?" Tom whispered.

"It stop bleeding, help pain."

They packed the poultices over the entrance and exit wounds. Vernon volunteered his shirt, and Tom tore it into strips, using them to tie the poultices into place.

"Uff," said Broadbent.

"I'm sorry, Father."

"Quit saying you're sorry, all of you. I want to groan without having to listen to apologies."

Philip said, "Father, you saved our lives back there."

"Lives that I put into danger in the first place."

"We'd be dead if you hadn't jumped on Hauser."

"The sins of my youth, come back to haunt me." He winced.

Borabay squatted on his heels and looked around at all of them. "I go now. I come back in half hour. If I no come back, when night come you wait till rain start and cross bridge without me. Okay?"

"Where are you going?" Vernon asked.

"To get Hauser."

He sprang up and was gone.

Tom hesitated. If he was going to go back for the Codex, it was now or never.

"There's something I have to do, too."

"What?" Philip and Vernon looked at him incredulously.

Tom shook his head. He couldn't find the words or the time to defend his decision. Maybe it wasn't even defensible. "Don't wait for me. I'll meet up with you at the bridge tonight, after the storm hits."

"Tom, have you gone crazy?" Max rumbled.

Tom didn't answer. He turned and slipped off into the jungle.

In twenty minutes he had crawled back out of the vine maze. He stood up to get his bearings. The necropolis of tombs was to the east: That much he knew. This close to the equator the late morning sun would still be in the eastern sky, and it gave him a general direction. He didn't want to think about the decision he had just made: whether it was right or wrong to leave his father and brothers, whether it was crazy, whether it was too dangerous. It was all beside the point: Getting the Codex was something he just had to do.

He went east.

74

Hauser's eyes scanned the ground ahead, reading it like a book: a seedpod pressed into the earth; a creased blade of grass; dew brushed from a leaf. He had learned how to track in Vietnam, and now every detail told him exactly where the Broadbents had gone as clearly as if they had left a trail of breadcrumbs. He followed their route rapidly but methodically, Steyr AUG at the ready. He felt better now, relaxed, if not at peace. Hauser had always found hunting a strangely compelling activity. And there was nothing to compare with the feeling of hunting the human animal. It was indeed the most dangerous game.

His worthless soldiers were still digging and blasting away at the far end of the city. Good. It would keep them busy. Tracking and killing Broadbent and his sons was a job for a lone hunter slipping unseen through the jungle, not for a noisy group of incompetent soldiers. Hauser had the advantage. He knew the Broadbents were unarmed, and he knew they would have to cross the bridge. It was only a matter of time before he caught up with them.

With them gone, he could loot the tomb at his leisure, bring out the Codex and the portable artworks, leave the rest for later. Now that he had softened up Skiba he was pretty sure he could extract more than fifty million from him, perhaps a lot more. Switzerland would be a good base to operate from. That was how Broadbent himself used to do it, launder questionable antiquities through Switzerland, claiming they were from an "old Swiss collection." The masterworks couldn't be sold on the open market—they were too famous and Broadbent's ownership too widely known—but they could be quietly placed here and there. There was always some Saudi sheik or Japanese industrialist or American billionaire who wanted to own a beautiful painting and who wasn't too particular where it came from.

Hauser abandoned these pleasant fantasies and turned his attention back to the ground. More dew swiped from a leaf; a spot of blood on the soil. He followed the traces into a ruined gallery and turned on his lamp. Moss scraped from a stone, an imprint in the soft ground—any idiot could follow these tracks.

He followed the signs as fast as he could, putting, as they said, as much pressure on the trail as possible. As he emerged into a broad forest, he saw one particularly clear trace, where they had stirred up some rotten leaves in their headlong flight.

Too clear. He froze, listened, and then crouched and minutely examined the ground ahead. Amateurish. The Viet Cong would laugh at this one: a bent sapling, a loop of vine hidden under leaves, an almost invisible trip wire. He took one careful step back, picked up a stick lying conveniently nearby, and lobbed it at the trip wire.

There was a snap, the sapling shot up, the loop jerked. And then Hauser felt a sudden breath of air and a tug on his pantleg. He looked down. Embedded in the loose crease of his pant was a small dart, its fire-hardened tip dribbling a dark liquid.

The poisoned dart had missed him by less than an inch.

For several minutes he remained frozen. He examined every square inch of ground around him, every tree, every limb. Satisfied there was no other trap, he leaned over and was about to pluck the dart out of his khakis when he stopped himself yet again—and just in time. The sides of the dart had imbedded in them two nearly invisible spines, also wet with poison, ready to prick the finger of whoever tried to grasp it.

He took a twig and flicked the dart off his pantleg.

Very clever. Three multilayered traps in one. Simple and effective. This was the Indian's work, no doubt about it.

Hauser moved forward, a little more slowly now, and with new-found respect.

75

Tom ran through the forest, speed taking precedence over silence, swinging wide of their earlier trail to avoid running into Hauser. His path took him through a maze of ruined temples buried under thick mats of vines. He had no light, and sometimes he had to feel his way down dark passageways or crawl under fallen stones.

He soon arrived at the eastern edge of the plateau. He paused, catching his breath, and then crept to the cliff and looked down, trying to orient himself. It seemed to him that the necropolis should lie somewhere to the south, so he went to the right, following the trail that skirted the cliffs. In another ten minutes he recognized the terrace and walls above the necropolis and found the hidden trail. He scurried down, listening at each switchback in case Hauser was still there, but he had long gone. A moment later he came to the dark opening to his father's tomb.

Their backpacks still lay in a pile on the ground where they had dropped them. Tom picked up his machete and resheathed it and then kneeled, rifling through the packs, taking out some reed bundles and a pack of matches. He lit one of the bundles and stepped into the tomb.

The air was pestilential. He breathed through his nose and ventured deeper inside. A tingle of horror crawled up his spine as he realized this was where his father spent the last month, locked up in pitch darkness. The flickering light illuminated a raised funeral slab of dark

stone, carved with skulls, monsters, and other strange motifs, surrounded by stacked boxes and crates banded with stainless steel and
bolted shut. This was no King Tut's tomb. It looked more like a
crowded, filthy warehouse.

Tom stepped closer, overcoming his sense of revulsion. Behind the
boxes his father had set up a crude living space. It looked as if he had
scraped together some dry straw and dust to form a kind of bed.
Along the back wall stood a row of clay pots, which evidently contained food and water; the stench of rot rose from them. Rats came
leaping out of the pots and fled before the light. Sick with fascination
and pity, Tom peered into one and found a scattering of dried plantains at the bottom; the food was crawling with greasy black cock-
roaches, which bumped and chittered in a panic from the torchlight.
Dead rats and mice floated in the water jugs. Against one wall was a
pile of rotting rats—obviously killed by his father in what must have
been the daily competition for food. In the back of the tomb Tom
could see the gleaming eyes of live rats, waiting for him to leave.

What his father had endured in here, waiting in the pitch-dark for
his sons who might not ever come . . . It was far more horrifying than
he could possibly imagine. That Maxwell Broadbent had endured and
lived—and even *hoped*—told Tom something about his father that he
had not known before.

He wiped his face. He needed to get the Codex and get out.

The boxes were stenciled and labeled, and it took Tom only a few
minutes to find the crate containing the Codex.

He dragged the heavy crate outside into the light and rested, gulp-
ing in the fresh mountain air. The box itself weighed eighty pounds,
and it contained other books besides the Codex. Tom examined the
quarter-inch bolts and wing nuts holding together the steel bands that
clamped down the fiberglass-wrapped wood sides of the box. The
wing nuts were tight and hard. It would take a wrench to unscrew
them.

He found a rock and gave one of the nuts a sharp blow, loosening
it. He repeated the process and in a few minutes had removed all the
wing nuts. He pulled off the steel bands. A few more massive blows
cracked the fiberglass covering, and Tom was able to wrench it free. A

half dozen precious books spilled out, all carefully wrapped in acid-free paper—a Gutenberg Bible, illuminated manuscripts, a book of hours. He shoved aside the books and reached in, grasped the buckskin-covered Codex, and pulled it out.

For a moment he stared at it. He remembered so clearly how it had sat in a little glass case in the living room. His father used to unlock the case every month or so and turn a page. The pages had pretty little drawings of plants, flowers, and insects, surrounded by glyphs. He remembered staring at those strange Mayan glyphs, the dots and thick lines and grinning faces, all wrapped and tangled around each other. He hadn't even realized it was a kind of writing.

Tom emptied one of their abandoned backpacks and shoved the book in. He shouldered the pack and started back up the trail. He decided to head southwest, keeping an eye out for Hauser.

He entered the ruined city.

76

Hauser followed the trail more carefully now, all his senses alert. He felt a tingling of excitement and fear. The Indian had been able to rig up a trap like that in less than fifteen minutes. Amazing. The Indian was still out there somewhere, no doubt readying another ambush for him. Hauser wondered at the rather interesting loyalty shown by this Indian guide to the Broadbents. Hauser never underestimated native skills in forestcraft, ambush, and killing. The Viet Cong had taught him respect. As he followed the Broadbents' trail he took every precaution against ambush, by walking off to one side and pausing every few minutes to examine the ground and undergrowth ahead, even smelling the air for human scent. No Indian up in a tree was going to surprise him with a poison dart.

He saw that the Broadbents were headed toward the center of the plateau, where the jungle was thickest. No doubt they hoped to hole up there and wait for nightfall. They would not succeed: Hauser had almost never encountered a trail he couldn't follow, particularly one made by a panicked group of people, one of whom was bleeding heavily. And he and his men had already thoroughly explored the entire plateau.

Soon the rainforest ahead became choked by a wild overgrowth of creepers and lianas. At first glance it looked impenetrable. He approached cautiously and peered down. There were small animal trails running every which way—mostly coatimundi trails. Fat, pendulous drops of water hung off every leaf, vine, and flower, waiting for the slightest vibration to fall. No one could walk through such a mine-field without leaving evidence of his passage in the form of leaves brushed clean of their dew. Hauser could see exactly where they had gone. He followed their trail into the dense overgrowth, where it seemed to vanish.

Hauser scrutinized the ground. There, in the damp litter of the for-est floor, were two almost invisible indentations, formed by a pair of human knees. Interesting. They had crawled into the heart of the creeper colony along the animal trails. He squatted and peered into the green darkness. He sampled the air with his nose. He examined the ground. Which trail had they taken? There, three feet in, was a tiny crushed mushroom, no bigger than a dime, and a scraped leaf. They had gone to earth in this mass of vegetation, waiting for nightfall. Without a doubt, Hauser thought, the Indian had set up his ambush in here. It was a perfect place. He stood back up and examined the lay-ers of rainforest. Yes, the Indian would be hiding somewhere on a branch above this warren of trails, poison dart at the ready, waiting for him to crawl past below.

What he had to do was to ambush the ambusher.

Hauser thought for a moment. The Indian was smart. He would already have anticipated this. He would know that Hauser would be expecting an ambush on this trail. Therefore, the Indian was not wait-ing in ambush on *this* trail. No. Rather, he expected Hauser to circle in and come around from the other side. Therefore, the Indian was wait-ing on the *other side* of the gigantic mass of growth to ambush Hauser.

Hauser slowly began circling the edge of the creeper colony, mov-ing as silently and smoothly as an Indian himself. If his assumptions were correct, the Indian would be found on the far side, probably up high, waiting for him to pass below. He would finish the Indian first—who was by far the greater danger—and then he would flush out the others and drive them toward the bridge, where they would be easily trapped and killed.

Hauser circled at a distance, stopping every few moments to scan the middle story of the jungle. If the Indian had done as he anticipated, he would be somewhere to his right. He moved with great caution. It took time, but time at least was on his side. He had at least seven hours until dark.

He moved forward, scanned again. There was something in a tree. He paused, moved a little, looked again. Just the corner of the Indian's red shirt was visible, on a limb about fifty yards to his right, and there—he could just see it—was the tip of a little reed blowgun aiming downward, waiting to nail Hauser as he came through.

Hauser moved sideways until he had more of the Indian's shirt in sight to make a target. He raised his rifle, took careful aim, and fired a single round.

Nothing. And yet he knew he had hit it. A sudden panic seized him: It was another trap. He flung himself sideways at the very moment the Indian came dropping down on him like a cat, sharpened stick in hand. Using a jujitsu move, Hauser threw himself forward and to the side, turning the Indian's own momentum against him, neatly throwing him off—and then he was up and placing an arc of automatic-weapon fire across where the Indian had been.

The Indian was gone, vanished.

He reconnoitered. The Indian had *still* been one step ahead of him. He glanced up and saw the tree with the little bit of red cloth, the tip of the blowgun dart, all still in place exactly where the Indian had put them. Hauser swallowed. Now was not the time for fear or anger. He had a job to do. He would no longer play the Indian's cat-and-mouse game, which Hauser now suspected he would lose. The time had come to flush out the Broadbents with brute force.

He turned and walked along the edge of the creeper colony, planted his feet, and took aim with the Steyr AUG. First one burst, then a second, and then he walked on, pouring fire into the thick vegetation. It had exactly the effect he anticipated: It flushed out the Broadbents. He could hear their panicked flight, noisy, like partridges. Now he knew where they were. He sprinted along the mass of growth to cut them off as they emerged and herd them toward the bridge.

There was a sudden sound behind him, and he spun toward the greater danger, squeezing the trigger and pouring firepower into the dense cover where the sound had come from. Leaves, vines, and twigs jittered off the branches and flew in all directions, and he could hear the *snick* and *thok* of bullets striking wood everywhere. He saw some movement and raked the vegetation with fire again—and then he heard a squeal and some thrashing.

Coatimundi, damn it! He had shot a coatimundi!

He turned now, focusing his attention ahead, lowered his gun, and fired in the direction of the fleeing Broadbents. He heard the coati squealing in pain behind him, the crackling of twigs, and then he realized, just in time, that this was no wounded coati—it was the Indian again.

He dropped, rolled, fired—not to kill, for the Indian had vanished into the vines, but to drive the Indian to his right, toward the open area in front of the bridge. He would drive him in the same direction as the Broadbents. He now had the Indian on the run, herding him together with the others. The trick was to keep them moving, firing steadily, preventing them from peeling off and coming back around behind him. He ran, crouching and firing short bursts, left and right, cutting off any possibility of escape back into the ruined city. By sweeping in from their left he was driving them ever closer to the chasm, crowding them, flushing them toward open ground. His clip empty, he paused to slam another in. As he ran, he heard, through the foliage ahead, the crash of the Broadbents in their flight in exactly the direction he hoped they would go.

He had them now.

77

Tom was already halfway back across the plateau when he heard the staccato fire from Hauser's gun. He instinctively ran toward the sound, fearful of what it might mean, knocking aside ferns and vines, jumping fallen logs, scrambling over wrecked walls. He heard the second and third bursts of gunfire, closer and more to his right. He veered toward it, hoping in some way to defend his brothers and father. He had a machete, he'd killed a jaguar and an anaconda with it—why not Hauser?

Unexpectedly he burst out of the foliage and into sunlight; fifty yards away lay the edge of the precipice, a sheer drop of more than a mile into a dark coil of mists and shadow. He was now at the edge of the great chasm. He looked to the right and saw the graceful catenary of the suspension bridge dangling over the canyon, swaying gently in the updrafts.

He heard more gunfire behind him and glimpsed movement. Vernon and Philip appeared out of the trees beyond the bridge, supporting their father, running as fast as they could. Borabay appeared a moment later farther back, catching up to them. A raking fire came past them, snipping off the heads of the ferns behind them, and too late Tom realized that he, too, was trapped. Tom ran toward them as another staccato peal of gunfire came out of the trees. Tom could now see that Hauser was several hundred yards behind, firing to their left and driving them toward the edge of the chasm and the bridge. Tom ran toward the bridgehead and reached it at the same time as the others. They paused, crouching. Tom could see that the soldiers on the other side, alerted by the gunfire, had already taken up covering positions and were blocking their escape.

"Hauser's *trying* to drive us out on the bridge," cried Philip.

Another burst of gunfire tore some leaves off a tree branch above them.

"We've no choice!" Tom cried.

In another moment they were running out on the swaying bridge, half-carrying, half-dragging their father. The soldiers on the far side dropped to their knees, blocking their exit, guns pointed.

"Just keep going," Tom shouted.

They were about a third of the way across when the soldiers in front of them fired a warning volley above their heads. At the same time a voice rang out from behind them. Tom turned. Hauser and several more soldiers were blocking their retreat at the other end of the bridge.

They were trapped in-between, all five of them.

The soldiers fired a second volley, this one lower. Tom could hear the bullets passing like bees above their heads. They had reached the middle of the bridge, and it was now swaying and jouncing from their motion. Tom looked back, looked forward. They stopped. There was nothing more they could do. It was over.

"Don't move," Hauser called out to them, strolling out on the bridge with a smile, weapon trained on them. They watched him approach. Tom glanced at his father. He was looking at Hauser with fear and hatred. The expression on his father's face frightened him even more than their situation.

Hauser stopped a hundred feet from them, steadying himself on the swaying bridge. "Well, well," he said. "If it isn't *old Max* and his three sons. What a nice family reunion."

78

During the twelve hours Sally had lain behind the tree trunk, her thoughts had, for some reason, turned to her father. That last summer of his life he had taught her how to shoot. After he died, she had continued to go down to the bluffs to practice shooting apples and oranges, and later pennies and dimes. She had gotten to be an excellent shot, but it was a useless skill—she had no interest in competition or hunting. She had simply enjoyed it. Some people liked to bowl, some liked Ping-Pong—she liked to shoot. Of course, in New Haven it was the most politically incorrect skill of all. Julian was horrified when he found out. He made her promise to give up shooting and keep it a secret—not because he was against guns but because it was déclassé. Julian. She pushed him out of her mind.

She shifted her cramped thighs and wiggled her toes, trying to limber up the stiffened muscles. She gave another handful of nuts to Hairy Bugger, who was still sitting grumpily in his vine cage. She was glad he had been there to keep her company these past hours, even if he was in a foul mood. The poor thing loved his freedom.

Bugger gave a squeak of alarm, and Sally was instantly alert. Then she heard it: some distant shots from the White City, a faint burst from an automatic weapon, then a second. With the binoculars she scanned the forest on the far side of the gorge. There were more shots, and still more, growing louder. A few minutes went by, and then she saw movement.

It was Tom. He had appeared at the edge of the cliffs, running. Philip and Vernon emerged out of the jungle ahead of him, supporting a wounded man between them—an old man in rags, Broadbent. Borabay was the last to appear, closest to the bridge.

There were more shots, and she now spied Hauser coming out of the trees from behind, flushing them out and driving them like game toward the bridge.

She lowered the binoculars and raised the gun, watching the drama through the scope of the Springfield. It couldn't be a worse situation. The Broadbents and Borabay were about to be trapped on the bridge. But they had no other choice, with Hauser behind them and the chasm to one side. They hesitated at the bridgehead, then ran out onto the span. Hauser was out of the trees and shouting to the soldiers on the far side, who kneeled and fired warning shots.

In a moment all five of the Broadbents, including Borabay, were trapped in the middle of the bridge, with Hauser and four soldiers at one end and four at the other. Totally trapped. The firing died down and all was silent.

Hauser, with a grimace on his face, now began walking along the precarious bridge toward them, his weapon leveled.

Sally felt her heart hammering in her chest. Her moment had come. Her hands were shaking, sweating. She remembered her father. *Calm your breathing. Allow your airflow to stop. Find your heartbeat. Shoot in between.*

Sally aimed at Hauser as he strolled along the bridge. The bridge was swaying, but she felt her chances of scoring a hit were better than fifty-fifty. They would be even better once he stopped walking.

Hauser advanced to within a hundred feet of the Broadbents and paused. She could kill him—she *would* kill him. She centered his torso in her crosshairs, but she did not squeeze the trigger. Instead, she asked herself: *What will happen* after *I kill Hauser?*

The answer wasn't hard to figure out. This was not *The Wizard of Oz*, and the Honduran soldiers on each side of the bridge would not lay down their guns saying, "Hail, Dorothy!" These were brutal mercenaries. If she shot Hauser, the soldiers would almost certainly open fire and massacre all the Broadbents on the bridge. There were ten soldiers—four at her end and now six at the other—and she couldn't hope to pick them all off, especially the six at the far end, who were virtually out of range. The chamber of the Springfield held only five shots, and when those were done she would have to pull back the bolt and manually reload five more, a long process. And she only had ten rounds anyway.

Whatever she did had to be done in five shots.

She felt a sense of panic. She had to think of a plan, a way to bring about an outcome where they all survived. Hauser was swaggering toward them with his rifle, and he clearly intended to kill them. Yes, she would have to kill him, and then it would be all over for the Broadbents.

Her mind reeled. There would be no misstep here, no second chance. She had to get this right. She played every option she could think of through her head, but they all ended the same way, with the Broadbents dead. Her hand shook; the figure of Hauser jittered in the scope. *If I kill Hauser, they're dead. If I don't kill Hauser, they're dead.*

She watched helplessly as Hauser aimed his weapon. He was smiling. He looked like a man about to enjoy himself.

79

Tom watched Hauser walk down the bridge, an arrogant smile of triumph on his face. He paused about a hundred feet from them. He swiveled the muzzle of the gun toward Tom. "Take off the pack and lay it down."

Tom carefully took off the pack but, instead of laying it down, held it over the gorge by a strap. "It's the Codex."

Hauser fired a round from his gun that snipped a piece of bamboo from the railing less than a foot from Tom. "*Lay it down.*"

Tom did not move. He continued holding the book over the gorge. "Shoot me and it goes over the side."

There was a silence. Hauser moved the muzzle of his gun toward Broadbent. "All right. Lay it down or Daddy dies. Last warning."

"Let him kill me," Broadbent growled.

"And after Dad there are your two brothers. Don't be stupid, and put it down."

After a brief moment Tom laid it down. He had no choice.

"The machete next."

Tom eased it out of its sheath and dropped it.

"Well, well," said Hauser, his face relaxing. He turned his gaze on their father. "Max. We meet again."

The old man, grasping his sons to help him stand, raised his head and spoke. "Your quarrel is with me. Let the boys go."

The smile on Hauser's face took on a frostier look. "On the

contrary, you're going to have the pleasure of seeing them die first."

Broadbent's head jerked a little. Tom tightened his grip. The bridge swayed slightly, the cold mists drifting upward. Borabay took a step forward but was stayed by Philip.

"Well then, who's first? The Indian? No, let's do him later. We'll go by age. Philip? Step away from the others so I don't have to kill you all at once."

After a brief hesitation Philip stepped to one side. Vernon reached out to him, grasped his arm, and tried to pull him back. He shook it off and took another step.

"You'll burn in hell, Hauser," roared Broadbent.

Hauser smiled pleasantly and raised the muzzle of his rifle. Tom looked away.

80

But the shot didn't come. Tom looked up. Hauser's attention had suddenly been diverted to something behind them. Tom turned around and saw a flash of black: An animal was bounding along one of the cables of the bridge toward them, a monkey racing along with his tail up—Hairy Bugger.

With a screech of joy Bugger leapt into Tom's arms, and Tom saw that he had a canister almost as large as himself tied to his midriff. It was the aluminum bottle of white gas from their backpacking stove. There was something scrawled on it—

I CAN HIT THIS S.

Tom wondered what the hell it meant, what Sally had in mind.

Hauser raised his gun. "Okay, everybody calm down. Everybody keep still. Now: Show me what it is the monkey just brought you. *Slowly.*"

All at once, Sally's plan came to Tom. He untied the canister.

"Hold it out at arm's length. Let me see it."

Tom held the cannister out. "It's a liter of white gas."

"Toss it over the side."

Tom spoke quietly. "There's a sharpshooter on our side who's got a bead on this bottle *as we speak.* As you know, white gas is explosively flammable."

Hauser's face showed no trace of emotion or reaction. He merely raised his gun.

"Hauser, if she hits this can, the bridge burns. You'll be cut off. You'll be trapped in the White City forever."

Ten electric seconds passed, and then Hauser spoke. "If the bridge burns, you'll die, too."

"You're going to kill us anyway."

Hauser said, "It's a bluff."

Tom did not respond. Seconds ticked by. Hauser's face betrayed nothing.

Tom said, "Hauser, she might just put a bullet through *you*."

Hauser raised his gun, and in that moment a bullet struck the bamboo bridge surface two feet in front of Hauser's boots with a *snick!* sending a spray of bamboo splinters up into his face. The report came a moment later, rolling across the chasm.

Hauser hastily lowered his gun muzzle.

"Now that we've established this is not bullshit, you tell your soldiers to let us pass."

"And?" said Hauser.

"You can have the bridge, the tomb, and the Codex. All we want is our lives."

Now Hauser shouldered his weapon. "My compliments," he said.

Tom, with slow movements, took the canister and, using a loose piece of twine from the bridge, tied it around one of the main cables.

"Tell your men to let us pass. You stay where you are. If anything bad happens to us, our sharpshooter shoots the canister and your precious bridge burns with you on it. Understand?"

Hauser nodded.

"I didn't hear the order, Hauser."

Hauser cupped his hands over his mouth. "Men!" he called in Spanish. "Let them leave! Do not molest them as they go! I am releasing them!"

There was a pause.

Hauser shouted, "I want a response to that order!"

"*Sí, señor,*" came the reply.

The Broadbents began walking off the bridge.

81

Hauser stood in the middle of the bridge, his mind having accepted the fact that a sharpshooter—no doubt that blond woman who had come with Tom Broadbent—had him in her crosshairs. *A useless old hunting rifle*, the soldier had told him. *Right*. She had placed a bullet at his feet at 350 yards. To think that she now had him in her sights was an unpleasant and yet oddly thrilling feeling.

He looked at the bottle tied to the cable. The distance from where he was standing to the bottle was less than one hundred feet. The sharpshooter was shooting from more than three hundred yards. The bridge was swaying in the updrafts. It would be a difficult shot, hitting a target moving through three dimensions. An almost impossible shot, in fact. In ten seconds he could reach the bottle, tear it off the cable, and drop it in the abyss. If he then turned and ran back toward the far end of the bridge, he would be a moving target rapidly going out of range. How likely would it be that she could hit him? He would be running fast along a *swaying* bridge—again moving in three spatial dimensions relative to her firing point. She would not be able to draw a bead on him. On top of that she was a woman. Obviously she could shoot, but no woman could shoot that well.

Yes, it could all be done quickly, before the Broadbents escaped, and she would never hit him or the canister. *Never.*

He crouched and sprang toward the can of white gas.

Almost instantly he heard the *snick!* of a bullet in front of him and then the report. He kept going and reached the can just as the second report reached his ears. Another miss. This was too easy. He had just put his hand on the can when he heard a *pop!* and saw a brilliant blossoming of light erupt in front of him with a *whoosh*, followed by a searing heat. He staggered back, waving his arm, surprised to see blue flames crawling all over him, his arms, his chest, his legs. He fell and rolled, thrashing around, beating at his arm, but he was like a blazing Midas and everything he touched seemed to turn to fire. He kicked, shrieked, rolled—and then suddenly he was like an angel, soaring on wings of air, and he closed his eyes and allowed the long, cool, delicious fall to happen.

82

Tom turned just in time to see the fiery human meteor that was Hauser streaking into the bottomless chasm, flickering dimly and silently as it hurtled down through layers of mist before disappearing, leaving nothing behind but a faint trail of smoke.

The entire midsection of the bridge where Hauser had been standing was on fire.

"Get off the bridge!" Tom cried. "Run!" He hesitated, then turned and ran back, snatched up the pack containing the Codex, and a moment later had caught up with his brothers, who were supporting their father, running as best they could toward the far end of the bridge. The soldiers guarding that end had retreated to terra firma, where they had turned and were now blocking the end, looking confused and uncertain.

They ran as best they could, supporting their father, advancing toward the four soldiers, who quickly retreated to terra firma but remained blocking the far end of the bridge. The soldiers looked confused, uncertain, guns raised, liable to do anything. Hauser's last order had been to let the Broadbents pass—but would they?

The leader of the group, a lieutenant, raised his weapon and cried, "Halt!"

"Let us pass!" Tom cried in Spanish. They kept coming.

"No. Get back."

"Hauser ordered you to let us pass!" Tom could feel the bridge trembling. The burning cable was going to go at any second.

"Hauser is dead," said the lieutenant. "I am now in charge."

"The bridge is burning, for God's sake!"

A smile crept up on the *teniente's* face. "Yes."

As if on cue the whole bridge jerked, and Tom and his father and brothers were thrown to their knees. One of the cables had parted, sending a shower of sparks into the abyss, while the bridge whipsawed under the sudden release of tension.

Tom struggled to his feet, helping his brothers raise their father.

"You must let us pass!"

The soldier answered with a burst of fire just above their heads. "You die with the bridge. That is my order! The White City is ours now!"

Tom turned; smoke and flames streamed from the bridge's midsection, fed by the updraft from below. Tom saw a second cable start to unravel, spilling burning bits of fiber into the air.

"Hang on!" he cried, gripping his father.

The cable parted with a violent lashing, and the entire deck of the bridge fell away like a curtain dropping. They clung to the two remaining cables, struggling to hold on to their weakened father. The bridge was whipsawing back and forth like a spring.

"Soldiers or no soldiers," said Tom, "let's get the hell off this bridge."

They began edging along the two remaining cables, their feet on the lower one, their hands on the upper one, helping Broadbent along.

The *teniente* and his three soldiers advanced two steps. "Get ready to fire!" They dropped to a stable firing position and took aim.

Tom and his family were now only twenty-five feet from land, and the soldiers would be firing at them from almost point-blank range. He knew they had no choice but to keep going toward the men who were about to kill them.

The third cable parted like a spring, sending a recoil through the bridge that almost knocked them all off. The wreckage of the bridge hung from the single remaining cable, swinging back and forth.

The *teniente* pointed his gun at them. "You die now," he said in English.

There was a hollow thud, but it was not from his gun. A surprised look came into the *teniente*'s face, and it was as if he were bowing down before them, a long arrow sticking out of the back of his head. This struck momentary confusion in the other five soldiers, and in that moment a bloodcurdling yell went up from the edge of the forest, followed by a huge shower of arrows. Tara warriors poured out of the jungle and raced across the flat area, leaping and shrieking, firing arrows on the fly. The remaining soldiers, caught by surprise on the flank, out in the open, threw down their guns in a panic to flee and were instantly transformed into human pincushions, struck with dozens of arrows simultaneously; they staggered about wildly like drunken porcupines before falling to the ground.

A moment later Tom and his brothers had reached land—just as the final cable parted in a great cloud of sparks. The two blazing ends of the bridge swung lazily toward the canyon walls and crashed into them with a shudder and a cascade of burning debris.

It was over. The bridge was gone.

Tom looked ahead and saw Sally stand up out of the brush in front and run toward them. They moved toward her, helping their father along, aided by Tara warriors. In a few moments they had reached her. Tom folded her in his arms and they hugged, while Hairy Bugger, now safe in Tom's pocket again, squeaked his displeasure at being squeezed in the middle.

Tom looked back. The two pieces of bridge were hanging over the chasm, still burning. A half dozen men had been left trapped in the white city. They stood on the edge of the precipice, staring at the dangling wreckage. The mists began to rise and, bit by bit, the silent, stupefied figures vanished.

83

The hut was warm and faintly perfumed with smoke and medicinal herbs. Tom entered, followed by Vernon, Philip, and Sally. Maxwell Broadbent was lying in a hammock with his eyes closed. Frogs peeped outside in the peaceful night. A young Tara medicine man was grinding herbs in one corner of the hut, under the watchful eye of Borabay.

Tom laid a hand on his father's forehead. His temperature was climbing. The gesture caused his father to open his eyes. His face was drawn, his eyes glittering with fever and the light of the fire. The old man mustered a smile. "As soon as I get better, Borabay's going to show me how to go spearfishing the Tara way."

Borabay nodded.

Broadbent's restless eyes moved over the company, seeking reassurance. "Eh, Tom? What do you say?"

Tom tried to say something but couldn't quite get the sounds out.

The young medicine man stood up and offered Broadbent a clay mug filled with some murky brown liquid.

"Not another of these," Broadbent muttered. "This is worse than the cod liver oil my mother used to force down my throat every morning."

"Drink, Father," said Borabay. "Good for you."

"What is it?" Broadbent asked.

"Medicine."

"I know that, but what *kind* of medicine? You can't expect me to swallow something without knowing what it is."

Maxwell Broadbent was proving a difficult patient.

Sally spoke. "It's *Una de gavilan, Uncaria tomentosa*. The dried root is an antibiotic."

"I suppose it can't hurt." Broadbent took the mug, swallowed. "We seem to have an excess of doctoring going on here. Sally, Tom, Borabay, and now this young witch doctor. You'd think I had something serious."

Tom glanced at Sally.

"The things we're going to do together when I get better!" Broadbent said.

Tom swallowed again. His father, seeing his discomfort—nothing ever escaped him—turned to him. "Well, Tom? You're the only real doctor around here. What's the prognosis?"

Tom tried to muster a smile. His father looked at him for a long time and then settled back with a sigh. "Who am I kidding?"

There was a long silence.

"Tom? I'm already dying of cancer. You can't tell me anything worse than that."

"Well," Tom began, "the bullet perforated your peritoneal cavity. You've got an infection, and that's why you have a fever."

"And the prognosis?"

Tom swallowed again. His three brothers and Sally were all looking at him intently. Tom knew his father would settle for nothing less than the plain, unadorned truth.

"Not good."

"Go on."

Tom couldn't quite bring himself to say it.

"That bad?" said his father.

Tom nodded.

"But what about these antibiotics this medicine man's giving me? And what about all those marvelous remedies in that codex you just rescued?"

"Father, the kind of infection you have, sepsis, can't be reached by any antibiotic. Nothing short of major surgery will fix it, and now it's probably too late even for that. Drugs can't do everything."

There was a silence. Broadbent turned and looked up. "Damn," he said at last, to the ceiling.

"You took that bullet for us," said Philip. "You saved our lives."

"Best thing I ever did."

Tom laid his hand on his father's arm. It was like a hot stick. "I'm sorry."

"So how long do I have?"

"Two or three days."

"Christ. That short?"

Tom nodded.

He lay back with a sigh. "The cancer would have gotten me in a few months anyway. Although it would have been damned nice having those months with my sons. Or even a week."

Borabay came over and laid his hand on his father's chest. "I sorry, Father."

Broadbent covered the hand with his. "I sorry, too." He turned and looked at his sons. "And I can't even look on the Lippi Madonna one more time. When I was in that tomb, I kept thinking about how if I could only look on that Madonna again, everything would be all right."

They spent the night in the hut watching over their dying father. He was restless, but the antibiotics were, at least for now, holding the infection at bay. When dawn broke the old man was still lucid.

"I need some water," he said, his voice hoarse.

Tom left the hut with a jug, heading for the nearby stream. The Tara village was just waking up. The cooking fires were being lit, and the beautiful French copper- and nickel-clad pots and pans and tureens were making their appearance. Smoke spiraled into the morning sky. Chickens scratched in the dirt plaza, and mangy dogs prowled about, looking for scraps. A toddler came teetering out of a hut, wearing a Harry Potter T-shirt, and took a pee. Even among a tribe this remote, Tom thought, the world was reaching in. How long would it be before the White City yielded up its treasures and its secrets to the world?

As Tom walked back carrying the water, he heard a sharp voice. The old crone, the wife of Cah, had come out of her hut and was gesturing toward him with a crooked hand. *"Wakha!"* she said, gesturing.

Tom paused warily.

Wakha!

He took a cautious step toward her, half expecting to have his hair yanked or his balls groped.

Instead the woman took him by the hand and pulled him toward her hut.

Wakha!

He reluctantly followed her bent form into the smoky hut.

And there, in the dim light, propped up against a post, stood the *Madonna of the Grapes* by Fra Filippo Lippi. Tom stared at the Renaissance masterpiece and took an uncertain step toward it, transfixed, hardly believing it could be real. The contrast between the shabby hut and the painting was too great. Even in the dark it fairly glowed with internal light, the golden-haired Madonna, barely a teenager, holding her baby, who was stuffing a grape into his mouth with two pink fingers. A dove floated above their heads, radiating gold leaf.

He turned to the old lady in astonishment. She was looking at him with a huge grin on her wrinkled face, her pink gums gleaming. She went over to the painting, picked it up, and thrust it in his arms.

Wakha!

She gestured for him to take it to his father's hut. She went behind, giving him little pushes with her hands. *"Teh! Teh!"*

Tom walked into the damp clearing with the painting cradled in his arms. Cah must have kept back the painting for himself. It was a miracle. He stepped into the hut and held the painting out. Philip glanced over, let out a cry, and fell back. Broadbent stared at it, his eyes widening. At first he said nothing, and then he lay back in his hammock, a look of fright on his face.

"Damn it, Tom! The hallucinations are starting."

"No, Father." He brought the painting close. "It's real. Touch it."

"No, don't touch it!" cried Philip.

Broadbent reached out a trembling hand and touched the painted surface anyway.

"Hello," he murmured. He turned to Tom. "I'm not dreaming."

"No, you're not dreaming."

"Where in the world did you get this?"

"She had it." He turned to the old woman, who stood in the doorway, a toothless grin on her face. Borabay began asking her questions, and she spoke at length. Borabay listened, nodding. Then he turned to his father.

"She say her husband greedy, keep back many things from tomb. Hide them in cave behind village."

"What things?" Broadbent asked sharply.

They spoke some more.

"She not know. She say Cah steal almost all treasure for tomb. He fill boxes with stones instead. He say he not want to put white man treasure in Tara tomb."

"Wouldn't you know it," said Broadbent. "When I was in the tomb, there were some crates that seemed hollower than they should be, almost empty. I couldn't get them open in the dark. That's what I was doing in the tomb just before Hauser showed up, checking to see if I could solve the mystery. That damned tricky old Cah. I should have known. He planned this whole thing from the start. Christ, he was as greedy as I was!"

Broadbent cast his eyes back on the painting. It reflected the light of the fire, the flickering glow playing over the Virgin's young face. There was a long silence as he looked at it. Then he closed his eyes and said, "Bring me a pen and paper. Now that I have something to leave you, I'm going to make out a new will."

84

They brought a pen and a roll of bark paper to Maxwell Broadbent.

"Shall we leave you?" asked Vernon.

"No. I need you here. You too, Sally. Come. Gather around."

They came and stood around his hammock. Then he cleared his throat. "Well, my sons. And—" he looked at Sally, "my future daughter-in-law. Here we are."

He paused.

"And what fine sons I have. Pity it took me so long to realize it." He cleared his throat. "I don't have a lot of wind left, and my head feels like a pumpkin, so I'll keep this short."

His eyes, still clear, traveled around the room. "Congratulations. You did it. You earned your inheritance, and you saved my life. You showed me what a goddamn fool of a father I've been—"

"Father—"

"No interruptions! I have some parting advice." He wheezed. "Here I am on my deathbed, how can I resist?" He took a deep breath. "Philip, of all my sons, you're the one most like me. I've seen, in these past years, how the expectation of a large inheritance has cast a shadow over your life. You're not naturally greedy, but when you're waiting for half a billion dollars, it has a corrosive effect. I've seen you living beyond your means, trying to play the rich, sophisticated connoisseur in your New York circle. You've got the same disease I had: needing to own beauty. Forget it. That's what museums are for. Live a simpler life. You have a deep appreciation for art, and that should be its own reward, not the recognition and fame. And I've heard you're one hell of a teacher."

Philip nodded curtly, not altogether pleased.

Broadbent took a couple of ragged breaths. Then he turned to Vernon. "Vernon. You're a seeker, and now I finally see just how important that choice is for you. Your problem is that you get taken in. You're an innocent. There's a rule of thumb here, Vernon: If they want money, the religion's bullshit. It doesn't cost anything to pray in a church."

Vernon nodded.

"And now Tom. Of all my sons you're the most different from me. I never really understood you. You're the least materialistic of my sons. You rejected me a long time ago, perhaps for good reasons."

"Father—"

"Quiet! Unlike me, you're disciplined in the way you live your life. I know what you really wanted to do was become a paleontologist and hunt dinosaur fossils. Like a fool, I pushed you into medicine. I know you're a good vet, although I've never understood why you're wasting your tremendous talents doctoring grade horses on the Navajo Indian reservation. What I've finally understood is that I must respect and honor your choices in life. Dinosaurs, horses, whatever. You do what you want with my blessing. What I have also come to see is your *integrity*. Integrity was something I never really had, and it upset me to see it so strongly in one of my sons. I don't know what you would have done with a big inheritance, and I expect you don't know, either. You don't need the money and you don't really want it."

"Yes, Father."

"And now, Borabay . . . you are my oldest and yet most recent son. I've only known you briefly, but in a strange way I feel I know you best of all. I've scoped you out, and I realize you're a little greedy like me. You can't wait to cut out of here and go to America and enjoy the good life. You don't really fit in with the Tara. Well, that's fine. You'll learn fast. You have an advantage here because you had a good mother and didn't have me for a father, messing you up."

Borabay was about to say something, but Broadbent raised his hand. "Can't a man give a deathbed speech around here without being interrupted? Borabay, your brothers will help you get to America and get citizenship. Once there you'll become more American than the natives, I have no doubt."

"Yes, Father."

Broadbent sighed and cast an eye on Sally. "Tom, this is the woman I never met but wished I had. You'd be a fool to let her slip away."

"I'm not a fish," said Sally sharply.

"Ah! That's just what I mean! A little prickly, perhaps, but an amazing woman."

"You're right, Father."

Broadbent paused, breathing heavily. It was an effort now to talk; the sweat stood out on his brow.

"I am about to write my last will and testament. I want each one of you to choose one thing from the collection in that cave. The rest, if you can get it out of the country, I'd like to donate to whatever museum or museums you choose. We'll go from oldest to youngest. Borabay, you start."

Borabay said, "I choose last. What I want is not in cave."

Broadbent nodded. "All right. Philip? As if I couldn't guess." His eyes strayed to the Madonna. "The Lippi is yours."

Philip tried to say something but could not.

"And now: Vernon?"

There was a silence, and then Vernon said, "I'd like the Monet."

"I thought that's what you'd say. I imagine you could get fifty million or more for it. And I hope you do sell it. But Vernon, please, *no* foundations. Don't give any money away. When you finally find what you're looking for, maybe then you'll have the wisdom to give a little bit of your money away, a *little* bit."

"Thank you, Father."

"I'm also going to send you back with a bagful of gems and coins so I can pay Uncle Sam."

"All right."

"And now, Tom, it's your turn. What's your pick?"

Tom glanced at Sally. "We'd like the Codex."

Broadbent nodded. "Interesting choice. It's yours. And now, Borabay, last but not least. What is this mysterious thing you want that isn't in the cave?"

Borabay came over to the bed and whispered in Broadbent's ear.

The old man nodded. "Excellent. Consider it done." He flourished his pen. His face was beaded with sweat, his breathing rapid and shallow. Tom could see he did not have much lucid time left. And he knew what death from sepsis was like.

"Now," he said, "give me ten minutes by myself to make out my last will and testament, and then we will gather witnesses and execute it."

85

Tom stood with his brothers and Sally in a cathedrallike grove of trees, watching the great funeral procession winding up the trail toward the tomb, which had been freshly chiseled in the limestone cliffs far above the village. It was an amazing sight. Maxwell Broadbent's body came at the head of the procession, borne upon a litter by four warriors. It had been embalmed using an ancient Mayan process. During the funeral ceremony the new chief of the village had transformed the corpse into El Dorado, the Gilded One of Indian legend—the way the Maya had once buried their emperors. They had smeared the body with honey and then sprinkled it with gold dust, coating it completely, to metamorphose it into the immortal form it would take in the afterlife.

Behind their father's litter came a long procession of Indians carrying grave goods for the tomb—baskets of dried fruits and vegetables, nuts, ollas of oil and water, then a slew of traditional Mayan artifacts such as jade statues, painted pots, beaten gold dishes and jugs, weapons, quivers full of arrows, nets, spears, everything that Maxwell Broadbent might need in the afterlife.

After that, hobbling around the bend, came an Indian carrying a painting by Picasso of a naked woman with three eyes, a square head, and horns, followed by the massive Pontormo scene of the Annunciation, carried by two sweating Indians, then the Bronzino portrait of Bia de' Medici, a pair of Roman statues, a few more Picassos, a

Braque, two Modiglianis, a Cezanne, more statues—twentieth-century grave goods. The bizarre procession wound its way up the hillside and into the grove.

And finally came the band, if that's what you could call it: a group of men playing gourd flutes, blowing long wooden trumpets, and beating sticks—with one young boy bringing up the rear, banging with all his might a shabby, Western-style bass drum. Hairy Bugger, who had been adopted by the tribe, rode on the boy's shoulder, enjoying the spectacle with a haughty look of disdain.

Tom felt a great mixture of sadness and catharsis. It was the passing of an era. His father was dead. It was the last good-bye to his childhood. Passing before his eyes were the things he knew and loved, the things he had grown up with. They were the things his father loved, too. As the procession went into the tomb darkness swallowed it all, men and grave goods alike—and then the men emerged, blinking and empty-handed. There his father's collection would be shut up, safe, dry, guarded and protected until the day when he and his brothers could return and claim what was theirs. The Mayan treasures, of course, would stay in the tomb forever, to ensure that Maxwell Broadbent lived a fine and happy life in the afterworld. But the Western treasures belonged to them, held in safekeeping by the Tara tribe. It was a funeral to end all funerals. Only the Mayan emperors had been buried like this, and not for at least a thousand years.

Three days after signing his last will and testament, Maxwell Broadbent passed away. He had had only one more day of lucidity before he sank into delirium, coma, and death. No death was pretty, Tom thought, but this one had had a certain nobility to it, if one could use that word.

It wasn't so much the death but the last lucid day of his father's life that Tom would never forget. The four sons had stayed with him. They hadn't talked much, and when they did it was of minor things— little memories, stories, forgotten places, laughs they'd had, people long gone. And yet that day of small talk had been more valuable than all the decades of important talk about the big things, the lectures, father-to-son exhortations, the advice and philosophizing and dinner-time discussions. After a lifetime at cross-purposes, Maxwell finally understood them and they understood him. And they could merely chat for the pleasure of it. It was as simple, and as profound, as that.

Tom smiled. His father would have loved his funeral. He would have been delighted to see this great procession through the forest, the giant wooden trumpets bellowing, the drums beating, the bamboo flutes playing, the women and men alternating singing and clapping. A great tomb had been freshly cut out of the rock, inaugurating a new necropolis for the Tara tribe. The White City had been cut off by the burning of the bridge, leaving six of Hauser's mercenaries behind. During the six weeks the new tomb was being built, the village buzzed daily with news of the trapped soldiers. They came down to the bridgehead from time to time, firing their guns, shouting, pleading, threatening. As the days and weeks passed the six had dwindled to four, three, and two. Now there was one, and he didn't shout or wave or fire his gun anymore. He just stood there, a small, gaunt figure, saying nothing, waiting for death. Tom had tried to convince the Tara to rescue him, but the Tara were adamant: Only the gods could rebuild the bridge. If the gods wanted to save him, they would.

But of course they didn't.

The boom of the bass drum brought Tom's thoughts back to the present spectacle. All the grave goods had been heaped in the tomb, and now it was time to close it up. The men and women stood in the forest, singing a forlorn, haunting tune while a priest waved a bundle of sacred herbs, the fragrant smoke drifting past them. The ceremony went on until the sun touched the western horizon, and then it stopped. The chief struck the end of the wooden key, and the great stone door of the tomb slid shut with a sonorous boom, just as the last rays vanished.

All was silent.

As they walked back to the village, Tom said, "I only wish Father had been able to see that."

Vernon put his arm around him. "He did, Tom. For sure, he did."

86

Lewis Skiba sat in the rocking chair on the crooked porch of the battenboard cottage, looking out over the lake. The hills were cloaked in autumnal glory, the water a darkened mirror reflecting the curve of evening sky. It was exactly as he remembered it. The dock ran crookedly into the water, with the canoe tied up at the end. The scent of warm pine needles drifted through the air. A loon called from the far shore, its forlorn cry dying among the hills, and it was answered by another loon at an immense distance, its voice as faint as starlight.

Skiba took a sip of fresh spring water and rocked back slowly, the chair and porch both creaking in protest. He had lost everything. He had presided over the collapse of the ninth largest pharmaceutical company in the world. He had watched its stock drop to fifty cents before trading was suspended forever. He had been forced into filing Chapter II, and twenty thousand employees saw their pension funds and life savings vanish. He had been fired by the board, vilified by shareholders and congressional committees, and made the butt of late-night television. He was under criminal investigation for accounting fraud, stock manipulation, insider trading, and self-dealing. Skiba had lost his home and his wife, and the lawyers had almost finished chewing through his fortune. Nobody loved him now except his children.

And yet Skiba was a happy man. No one could understand this happiness. They thought he had lost his mind, that he was having some kind of breakdown. They did not know what it was like to be pulled out of the very flames of hell.

What was it that had stayed his hand, three months ago, in that dark office? Or in the three months that followed? Those three months of silence from Hauser had been the darkest months of Skiba's life. Just when it seemed the nightmare would never end, suddenly there was news. The *New York Times* had run a little article, buried in the B section, which announced the creation of the Alfonso Boswas Foundation, a nonprofit organization devoted to translating and publishing a certain ninth-century Mayan codex found in the collections of the late Maxwell Broadbent. According to the foundation's president, Dr. Sally Colorado, the Codex was a Mayan book of healing that would prove tremendously useful in the search for new drugs. The foundation had been established and funded by the four sons of the late Maxwell Broadbent. The article noted that he had passed away unexpectedly while on a family holiday in Central America.

That was all. There was no mention of Hauser, the White City, the lost tomb, the crazy father burying himself with his money—nothing. A few days later he had noted another curious article in the *Times,* one that he had almost passed over before the significance struck him. There had been a minor scandal up at Yale—a professor had lost his position and had been sued by the giant Swiss pharmaceutical company Hartz, which claimed that he had defrauded the company of a million dollars over a non-existent Mayan "herbal" manuscript. Someone else, it seemed, had been hoping to get rich on the Codex.

Skiba had felt as if the weight of the world had been lifted from his shoulders. The Broadbents were alive. They had not been murdered. Hauser had failed to get the Codex and, most important, had failed to kill them. Skiba would never know what happened, and it would be too dangerous to inquire. The only thing he knew was that he was not guilty of murder. Yes, he was guilty of terrible crimes and he had much to atone for, but the irrevocable taking of a human life—even his own—wasn't among them.

There was one other thing. By being stripped of everything— money, possessions, reputation—he could finally see again. The scales had fallen. He could see as clearly as if he were a child once more: all

the bad things he had done, the crimes he had committed, the selfish-
ness and greed. He could trace in perfect clarity now the spiraling eth-
ical descent he had made in his successful career in business. It was so
easy to become confused, to conflate prestige with honesty, power
with responsibility, sycophancy with loyalty, profit with merit. You
had to be an exceptionally clear-minded human being to keep your
integrity in such a system.

Skiba smiled as he gazed out over the mirrored surface of the lake,
watching it all disappear in the evening twilight, everything he had
worked for, everything that had once been so important to him. In the
end, even the battenboard cabin would have to go, and he would never
gaze on this lake again.

It didn't matter. He had died and been reborn. Now he could begin
his new life.

87

Officer Jimmy Martinez of the Santa Fe Police Department settled back in his chair. He had just laid down the telephone. The leaves on the cottonwood tree outside the window had turned a rich, golden yellow, and a cold wind swept down from the mountains. He glanced at his partner, Willson.

"The Broadbent place again?" Willson asked.

Martinez nodded. "Yeah. You'd think those neighbors would've gotten used to it by now."

"These rich people—who can figure 'em out?"

Martinez snorted his agreement.

"Who do you think that character up there really is? Have you ever seen anything like it? A tattooed Indian from Central America, going around in the old man's suits, smoking his pipe, riding his horses around that thousand-acre ranch, bossing the servants, playing the country gentleman, insisting everyone call him *sir?*"

"He owns the place," said Martinez. "It checks out, all legal."

"Sure he owns the place! But my question is: How the hell did he get his hands on it? That estate's worth twenty, thirty million. And then to run it, shit, must be a couple of mil a year. Do you really think a guy like that has money?"

Martinez smiled. "Yeah."

"Whaddya mean, yeah? Jimmy, the guy has filed teeth. He's a frigging *savage.*"

"No, he isn't. He's a Broadbent."

"Are you nuts? You think that Indian with earlobes dragging on the ground is a Broadbent? Get out, Jimmy, what've you been smoking?"

"He looks just like them."

"You ever met them?"

"I met two of the sons. I'm telling you, he's another one of the old man's sons."

Willson stared at him, astonished.

"The man had a reputation in that way. The other sons got the art, he got the house and a shitload of money. Simple."

"An *Indian* son of Broadbent?"

"Sure. I bet the old man boned some woman in Central America on one of his expeditions."

Willson sat back in his chair, deeply impressed. "You're gonna make detective lieutenant someday, you know that, Jimmy?"

Martinez nodded modestly. "I know."

Look for Douglas Preston's
new novel, coming September 2005!

0-765-31104-6 • $24.95/$33.95 Can.

After surviving a murderous ordeal in Costa Rica's jungles,
Tom and Sally Broadbent return home, seeking
peace and quiet in the arid canyons of New Mexico.
Unfortunately, they will find unimaginable horror
in the very place they sought solace....

The greatest scientific discovery of all time
will lead a gifted, murderous scientist, a mysterious CIA agent
turned monastery monk, a renegade federal agent,
and a shadowy agency with a deadly mission
down the same unearthly path to...*TYRANNOSAUR CANYON.*